BEVERLY BARTON
Witness

HQN™

ISBN-13: 978-0-373-77503-3

WITNESS

Copyright © 2010 by Harlequin Books S.A.

The publisher acknowledges the copyright holder of the individual works as follows:

DEFENDING HIS OWN
Copyright © 1995 by Beverly Beaver

GUARDING JEANNIE
Copyright © 1995 by Beverly Beaver

Recycling programs for this product may not exist in your area.

Printed in U.S.A.

CONTENTS

DEFENDING HIS OWN

PROLOGUE

She must have taken the wrong turn off Cotton Lane. There was nothing out here but a bunch of cotton fields and an endless stretch of dirt road, apparently leading nowhere except in and out of the fields.

Deborah Vaughn slowed her dark blue Cadillac to a stop, shifted the gears into Park and picked up the piece of paper on which she'd written the directions. Despite the protection of her sunglasses, Deborah squinted against the sun's blinding glare. Holding up her hand to shield her eyes, she glanced down at the map and instructions she'd brought along to help her find the new development property her real estate firm had just purchased. Damn! She had turned off too soon.

Glancing around, she didn't see anywhere to make a turn, and she certainly had no intention of backing her car all the way to Cotton Lane. She'd just have to go a little farther and find some place to turn around.

Shifting the gears into Drive, she drove on. Within a few minutes she spotted what appeared to be the burned-out remains of an old shack. A wide, weed-infested path, marred with deep ruts, ran straight from the dirt road to where a shiny black Ford pickup had parked in knee-high grass behind the still-standing brick chimney.

Loud, pulse-pounding country music blared from the truck's radio.

Deborah assumed the truck belonged to the farmer who had planted the acres of cotton. She drove her Cadillac onto the path, intending to back up and head out the way she had come.

The sun's glare blocked her vision, allowing her only a partial view of the open truck door. A man jumped out of the driver's side, and yelled a warning. She glanced toward the back of the truck where two men stood, one holding a gun to the other's head.

Sunshine reflected off the metal on the gun in the killer's hand. The gun fired. The wail of a steel guitar blasted from inside the truck. Deborah screamed. Blood splattered from the dead man's head. The killer turned abruptly and stared at the Cadillac, at the woman inside, then released his hold on the body. His victim slumped to the ground.

Deborah recognized the killer from his picture in the paper. She couldn't remember his name, but she knew he was somehow connected to that outlaw gang headed by Buck Stansell.

The man who'd leaped out of the truck pointed toward Deborah's car.

Dear God, she had to get away! Shifting the car into reverse, she backed out of the bumpy path and then headed the Cadillac toward Cotton Lane. She heard the truck's engine roar to life. Glancing back she saw the killer aim his gun out the window.

The Caddy sped down the dirt road, the black truck in hot pursuit. While the driver veered the truck off the side of the dirt road, partially into the open field, the killer aimed his gun toward Deborah. The truck closed in on the car, the truck's hood parallel to the Cadillac's left rear bumper. The killer fired; the bullet shattered the outside mirror. Deborah cried out, but didn't slow her escape, didn't take her eyes off the road ahead of her.

A cloud of dust flew up behind the Cadillac, providing a thin veil of protection between her and the men determined to overtake her. The truck picked up speed just as Deborah saw Cotton Lane ahead of her. Another bullet ripped through the driver's door.

They intended to kill her. She had no doubt in her mind.

She'd seen the killer's face, the man who had murdered another in cold blood. She could identify him. And he knew it.

The minute she turned the Caddy onto Cotton Lane, she sped away from the truck. She had to escape. Had to find help. But who? Where? The police!

She didn't dare slow down enough to use her cellular phone. She had to make it to the police station before her pursuers caught her.

Where the hell was the police station in Leighton? *Think, dammit, Deborah! Think!*

She crossed Highway 72, paying little attention to whether or not traffic was coming from the other direction. The sleepy little town of Leighton, Alabama lay straight ahead. The truck breathed down her neck like a black dragon, the killer's gun spitting deadly lead fire.

A bullet sailed through the back glass, embedding itself in the dashboard. Deborah ran the Caddy straight through the town's one red light. The black truck slowed, but continued following her.

Deborah brought her car to a screeching halt at the side of the police station, a small metal building on the right side of the narrow street. Glancing behind her, she saw the black truck creep by. Lying down in the front seat, she eased open the door, crawled out and made a mad dash to safety.

A young officer jumped up from behind a metal desk when Deborah ran inside the station. "What the hell's going on, lady? You look like the devil's chasing you."

"He is." Deborah panted, wiping the perspiration from her face with the palm of her hand. She grabbed the approaching officer's shoulders. "I just witnessed a murder."

"You what?" The young officer's face paled. "Come on in and sit down."

"I don't want to sit down," Deborah screamed. "They're out there. Two of them. The killer and the man who was driving the truck. They followed me all the way into town. They shot at me. They were trying to kill me!"

"Good God!" He shoved Deborah aside, drew his 9 mm handgun and rushed outside.

The female officer who'd been listening to the conversation rushed over to Deborah and followed her when she headed for the door. Looking up and down the street, Deborah didn't see the truck. She leaned against the doorpost.

"Are you all right?" the woman officer asked.

"I will be."

The male officer let out a long, low whistle when he saw Deborah's Cadillac. "Good thing they didn't get a lucky shot or you'd be dead, ma'am."

"They're gone, aren't they?" Deborah asked, realizing they wouldn't have hung around, making it easy for the police to arrest them.

"Yes, ma'am, looks that way." He walked toward her, shaking his head. "Just where did this murder take place?"

"Out past some cotton fields, somewhere off Cotton Lane."

"Don't suppose you recognized either man in the truck or the man you say they murdered?"

"I only recognized one of them," Deborah said. "The killer. He's one of Buck Stansell's gang. I remember seeing his picture in the paper when he went to trial a few months ago on drug-related charges."

"Lon Sparks?" the officer asked. "You saw Lon Sparks kill a man?"

"Yes, if that's his name...I saw him kill a man. Shot him in the head. Blood everywhere. All over the dead man. All over the killer." Deborah trembled, her hands shaking uncontrollably.

"Damn, ma'am, I sure wouldn't want to be in your shoes. Lon Sparks is a mean bastard, if you'll pardon me saying so." The officer returned his gun to his holster.

"Shut up, Jerry Don, can't you see she's already scared out

of her wits." Putting an arm around Deborah's shoulder, the female officer led her back inside the station. "We'd better get hold of the chief and then call the sheriff. If the killing took place out past Cotton Lane, then it's a county matter."

"Everything will be all right," Jerry Don said. "You're safe here with us, Miss...er... Miss...?"

"Deborah Vaughn."

"Come on over and sit down, Miss Vaughn, and tell me exactly what happened," The female officer said.

"May I use your phone first?" Deborah picked up the telephone on the officer's desk. "I'm expected at home for dinner and my mother will worry if I'm late."

Her hands trembled as she dialed the number. "Mother, I'm afraid I'll be running a little late. You and Allen go ahead and have dinner without me. No. No, everything's all right. I just ran into a little car trouble out here in Leighton. Nothing I can't handle."

Nothing she couldn't handle. That's right, Deborah. You're tough, aren't you? You can handle anything that's thrown your way. You don't need anyone to take care of you. You've been taking care of everyone else for so long, you wouldn't know how it felt to admit you needed someone.

Well, it looked like the time had come. If the police wanted her to live long enough to testify against a cold-blooded killer, someone was going to have to protect her from Buck Stansell's outlaws.

CHAPTER ONE

HE HAD SWORN he'd never come back to Sheffield, Alabama. But never say never. Ashe McLaughlin had discovered that anyone so absolutely certain often wound up eating his own words. And in his case, the taste was mighty bitter.

He had been gone eleven years, and little had changed. Except him. He had changed. He was older. Smarter. Harder.

He chuckled to himself. Harder? Hell, folks in northwest Alabama had considered him a real bad boy, one of those McLaughlins from Leighton, his daddy nothing but a white trash outlaw. But Ashe hadn't been as tough as everyone thought. He had hated the legacy of poverty and ignorance his family had given him. He'd wanted more. He'd fought long and hard to better himself. But Wallace Vaughn had destroyed Ashe's dreams of being accepted in Colbert County.

Eleven years ago he'd been told to leave town or else—or else he would have done jail time.

Now, here he was returning to a town that hadn't wanted his kind. He couldn't help wondering if anyone other than his grandmother would welcome him home. He supposed Carol Allen Vaughn would be glad to see him. After all, she'd been the one who'd asked him to take this job. He was probably a fool for agreeing to act as Deborah's bodyguard.

Deborah Vaughn. No amount of time or distance had been able to erase her from Ashe's memory.

He parked his rental car in the circular drive in front of the old Allen home, a brick Greek Revival cottage on Montgomery

Avenue. His grandmother had once been the housekeeper here
for the Vaughn family.

Walking up to the front door, he hesitated before ringing the
bell. He'd never been allowed to enter the house through the
front door but had always gone around to the back and entered
through the kitchen. He remembered sitting at the kitchen table
doing his homework, sharing milk and cookies with Deborah,
and sometimes her older cousin Whitney. That had been a lifetime ago.

He rang the doorbell. What the hell was he doing here? Why
had he allowed Carol Vaughn's dare to goad him into returning
to a town he hated? *Deborah needs you*, she'd said. *Are you
afraid to see her again?* she had taunted him.

He was not afraid to see Deborah Vaughn again. After ten
years as a Green Beret, Ashe McLaughlin was afraid of nothing, least of all the girl who had betrayed him.

A plump, middle-aged woman opened the door and greeted
him with a smile. "Yes, sir?"

"I'm Ashe McLaughlin. Mrs. Vaughn is expecting me."

"Yes, please come inside. I'll tell Miss Carol you're here."

Ashe stepped into the gracious entrance hall large enough
to accommodate a grand piano as well as a large mahogany
and gilt table with an enormous bouquet of fresh flowers in the
center. A sweeping staircase wound upward on the left side of
the room.

"If you'll wait here, please." The housekeeper scurried down
the hall toward the back of the house.

He'd been summoned home. Like a knight in the Queen's
service. Ashe grinned. Better a knight than a stable boy, he
supposed. Why hadn't he just said no? *I'm sorry, Mrs. Vaughn,
but whatever trouble Deborah has gotten herself into, you'll
have to find someone else to rescue her.*

God knows he had tried to refuse, but once he'd heard that
Deborah's life was in real danger, he had wavered in his resis-

tance. And Carol Vaughn had taken advantage of the weakness she sensed in him.

"Ashe, so good of you to come, dear boy." The voice still held that note of authority, that hint of superiority, that tone of Southern gentility.

He turned to face her, the woman he had always thought of as the personification of a real lady. He barely recognized the woman who stood before him. Thin, almost gaunt, her beautiful face etched with faint age lines, her complexion sickly pale. Her short blond hair was streaked with gray. She had once been full-figured, voluptuous and lovely beyond words.

She couldn't be much more than fifty, but she looked older.

Caught off-guard by her appearance, by the drastic change the years had wrought, Ashe stared at Carol Vaughn. Quickly recovering his composure, he took several tentative steps forward and held out his hand.

She clasped his big, strong hand in her small, fragile one and squeezed. "Thank you for coming. You can't imagine how desperately we need your help."

Ashe assisted Carol down the hallway and into the living room. The four-columned entry permitted an unobstructed view of the room from the foyer. The hardwood floors glistened like polished metal in the sunlight. A blend of antiques and expensive reproductions bespoke of wealth and good taste.

"The sofa, please, Ashe." She patted his hand. "Sit beside me and we'll discuss what must be done."

He guided her to the sofa, seated her and perched his big body on the edge, not feeling comfortable in her presence. "Does Deborah know you sent for me?"

"I haven't told her," Carol said. "She's a stubborn one, that girl of mine. She's always had a mind of her own. But she's been a dutiful daughter."

"What if she doesn't agree to my being here?" He had known Deborah when she was seventeen, a plump, pretty girl who'd had a major crush on him. What would she look like now? And how did she feel about him after all these years?

"Mazie, please bring us some coffee," Carol instructed the housekeeper who stood at the end of the hallway. "And a few of those little cakes from the bakery. The cinnamon ones."

"Refreshments aren't necessary, Mrs. Vaughn. Really." Ashe felt ill at ease being entertained, as if his visit were a social call. "I'm here on business. Remember?"

"Mazie, go ahead and bring the coffee and the cakes, too." Carol turned her attention to Ashe. "Times change, but good manners don't. Of course my mother would be appalled that I had welcomed a gentleman, unrelated to me and not a minister, into my home when I am quite alone."

"Coffee will be fine, Mrs. Vaughn."

"You used to call me Miss Carol. I much prefer that to the other. Your calling me Mrs. Vaughn makes us sound like strangers. And despite your long absence from Sheffield, we are hardly strangers, are we, Ashe?"

"No, ma'am, we're not strangers."

"Mazie has prepared you a room upstairs. I want you with Deborah at all times." Carol blushed ever so lightly. "Or at least close by."

"Has she received any more threats since we spoke two days ago?"

"Mercy, yes. Every day, there's a new letter and another phone call, but Charlie Blaylock says there's nothing more he can do. And I asked him why the sheriff was incapable of protecting innocent citizens."

"Has a trial date been set for Lon Sparks?" Ashe asked.

"Not yet. It should be soon. But not soon enough for me. I can't bear the thought of Deborah being in danger."

"She just happened to be in the wrong place at the wrong time." Ashe knew what that was like. And he knew as well as anyone in these parts just how dangerous Buck Stansell and his band of outlaws could be. For three generations, the

Stansell bunch, along with several other families, had cornered the market on illegal activities. Everything from prostitution to bootlegging, when the county had been dry. And nowadays weapons and drugs dominated their money-making activities.

"She insists on testifying." Carol glanced up when she saw Mazie bringing the coffee. "Just put it there on the table, please."

Mazie placed the silver service on the mahogany tea table to the left of the sofa, asked if there would be anything else and retreated to the kitchen when told all was in order.

"Do you prefer your coffee black?" Carol asked.

"Yes, ma'am. Thank you." When his hostess poured the coffee and handed it to him, Ashe accepted the Haviland cup.

"I will expect you to stay in Sheffield until the trial is over and Deborah is no longer in danger."

"I've already assured you that I'll stay as long as is necessary to ensure Deborah's safety."

"And I will send the sum we agreed upon to your agency in Atlanta on a weekly basis."

"You and I have come to an agreement on terms," Ashe said. "But unless Deborah cooperates—"

"She will cooperate."

Ashe widened his eyes, surprised by the vigor of Carol Vaughn's statement. Apparently her fragile physical condition had not extinguished the fire in her personality.

The front door flew open and a tall, gangly boy of perhaps twelve raced into the living room, tossing a stack of schoolbooks down on a bowfront walnut commode.

"I made a hundred on my math test. See. Take a look." He dashed across the room, handed Carol his paper and sat down on the floor at her feet. "And guess what else, Mother? My team beat the hel…heck out of Jimmy Morton's team in PE today."

Carol caressed the boy's blond hair, petting him with deep affection. "I'm so proud of you, Allen."

The boy turned his attention to Ashe, who stared at the child, amazed at his striking resemblance to Deborah. Ashe's grandmother had mentioned Allen from time to time in her letters and phone calls. He'd always thought it odd that Wallace and Carol Vaughn had had another child so late in life. When Wallace Vaughn had run Ashe out of town eleven years ago, the Vaughns had had one child—seventeen-year-old Deborah.

"Who's he?" Allen asked.

"Allen, this is Mr. McLaughlin. He's an old friend. He and Deborah went to school together."

"Were you Deborah's boyfriend?" Allen scooted around on the floor until he situated himself just right, so he could prop his back against the Queen Anne coffee table.

"Allen, you musn't be rude." Carol shook her index finger at the boy, but she smiled as she scolded him.

"I wasn't being rude. I was just hoping Mr. McLaughlin was here to ask Deborah for a date. She never goes out unless it's with Neil, and she told me that he isn't her boyfriend."

"I must apologize for Allen, but you see, he is very concerned that Deborah doesn't have a boyfriend," Carol explained. "Especially since he's going steady himself. For what now, Allen, ten days?"

"Ah, quit kidding me." Allen unlaced his shoes, then reached up on top of the tea table to retrieve a tiny cinnamon cake. He popped it into his mouth.

Ashe watched the boy, noting again how much he looked like Deborah as a young girl. Except where she had been short and plump with small hands and feet, Allen was tall, slender and possessed large feet and big hands. But his hair was the same color, his eyes an almost identical blue.

"Hey, what do we know about Mr. McLaughlin? We can't let Deborah date just anybody." Allen returned Ashe's penetrating stare. "If he gets serious about Deborah, is he the kind of man who'd make her a good husband?"

The front door opened and closed again. A neatly attired young woman in a navy suit and white blouse walked into the entrance hall.

"Now, Allen, you're being rude again," Carol said. "Besides, your sister's love life really isn't any of our business, even if we did find her the perfect man."

"Now what?" Deborah called out from the hallway, not even looking their way. "Mother, you and Allen haven't found another prospect you want me to consider, have you? Just who have you two picked out as potential husband material this time?"

Carrying an oxblood leather briefcase, Deborah came to an abrupt halt when she looked into the living room and saw Ashe sitting beside her mother on the sofa. She gasped aloud, visibly shaken.

"Come in, dear. Allen and I were just entertaining Ashe McLaughlin. You remember Ashe, don't you, Deborah?"

"Was he your old boyfriend?" Allen asked. "Mother won't tell me."

Ashe stood and took a long, hard look at Deborah Vaughn… the girl who had proclaimed her undying love for him one night down by the river, eleven years ago. The girl who, when he gently rejected her, had run crying to her rich and powerful daddy.

The district attorney and Wallace Vaughn had given Ashe two choices. Leave town and never come back, or face statutory rape charges.

"Hello, Deborah."

"What are you doing here?"

She had changed, perhaps even more than her pale, weak mother. No longer plump but still as lovely as she'd been as a teenager, Deborah possessed a poise and elegance that had eluded the younger, rather awkward girl. She wore her long, dark blond hair tucked into a loose bun at the nape of her neck. A pair of small golden earrings matched the double gold chain around her neck.

"Your mother sent for me." Ashe noted the astonished look on her face.

Deborah, still standing in the entrance hall, gazed at her mother. "What does he mean, you sent for him?"

"Now, dear, please come in and let's talk about this matter before you upset yourself."

"Allen, please go out in the kitchen with Mazie while I speak with Mother and Mr. McLaughlin."

"Ah, why do I have to leave? I'm a member of this family, aren't I? I shouldn't be excluded from important conversations." When his sister remained silent, Allen looked pleadingly at his mother, who shook her head.

"Do what Deborah says." Carol motioned toward the hall-way. "This is grown-up talk and although you're quite a young man, you're still not old enough to—"

"Yeah, yeah. I know." Allen jumped up and ran out of the room, his eyes downcast and his lips puckered into a defiant pout.

"What's going on?" Deborah marched into the living room, slamming her briefcase down atop Allen's books on the antique commode. She glared at Ashe. "What are *you* doing here?"

"As Ashe said, I sent for him." Tilting her chin upward, Carol straightened her thin shoulders.

"You what?"

"Calm yourself," Carol said.

"I am calm." Deborah spoke slowly, her teeth clenched tightly.

"Ashe works for a private security firm out of Atlanta." Carol readjusted her hips on the sofa, placing her hand down on the cushion beside her. "I've hired him to act as your bodyguard until the trial is over and you're no longer in any danger."

"I can't believe what I'm hearing." Deborah scowled at

Ashe. "You've brought this man back into our lives. Good God, Mother, do you have any idea what you've done?"

"Don't speak to me in that tone of voice, Deborah Lu-ellen Vaughn! I've done what I think is best for everyone concerned."

"And you?" Deborah looked directly at Ashe. "Why would you come back to Sheffield after all these years? How on earth did my mother persuade you to return?" Deborah's rosy cheeks turned pale, her lips quivered. "What—what did she tell you?"

"I told him that your life had been threatened. I explained the basic facts." Carol turned to Ashe. "This is what he does for a living, and I'm paying him his usual fee, isn't that right, Ashe?"

"This is strictly a business arrangement for me," Ashe replied. "My services are for hire to anyone with enough money to afford me."

Where was the sweet girl he'd once known? The laughing, smiling girl who'd been his friend long before she'd become his lover one hot summer night down by the river. He had never regretted anything as much as he had regretted taking Deborah's virginity. He'd been filled with rage and half drunk. Deborah had been with him that night, trying to comfort him, and he had taken advantage of her loving nature. But she'd paid him back.

"I don't want you here. Keep a week's salary for your trouble." Deborah nodded toward the door. "Now, please leave."

"No!" Reaching out, Carol grabbed Ashe by the arm. "Please, don't leave. Go in the kitchen and have some cookies with Allen."

"Mother! Think what you're saying."

"Please, Ashe. Go out into the kitchen for a few minutes while I speak with Deborah."

Ashe patted Carol on the hand, then pulled away from her.

"I won't leave, Miss Carol. It would take an act of congress to get me out of Sheffield."

He smiled at Deborah when he walked past her, halting briefly to inspect her from head to toe, then proceeding down the hallway and through the door leading to the kitchen.

Heat and cold zigzagged through Deborah like red-hot and freezing blue shafts of pain. Ashe McLaughlin. Here in Sheffield. Here in her home. And he'd seen Allen!

"He can't stay."

"Come over here, dear." Carol patted the sofa seat. "You've needed him for such a long time, Deborah, but now more than ever. You know I disagreed with your father's assessment of Ashe, but I loved your father and never would have gone against his wishes. But once Wallace died, I begged you to let me contact Ashe. He's kept in touch with Mattie all these years. We could have asked him to come home at any time."

"He kept in touch with his grandmother, not with us. He left this town and didn't look back. He never once called me or wrote me or…" Deborah crossed the room, slumped down on the sofa beside her mother and folded her hands in her lap. "I need to phone the office and let them know I won't be back in this afternoon. I had planned to just drop Allen off, but I saw the car in the drive and wondered who… I don't want Ashe McLaughlin here."

"But I do." Carol's blue eyes met her daughter's blue eyes, stubborn, determined and equally strong. "We both know that I'm only in remission. The cancer could worsen at any time and I'll have to go in for more surgery. I could die without ever seeing you happy."

"You honestly think Ashe McLaughlin can make me happy? Get real, Mother." Deborah lowered her voice to a snarling whisper. "The man seduced me when I was seventeen, dropped me like a hot potato and left town two months later, never bothering to find out whether or not he'd gotten me pregnant."

"I think you should know that—"

"If you're convinced I need a bodyguard then have the private security agency send someone else. Tell them we want someone older or younger or… Hell! Tell them anything, but get rid of Ashe."

"I believe he still cares about you." Carol smiled, deepening the faint lines in her face.

"Mother!"

"It's been eleven years, Deborah, and you haven't had one serious relationship in all that time. Doesn't that tell you anything about your own feelings?"

"Yes. It tells me that I'm a smart girl. I learn from my mistakes."

"It tells me that you've never gotten over Ashe McLaughlin, that somewhere deep down, in your heart of hearts, you're still in love with him."

Deborah couldn't bear it. Her mother's words pierced the protective wall she had built around her heart. She didn't love Ashe McLaughlin. She hated him. But she knew only too well how fine a line there was between love and hate.

"I've hardly had time to date, let alone find the man of my dreams. Have you forgotten that I was in my senior year of college when Daddy died and I had to complete my courses for my degree and step in at Vaughn & Posey?" Deborah paused, waiting for her mother to comment. Carol said nothing.

"Then I had to earn my Realtors' license and work damn hard to fill Daddy's shoes at the firm," Deborah said. "Over the last few years while other firms have floundered, I've kept Vaughn & Posey in the black, making substantial gains each year. Over the last five years, we've been involved in two different subdivision developments."

Carol held up her hand, signaling acquiescence. "I know what a busy young woman you've been. But other people lead busy lives and still find time for romance."

"I don't need any romance in my life. Have you also forgotten how my foolishly romantic illusions about love nearly destroyed my life eleven years ago?"

"Of course I haven't forgotten. But there's more at stake than my desire to see you and Ashe settle things between you. Your life is in danger—real danger. Charlie Blaylock can only do so much. You need twenty-four-hour-a-day protection, and Ashe is highly qualified to do the job I've hired him to do."

"What makes him so highly qualified?"

"He was a Green Beret for ten years and joined, what I am told, is the best private security agency in the South. If you won't agree to his staying here for any other reason, do it for me. For my peace of mind."

"Mother, really. You're asking a great deal of me, aren't you? And you're putting Allen at risk. What if Ashe were to suspect the truth? Do we dare take that kind of chance? How do you think Allen would react if he found out that everything we've told him is a lie?"

Tears gathered in the corners of Deborah's eyes. She blinked them away. No tears. Not now. She cried only when she was alone, where no one could see her. Where no one would know that the strong, dependable, always reliable Deborah Luellen Vaughn succumbed to the weakness of tears. Since her father died, she had learned to be strong—for her mother, for Allen, for those depending upon Vaughn & Posey for their livelihoods.

"Even if Ashe learns the truth, he would never tell Allen."

"How can you be so sure?"

"Intuition."

Deborah groaned. Sometimes her mother could be incredibly naive for a fifty-five-year-old woman. "I don't want Ashe McLaughlin to become a part of our lives."

"He's always been a part of our lives." Carol glanced up at the oil painting of Allen at the age of three, hung over the fireplace beside the portrait of a three-year-old Deborah. "All I ask is that you allow him to stay on as your bodyguard until after Lon Sparks's trial. If you feel nothing for Ashe except hatred, then his being here should do nothing more than annoy you. Surely you can put up with a little annoyance to make your dying mother happy."

"You aren't dying!"

"Please, dear, just talk to Ashe."

Sighing deeply, Deborah closed her eyes and shook her head. How could she say no to her mother? How could she explain what the very sight of Ashe McLaughlin had done to her? Wasn't she already going through enough, having to deal with testifying against a murderer, having to endure constant threats on her life, without having to put up with Ashe McLaughlin, too?

"Oh, all right, Mother. I'll talk to Ashe. But I'm not promising anything."

"Fine. That's all I ask." Gripping the arm of the sofa for support, Carol stood. "I'll go in the kitchen and see how Ashe and Allen are getting along, then I'll send Ashe out to you."

Standing, Deborah paced the floor. Waiting. Waiting to face the man who haunted her dreams to this very day. The only man she had ever loved. The only man she had ever hated. Stopping in front of the fireplace, she glanced up at Allen's portrait. He looked so much like her. Their strong resemblance had made it easy to pass him off as her brother. But where others might not see any of Ashe in Allen's features, she could. His coloring was hers, but his nose was long and straight like Ashe's, not short and rounded like hers. His jaw tapered into a square chin unlike her gently rounded face.

Now that Allen was ten, it was apparent from his size that he would eventually become a large man, perhaps as big as Ashe, who stood six foot three.

But would Ashe see any resemblance? Would he look at Allen and wonder? Over the years had he, even once, asked himself whether he might have fathered a child the night he had taken her virginity?

"Deborah?"

She spun around to face Ashe, who stood in the hallway. Had he noticed her staring at Allen's portrait?

"Please come in and sit down."

He walked into the living room, but remained standing. "I came back to Sheffield as a favor to your mother." *And because she dared me to face the past.* "She sounded desperate when she called. My grandmother told me about Miss Carol's bout with cancer. I—"

"Thank you for caring about my mother."

"She was always good to Mama Mattie and to me. Despite what happened between the two of us, I never blamed your mother."

What was he talking about? What reason did he have to blame anyone for anything? He'd been the one who had left Sheffield, left an innocent seventeen-year-old girl pregnant.

"Mother has gotten it into her head that I need protection, and I don't disagree with her on that point. I'd be a fool to say I'm not afraid of Buck Stansell and his gang. I know what they're capable of doing. I saw, firsthand, how they deal with people who go against them."

"Then allowing me to stay as your bodyguard is the sensible thing to do."

How was it, he wondered, that years ago he'd thought Whitney Vaughn was the most beautiful, desirable creature on earth, when all along her little cousin Deborah had been blossoming into perfection? Although Whitney had been the woman he'd wanted, Deborah was the woman he'd never been able to forget.

"I would prefer your agency send another representative. That would be possible, wouldn't it? Surely, you're no more eager than I am for the two of us to be thrown together this way."

"Yes, it's possible for the Dundee Agency to send another agent, but your mother wants me. And I intend to abide by her wishes."

Deborah glared at him, then regretted it when he met her gaze head-on. She didn't like the way he was looking at her. As if…as if he found her attractive.

"You could speak to Mother, persuade her to agree to another agent."

"Yes, I could speak to your mother, but I don't think anything I say will dissuade her from having me act as your personal bodyguard." Ashe took a tentative step toward Deborah. She backed away from him. "Why is it that I get the feeling Miss Carol would like to see something romantic happen between you and me?"

Deborah turned from him, cursing the blush she felt creeping into her cheeks. When he placed his hands on her shoulders, she jerked away from him, rushing toward the French doors that opened up onto a side patio. She grasped the brass handle.

"I'm not interested in forming any kind of relationship with you other than employer and employee," Ashe said. "I agreed to act as your bodyguard because a fine, dear lady asked me to, as a personal favor to her. That's the only reason I'm here. You don't have to worry that I'll harass you with any unwanted attention."

Deborah opened the French doors, walked outside and gazed up at the clear blue sky. Autumn sky. Autumn breeze. A hint of autumn colors surrounded her, especially in her mother's chrysanthemums and marigolds that lined the patio privacy wall.

Why should Ashe's words hurt her so deeply? It wasn't as if she still loved him. She had accepted the fact, long ago, that she had meant nothing to him, that Whitney had been the woman he'd wanted. Why would she think anything had changed?

Ashe followed her out onto the side patio. "It wasn't easy for me to come back. I never wanted to see this place again as long as I lived. But I'm back and I intend to stay to protect you."

"As a favor to my mother?"

"Partly, yes."

She wouldn't face him; she couldn't. "Why else would you come back to Sheffield?"

"Your mother asked me if I was afraid to face the past. She dared me to come home."

"And were you afraid to face the past?"

"I'm here, aren't I? What does that tell you?"

"It tells me that you have a soft spot in your heart for my mother because she was kind to your grandmother and you and your cousin, Annie Laurie. And it tells me that you're the type of man who can't resist a dare."

"If I'm willing to come back to Sheffield, to act as your personal bodyguard because it's what Miss Carol wants, then it would seem to me that you should care enough about her to agree to her wishes. All things considered." He moved over to where Deborah stood near the miniature waterfall built into the privacy wall.

Turning her head slightly, she glanced at him. He had changed and yet he remained the same. Still devastatingly handsome, a bit cocky and occasionally rude. The twenty-one-year-old boy who'd made love to her had not completely vanished. He was there in those gold-flecked, green eyes, in that wide, sensuous mouth, in those big, hard hands. She jerked her gaze away from his hands. Hands that had caressed her intimately. Hands that had taught her the meaning of being a sexual woman.

How could she allow him to stay in her home? How could she endure watching him with Allen, knowing they were father and son?

Was there some way she could respect her mother's wishes and still keep the truth from Ashe?

"Let's understand something up front," Deborah said, facing him, steeling herself not to show any emotion. "I don't want you here. I had hoped I'd never see you again as long as I lived. If I agree to your acting as my bodyguard until the end of the trial, to please Mother, you must promise me, here and now, that once I am no longer in any danger, you'll leave Sheffield and never return."

"Do you honestly think I'd want to stay?"

"Promise me."

"I don't have to promise you anything. I don't owe you anything." He glared at her, into those bright, still innocent-looking blue eyes and wanted to grab her and shake her until her teeth rattled. Who the hell did she think she was, giving him orders, demanding promises from him?

"You're still as stubborn, as bullheaded, as aggravating as you ever were," she said.

"Guilty as charged." He wanted to shout at her, to tell her she seemed to be the same little girl who wanted her own way. But this time she couldn't go running to Daddy. This time Wallace Vaughn couldn't force him to leave town. Nobody could. Most certainly not Deborah.

"We seem to be at an impasse."

"No, we're not. Once I settle in, pay a few visits on family and get the lay of the land, so to speak, you're stuck with me for the duration." When she opened her mouth to protest, he shook his head. "I won't promise you anything, but I can tell you this, I don't intend to stay in Alabama one day longer than necessary. And while I'm here, you don't have anything to fear from me. My purpose is to protect you, not harm you."

They stared at each other, face-to-face, two determined people, neither giving an inch. Finally Deborah nodded, then looked away.

"Dinner is at six-thirty, if you care to join us," she said.

"Fine. I'll be back from Mama Mattie's before then." Ashe hesitated momentarily, overwhelmed with a need to ask Deborah why. Why had she gone running to her daddy eleven years ago? Had his rejection made her hate him that much?

"I'll have Mazie prepare you a room, if Mother hasn't already seen to it."

"Thanks." There was no reason to wait, no reason to keep

looking at her, to continue wondering exactly what it was about this woman that had made her so unforgettable. He tried to smile, but the effort failed, so he turned and walked back inside the house.

Deborah balled her hands into fists. Taking and releasing a deep breath, she said a silent prayer, asking God to keep them all safe and to protect Allen from the truth. A truth she had kept hidden in her heart since the day he was born, since the day she agreed to allow her son to be raised as her brother.

CHAPTER TWO

As ASHE DROVE his rental car up Montgomery Avenue, into the downtown area of Sheffield, he noticed the new businesses, mostly restaurants—Louisiana, Milestones and New Orleans Transfer. Come what may, Southerners were going to eat well. Mama Mattie's homespun philosophy had always been that if folks spent their money on good food, they wouldn't need to spend it on a doctor.

Mama Mattie. How he loved that old woman. She was probably the only person he'd ever truly loved. The only person who had ever really loved him. He could barely remember a time during his growing up years when he hadn't lived with her. He had faint memories of living in a trailer out in Leighton. Before he'd started school. Before his daddy had caught his mama in bed with another man and shot them both.

The courts had sentenced JoJo McLaughlin to life in prison, and that's where he'd died, seven years later.

Mama Mattie had tried to protect Ashe from the ugly truth, from the snide remarks of unthinking adults and the vicious taunts of his schoolmates. But his grandmother had been powerless to protect him from the reality of class distinction, from the social snobbery and inbred attitudes of elite families, like the Vaughns, for whom she worked.

If he'd had a lick of sense, he would have stayed in his place and been content to work at the service station during the day and at the country club as a busboy on weekend nights. But no, Ashe McLaughlin, that bad boy who'd come from white trash outlaws, had wanted to better himself. It didn't matter to anyone that he graduated salutatorian of his high school class or that he attended the University of North Alabama on an academic scholarship. He still wasn't good enough to associate with the *right people*.

He had thought Whitney Vaughn cared about him, that their passionate affair would end in marriage. He'd been a fool. But he'd been an even bigger fool to trust sweet little Deborah, who professed to be his friend, who claimed she would love him until the day she died.

Crossing the railroad tracks, Ashe turned off Shop Pike and drove directly to Mama Mattie's neat frame house.

When he stepped out of the car, he saw her standing in the doorway, tall, broad-shouldered, her white hair permed into a halo of curls around her lean face.

He had sent her money over the years. Wrote her occasionally. Called her on her birthday and holidays. Picked up special gifts for her from around the world. She had asked him to come home a few times during the first couple of years after he joined the army, but she'd finally quit asking.

She wrote him faithfully, once a month, always thanking him for his kindness, assuring him she and Annie Laurie were well. Sometimes she'd mention that Miss Carol had dropped by for a visit, and told him what a precious little boy Allen Vaughn was. But she never mentioned Deborah. It was as if she knew he couldn't bear for her name to be mentioned.

Mattie Trotter opened the storm door, walked out onto the front porch and held open her arms. Ashe's slow, easy gait picked up speed as he drew closer to his grandmother. Taking the steps two at a time, he threw his arms around Mama Mattie, lifting her off her feet.

"Put me down, you silly boy! You'll throw out your back picking me up." All the while she scolded, she smiled, that warm, loving smile Ashe well remembered from his childhood.

Placing her on her feet, he slipped his arm around her waist, hugging her to his side. She lacked only a few inches being as tall as he was. "It's so good to see you again, Mama Mattie."

"Come on inside." She opened the storm door. "I've made those tea cakes you always loved, and only a few minutes ago, I put on a fresh pot of that expensive coffee you sent me from Atlanta."

Ashe glanced around the living room. Small, not more than twelve by fourteen. A tan sofa, arms and cushions well-worn, sat against the picture window, a matching chair to the left. The new plaid recliner Ashe had sent her for Christmas held a fat, gray cat, who stared up at Ashe with complete disinterest.

"That's Annie Laurie's Mr. Higgins. She's spoiled him rotten," Mattie said. "But to be honest, I'm pretty fond of him myself. Sit down, Ashe, sit down."

He sat beside her on the sofa. She clasped his hands. "There were times when I wondered if I'd ever see you again. I'm an old woman and only God knows how much longer I'm going to be in this world."

"Don't talk like that. You'll live to be a hundred."

Releasing his hands, she looked directly into his eyes. "Have you seen Deborah?"

"Yeah, Mama Mattie, I've seen Deborah Vaughn."

"She turned out to be a beautiful woman, didn't she?"

"She was always beautiful, just not...not finished."

"Miss Carol looks bad, doesn't she?" Mattie shook her head sadly. "That bout she had with cancer a while back took its toll on her. She's in remission now, but we all live in fear she'll have a relapse."

"She aged more than I'd expected," Ashe said, recalling how incredibly lovely Carol Vaughn had once been. "But nothing else has changed about her. She's still a very kind lady."

"So is Deborah."

"Don't!" Ashe stood abruptly, turning his back on his

grandmother, not wanting to hear her defend the woman who had been responsible for having him run out of town eleven years ago.

Mattie sighed. "I still say you judged her wrong. She was just a child. Seventeen. You rejected all that sweet, young love she felt for you. If she went to her daddy the way you think she did, then you shouldn't hold it against her. My God, boy, you took her innocence and then told her you didn't want her."

"It wasn't like that and you damn well know it." Ashe needed to hit something, smash anything into a zillion pieces. He hated remembering what he'd done and what his stupidity had cost him.

"Don't you swear at me, boy." Mattie narrowed her eyes, giving her grandson a killing look.

"I'm sorry, Mama Mattie, but I didn't come by to see you so we could have that old argument about Deborah Vaughn." Ashe headed toward the kitchen. "Where are those tea cakes?"

Mattie followed him, busying herself with pouring coffee into brown ceramic mugs while Ashe devoured three tea cakes in quick succession. He pulled out a metal and vinyl chair and sat down at the table.

"They taste just the same. As good as I remember."

He would never forget walking into the Vaughns' kitchen after school every day, laying his books on the table and raiding Mama Mattie's tea cake tray. More often than not, he and Annie Laurie rode home with Miss Carol when she picked up Deborah and Whitney from school.

Whitney had ignored him as much as possible, often complaining to her aunt that she thought it disgraceful they had to be seen with *those children*. He supposed her haughty attitude had given him more reason to want to bring her down to his level, and eventually he'd done just that. He hadn't been Whitney's first, but he hadn't cared. She'd been hot and eager and he'd thought she really loved him.

All the while he'd been drooling over Whitney, he hadn't missed the way Deborah stared at him, those big blue eyes of hers filled with undisguised adoration.

"Thinking about those afternoons in the Vaughn kitchen?" Mattie asked.

"What is it with you and Miss Carol? Both of you seem determined to resurrect some sort of romance between Deborah and me." Ashe lifted the coffee mug to his lips, sipped the delicious brew and held his mug in his hand. "Deborah and I were never sweethearts. We weren't in love. I liked her and she had a big teenage crush on me. That's all there ever was to it. So tell me what's going on?"

"Neither one of you has ever gotten married."

"Are you saying you'd like to see me married to Deborah?" Ashe's laughter combined a snicker, a chuckle and a groan. "It's never going to happen. Not in a million years. Wherever did you get such a crazy idea?"

"You came back home when Miss Carol called and told you that Deborah was in trouble, that her life was in danger," Mattie said. "In eleven years nothing I've said or done could persuade you to return. And don't try to tell me that you came back because of Miss Carol. You could have sent another man from that private security place where you work. You didn't have to come yourself and we both know it."

"Miss Carol asked for me, personally. I knew how sick she'd been. You've told me again and again that you were afraid she might die."

"So knowing Buck Stansell is probably out to stop Deborah from testifying didn't have anything to do with your coming home? You don't care what happens to her?"

"I didn't say I don't care. I wouldn't want anything to happen to her." When Miss Carol had first telephoned him and explained the situation, his blood had run cold at the thought of anyone harming Deborah. Despite what she'd done to him, he couldn't help remembering the sweet, generous, loving girl he'd known since she was a small child. He had thought she didn't matter to him, that he didn't even hate her anymore. But he'd been wrong. He cared. He cared too damned much. Now that he'd seen Deborah again, he was worried that he couldn't act as her bodyguard and keep their relationship on a purely business level. And that could be dangerous for both of them. If he was smart, he'd call Sam Dundee and tell him to put another agent on the first available flight out of Atlanta.

But where Deborah Vaughn was concerned, he'd never been smart. Not when he had ignored her to pay court to her older cousin. Not when he'd accepted her comfort and love when Whitney had rejected him. And not when he'd been certain she would never betray him to anyone, least of all her father.

Mattie poured herself a second cup of coffee, broke a tea cake in two and popped half into her mouth. Chewing slowly, she watched Ashe. When he turned around and caught her staring at him, he smiled.

"All right. I admit it. Part of the reason I agreed to Miss Carol's request was because I don't want to see anything happen to Deborah. There. I said it. Are you satisfied?"

Mattie grinned, showing her perfect, white dentures. "You ought to go have a talk with Lee Roy and Johnny Joe. They're working for Buck Stansell, you know."

"Yeah, I figured as much, since their daddy and mine were both part of that gang years ago, along with Buck's daddy."

"Well, I don't trust Johnny Joe, but I always saw something in Lee Roy that made me think he was a mite better than that bunch of trash he came from."

"Hey, watch what you're saying, Mama Mattie. You're talking about my family." Ashe grinned.

"Your daddy's family, not mine, and not yours. I think Johnny Joe took after his daddy and his Uncle JoJo, where Lee Roy reminds me a bit of your daddy's sister. She wasn't such a bad girl. She and your mama always got along."

"You think Lee Roy and Johnny Joe know something about the threats against Deborah?" Ashe asked.

"Can't nobody prove nothing, but folks know that Buck Stansell was behind that killing Deborah witnessed. Whoever's been sending her those notes and making those phone calls, you can bet your bottom dollar that Buck's behind it all."

"What do you know about this Lon Sparks? I don't remember him."

"No reason you should. He showed up around these parts a few years back. I hear he come up from Corinth with a couple of other guys that Buck recruited when he expanded his drug dealings."

"How do you know so much, old woman?" Ashe laid his hand over his grandmother's where it rested beside her coffee cup.

"Everybody hears things. I hear things. At the beauty shop. At the grocery store. At church."

"After I've settled in and made my presence known, I'll take a ride out to Leighton and see how my cousins are doing."

"You be careful, Ashe. Buck Stansell isn't the kind of man to roll over and play dead just because Deborah's got herself a bodyguard."

"Don't you worry. I'm not stupid enough to underestimate Buck. I remember him and his old man. I've come up against their type all over the world."

"While you're taking care of Deborah and Miss Carol and that precious little Allen, make sure you take care of yourself, too." Mattie squeezed her grandson's big hand.

The back door swung open and a tall, thin young woman in a sedate gray pantsuit walked in and stopped dead still when she saw Ashe.

"Oh, my goodness, it's really you!" Annie Laurie threw herself into Ashe's arms. "Mama Mattie said you'd come home, but I wasn't so sure. You've been away forever and ever."

Mr. Higgins sneaked into the kitchen, staring up at Annie Laurie, purring lightly.

Ashe held his cousin at arm's length, remembering the first time he'd seen her. She'd been a skinny eight-year-old whose parents had been killed in an automobile accident. Mama Mattie, Annie Laurie's mother's aunt, had been the child's closest relative and hadn't hesitated to open her home and heart to the girl, just as she had done for Ashe. "Here, let me have a good look at you. My, my. You sure have grown. And into a right pretty young lady."

Blushing, Annie Laurie shoved her slipping glasses back up her nose. "You haven't seen me since I was thirteen."

Hearing a car exit the driveway, Ashe glanced out the window in time to see a black Mercedes backing up, a familiar-looking redheaded guy driving.

"Your boyfriend bring you home from work?" Ashe asked.

Annie Laurie's pink cheeks flamed bright red. She cast her gaze down toward the floor, then bent over, picked up Mr. Higgins and held him in her arms.

"Stop teasing the girl," Mattie said.

"He's not your boyfriend?" Ashe lifted her chin.

"He's my boss."

"Your boss?"

"That was Neil Posey," Mattie said. "You remember him. He's Archie Posey's son. He's partners with Deborah in their daddies' real estate firm."

"You work for Vaughn & Posey Real Estate?" Ashe asked. "I guess Mama Mattie told me and I'd just forgotten."

"I'm Neil's…that is, Mr. Posey's secretary. And he's not my boyfriend. He's Deborah's…I mean, he likes her."

"What?" Ashe laughed aloud. Neil Posey was Deborah's boyfriend? That short, stocky egghead with carrot red hair and trillions of freckles.

"I've tried to tell Annie Laurie that Deborah isn't interested in Neil just because he follows her around like a lovesick puppy dog." Mattie shook her head, motioning for Ashe to let the subject drop. "Are you staying for supper? I've got some chicken all thawed out. It won't take me long to fry it up."

"Sorry, Mama Mattie, I'm expected for dinner at the Vaughns', but I'm looking forward to some of your fried chicken while I'm home."

"You be sure and tell Deborah and Miss Carol I asked about them," Mattie said. "And, here, take Allen some of my tea cakes. He loves them as much as you used to when you were his age."

Ashe caught an odd look in his grandmother's eyes. It was as if she knew something she wanted him to know, but for some reason didn't see fit to tell him. He shook off the notion, picked up his coffee mug and relaxed, enjoying being home. Back in his grandmother's house. Back with the only real family he'd ever known.

DEBORAH CHECKED HER appearance in the cheval mirror, tightened the backs of her pearl earrings and lifted the edge of her neckline so that her pearl necklace lay precisely right. Ashe McLaughlin's presence at their dinner table tonight had absolutely nothing to do with her concern about her appearance, she told herself, and knew it was a lie. Her undue concern *was* due to Ashe, and so was her nervousness.

Didn't she have enough problems without Ashe reappearing in her life after eleven years? How could her mother have thought that bringing that man back into their lives could actually help her? She'd almost rather face Buck Stansell alone than have to endure weeks with Ashe McLaughlin at her side twenty-four hours a day.

Of course, her mother had been right in hiring a personal bodyguard for her. She had to admit that she'd considered the possibility herself. But not Ashe!

Ever since she had inadvertently driven up on the scene of

Corey Looney's execution, she had been plagued by nightmares. Both awake and asleep. Time and again she saw the gun, the blood, the man's body slump to the ground. Even in the quiet of her dark bedroom, alone at night, she could hear the sound of the gun firing.

Shivers racked Deborah's body. Chill bumps broke out on her arms. The letters and telephone calls had begun the day the sheriff arrested Lon Sparks. At first she had tried to dismiss them, but when they persisted, even the local authorities became concerned.

Colbert County's sheriff and an old family acquaintance, Charlie Blaylock, had assigned a deputy to her before and during the preliminary hearing, but couldn't spare a man for twenty-four-hour-a-day protection on an indefinite basis. Charlie had spoken to the state people, the FBI and the DEA, hoping one or more of the agencies' interest in Buck Stansell's dealings might bring in assistance and protection for Deborah.

But there was no proof Buck Stansell was involved, even though everyone knew Lon Sparks worked for Stansell. The federal boys wanted to step in, but murder in Colbert County was a local crime. They'd keep close tabs on the situation, but couldn't become officially involved.

Charlie had been the one to suggest hiring a private bodyguard. Deborah had agreed to consider the suggestion, never dreaming her mother would take matters into her own hands and hire Ashe McLaughlin.

Closing the door behind her, Deborah stepped out into the upstairs hallway, took a deep breath and ventured down the stairs. When she entered the foyer, she heard voices coming from the library, a room that had once been her father's private domain. Her mother had kept the masculine flavor of the room, but had turned it into a casual family retreat where she or Deborah often helped Allen with his homework. The old library was more a family room now.

She stood in the open doorway, watching and listening,

totally unnoticed at first. Her mother sat in a tan-and-rust floral print chair, her current needlepoint project in her hand. She smiled, her gaze focused on Allen and Ashe, who were both sitting on the Tabriz rug, video-game controls in their hands as they fought out a battle on the television screen before them.

"You're good at this," Allen said. "Are you sure you don't have a kid of your own you play with all the time?"

Deborah sucked in a deep breath, the sting of her son's words piercing her heart. She couldn't bear the way Allen looked at Ashe, so in awe of the big, friendly man he must never know was his father.

"I don't have any kids of my own." Ashe hadn't thought much about having a family. His life didn't include a place for a wife and children, although at one time, a family had been high on his list of priorities—eleven years ago when he'd thought he would marry Whitney Vaughn and carve a place for himself in local society. Hell, he'd been a fool in more ways than one.

"You should be thinking about a family, Ashe," Carol Vaughn said, laying aside her needlework. "You're how old now, thirty-two? Surely you've sowed all the wild oats a man would need to sow."

Ashe turned his head, smiled at Carol, then frowned when he caught sight of Deborah standing in the doorway. "I haven't really given marriage a thought since I left Sheffield. When a man puts his trust in the wrong woman, more than once, the way I did, it makes him a little gun-shy."

Deborah met his fierce gaze directly, not wavering the slightest when he glared at her with those striking hazel eyes…gold-flecked green eyes made even more dramatic since they were set in a hard, lean, darkly tanned face.

Ashe realized that he could not win the game of staring her down. Deborah Vaughn had changed. She was no longer the shy, quiet girl who always seemed afraid to look him in the eye. Now she seemed determined to prove to him how tough she was, how totally immune she was to him.

With that cold, determined stare she told him that he no longer had any power over her, that the lovesick girl she'd once been no longer existed. Her aversion to him came as no great surprise, but what did unsettle him was her accusatory attitude, as if she found him at fault.

All right, he had taken her innocence when he'd had no right to touch her, but he'd told her he was sorry and begged her to forgive him. He had rejected her girlish declaration of love as gently as he'd known how. If he'd been a real cad, he could have taken advantage of her time and again. But he'd cared about Deborah, and his stupidity in taking her just that one time had made him heartsick.

But he had not ruined her life. It had been the other way around. She had almost ruined his a couple of months later by running to her daddy. Why had she done it? Had she hated him that much? Did she still hate him?

Carol glanced at her daughter. "Deborah, come join us. Mazie tells me dinner will be ready promptly at six-thirty."

"She's always punctual. Dinner's at six-thirty every night," Deborah said.

"She's prepared Allen's favorite. Meat loaf with creamed potatoes and green peas," Carol said.

"Hey, pal, that's my favorite, too." Ashe elbowed Allen playfully in the ribs.

Allen leaned into Ashe, toppling the big man over onto the rug. Within seconds the two were wrestling around on the floor.

Deborah looked from father and son to her mother. Nervously she cleared her throat. When no one paid any heed to her, she cleared her throat again.

"Come sit down." Carol gestured toward the tufted leather sofa. "Let the boys be boys. They'll tire soon enough."

When Deborah continued staring at Allen and Ashe rolling around on the floor, both of them laughing, Carol stood and walked over to her daughter.

"Allen needs a man in his life." Carol slipped her arm around Deborah's waist, leading her into the room. "He'll soon be a teenager. He's going to need a father more than ever then."

"Hush, Mother! They'll hear you."

Carol glanced over at the two rowdy males who stopped abruptly when their roughhousing accidently knocked over a potted plant.

"Uh-oh, Allen, we'll be in trouble with the ladies now." Rising to his knees, Ashe swept up the spilled dirt with his hands and dumped it back into the brass pot.

"Don't worry about it," Carol said. "I'll ask Mazie to run the vacuum over what's left on the rug."

Deborah glanced down at her gold and diamond wristwatch. "It's almost six-thirty. I'll check on dinner and tell Mazie about the accident with the plant."

The moment Deborah exited the room, Allen shook his head, stood up and brushed off his hands. "What's the matter with Deborah? She's acting awful strange."

"She's nervous about the upcoming trial, but you know that, Allen." Carol smiled, first at Allen and then at Ashe. "Our lives have been topsy-turvy for weeks now."

"No, I'm not talking about that." Allen nodded toward Ashe. "She's been acting all goofy ever since Ashe showed up here today." He turned to Ashe. "Nobody ever answered my question about whether you and Deborah used to be an item."

"Allen—" Carol said.

"Deborah and I were good friends at one time." Ashe certainly couldn't say anything negative about his sister to the boy. "I'm four years older, so I dated older girls."

"Deborah had a crush on Ashe for years," Carol said.

When Ashe glanced at Carol, she stared back at him, her look asking something of him that Ashe couldn't comprehend.

"She liked you, but you didn't like her back?" Allen asked.

"Boy, were you dumb. Deborah's pretty and about the nicest person in the world."

"Yeah, Allen, I was pretty dumb all right. I'm a lot smarter now."

"Well, if Deborah gives you a second chance this time, you won't mess things up, will you?" Allen looked at him with eyes identical to Deborah's, the purest, richest blue imaginable.

"I'm not here to romance your sister," Ashe said. "I'm here to protect her, to make sure—"

Carol cleared her throat; Ashe realized he was saying too much, that they wanted the boy protected from the complete, ugly truth.

"Ashe is here to act as Deborah's bodyguard. You know, the way famous people have bodyguards to protect them from their overzealous fans. Well, Ashe is going to make sure the reporters and people curious about the trial don't interfere with her life in any way."

"The kids at school say Buck Stansell will try to kill Deborah if she tells in court what she saw that man do," Allen said, looking directly to Ashe for an explanation. "Is that true?"

"No one is going to hurt Deborah while I'm around." Ashe placed his hand on the boy's shoulder. "And I'll be here until after the trial, maybe a little longer."

Carol Vaughn sighed. Ashe glanced at the doorway. Deborah had returned and was looking straight at him, her eyes filled with pain and fear and something indiscernible. Longing? Ashe wondered. Or perhaps the remembrance and regret of longing?

Deborah willed herself to be strong, to show no sign of weakness in front of Allen and her mother or in Ashe's presence. She'd heard Ashe say that no one would hurt her while he was around. For one split second her heart had caught in her throat. He had sounded so determined, so protective, as if he truly cared what happened to her.

"Dinner is ready." Damn, her voice shouldn't sound so unsteady. She had to take control. "Is everything all right?"

"Fine," Carol and Ashe said in unison.

Rushing across the room, Allen threw his arms around Deborah. "I'll help Ashe protect you. You'll have two men in your life now, and we'll make sure nobody bothers you."

Deborah hugged her son to her, threading her fingers through his thick blond hair. "I feel very safe, knowing that I have you two guys looking out for me."

Carol Vaughn steered Allen and Ashe into the hall. "You two wash up and meet us in the dining room." She slipped her arm around Deborah's waist. "Come, dear."

Carol managed to keep the conversation directed on Allen during the meal, telling Ashe about the boy's exploits since early childhood. Deborah wished her mother didn't have her heart set on reuniting them all. There was no way it would ever happen. She and Ashe didn't even like each other. She certainly had good reason not to like Ashe, and it seemed he thought he had reason to dislike her.

"I told Mazie to save the apple pie for tomorrow night's dinner," Carol said. "Ashe brought us some of Mattie's delicious homemade tea cakes."

"I love Mama Mattie's tea cakes," Allen said.

Jerking his head around, Ashe stared at Allen. Had he heard correctly? Had Allen Vaughn referred to Ashe's grandmother as Mama Mattie?

"Mattie insisted Allen call her Mama Mattie." Carol laid her linen napkin on the table. "She said that she liked to think of Allen as a grandchild."

Deborah strangled on her iced tea. Lifting her napkin to her mouth, she coughed several times. Her faced turned red. She glared at her mother.

"Let's have Mazie serve the tea cakes in the library with coffee for us and milk for Allen." Easing her chair away from the table, Carol stood.

Allen followed Carol out of the dining room, obviously eager for a taste of Mattie Trotter's tea cakes. Deborah hesitated, waiting for Ashe. He halted at her side as he walked across the room.

"You look lovely tonight," he said. What the hell had prompted that statement? He'd thought it, and made the remark before thinking.

"Thank you."

She wore blue silk, the color of her eyes. And pearls. A lady's jewel. Understated and elegant.

"We've tried to protect Allen from the complete truth," she said. "He's so young. And he and I are very close. He was only four when Daddy died, and he tries to be our little man."

"He knows more than you think." Ashe understood her need to protect the boy; on short acquaintance he felt an affinity with Deborah's brother and a desire to safeguard him. "Anything made public, he's bound to hear sooner or later. You're better off being up front with him."

"Just what do you know about ten-year-old boys?"

"I know they're not babies, that a boy as smart as Allen can't be fooled."

"It's not your place to make decisions where—"

The telephone rang. Deborah froze. Ashe wished he could erase the fear he saw in her eyes, the somber expression on her face. "Have you had your number changed? Unlisted?"

"Yes." She swallowed hard.

"It's for you, Miss Deborah." Mazie stood in the doorway holding the portable phone. "It's Mr. Posey."

Letting out a sigh, Deborah swayed a fraction. Ashe grabbed her by the elbow.

"Are you all right?" he asked.

Deborah took the phone from Mazie, placed her hand over the mouthpiece and looked at Ashe. "Go ahead and join Mother and Allen in the library."

"Neil Posey?" Ashe asked. "Has he changed any or do his buddies still call him Bozo?"

Deborah widened her eyes, glaring at Ashe as if what he'd said had been sacrilege. *Go away. Now.* She mouthed the words. Grinning, Ashe threw up his hands in a what-did-I-say gesture, then walked out of the room.

"Neil?"

"I thought perhaps you'd like to take a drive," he said. "It's such a lovely autumn night. We could stop by somewhere for coffee later."

"Oh, that's such a sweet thought, but I'm afraid… Well, tonight just isn't good for me. We…that is, Mother has company tonight."

"I see. I'm disappointed of course, but we'll just make it another night."

"Yes, of course."

"See you tomorrow," Neil said. "Yes. Tomorrow." Deborah laid the phone down on the hall table.

Before she took three steps, the telephone rang again. She eyed it with suspicion. *Don't do this to yourself. Answer the damned thing. It's not going to bite you.*

"Hello. Vaughn residence."

"Deborah?" the man asked.

"Yes."

"Telling the sheriff what you saw was your first mistake. Testifying in court will be your last mistake."

"Who is this?" Sheriff Blaylock had put a tap on their telephones, the one in her bedroom and the one in the library. Damn, why hadn't she remembered not to answer the portable phone?

"This is someone concerned for your safety."

"How did you get our number?" She gripped the phone with white-knuckled ferocity.

"Change it as many times as you want and we'll still keep calling."

"Leave me alone!" Deborah's voice rose.

Ashe appeared before her, grabbed the phone out of her hand and shoved her aside. She stared at him in disbelief.

"Ms. Vaughn won't be taking any more phone calls." He ended the conversation, laid the phone on the hall table, then grabbed Deborah by the arm. "From now on, you're not to answer the phone. Mazie or I will screen all the incoming calls."

The touch of his big hand on her arm burned like fire. He was hard, his palm warm. She looked up at him, saw the genuine concern in his eyes and wanted nothing more than to crumple into his arms. It would be so easy to give in to the fear and uncertainty that had plagued her since she had witnessed Corey Looney's death. Ashe was big and strong, his shoulders wide enough to carry any burden. Even hers. She wanted to cry out to him "Take care of me," but she couldn't. She had to be strong. For herself. For her mother and Allen.

"Please, don't mention the phone call to Mother. It will only worry her needlessly."

"Needlessly?" Ashe grabbed Deborah by the shoulders. "You're so cool and in control. You're not the girl I used to know. She would have been crying by now. What changed you so much?"

You did. The words vibrated on the tip of her tongue. They would be so easy to say, so difficult to explain. "I grew up. I took on the responsibilities Daddy left behind when he died so suddenly."

Ashe ran his hands up and down her arms. She shivered. For one instant he saw the vulnerable, gentle girl he'd once liked, the Deborah who had adored him. "You won't answer the telephone, at home or at work."

"All right."

"And I won't mention this call to Miss Carol."

"Thank you."

He could barely resist the urge to kiss her. She stood there facing him, her defiant little chin tilted, her blue eyes bright, her cheeks delicately flushed. God, but she was beautiful. But then she always had been. Even when he'd fancied himself in love with Whitney, he hadn't been immune to Deborah's shy, plump beauty.

"If you ever need to let down your defenses for a few minutes, to stop being strong all the time for your mother and brother, I'll be around." He released her, but continued looking directly at her.

She nodded her head, turned and walked away from him.

He didn't want to care about her. Dammit! All these years he'd never been able to forget her. Or the fact that she had betrayed him to her father. Or that she had been a virgin and he had taken advantage of her. And he could never forget when she'd told him she loved him that night, he had seen a depth of emotion on her face he'd never seen again.

He waited in the entrance hall for a few minutes, wondering how the hell he was going to do his job protecting Deborah from the bad guys, when what she desperately needed was protection from him.

CHAPTER THREE

"MOTHER HAD MAZIE put your bag in here," Deborah said. "One of the guest rooms. It's right across the hall from mine."

"I'm sure it'll be fine." Ashe followed her into the room. Over the years he had stayed in some fancy places. It wasn't as if the finer things in life impressed him the way they once had. But even now, after all these years, he couldn't suppress the satisfaction of knowing he'd be sleeping in a guest room at the Vaughns' house.

Deborah flipped on the overhead light, revealing a room done tastefully in shades of tan and green. The antique oak bedroom suite, masculine in its heavy lines and massive size, would have overwhelmed a smaller room.

"Mother's room is to the right." Deborah returned to the hall. Ashe stood in the doorway. "And that's Allen's room." She pointed to the open door from which a blast of loud music came, then quieted. "He forgets and plays it too loud sometimes, but he's trying to be more considerate, for Mother's sake."

"I suppose it's been difficult for her trying to raise a young boy, alone, especially at her age." Ashe caught a glimpse of Allen darting around in his room, apparently straightening things.

"Mother is an incredible lady, but she hasn't been alone in raising Allen. I've been with her, taking as much responsibility for him as I possibly could."

"I'm sure you have. I just meant she's raised him without a father, without a man around to help her."

Deborah noticed Ashe watching their son. No! She had to stop thinking that way. Allen Vaughn was her brother.

"He's picking up because he plans to invite you in. He has a lot of questions to ask you about being a bodyguard."

"He's quite a boy, isn't he?" Ashe looked at Deborah. "He reminds me of you. Same coloring. Same quick mind."

"Yes, Allen and I are very much alike." But there are things about him that remind me of you, she wanted to say. Even before Ashe had come back into their lives, she had found similarities between Allen and the man who had fathered him. Now that they'd be together all the time, would those similarities become even more apparent?

"He's big for his age, isn't he?" Ashe asked. He'd thought it strange that Allen was so tall for a ten-year-old. Deborah couldn't be more than five-four, about the same height as Miss Carol; and Wallace Vaughn had been short and stocky.

"Yes." She smiled, thinking about how Ashe had looked as a boy of ten. He had been a part of her life for as long she could remember. He'd come to live with Mattie Trotter when he was only six, right after his mother's death. Deborah had grown up accustomed to seeing Ashe in the kitchen and out in the garden, during the summers and after school, until he'd grown old enough for part-time jobs.

"What are you thinking about?" Ashe couldn't quite discern that faraway look in her eyes. Whatever thoughts had captured her, they must have been pleasant.

"I was thinking about when we were kids. You and little Annie Laurie, Whitney and I." She could have lied, but why should she? They could not change the past, neither the good nor the bad. What had happened, had happened.

"How is Whitney?"

Deborah hadn't thought Ashe's interest in her cousin would create such a sharp pain inside her heart. *Don't do this to yourself! It doesn't matter any more. Whitney is not your rival. You don't love Ashe McLaughlin.*

"She's as well as anyone could be married to George Jamison III."

"What does that mean, exactly?"

"It means that George is quite content to live off Whitney's money, and the two of them have never had children because Whitney is too busy trying to raise the little boy she married."

"I'd say Whitney got what she deserved, wouldn't you?" He could remember a time when he had longed to make Whitney Vaughn his wife. He'd been a fool. She had wanted Ashe for one thing and one thing only. She had enjoyed the sense of danger and excitement she found having an affair with a bad boy her friends considered beneath them.

"She could have married you, couldn't she? You never would have deserted *her*. And you wouldn't have lived off her inheritance." Deborah turned toward her room.

Ashe gripped her by the elbow, pulling her toward him. Jerking her head around, she glared at him. "Your cousin didn't want to marry me. Remember?" he said. "She thought I wasn't good enough for her. But you didn't think that, did you, Deborah?"

He said her name all soft and sexy and filled with need. The way he'd said it that night. She tried to break away, to force herself into action, to terminate the feelings rising within her. No, she had never thought she was too good for Ashe. She had adored him for as long as she could remember and held her secret love in her heart until the night he'd turned to her for comfort.

He had taken the comfort she'd offered—and more. He'd taken all she had to give. And left her with nothing.

No, that wasn't true. He had left her with Allen.

"Did you change your mind, later? After—" Ashe began.

"No, I… The difference in our social positions isn't what kept us apart and we both know it."

"What about now?" he asked.

"What do you mean?" She looked at him, questioning his statement, daring him to ask her what she thought of the man who had come back into her life after deserting her eleven years ago.

"I'm the hired help around here." His lips were so close that his breath mingled with hers. "Would Miss Deborah ever fool around with the hired help?"

"You're being offensive." She tried to pull away from him; he held fast. Her heartbeat drummed in her ears.

They stared at each other. Defiant. Determined. Neither backing down.

"Hey, Ashe, come in my room and let me introduce you to Huckleberry," Allen called out from down the hallway.

Allen's interruption immediately broke the tense spell. Deborah breathed a sigh of relief; Ashe loosened his hold on her arms.

"Allen, does Mother know you've brought Huckleberry inside?" Deborah asked as she eased her body away from Ashe.

A large tan Labrador retriever stood beside Allen, the dog's tongue hanging out, his tail wagging as the boy stroked his back.

Ashe grinned. "Where does Huckleberry usually stay?"

"Outside," Deborah said. "But occasionally Mother allows Allen to bring him inside."

"Come on." Allen waved at Ashe. "I want to show you my room. Deborah helped me redo the whole thing last year. It's a real guy's room now and not a baby's room anymore."

"Is your mother having a difficult time letting Allen grow up?" Ashe asked.

"Yes, I suppose she is. But he is the baby, after all."

"Come on, Ashe." Allen motioned with his hand.

"Coming?" Ashe asked Deborah.

"Yes, in a minute. You go ahead."

Ashe gave Huckleberry a pat on the head when he entered

Allen's domain. He'd speak to Deborah and Miss Carol about allowing the dog to remain inside. A dog as big as Huckleberry could act as a deterrent to anyone foolish enough to break into the house.

Allen's room was indeed a *real guy's room*. Posters lined one wall. Dark wooden shutters hung at the windows. A sturdy antique bed, covered in blue-and-green plaid, and a huge matching dresser seemed to be the only antique items in the room. A color television, a CD player, a VCR and a tape recorder filled a wall unit beside a desk that held a computer, monitor and printer.

"This is some room, pal. I'd say your sister made sure you had everything a guy could want."

"Yeah, she let me get rid of everything babyish." Allen grabbed Ashe by the hand. "Come take a look at these. This is one of my hobbies."

Allen led Ashe over to a shiny metal trunk sitting at the foot of his bed. Lying atop the trunk were two brown albums.

"What have you got here?"

"My baseball card collection."

Deborah stood in the hallway, listening, waiting. How was she going to protect Allen from Ashe McLaughlin when she was finding it difficult to protect herself from him? The moment he'd pulled her close, the moment he'd said her name in that husky, sexy voice of his, she'd practically melted. No other man had ever made her feel the way Ashe did.

Damn him! Damn him for having the same dizzying effect on her he'd always had. Eleven years hadn't changed the way she wanted him. If she thought she would be immune to Ashe's charms, then she'd been a total fool. If she wasn't careful, she'd wind up falling in love with him all over again.

She couldn't let that happen. And she couldn't allow Ashe to find out that Allen was his son.

Deborah walked down the hall, stopping in the doorway to Allen's bedroom. Ashe and Allen sat on the bed, Huckleberry curled up beside them, his head resting on a pillow. A lump formed in Deborah's throat.

Please, dear Lord. Don't let anyone else notice what I see so plainly—the similarities in boy and man.

"How long were you a Green Beret?" Allen asked.

"Ten years."

"Wow, I'll bet that's one exciting job, huh? Did you ever kill anybody?"

Deborah almost cried out, not wanting Ashe to discuss his life in the special forces with their ten-year-old son. She bit her lip and remained silent, waiting for Ashe's reply.

"Yes, Allen, I've killed. But it isn't something I like to talk about. It was my job to get rid of the bad guys, but killing is never easy."

"That's what you're here in Sheffield to do, isn't it?" Allen asked. "You're here to protect Deborah against the bad guys, and if you have to, you'll kill them, won't you?"

"I hope it doesn't come to that," Ashe said. "But, yes, I'll do whatever it takes to keep Deborah safe."

"How long have you been a bodyguard?"

"I started working for Sam Dundee last year, right after I left the army."

"Why'd you leave the Green Berets?"

Deborah cleared her throat, stepped inside Allen's room and gave him a censuring stare. "I think you've asked Ashe enough questions for one night. Save a few for later."

"Ah, Deborah, can't he stay just a little while longer?" Allen whined in a typical childlike manner. "I was going to ask him about the two of you when you were kids." Allen turned his attention to Ashe. "Did you ever kiss Deborah when you two were teenagers?"

"Allen!" Deborah scolded, her voice harsher than she had intended.

"Yes, I kissed Deborah." Ashe watched her closely, noting

that she wouldn't look at him, that she had balled her hands into fists and held them rigidly at her hips.

"I knew it! I knew it!" Allen bounced up and down on the bed. "You two were a thing, weren't you?"

"No, Allen." Deborah trembled inside, and prayed the shivers racing through her body didn't materialize externally. "Stop jumping up and down on the bed."

"You sure are being a grouch." Settling back down on the side of the bed, Allen glanced back and forth from Deborah to Ashe. "What's the big secret about you two being an item when you were teenagers? Is it a big deal that Ashe was your boyfriend?"

"We've told you that Ashe wasn't my boyfriend," Deborah said. No, he'd never been her boyfriend, just her lover for one night. One night that had changed her life forever. "We were friends."

"Then why did he kiss you?" Allen asked.

Deborah looked to Ashe, her gaze pleading with him, then she glanced away quickly. "Sometimes an occasion arises when a friend might kiss another friend," Deborah said.

The look on Allen's face plainly said he didn't believe a word of it.

"Deborah and I were friends all our lives," Ashe explained. "Then not long before I left Sheffield, we thought we could be more than friends. That's when I kissed her. But it didn't work out. So you see, Allen, your sister was never actually my girlfriend."

"Do you have a girlfriend now?"

"Allen!" Rolling her eyes heavenward, Deborah shook her head in defeat. "Enough questions for one night."

Ashe laughed. "I remember being the same way when I was his age. I used to drive Mama Mattie nuts asking her so many questions. I guess it's the age. The whole world is a mystery when you're ten."

"I guess it's a guy thing, huh, Ashe?"

Allen looked at Ashe McLaughlin with such adoration in his eyes that Deborah almost cried. There had been a time when she, too, had adored Ashe. It was so easy to fall under his spell, to succumb to his charm. Maybe her son had inherited her weakness.

"Curiosity isn't a guy thing," Ashe said. "I remember a time when your sister's curiosity got the minister in big trouble."

"What?" Allen grinned, stole a quick glance at Deborah and burst into laughter. "Deborah did something she wasn't supposed to do? I can't believe it. She always does the right thing."

"Well, she made the mistake of walking in on Reverend Bently and the new choir director, a very attractive lady," Ashe said.

"I asked Mother, right in the middle of her study club meeting, why Reverend Bently would kiss Miss Denise." Deborah smiled, remembering the utter horror on her mother's face and the loud rumble of ladies' voices rising in outrage as they sat in Carol Vaughn's garden, dropping their finger sandwiches and spilling their tea.

"How'd you know, Ashe? Were you there? Did you see it happen?"

"Allen, that's enough questions," Deborah said. "You've got school tomorrow and I have work. Besides, Ashe hasn't even settled in yet. Save the rest of your million and one questions for another day."

"Ah…ahh… All right."

"Deborah told me all about it when I stopped by to pick up Mama Mattie that evening after I got off from work. Your sister was only twelve then, and at that age she used to tell me everything."

Not everything, Deborah thought. Not then, not later, and certainly not now. She never told him how much she loved him. Not until that night by the river. But he'd known she had a crush on him, just as he was aware, now, that she was afraid of him, afraid of how he made her feel.

"Deborah's right, pal. It's getting late." Ashe ruffled the boy's thick blond hair, hair the exact shade Deborah's had been as a child. "I'll be around for several weeks. You'll have a chance to ask me a lot more questions."

Deborah waited in the hallway until Ashe walked past her and toward his own room. He hesitated in the doorway.

"You were always special to me," he said. "I trusted you in a way I didn't trust another soul."

She stood in the hall, staring at his back as he entered his room and closed the door. She shivered. What had he meant by that last statement? Was he accusing her of something? He had trusted her. Well, she had trusted him, too. And he had betrayed her. He had taken her innocence, gotten her pregnant and left town.

Whatever had gone wrong between them hadn't been her fault. It had been his. He hadn't loved her. He'd used her. And afterward, when she'd poured out her heart to him, he'd said he was sorry, that he never should have touched her.

Ashe McLaughlin had regretted making love to her. She could never forget the pain that knowledge had caused her. Even if she could forgive him, she could never forget what he'd said to her eleven years ago… *But I don't love you, Deborah. Not that way. What we did tonight shouldn't have happened. I'm sorry. It was all my fault. Forgive me, honey. Please forgive me.*

Tears gathered in the corners of her eyes. She walked the few steps to her open bedroom door, crossed the threshold, closed the door quietly and, once alone, wiped away her tears.

"ALL OF MS. VAUGHN'S calls are to be screened. That means the caller must identify him or herself and must be someone Ms. Vaughn knows. Otherwise the call will be directed to me. Is that understood?"

Ashe McLaughlin issued orders to the office staff of Vaughn & Posey, the men obviously intimidated, the women enthralled. Standing six-foot-three, broad-shouldered and commanding in his gray sport coat, navy slacks and white shirt, Ashe was the type of man to whom no one dared utter a word of protest.

Listening to Ashe give orders, Deborah waited in her office doorway, Neil Posey at her side. When the staff, one by one, turned their heads in her direction, she nodded her agreement with Ashe. He'd made it perfectly clear to her before they arrived at work that he would be in charge of her life, every small detail, until she was no longer in danger.

Ashe turned to Annie Laurie, who had worked as Neil's secretary for the past five years, and was doing double duty as Deborah's secretary while hers was out on maternity leave. "Carefully check all of Deborah's mail. Anything suspicious, bring to me. And I'll open all packages, no matter how innocent looking they are. Understand?"

"Of course, Ashe." Despite her mousy brown hair and out-of-style glasses, plain little Annie Laurie had grown into a lovely young woman.

Deborah tried not to stare at Ashe, but she found herself again inspecting him from head to toe as she had done at breakfast this morning. No wonder all the females in the office were practically drooling. Although his clothes were tailored to fit his big body, on Ashe they acquired an unpretentious casualness. He wore no tie and left the first two buttons of his shirt undone, revealing a tuft of dark chest hair.

"Who does he think he is coming in here issuing orders right and left?" Neil Posey whispered, his tone an angry hiss. "When you introduced him as your bodyguard, I assumed you would be giving him orders, not the other way around."

"Ashe can't do the job Mother hired him to do unless I cooperate." Deborah patted Neil on the shoulder. "Ashe is here to protect me. He's a trained professional."

"He hasn't changed. He's as damn sure of himself as he ever

was." Neil took Deborah's hand in his. "I don't like the idea of that man living in your house, sleeping across the hall from you."

"He could hardly protect me if he stayed at a motel."

"Why Ashe McLaughlin? Good grief, Deb, you were in love with the guy when we were in high school." Neil's eyes widened. He stared directly at Deborah. "You don't still...the man doesn't mean anything to you now, does he?"

"Lower your voice." She had told Neil time and again that she couldn't offer him more than friendship. She'd never led him on or made him any promises. Perhaps it was wrong of her to go out with him from time to time, but he was such a comfortable, nonthreatening date.

"I'm sorry," Neil said. "It's just I'd hate to see him break your heart. You mooned around over him for years and all he could see was Whitney."

"Yes, Neil, I know. Can we please change the subject?"

Deborah caught a glimpse of Ashe going from desk to desk, speaking personally to each Vaughn & Posey employee. Ashe looked up from where he was bent over Patricia Walden's desk and smiled at Deborah. He'd seen her staring at him, watching while Patricia fluttered her long, black eyelashes at him. Deborah forced a weak smile to her lips.

"Look at him flirting with Patricia, and her a married woman!" Neil sucked in his freckled cheeks, making his long, narrow face appear even more equine than usual.

"Neil, close the door, please. We need to discuss the Cotton Lane Estates. I'm afraid we've allowed my situation to interfere in our moving ahead on this project."

Neil closed the door, followed Deborah across the room, waited until she sat, then seated himself. "We have the surveyor's report. No surprises there. I've had Annie Laurie run a check on the deed. Everything is in order. Mr. and Mrs. McCullough have agreed to our last offer. I'd say, despite your problems, things are moving ahead quite smoothly."

"We should have had this deal wrapped up a week ago. Have Mr. and Mrs. McCullough come in today and let's get everything signed, sealed and delivered. We've still got several months of good weather, so if we can give Hutchinson the go-ahead, he can move his crews in there and cut the roads we'll need before we divide the land into one-acre lots."

"I'll give the McCulloughs a call. Since he's retired, they shouldn't have any problem driving down from Decatur this afternoon."

"Fine. And thanks for handling things while my life has been turned upside down lately."

Neil smiled, that widemouthed grin that showed all his teeth. "You know I'd do anything for you, Deb. Anything."

The door opened and Ashe McLaughlin walked in, making no apologies for interrupting. "Make time at lunch to go with me to see Sheriff Blaylock. I want to arrange for one of his men to keep an eye on you tomorrow while I do a little investigating on my own."

"I don't think that's necessary," Neil said. "Whenever you need to do your *investigating,* I'll be more than happy to stay with Deborah.

"Neil—" Deborah wanted to caution her friend, but she didn't get the chance.

"Look, Posey, I appreciate the fact you're Deborah's friend, but you're a realtor. I'm a professional bodyguard. If I can't be at Deborah's side, I want another professional to be there. One of the sheriff's deputies."

"I can assure you that I'd die to protect Deborah."

"That may be so, but once they kill you, what would keep them from killing her?" Ashe ignored Deborah's pleading look that said not to crush Neil Posey's ego. But Ashe didn't give a damn about Posey's ego. He simply wanted to make sure the man understood he wasn't equipped to play hero. "Do you own a gun? Do you carry it with you? Have you ever killed a man?"

"No, I don't own a gun and I most certainly have never killed another human being." Neil shuddered, obviously offended at the thought.

"It's all well and good to be willing to die to protect Deborah, but it's just as important to be willing to kill, or at least maim an assailant, in order to protect her."

"I'll arrange to go with you to see Charlie Blaylock," Deborah said, her tone sharp. She wanted Ashe to know how displeased she was with him. There had been no need to humiliate Neil. "Thank you for your offer, Neil. I'd feel completely safe with you, but…" She nodded in Ashe's direction. "Mother is paying Mr. McLaughlin a small fortune, so I plan to get our money's worth out of him."

"Yes, well…I understand." With shoulders slumped, Neil slinked out of Deborah's office like a kicked dog.

She marched across the room, slammed shut the door and turned on Ashe. "How dare you make Neil feel less than the man he is! What gave you the right to humiliate him that way?"

"My intention wasn't to humiliate Neil. Hell, I have no reason to dislike the man, to want to hurt him. My intention was to show him that he's useless as a bodyguard."

"Did you have to do it in front of me?" She looked down at her feet. "Neil has a crush on me."

Ashe laughed. "That must be the reason Annie Laurie can't get to first base with him."

Deborah snapped her head up, her eyes making direct contact with Ashe's. She smiled. "I've done everything but offer to pay for their wedding to get Neil interested in Annie Laurie. He can't seem to see past me to take notice of what a wonderful girl Annie Laurie is and how much she adores him."

Ashe stared at Deborah, his expression softening as he remembered another stupid man who had been so blinded by his passion for one woman that he'd allowed a treasure far more rare to slip through his fingers. Unrequited love was a bitch.

"I'm sorry if you think I was too rough on Neil. Annie Laurie had told me he liked you, but I had no idea he fancied himself in love with you. I'll tread more lightly on his ego from now on."

"Thank you, Ashe. I'd appreciated it."

A soft knock sounded at the door, breaking the intensity of Deborah's and Ashe's locked stares.

"Yes?"

Annie Laurie cracked open the door, peeked inside and held out a bundle of mail. "I've checked through these. The one I put on top looks odd to me. Whoever sent it used one of Deborah's business cards as a mailing label."

"Hand me that letter and place the others on the desk," Ashe said.

Annie Laurie obeyed Ashe's command. Deborah glanced from Annie Laurie's worried face to the letter in Ashe's hand. She waited while he turned the envelope over, inspecting it from every angle. He held it up to the light.

"Does this look pretty much like the other letters you've received?" he asked.

"The others were typed," Deborah said. "This is the first time they've used my business card."

Ashe walked over to Deborah's desk, picked up her letter opener and sliced the envelope along the spine. Lifting out a one-page letter, he laid the opener down, spread apart the white piece of stationery and read aloud the message, which had been typed.

"Don't show up in court. If you do, you'll be sorry."

Deborah glanced at Annie Laurie who seemed to be waiting for something. "Is there something else?" she asked.

Tilting her head to one side and casting her gaze downward, Annie Laurie smiled. "Megan stopped by to see you. She's got Katie with her."

"Oh." Deborah returned Annie Laurie's smile. "I suppose

everyone's passing Katie around as if she were a doll. Tell Megan I'll be out in just a minute."

Annie Laurie slipped out of the office, silently closing the door behind her.

"What was that all about? Who are Megan and Katie?"

"Megan is my secretary. She's on maternity leave. Katie is her two-week-old baby girl."

Ashe shook his head. "You've just received another threatening letter and you're concerned with coochie-cooing over your secretary's new baby?"

"I've received a letter very similar to the one you hold in your hand every day since Lon Sparks was arrested," Deborah said. "And I get at least one threatening phone call a day. But it isn't every day that Katie goes for her two-week checkup and Megan brings her by to see us."

Ashe grinned. God bless her, Deborah hadn't really changed. Not nearly as much as he thought she had. And certainly nowhere near as much as she tried to make everyone think. Underneath all that tough, career-woman exterior lay the heart of the sweet, caring girl she'd been years ago. He supposed he should have realized that Deborah was perfectly capable of handling both roles, that sophistication and success didn't exclude the more nurturing qualities that made Deborah such a loving person.

"You go visit with mother and baby," Ashe said. "I'll phone Sheriff Blaylock and let him know we'll be stopping by around noon. We'll let him add this letter to his collection."

"It won't do any good." Deborah opened the door. "There are never any fingerprints, nothing unique about the stationery. They're all mailed from Sheffield. And the typewriter isn't much of a clue. Hundreds of people in this area have access to the same brand."

"Whoever's doing this is experienced. He's no amateur."

"Buck Stansell may be a redneck outlaw, but he's a professional redneck outlaw."

"Yeah, his family's been in the business for several genera-tions." Ashe glanced around Deborah's office. "Kind of like the Vaughns have been in real estate for three generations."

"Don't assume that I'm taking the threats lightly," she said, her hand on the doorpost. "I'm shaking in my boots. But I have a business to run, people who count on Vaughn & Posey for their livelihoods. And I have a mother who's in bad health and a ch…a brother who's only a child."

"Who has access to your business cards?"

"What?"

"Could just anybody get one of these cards?" Ashe waved the envelope in the air.

"Oh, yes, anybody could get one." Deborah walked into the outer office. "Megan, we're so glad you stopped by. Who's got Katie? Come on, Helen, give her to me."

Ashe stood in the doorway, watching Deborah hold her sec-retary's baby. She looked so natural, as if cuddling a baby in her arms was something she did all the time. Why wasn't she married, with children of her own? A woman like Deborah shouldn't be single, still living at home with her mother and little brother. She should be hustling a pack of kids off to school and baseball games and cheerleader practice. She should be holding her own child in her arms.

Ashe didn't mean to eavesdrop, but when Megan pulled Deborah aside into the corner near her office, he remained standing just behind the partially closed door.

"I want to thank you again for the bonus you gave me," Megan said. "Bennie is so proud, he would never have accepted the money if you hadn't convinced him it was a bonus and that Mr. Posey had given the same amount to his secretary. Annie Laurie even went along with our little fib."

"It was a bonus," Deborah said. "A baby bonus. I think every baby should have a fully equipped nursery."

"We could never have afforded everything without that bonus. And after that, you didn't have to bring another gift to the hospital." Megan looked down at the pink-and-white ruffled dress her daughter wore. "It looks beautiful on her, don't you think?"

Ashe closed the door. Still the do-gooder. Still the tender-hearted pushover. No, Deborah hadn't changed. She was older, more beautiful, more experienced and certainly more sophisticated. But she was still the girl he'd considered his friend, the girl with whom he would have trusted his soul.

Was it possible that she had no idea what her father had done to him? Had he misjudged her all these years? Maybe she hadn't run to Wallace Vaughn and cried rape. But even if she hadn't falsely accused him, she'd still told her father that the two of them had made love. Surely she would have known how her father would react.

Even after Ashe had left town, Wallace Vaughn had slandered him. It had become public knowledge that Deborah's father had run Ashe McLaughlin out of Sheffield.

All the old feelings came rushing back, bombarding him with their intensity. All the love, the hate, the fear and the uncertainty. Maybe Carol Vaughn had been right. He hadn't returned to Sheffield before now because he was afraid to face the past, to find out the truth, to confront Deborah and Whitney.

But he was back now, and there was no time like the present to meet the ghosts of his past head-on.

CHAPTER FOUR

CHARLIE BLAYLOCK HAD been a friend of her father and Deborah suspected he'd always had a soft spot in his heart for her mother. He asked about Carol every time he ran into Deborah, and his concern certainly seemed a bit more than neighborly.

Deborah tried to relax as she sat in Charlie's office listening to him explain the details of the Lon Sparks case to Ashe, and exactly what he could and could not do to protect Deborah against Buck Stansell and his bunch of outlaws.

"When Carol asked my advice about hiring a private bodyguard for Deborah, I was all for it." Charlie gazed out the window that overlooked the parking area. He moved with a slow, easy stride, all six feet five inches, three hundred pounds of him. "We don't have a smidgen of proof that Buck and his boys are involved in the threats Deborah's been receiving. If we had any proof, we could make a move to stop them. But even if we caught the guy who's making the phone calls, Buck would just have somebody else take up where he left off."

"I'm planning on paying a visit to Lee Roy and Johnny Joe." Ashe stood, walked across the room, and stopped at Charlie's side. "I want you to have one of your men stay with Deborah while I drop in on my cousins."

Charlie lifted his eyebrows. "When were you planning on visiting the Brennan brothers?"

"Tomorrow. Bright and early."

"I've tried to tell Ashe that I've survived for a couple of weeks now without his constant protection." Deborah squirmed around in the uncomfortable straight-back chair in which she sat. "I'll be perfectly all right at the office for a couple of hours."

"I'll have somebody stop by the house around seven in the morning and stay with Deborah until you finish your business and get back to Sheffield." Charlie laid his big hand on Ashe's shoulder, gripping him firmly. "I was surprised when Carol told me she was hiring you. Last I'd heard, you were still in the army. The Green Berets, wasn't it?"

"I left over a year ago." Ashe looked down at Charlie's hand resting on his shoulder, all friendly like.

Ashe figured Charlie Blaylock knew exactly what his old friend, Wallace Vaughn, had done to him eleven years ago. Although Charlie had been sheriff even then, Wallace had brought the district attorney with him when he'd had his little talk with Ashe. And Sheffield's chief of police had been waiting right outside the door, waiting to arrest Ashe if he hadn't agreed to leave town and never return. But Charlie would have known what Wallace had been up to, perhaps had even given him a little advice on how to get rid of that white-trash boy who had dared to violate Wallace's precious daughter.

Charlie gave Ashe's shoulder another tight squeeze, then released him. "Carol wants you here. She's convinced herself that nobody else can protect Deborah. I'll do everything I can to cooperate with you."

"I'll keep that in mind."

Removing the most recent threatening letter from his coat pocket, Ashe dropped it on Charlie's desk. "You might want to have this examined, but I'd say it's clean."

"Another one?" Charlie asked. "This has become a daily occurrence, hasn't it?"

"I expect you'll notify the big boys, keep them informed on every detail. Let them know that I've arrived, if you haven't already called them." Walking across the room, Ashe held out his hand to Deborah. "Let's go get a bite of lunch."

Deborah started to take his hand, then hesitated when Charlie spoke.

"What makes you think anybody else is involved in this case?" Charlie picked up the envelope from his desk, glancing at it casually as he turned it over.

"Buck Stansell has the drug market cornered in this county. And if Corey Looney's death was drug related, the DEA is already unofficially involved." Ashe dropped the hand he'd been holding out to Deborah.

She glanced back and forth from Charlie's flushed face to Ashe's cynical smile. The big boys? The DEA? No one had told her that Corey Looney had been executed because of a drug deal.

"What are y'all—" Deborah began.

"I don't know what you're talking about." Charlie laid the envelope on his desk, rested his hand on the back of his plush leather chair and looked Ashe straight in the eye.

"My boss is a former agent," Ashe said. "All Sam Dundee had to do was make a phone call. I know everything you know, Blaylock. Everything."

"Stop it, both of you!" Deborah jumped up, slammed her hands down on her hips and took a deep breath. "I have no idea what y'all are talking about, but I'm tired of you acting as if I'm not in the room. I'm the person whose life is in danger. *I'm* the one who should know *everything!*"

Ashe grabbed her by the elbow, forcing her into action as he practically dragged her out of Charlie's office. "I'll tell you whatever you need to know at lunch."

"Whatever I need to know!" She dug in her heels in the hallway.

Ashe gave her a hard tug. She fell against him and he slipped his arm around her. "It's a beautiful fall day. Let's pick up something and take it down to Spring Park for a picnic."

Deborah jerked away from him. She couldn't bear being this close to him. Despite their past history, she could not deny the way Ashe made her feel—the way no other man had ever made her feel.

"What was all that between you and Charlie?" Deborah stood her ground, refusing to budge an inch, her blue eyes riveted to Ashe's unemotional face. "For a minute there I thought he wanted to take a punch at you."

Ashe glanced around the corridor, listening to the sound of voices from the adjoining offices. "This isn't the time or the place."

"Just tell me this, is the DEA involved in this case?"

"Unofficially." Ashe grabbed her by the arm again. "Come on. We'll get lunch, go to the park and talk."

"All right." She followed his lead, outside and into the parking lot.

She didn't resist his manhandling, macho jerk that he was. Ashe's brutally masculine qualities had fascinated her as a teenager. Now they irritated and annoyed her. Yet she had to admit, if she was totally honest with herself, that she couldn't imagine any other bodyguard with whom she'd feel more secure.

There was a strength in Ashe that went beyond the normal male quality. It had been there, of course, years ago, but she recognized it now for what it was. Primitive strength that came from the core of his masculinity, the ancient need to beat his chest and cry out a warning to all other males.

Deborah shivered. Everything male in Ashe called to all that was female within her. If he claimed her, as he once had done, would she be able to reject him? A need to be possessed, protected and cherished coursed through her veins like liquid fire, heating her thoughts, warming her femininity.

When he opened the passenger door of his rental car and assisted her inside, she glanced up at him. Her heartbeat roared in her ears. Ashe hesitated just a fraction of a second. He looked at her lips. She resisted the urge to lick them.

"Where's a good place to get take-out close by?" He shut

the door, walked around the hood of the car and got in on the driver's side.

"Stephano's on Sixth Street has good food." She clutched her leather bag to her stomach. "It's on the left side of the street, so you may want to turn off on Fifth and make the block."

When she returned home this evening, she'd tell her mother that this wasn't going to work, having Ashe as her bodyguard. Even if he kept her safe from Buck Stansell, another few weeks of being near Ashe would drive her insane.

Ashe picked up a couple of meatball subs, colas and slices of sinfully rich cheesecake. Gazing down into the bag, Deborah shook her head.

"This is too much food. I can't eat all of this. I have to watch my…" She left the sentence unfinished. She'd been about to tell Ashe McLaughlin that she had to watch her weight. Of course she had no need to tell him; he could well remember what a plump teenager she'd been.

"Splurging one day won't spoil that knockout figure of yours." Ashe kept his gaze focused on the road as he turned the car downward, off Sixth Street, and into the park area beneath the hill.

He thought she had a knockout figure? Was that the reason he couldn't seem to take his eyes off her all morning? Why he watched every move she made at the office? The thought of Ashe approving of her figure sent pinpricks of excitement rushing through her. Idiot! She chastised herself. You shouldn't care what he thinks. You shouldn't care what any man thinks, least of all Ashe. He didn't want you when you were a plump teenager, and you don't want him now. So there.

Liar! Good or bad. Right or wrong. You still want Ashe McLaughlin. You've never wanted anyone else.

"Is there a woman in your life back in Atlanta?" She heard herself ask, then damned herself for being such a fool. How could she have asked him such a question?

Ashe parked the car in the shade, opened his door and turned to take their lunch bag from Deborah. "No one special," Ashe said. "Women come and go, but there's been no one special in my life since I left Sheffield eleven years ago."

Whitney, Deborah thought. Her cousin had been the only special woman in Ashe's life. Jealousy and pity combined to create a rather disturbing emotion within Deborah. Both feelings constituted an admission that she still cared about Ashe.

And she didn't want to care. God in heaven, she didn't dare care. He had taken her innocence, broken her heart and left her pregnant. What woman in her right mind would give a man like that a second chance?

But then, Ashe hadn't said or done anything to indicate he wanted a second chance.

"This place hasn't changed much, has it?" Ashe looked around Spring Park, a small area of trees, playground equipment and picnic tables surrounding a small lake fed by an ancient underground spring.

"It's a bit lonely this time of day and this late in the season. Most of the activity takes place over there—" Deborah pointed to the south of the park "—at the golf course."

Ashe chose a secluded table on the west side of the park, near a cove of hedge apple trees, their bare branches dotted with mistletoe. The spring's flow meandered around behind them on a leisurely journey toward Spring Creek. Laying down the paper sack, Ashe removed the white napkins and spread out their lunch. He handed Deborah a cup and straw. She avoided touching his hand when she accepted the offering.

"Are you afraid of me?" he asked, swinging his long legs under the picnic table.

Deborah sat across from him, gripping the plastic container of food as she placed the cola on the concrete table. "Why should I be afraid of you? You're here to protect me, aren't you?"

"I wasn't asking if you were afraid that I might physically harm you. We both know that's ridiculous. I'm asking why your hands tremble whenever you think I might touch you. And why you have a difficult time looking directly at me. Your eyes give you away, honey."

She undid the plastic covering her meatball sandwich. "I feel awkward around you, Ashe. I guess I'm just not as sophisticated as the women you're accustomed to these days. Maybe what happened between us in the past didn't affect your life the way it did mine."

No, Ashe didn't suppose what had happened between them had affected his life the way it had hers. She had gone on as if nothing had happened, secure in her family's love and support and Wallace Vaughn's money. Maybe she'd suffered a broken heart for a while until she'd found another boyfriend. But he had paid a high price for their night of passion. He had lost his dream. His big plans of becoming one of the area's movers and shakers had turned sour.

"You don't look like you've fared too badly." Ashe surveyed her from the top of her golden blond hair, all neatly secured in a fashionable bun at the nape of her neck, to the length of shapely legs partially hidden beneath the picnic table. "You're successful, beautiful and rich."

Did he actually have no idea what he'd done to her? Of course he didn't know about the child they had created together, but how could he have forgotten his adamant rejection, his cruel words of regret, his deliberate avoidance of her in the days and weeks following their lovemaking?

"Whenever we're together, I can't seem to stop thinking about… I suppose it's true what they say about a woman never forgetting her first lover."

Her words hit him like a hard blow to the stomach. He sucked in air. Why did she sound so innocent, so vulnerable? After all this time, why did the memories of that night haunt him? Why did the thought of a young girl's passionate cries still echo in his mind? "And a guy never forgets what it's like to take a virgin, to be her first. I never meant for it to happen. One minute you were comforting me and the next minute—"

"You don't have to tell me again that you wished it hadn't happened, that you regretted making love to me the minute it was over. You made that perfectly clear eleven years ago! Do you think I don't know that you were pretending I was Whitney all the while you were…"

Deborah lifted her legs, swung them around and off the concrete bench and jumped up, turning her back to Ashe. The quivering inside her stomach escalated so quickly it turned to nausea.

Dammit! Is that what she actually thought? That he had pretended she was Whitney? Yes, he'd thought he was in love with Whitney, but the minute she announced her engagement to George Jamison III, there at the country club where he worked, he'd begun to doubt his love. And when she had laughed in his face and told him he'd been a fool to think she'd ever marry a loser like him, all the love inside him had died. Murdered by her cruelty.

Ashe got up and walked over to Deborah. He wanted to touch her, to put his arms around her and draw her close. She stood there, her shoulders trembling, her neck arched, her head tilted upward. Was she crying? He couldn't bear it if she was crying.

"Deborah?"

She couldn't speak; unshed tears clogged her throat. Shaking her head, she waved her hands at her sides, telling him to leave her alone.

"I did not pretend you were Whitney." He reached out to touch her, but didn't. He dropped his hand to his side. "I might've had a few drinks to dull the pain that night, but I knew who you were and I knew what I was doing."

"You were—" she gasped for air "—using me."

How could he deny the truth? He had used her. Used her to forget another woman's heartless rejection. Used her to salve his bruised male ego. Used her because she'd been there at his side, offering her comfort, her love, her adoration.

"Yeah, you're right. I used you. And that's what I regretted. I regretted taking advantage of you, of stealing your innocence. But I didn't regret the loving."

The unshed tears nearly choked her. The pain of remembrance clutched her heart. He didn't regret the loving? Was that what he'd just said?

He grabbed her shoulders in a gentle but firm hold. She tensed, every nerve in her body coming to full alert. She couldn't bear for him to touch her, yet couldn't bring herself to pull away.

"I told you I was sorry for what happened, that I regretted what I'd done." Ashe couldn't see Deborah's face; she kept her back to him. But in his mind's eye he could see plainly her face eleven years ago. There in the moonlight by the river, her face aglow with the discovery of sexual pleasure and girlish love, she had crumpled before his very eyes when he'd begged her to forgive him, told her that what happened had been a mistake. She had cried, but when he'd tried to comfort her, she had lashed out at him like a wildcat. He'd found himself wanting her all over again, and hating himself for his feelings.

"I've never felt so worthless in my life as I did that night." Deborah balled her hands into fists. She wanted to hit Ashe, to vent all the old bitterness and frustration. She wanted to scream at him, to tell him that he'd left her pregnant and she hated him for not caring, for never being concerned about her welfare or the child he had given her.

He turned her around slowly, the stiffness in her body unyielding. She faced him, her chin lifted high, her eyes bright and glazed with a fine sheen of moisture.

"When I took you, I knew it was you. Do you understand? I wanted you. Not Whitney. Not any other woman."

"But you said...you said—"

"I said it shouldn't have happened. It shouldn't have. I didn't love you, not like I should have. I couldn't offer you marriage. What I did was wrong."

She quivered from head to toe, clinching her jaws tightly, trying desperately not to cry. She glared at him, her blue eyes accusing him.

Dear God, he had hurt her more than he'd ever known. After all these years, she hadn't let go of the pain. Was that why she'd gone to her father? Is that why she'd accused him of raping her? Or had she accused him? Was it possible that the rape charges had been Wallace's idea? The thought had crossed his mind more than once in the past eleven years.

"Neither of us can change the past," he said. "We can't go back and make things right. But I want you to know how it really was with me. With us."

"It doesn't matter. Not any more." She tried to pull away from him; he held her tight.

"Yes, it does matter. It matters to me and it matters to you."

"I wish Mother had never brought you back." Deborah closed her eyes against the sight of Ashe McLaughlin, his big hands clasping her possessively.

"She's doomed us both to hell, hasn't she?" Ashe jerked Deborah into his arms, crushing her against him. "I would have made love to you a second time that night and a third and fourth. I wanted you that much. Do you understand? I never wanted anything as much as I wanted you that night. Not Whitney. Not my college degree. Not being successful enough to thumb my nose at Sheffield's elite."

Her breathing quickened. Her heart raced wildly. She wanted to run. She wanted to throw her arms around Ashe. She wanted to plead with him to stop saying such outrageous things. She wanted him to go on telling her how much he'd wanted her, to tell her over and over again.

"Why…why didn't you tell me? That night? All you kept

saying was that you were sorry." Deborah leaned into him, unable to resist the magnetic pull of his big body.

"You wanted me to tell you I loved you. I couldn't lie to you, Deborah. I'd just learned that night that I didn't know a damned thing about love."

"Ashe?"

He covered her lips with his own. She clung to him, returning his kiss with all the pent-up passion within her. The taste of her was like a heady wine, quickly going to his head. It had been that way eleven years ago. The very touch of Deborah Vaughn intoxicated him.

He thrust his tongue into her mouth, gripped the back of her head with one hand and slipped the other downward to caress her hip. He grew hard, his need pulsing against her. She wriggled in his arms, trying to get closer. Their tongues mated in a wet, daring dance. A prelude to further intimacy.

When they broke the kiss to breathe, Ashe dropped his hand to her neck, circling the back with his palm. His moist lips sought and found every sweet, delicious inch of her face.

Deborah flung her head back, exposing her neck as she clung to him, heat rising within her, setting her aflame. Ashe delved his tongue into the V of her blouse, nuzzling her tender flesh with his nose. Reaching between them, he undid the first button, then the second, his lips following the path of his fingers.

A loud blast rent the still autumn air. Ashe knocked Deborah to the ground, covering her body with his as he drew his 9 mm out of his shoulder holster.

"Keep down, honey. Don't move."

"Ashe? What happened? Did—did someone shoot at us?" She slipped her arms around his waist.

Lifting his head, Ashe glanced around and saw nothing but an old red truck rounding the curve of the road, a trail of exhaust smoke billowing from beneath the bed. He let out a sigh of relief, but didn't move from his position above Deborah. He waited. Listening. Looking in every direction, lifting himself on one elbow to check behind them.

"Ashe, please—"

"It's all right." After returning his gun to its holster, he lowered himself over her, partially supporting his weight with his elbows braced on the ground. "I'm pretty sure the noise was just a truck backfiring."

"Oh." She sighed, then looked up into Ashe's softening hazel eyes. Eyes that only a moment before had been clear and trained on their surroundings. Now he was gazing down at her with the same undisguised passion she'd seen in them when he had unbuttoned her blouse.

Her diamond-hard nipples grazed his chest. His arousal pressed against her. She needed Ashe. Needed his mouth on her body. Needed him buried deep inside her. Needed to hear him say that he wanted her more than he'd ever wanted anything or anyone.

"It's safe for us to get up now, isn't it?" She heard her own breathless voice and knew Ashe would realize how needy she was.

"I don't think it's safe for us anywhere, honey. We're in danger from each other here on the ground or standing up."

When he lowered his mouth, brushing her lips with his, she turned her head to the side. But she still held him around the waist, her fingers biting into his broad back.

"Eleven years ago, you weren't much more than a girl. What you felt was puppy love. And I was a confused young man who didn't have the foggiest idea what love was all about. But I was older and more experienced. I take the blame for everything." Ashe kissed her cheek, then drew a damp line across to her ear. "We're both all grown up now. Whatever happens between us, happens between equals. No regrets on either side. No apologies. I want you. And you want me."

She shook her head, needing to deny the truth. If she admitted she wanted him, she would be lost. If they came together again, for him it would be sex, but for her it would be love. Just like last time. She couldn't have an affair with Ashe and just let him walk out of her life after the trial. She couldn't give herself to him and risk having her heart broken all over again.

"Please, let me get up, Ashe. I'm not ready for this." She shoved against his chest. He remained on top of her, unmoving, his eyes seeking the truth of her words.

Nodding his head, he lifted himself up and off her, then held out his hand. She accepted his offer of assistance, taking his hand and allowing him to pull her to her feet. She brushed the blades of grass and crushed leaves from her dress, redid the open buttons and straightened the loose strands of her hair.

"I need to get back to work," she said, not looking directly at him. "Let's take this food back to the office with us. We'll be safer there. We won't be alone."

Without a word, Ashe gathered up their sandwiches, returning them to the paper bag. She was right. They'd both be a lot safer if they weren't alone. He intended to do everything in his power to protect Deborah, to make sure no harm came to her. But could he protect her from what they felt for each other? From the power of a desire too powerful to resist?

LATER THAT DAY Ashe stood in the doorway of Allen's room watching Deborah help the boy with his homework. She played the part of his mother convincingly. He wondered how long she had substituted for Miss Carol. Ever since illness had sapped Miss Carol's strength and she lived in constant fear the cancer would return?

No one seeing Deborah and Allen together could deny the bond between sister and brother. Her whole life seemed to revolve around the boy, and he so obviously adored her.

While Allen struggled with the grammar assignment, he eased his right hand down to stroke Huckleberry's thick, healthy coat.

"Remember, Allen, it's rise, rose, risen," Deborah said. "Do this one again."

Nibbling on the tip of his pencil eraser, Allen studied the sentence before him. "Hmm-hmm."

Ashe remembered how Deborah had struggled with algebra. When he had tutored her, downstairs at the kitchen table, she'd sat there nibbling on her eraser, a perplexed look on her face identical to Allen's. Ashe had been the one who'd had trouble with grammar, and Deborah had helped him write more than one term paper.

Gripping his pencil in his left hand, Allen scribbled the sentence across the sheet of notebook paper, then looked up at Deborah. "Is that right?"

Checking his work, she smiled. "Yes, it's right. Now go on to the next one." She glanced up and saw Ashe. Her smile vanished. Standing, she moved her chair from Allen's right side to his left, shielding him from Ashe's view.

Why had she moved? he wondered. It was as if she were protecting Allen. But from what? Surely not from him.

Ashe walked into the room. Huckleberry lifted his head from the floor, gave Ashe a quick glance, recognized him as no threat and laid his head back down, his body pressed against Allen's foot.

"Hey, Ashe." Allen looked up from his homework paper. "I'm almost finished here, then we can play a video game on the computer."

"Maybe Ashe doesn't want to play," Deborah said, standing up, placing her body between Ashe and her brother. "We've had a long day. Maybe he wants to read or watch TV alone for a while."

"I'm alone all the time in my apartment in Atlanta," Ashe said. "I like being part of a family. Allen and I are pals. I think we enjoy doing a lot of the same things."

"Oh. I see." Did he spend all his time in his Atlanta apartment alone? She doubted it. A man like Ashe wouldn't be long without a woman. She pictured the entrance to his apartment. The thought of a revolving door flashed through her mind.

"Your sister used to have a problem with algebra," Ashe said, walking around Deborah to sit down in the chair she had vacated. "English grammar seems to be your downfall just like it was mine. I guess guys have a difficult time choosing the right words, huh?" Ashe glanced up at Deborah, who glared down at him.

"I don't have to sweat making good grades in anything except this." Allen punched his paper with the tip of his pencil. "I've got three more sentences to go, then watch out, Indiana Jones!"

Allen leaned over his desk, reading from his book. He jotted down the sentence, choosing the correct verb tense. Ashe watched the way his untutored handwriting spread across the page, like so much hen scratch. The boy's penmanship was no better than his own. Another shortcoming a lot of guys had in common.

Ashe noticed a crossword puzzle book lying on the edge of the desk. He loved working the really tough ones, the ones that often stumped him and stimulated his mind. He'd been a dud at English grammar, but he was a whiz at figuring out puzzles, even word puzzles.

Ashe picked up the book. "Have you got an extra pencil?"

Allen opened his desk drawer, retrieved a freshly sharpened number two and handed it to Ashe. "You like crossword puzzles, too?"

"Love 'em." Taking the pencil and sticking it behind his ear, Ashe opened the book, found the most complicated puzzle and studied it.

He felt Deborah watching him. What the hell was the matter with her? "Are you planning on hanging around and cheering us on while we play Indiana Jones and the Last Crusade?"

"No. I just want to make sure Allen finishes his homework."

"I'll make sure he does. Go wash out your lingerie or something. Read a good book. Call your boyfriend." Ashe's expression didn't alter as he named off a list of alternatives to standing guard over her brother.

"I told you Deborah doesn't have a boyfriend. She won't give any guy the time of day." Allen never looked up from his paper.

Ashe glanced down at the puzzle. "What's another word for old maid?"

Allen smothered his laughter behind his hand, sneaking a peek at Deborah out of the corner of his eye.

"Try the word *smart*," Deborah said. "As in any smart woman dies an old maid, without having to put up with a man trying to run her life."

"Spinster." Ashe acted as if he hadn't heard Deborah's outburst. Jerking the pencil from behind his ear, he printed the letters into the appropriate boxes.

"Hey, you're left-handed just like me," Allen said, his face bursting into a smile.

Deborah's heart sank. No. She mustn't panic. A lot of people were left-handed. There was no reason for Ashe to make the connection.

"We seem to have a lot in common." Ashe couldn't explain the rush of emotion that hit him. Like a surge of adrenaline warning him against something he couldn't see or hear, touch, taste or feel. Something he should know, but didn't. And that sense of the unknown centered around Allen Vaughn. Ashe found himself drawn to the boy, in a way similar yet different from the way he'd been drawn to Deborah when they'd been growing up together.

"Ashe, I... We need to talk," Deborah said.

He glanced up at her. Her face was pale. "Can't it wait until later? Allen and I are looking forward to our game."

"This won't take long." She nodded toward the hallway.

He laid down the puzzle book and pencil, stood up and

patted Allen on the back. "You finish your homework while I see what Deborah wants that's so important it can't wait."

"Hurry," Allen said. "I'm almost through."

Deborah led Ashe out into the hallway, closing Allen's bedroom door behind him. "Please don't let Allen become too fond of you. He's at an age where he wants a man around, and he seems to idolize you. He thinks you're something special."

"So what's the problem?" Ashe asked. "I like Allen. I enjoy spending time with him. Do you think I'm a bad influence on him?"

"No, that isn't it."

"Then what is it?"

"If you two become close—too close—it'll break his heart when you leave Sheffield. He's just a little boy. I don't want to see him hurt."

Ashe pinched her chin between his thumb and forefinger, tilting her downcast eyes upward, making her look directly at him. "Who are you afraid will get too close to me? Who are you afraid will be brokenhearted when I leave? Who, Deborah? You or Allen?"

She hardened her stare, defying him, standing her ground against the overwhelming emotions fighting inside her. "You won't ever break my heart again, Ashe McLaughlin. I know you aren't here to stay, that you're in Sheffield on an assignment, just doing your job. But Allen is already forming a strong attachment to you. Don't encourage him to see you as a…a…big brother."

"A father figure, you mean, don't you? Allen needs a father. Why hasn't Carol ever remarried and given him a father? Or why haven't you married and given him a brother-in-law?"

"I don't think my personal affairs or my mother's are any of your business."

"You're right." He released her chin.

"Please don't spend so much time with Allen. Don't let him

start depending on you. You aren't going to be around for very long."

"What should I do to entertain myself at night?" he asked. "Should I play bridge with your mother and her friends? Should I watch the Discovery channel on TV downstairs in the library? Should I invite a lady friend over for drinks and some hanky-panky in the pool house? Or should I come to your bedroom and watch you undress and see your hair turn to gold in the moonlight? Would you entertain me to keep me away from Allen?"

Her hand itched to slap his face. She knotted her palm into a fist, released it, knotted it again, then repeated the process several times.

"If you hurt my…my brother, I'll—"

He jerked her into his arms, loving the way she fought him, aroused by the passion of her anger, the heat of her indignation. "I'm not going to hurt Allen. You have my word."

Ceasing her struggles, she searched his face for the truth. "And I don't want to hurt you, Deborah. Not ever again. No matter what we've done to each other in the past, we don't have to repeat our mistakes."

"You're right," she said breathlessly. "Do your job. Act as my bodyguard until the trial is over and the threats stop. There's no need for you to become a temporary member of the family. None of us need a temporary man in our lives."

Was that what he was? Ashe wondered. A temporary man. Never a permanent part of anything. Just there to do a job. It hadn't mattered before, that he didn't have a wife or children. That his life held so little love, so little commitment. Why had being back in Sheffield changed all that? Being around families again, his family and Deborah's, brought to mind all his former hopes and dreams. Dreams of living in one of the big old houses in Sheffield, of becoming a successful businessman, of showing this town how far he'd come—from the depths of white trash, from the McLaughlins of Leighton. And the biggest part of his dream had been the society wife and the children she'd give him. Children who would never know the shame he'd felt, would never face the prejudice he'd fought, would never be looked at as if they were nothing.

"I'll do my job. I'll be careful not to let Allen become too attached to me. And I won't come into your bedroom and make slow, sweet love to you. Not unless you ask."

He didn't give her a chance to say a word. Turning, he marched down the hall, opened Allen's door and walked in, never once looking back at Deborah.

"Hell will freeze over, Ashe McLaughlin, before I ever ask you to make love to me again!" she muttered under her breath.

CHAPTER FIVE

A PASSEL OF hounds lay in the dirt yard surrounding the double-wide trailer. A brand-new cherry red Camaro, parked beside an old Ford truck, glistened in the morning sun. A long-legged, large-breasted brunette with a cigarette dangling from her lips flung open the front door and ushered three stair-step-size children onto the porch. Her voice rang out loud and clear.

"Get your rear ends in the car. I ain't got all morning to get you heathens to school."

The children scurried toward the Camaro. The woman turned around, surveyed Ashe from head to toe and grinned an I'd-like-to-see-what-you've-got-in-your-pants-honey kind of grin.

Ashe leaned against the hood of the rented car he had parked several feet off the gravel drive leading to Lee Roy Brennan's home. He eyed the smiling woman.

"Well, hello." She gave the youngest child a shove inside the car, never taking her eyes off Ashe. "You here to see Lee Roy?"

"Yeah. Is he around?"

"Could be." She ran her hand down her hip, over the tight-fitting jeans that outlined her shapely curves. "Who wants to know?"

"How about you go tell Lee Roy that Ashe McLaughlin wants to see him?"

"Well, Mr. Ashe McLaughlin, you sure do look like you're everything I ever heard you were." She stared directly at his crotch, then moved her gaze up to his face. "Lee Roy says you been in the army. One of them Green Berets. A real tough guy."

Ashe glanced at the three children in the Camaro. People like this didn't care what they said or did in front of their kids. He had vague memories of his old man cursing a blue streak, slapping his mother around and passing out drunk. Yeah, Ashe knew all about the low-class people he'd come from and had spent a lifetime trying to escape.

"Go tell Lee Roy his cousin wants to see him," Ashe said.

The woman's smile wavered, her eyes darting nervously from Ashe to the trailer. "Yeah, sure. He heard you was back in these parts."

Ashe didn't move from his propped position against the hood of his car while Lee Roy's wife went inside the trailer. Three pairs of big brown eyes peered out the back window of the Camaro. Ashe waved at the children. Three wide, toothy smiles appeared on their faces.

"Hey, cousin. What's up?" Lee Roy Brennan stepped out onto the wooden porch connected to his trailer, his naked beer belly hanging over the top of his unsnapped jeans.

"Just paying a social call on my relatives." Ashe lowered his sunglasses down on his nose, peering over the top so that his cousin could see his eyes. Ashe had been told that he possessed a look that could kill. Maybe not kill, he thought, but intimidate the hell out of a person.

"You run them kids on to school, Mindy." Lee Roy swatted his wife's round behind.

She rubbed herself against the side of his body, patting him on his butt before she sauntered off the porch and strutted over to the car. She gave Ashe a backward glance. Although he caught her suggestive look in his peripheral vision, he kept his gaze trained on Lee Roy.

"Come on in and have a cup of coffee. Johnny Joe just got up. He's still in his drawers, but he'll be glad to see you."

Standing straight and tall, Ashe accepted his cousin's invitation. Lee Roy slapped Ashe on the back when they walked inside the trailer.

"Didn't think I'd ever see you around these parts again. Not after the way old man Vaughn run you out of the state."

Ashe removed his sunglasses, dropped them into the inside pocket of his jacket and glanced over at the kitchen table where Johnny Joe, all five feet eight inches of him, sat in a wooden chair. Swirls of black hair covered his stocky body, making him look a little like an oversize chimpanzee.

"Heard you was back. What the hell ever made you agree to hire on as a bodyguard for that Vaughn gal?" Johnny Joe picked up a mug with the phrase Proud to be a Redneck printed on it. "I figured you wouldn't have no use for that bunch."

Lee Roy wiped corn flake crumbs out of a chair, then turned to lift a mug off a wooden rack. "Have a seat. You still like your coffee black?"

"Yeah." Ashe eyed the sturdy wooden chair, a few crumbs still sticking to the side. Sitting down, he placed his hands atop the table, spreading his arms wide enough apart so that his cousins could get a glimpse of his shoulder holster.

Lee Roy handed Ashe a mug filled with hot, black coffee, then sat down beside his brother. "You're working for some fancy security firm in Atlanta now, huh? Got your belly full of army life?"

"Something like that," Ashe said. "And private security work pays better, too."

The brothers laughed simultaneously. Ashe didn't crack a smile.

"You bleeding old lady Vaughn dry?" Johnny Joe asked. "After what her old man almost did to you, I figure you got a right to take 'em for all you can get."

Ashe glared at Johnny Joe, the hirsute little weasel. He hadn't taken after the McLaughlin side of the family in either size, coloring or temperament. No, he was more Brennan. Little, dark, smart-mouthed and stupid.

"Shut up, fool." Lee Roy swatted his younger brother on his head. "Ashe wouldn't have come back to take care of Deborah Vaughn just for the money."

"You doing her again, Ashe?" Johnny Joe snickered.

Lee Roy slapped him upside his head again, a bit harder.

"What the hell was that for?" Johnny Joe whined.

"Don't pay no attention to him." Lee Roy looked Ashe square in the eye. "It's good to see you again. We had some fun together, back when we was kids. You and me and Evie Lovelady."

"Yeah, we had some good times." Ashe had liked Lee Roy better than any of his McLaughlin relatives and the two of them had sowed some pretty wild oats together. Fighting over Evie Lovelady's favors. Getting drunk on Hunter McGee's moonshine in the backseat of Lee Roy's old Chevy. Getting into fights with Buck Stansell when he cheated at cards.

Another life, a lifetime ago.

"This ain't just a social call to get reacquainted with relatives," Lee Roy said. "Spit it out, whatever it is you come here to say."

"I understand you two are working for Buck Stansell. Is that right?"

Johnny Joe opened his mouth to respond, but shut it quickly when his older brother gave him a warning stare.

"Buck took over the business when his old man died a few years back." Lee Roy picked up his coffee mug, took a swig, then wiped his mouth with the back of his big hand. "Our old man and yours both worked for Buck's daddy."

"I know who my daddy worked for and what he did for a living," Ashe said, laying his palms flat on the table. "I've chosen to work on the other side of the law. And right now, my main concern is Deborah Vaughn's safety."

"I see." Lee Roy studied the black liquid in his mug.

"She ain't in no danger as long as she keeps that pretty little mouth of hers shut," Johnny Joe said.

"Dammit, man, you talk too much." Lee Roy turned to Ashe. "You ought to stay out of things that ain't none of your business. What happens to Deborah Vaughn shouldn't be your concern."

Ashe leaned over the table, glanced back and forth from one brother to the other, finally settling his hard stare on Lee Roy. "Deborah Vaughn is very much my concern, and what happens to her is my personal business."

"Are you saying that there's still something between the two of you? Hell, man, I'd have figured—"

"I will take it personally if anything happens to her. If one hair on her head is harmed, I'll be looking for the guy who did it. Do I make myself clear?"

"Why are you telling us?" Lee Roy asked.

"I'm asking you to relay the message." Ashe shoved back the chair and stood, towering over his seated cousins. "Tell Buck Stansell that Deborah Vaughn is my woman. She's under my protection. This isn't just another job to me."

"You sure you want to tangle with ol' Buck?" Johnny Joe grinned, showing his crooked teeth, three in a row missing on the bottom.

"I've trapped and gutted meaner bastards than Buck Stansell, and you can tell him that. Buck and his friends don't want to tangle with me. If I have to come after them, I will."

"You sure do talk big," Johnny Joe said. "But then you always did. Just 'cause you been in the Green Berets—"

"Shut up!" Lee Roy said.

"I know that the local, state and federal authorities would all like to see Buck behind bars." Ashe walked toward the door. "So would I. But you tell him that my only interest in him and his business is my woman's safety. If he leaves her alone, I'll leave him alone. Pass that advice along."

"Yeah, I'll do that," Lee Roy said. "Can't say whether or not

Buck will take the advice, but it's possible that whoever's out
to get Deborah Vaughn might listen. Her being your woman
just might make a difference. To certain people."

Ashe smiled then, nodded his head and walked out the door.
He'd bet money that before he was halfway back to Sheffield,
Lee Roy and Johnny Joe would be on their way to see Buck
Stansell.

ASHE PARKED HIS rental car in the lot adjacent to Vaughn &
Posey Real Estate. Walking up the sidewalk, he almost laughed
aloud when he saw the sheriff's deputy pacing back and forth
just inside the office entrance. The fresh-faced kid looked like
a posted sentry marching back and forth.

When Ashe opened the door, the deputy spun around, taking
a defensive pose, then relaxed when he recognized Ashe.

"No problems here, Mr. McLaughlin. Not even a phone call
or a letter."

"Good. Tell Sheriff Blaylock that I said you did a fine job.
Thanks—" Ashe glanced at the boy's name tag "—Deputy
Regan."

The young man grinned from ear to ear. "Ms. Vaughn's
taking care of some personal business right now, but she agreed
to keep her door open so she wouldn't be out of my sight."

Ashe slapped the deputy on the back. "I'll take over now.
I appreciate your diligence in keeping Ms. Vaughn safe for
me."

Ashe noticed Deborah in her office, standing to the side of
another woman, whose back was to him. Deborah glanced at
him, her face solemn.

The young deputy backed out of the office like a servant
removing himself from the presence of his king. Ashe nodded
a farewell to the boy, then focused all his attention on Deborah
and the other woman.

He heard a rather loud hiss, then someone cleared their

throat. Looking around, he saw Annie Laurie motioning for him to come to her.

"What's up?"

"Shh…shh." She flapped her hands in the air and shook her head. "Whitney Jamison—" Annie Laurie pointed to Deborah's office "—is in there right now. She came prancing in here with her nose in the air, looking all over the place for you."

Ashe sat down on the edge of Annie Laurie's desk, leaned over and whispered, "What makes you think she was looking for me?"

"She said so, that's how I know." Annie Laurie kept her voice low. "She took one look at the deputy and asked what he was doing here. Deborah told him he was on temporary guard duty. Then Whitney asked what was the problem, had you already deserted her? Then that bitch laughed. I wish Deborah had slapped her face."

"Aren't you overreacting just a little?"

"No, I don't think I am. Do you suppose for one minute that Whitney will let Deborah forget that you once asked Whitney to marry you and she dumped you, that she made you look like a fool?"

"Maybe I'd better go on in there and make sure there's not a catfight." Ashe grinned.

"Wipe that stupid grin off your face," Annie Laurie said. "Deborah Vaughn is not the type of lady to get into a catfight over any man, not even you, cousin dear."

Ashe laughed, but took note of Annie Laurie's words. She was right. Deborah wasn't the catfight type by any stretch of the imagination. But if she was, and she did choose to go one-on-one with Whitney, he'd place all his money on Deborah.

Ashe walked into Deborah's office, stopping directly behind Whitney, who was obviously unaware of his presence.

"It's going to be a delightful evening. Simply everyone will be there. You must come. If you don't, I'll never forgive you.

After all, George's fortieth birthday celebration should be something for him to remember."

"Of course I'll be there," Deborah said. "I wouldn't miss it."

Deborah looked over her cousin's shoulder, making direct eye contact with Ashe, who couldn't seem to erase the lopsided grin off his face. The very sound of Whitney's voice grated on his nerves. Why had he never noticed how whiny she sounded?

"You mean we'll be there, don't you?" Ashe stepped to one side, placing himself beside Deborah's desk.

Whitney spun around, a cascade of long black curls bouncing on her shoulders, settling against her pink silk blouse. "Ashe!"

She stared at him, her eyes hungry, her mouth opening and then closing as she bit down on her bottom lip. Whitney Vaughn Jamison was still beautiful, erotically beautiful with her dark hair and eyes and slender, delicate body.

Over the years there had been a few times when he'd wondered how he'd feel if he ever saw her again. Now he knew. He didn't feel a damned thing. Except maybe grateful she'd rejected him. Despite her beauty, there was a noticeable hardness in her face, a lack of depth in those big, brown eyes. He'd been too young and foolish to have seen past the surface eleven years ago.

"Whitney, you haven't changed a bit." It was only a small lie, a partial lie. She'd grown older, harder, hungrier.

"Well, darling, you've certainly changed. You've gotten bigger and broader and even better looking." Rushing over to him, she slipped her arms around his neck and kissed him boldly on the mouth.

She all but melted into him. Ashe did not return her kiss. He eased her arms from around his neck, held her hands in his for a brief moment, then released her and took a step over toward Deborah.

"What's this big event you've invited Deborah and me to attend? Something special for ol' George's birthday?" Ashe took another step in Deborah's direction.

"His fortieth birthday." Whitney pursed her lips into a frown. "And he's being a beast about getting older. I think it really bothers him that I'm so much younger."

"Not that much younger," Ashe said. "If I recall, you're thirty-four."

Whitney gasped, then smiled and purred as she gave Ashe another hungry look. "Of course you'd remember. You probably remember a lot of things about me, don't you, Ashe?"

"Not really, Whitney. To be honest, I haven't given you more than a passing thought over the years."

Ashe slipped his arm around Deborah's waist. Glaring at him, she opened her mouth to protest. He tightened his hold on her. She wriggled, trying to free herself.

"Deborah, on the other hand, I never forgot." He pulled her close to his side, smiled at her and barely kept himself from laughing out loud when he saw the stricken look on her face.

"Well, don't tell me you were cheating on me with my little cousin behind my back." Whitney pasted a phony smile on her heavily made-up face.

"Sort of like the way you cheated on me with George?" Ashe asked.

"That was years ago. Surely you don't still hold that against me?" Whitney fidgeted with the shoulder strap on her beige leather purse.

"Whitney, I appreciate your stopping by to invite me—" Deborah gasped when Ashe squeezed her around the waist "—us to George's birthday party." She glared at Ashe. "We'll be there."

"I'll be looking forward to seeing you again, Ashe. The party's at the country club." Whitney's genuine smile returned with a vengeance.

When she didn't receive the reaction from Ashe she'd hoped

to evoke, she waved at him with her index finger. "Until next Saturday night."

The moment Whitney exited the office, Deborah jerked out of Ashe's embrace, stormed across the room and slammed the door.

"Just what was that all about?" Deborah anchored her hands on her hips.

"I think your cousin was coming on to me. What do you think?"

"Of course, she was coming on to you. My God, I expected her to drag you down on my desk and jump on top of you at any minute."

Ashe chuckled, then coughed and covered his mouth when he noticed Deborah's face reddening and her eyes widening.

"I was not referring to the way Whitney threw herself at you," Deborah said. "I was talking about your dragging me into your arms, accepting her invitation on *our* behalf and telling her that I was the one you never forgot."

"Oh, that."

"Yes, that!"

"You had already accepted her invitation when I walked in, hadn't you? All I did was let Whitney know that you didn't go anywhere without me these days."

"I could have, and would have, explained to her that as my bodyguard, you'd have to accompany me." Deborah dropped her hands to her sides. "That doesn't explain your manhandling me in front of Whitney or your reason for saying what you did."

"I put my arm around you because I wanted Whitney to think that there's more than a business arrangement between the two of us."

"But there isn't."

"Of course there is. Do you honestly think I came back to Sheffield, to a town I swore had seen the last of me, to lay my life on the line for a woman who pretends she hates me, simply as a favor to a woman who was once kind to me and my grandmother?"

"Yes. That's what you told me."

"Doing a favor for Miss Carol was only part of my reason for accepting this job." Ashe realized that he'd been lying to himself as well as Deborah about his reasons for accepting Carol Vaughn's dare. "I wasn't lying when I told Whitney that you were the one I never forgot."

Deborah's vision blurred. Her ears rang with the pounding of her heart. "Don't—" she threw up her hands in front of her as if to ward him off "—please, don't. Whitney was the one. You loved her. Don't you dare lie to me!"

"You and I need to have a long talk and get a few things straight, but I doubt this is the time or the place." Ashe heard the phones in the outer office ringing and the buzz of voices. "Whitney doesn't mean a damn thing to me. You, on the other hand, do. I'm here to protect you. And you'll be a lot safer if everyone thinks you're—"

A loud knock on the outer office door interrupted Ashe midsentence. Opening the door, Annie Laurie walked in with a package in her hands.

"This just came for Deborah. There's no return address." Annie Laurie held the square box out in front of her. "Something inside there is ticking!"

Deborah stood deadly still staring at the box. Ashe took the package out of Annie Laurie's hands. Listening, he heard the steady *tick, tick, tick* coming from inside the cardboard container.

"Don't panic, and don't scare the others in the office," Ashe said. "Go back to your desk and call the Sheffield police. Talk to Chief Burton. Tell him to send whatever kind of bomb squad he has over here, pronto."

"You think it's a bomb?" Annie Laurie gulped, then started backing out of the office. "What do we do?"

"You and Deborah get everyone outside. Tell them you'll

explain once you're out. Walk them across the street. And make sure everyone stays there."

"What about you?" Deborah asked.

"I'm going to set this box down on your desk and follow you all outside."

Deborah shoved a stricken Annie Laurie out of the office, then rounded all her employees together and ushered them outside, while Annie Laurie phoned the police. Deborah started into Neil's office, but Annie Laurie reminded her that Neil was in Florence at a realtor's brunch.

Ashe set the ticking box down on Deborah's desk. His gut instincts told him that this wasn't a bomb, but his instincts had been wrong a few times and it had nearly cost him his life. He didn't take chances anymore. Not with other people's lives. Certainly not with Deborah's life.

Within five minutes Chief Burton and his bomb squad arrived. The employees of Vaughn & Posey stood across the street in front of the bank, their evacuation and the presence of several police vehicles garnering attention from passersby. A small crowd of spectators gathered on the corner.

Ashe stayed beside Deborah, who stood ramrod straight, her vision focused on her office building. She gripped Ashe's hand tightly, but he was certain she had no idea what she was doing.

A member of the bomb squad walked through the front door, holding the open box in his hands. "Somebody's got a real warped sense of humor, Chief. Take a look at this."

Ashe held on to Deborah's hand as she dashed across the street.

"Everybody can go back to work," Chief Burton said. "There's no bomb."

"What was ticking?" Deborah asked.

The chief held out the box. "Take a look, Ms. Vaughn."

Inside the hand-delivered package lay an ordinary alarm clock, tightly wound. Positioned on all four sides of the box, surrounding the ticking clock, were unlit sticks of dynamite. A small white card was stuck to the face of the clock, the message typed. "Next time, boom!"

Ashe could almost hear a man's insidious laughter. Buck Stansell's crazy, sharp laugh. Ashe remembered the man's diabolical sense of humor. Buck had not meant to harm Deborah, only to frighten her. If Buck had wanted Deborah dead, he would have killed her before Ashe had come into the picture.

But what would happen if Deborah couldn't be scared off, if she showed up in court to testify against Lon Sparks? With a man like Buck Stansell, anything was possible. All Ashe knew was that whatever happened, he was going to take care of Deborah.

"A clock!" Deborah balled her hands into fists. "A stupid alarm clock!"

"Looks like another warning," Chief Burton said. "I'll see that Charlie's people get a look at this. I doubt we'll be able to trace it to anybody, but we'll see what we can do. Maybe somebody at the messenger service will remember who sent it, but I've got my doubts. Anybody could've paid a kid off the street to run a package by the office."

"It's not going to stop, is it?" Deborah looked to Ashe for an answer. He grasped her by the shoulders. She trembled.

"I'm not going to lie to you," he said. "The phone calls and letters aren't going to stop. But I'm screening them. You don't have to deal with them at all. And from now on, any UPS deliveries will come directly to me, too. You don't even have to know about them."

"Unless you think it's another bomb and we have to evacuate the office again." Deborah wanted to walk into Ashe's arms, to lay her head on his chest and cry. Instead she pulled away from him, turning to her employees, still standing around outside on the sidewalk. "Let's get back to work." Then she held out her hand to Chief Burton, thanked him for arriving so promptly and took one last look at the gag gift she'd been sent.

She walked back into the building, her head held high. At that moment Ashe didn't think he'd ever been as enthralled by a woman's show of strength. He knew she'd been scared to death, had felt her trembling beneath his hands, but despite her anger and uncertainty, she was not defeated.

Ashe waited around outside for a few minutes until the police left and the crowd cleared. He found Deborah in her office, alone, her elbows propped up on her desk, her hands covering her face.

He closed the door behind him. Dropping her hands, she stared up at him, her eyes damp but without any real tears.

He walked over, knelt down beside her swivel chair and took her hands into his. "It's all right if you want to cry or scream or hit something. Nobody can be strong all the time."

"I have to be," she said, her voice flat and even, masking her emotions. She looked down at her lap where he held her hands. "Mother and Allen have no one else but me. If I fall apart…if I…" Pausing, she swallowed. "I have to keep Vaughn & Posey going. So many people depend on this business. And since Mother's illness, she's become very fragile emotionally."

"Then put up a brave front for Miss Carol and Allen. Even let your employees go on thinking you're superwoman. But I've got some broad shoulders, Deborah. And they're here for you to lean on any time you feel the need."

She looked at him, her blue eyes softening just a fraction. "Part of the job, Mr. McLaughlin? I thought you were supposed to protect me. Giving comfort is extra, isn't it? How much more will that cost me?"

He stood and jerked her up into his arms in one swift move. She gasped as she fell against him and he trapped her body, holding her securely in his arms. He lowered his head until their breaths mingled.

She closed her eyes, blocking out the sight of him, telling herself she was a fool to succumb to his easy charm.

"The comfort is free, Ms. Vaughn." He whispered the words against her lips. "If you're woman enough to accept it."

Sucking in a deep breath, she opened her eyes. He released his hold on her and gave her a slight push away from him. Turning his back on her, he headed for the door.

"Ashe?"

"I'm just going to get a cup of coffee. I'm not leaving you, even if right now I'd like nothing better than to walk out that door and not come back."

"No one is stopping—"

He pivoted around, glaring at her. "No, that's not true. I don't want to walk out on you and never come back. What I want, more than anything, is to shove all that stuff off your desk, lift you up on it and—"

"I think you're confusing me with Whitney," Deborah said.

"No, honey, that's something I've never done. It's your legs I'd like to slide between and your body I'd like to claim, not your cousin's."

Ashe turned, walked out of the office and closed the door behind him.

Deborah stood beside her desk, trembling. Visions of her lying on top of her desk flashed through her mind. She shook her head trying to dislodge the thoughts of Ashe McLaughlin leaning over her body, lifting her hips and burying himself inside her.

She covered her mouth with her hand to still her cry, then bit down on the side of her finger as shivers of desire rippled through her.

CHAPTER SIX

DEBORAH HAD THOUGHT about making a fire in her sitting-room fireplace, but had neither the strength nor the determination. Although the October night was chilly, it wasn't really cool enough for a fire. She'd simply thought a cosy glowing fire would be soothing. Instead she had settled for a nice warm bath and a cup of cinnamon tea.

She curled up on the huge padded window seat beneath the stained-glass window in her sitting room alcove. Her room was her haven. Since early childhood, she had escaped into this luxurious old room with its high ceilings and aged wooden floors. Many days she had sat where she sat now, watching the way the sun turned the colors in the stained-glass window to sparkling jewels.

She had written silly, girlish poems about love and life and Ashe McLaughlin. She had long ago burned those poems. Even now she could feel the tears on her face, the tears she had shed the night she'd tossed those hopeless professions of love into the fireplace and watched her youthful dreams go up in smoke.

She shouldn't be dwelling on the past, not with so many problems facing her in the present. Between the constant harassing threats and Ashe's presence, her nerves were raw. She wanted to scream, to cry, to break something—anything—into a thousand pieces.

She wanted Ashe to go away; she wanted Ashe to never leave her. She fantasized about telling Ashe that Allen was his son; she lived in fear Ashe would discover the truth.

Deborah set her teacup on the mahogany tea table beside the

window bench, pulled the cream crocheted afghan over her legs and rested her head against the window frame. She should have been in bed an hour ago, but she knew she wouldn't be able to sleep. The simple, orderly life she had worked out for herself had suddenly and irrevocably fallen apart. She had turned off on the wrong road, witnessed a murder and her life would never be the same again. Not only was her life being threatened by the most notorious hoodlums in the state, but the very man determined to protect her posed the greatest threat of all. How ironic, she thought, that she should fear Ashe McLaughlin even more than she feared Buck Stansell.

She heard a soft rap on her door. Her mother? Had she taken ill? Or Allen, who usually slept soundly the whole night through? No. Not her mother. Not Allen.

Ashe.

Dropping the afghan to the floor, she walked across the room, her heart hammering away in her chest. Just before opening the door, she readjusted her silk robe, tightening the belt around her waist.

Ashe McLaughlin stood in the hallway, one big hand braced against the doorpost. He still wore his charcoal gray slacks and his dove gray linen shirt, but the shirt was completely unbuttoned and the hem hung loose below his hips.

"May I come in? We need to talk."

"It's late, Ashe. After midnight. I'm tired." She didn't want him in her room, didn't want to be alone with him. "Can't this wait until morning?"

"It could, but since we're both awake, I see no reason to postpone our conversation." He dropped his hand from the doorpost, leaned toward her and looked her over from head to toe. "Are you going to let me in?"

If she said no, he would think she was afraid of him, that he still held some kind of power over her. She couldn't let him think she cared, that he… Oh, who was she kidding? Any fool could see that Ashe McLaughlin made her act like a silly, lovesick schoolgirl.

"Come on in." She stepped back, allowing him entrance.

He followed her into the sitting room, glancing around, taking note of the lush femininity of the room. All muted cobalt blues and faded rose colors with splashes of rich cream. Ruffles and lace and dainty crocheted items whispered "Lady."

"Won't you sit down?" She indicated the antique rocker covered in a vibrant floral pattern.

Ashe eyed the delicate chair, wondering if it would hold his weight. Deborah sat on the wide, plush window seat. Without asking permission, he walked over and sat down beside her. She jumped, then glared at him.

"I was afraid I'd break that little rocker," he said, smiling.

"You could have sat in the arm chair, there by the fireplace." She indicated the wing chair, a wide-brimmed, lace hat hanging from one wing.

"I'd rather sit beside you." He knew he made her nervous, and he thought he knew why. No matter what had happened between them eleven years ago, no matter how betrayed either of them felt, the spark that had ignited a blazing fire between them that one night down by the river still burned inside both of them.

"Fine, sit beside me." She glanced over at the tea service. "Would you care for some cinnamon tea?"

"No, thanks."

"What was so urgent that you couldn't wait until tomorrow to discuss it with me?" Feeling her robe slipping open across her thigh, she grabbed the blue silk and held it in place.

"Are you all right, Deborah?" he asked. "I mean really all right. You've had a rough day, and you barely said ten words at dinner. Miss Carol is worried. So is Allen."

"I'm fine, and I'll make sure Mother and Allen both know it. Now, if that's all you came to say—" she started to rise.

"Sit down."

She eased back down onto the bench.

"As you know, I paid a visit to Lee Roy and Johnny Joe, a couple of my cousins who work for Buck Stansell."

Her eyes, wide and overly bright, looked right at him. Damn her, she was working hard at being brave, at pretending she wasn't slowly falling apart. And he figured having him around wasn't helping her any. But he couldn't leave, couldn't let Sam Dundee send another agent to protect her. Deborah was his responsibility, his to protect, his to defend against whatever harm came her way.

"What happened?" Deborah asked. "I'm sure they didn't admit that Buck Stansell was harassing me, trying to convince me that he'd have me killed if I testify against Lon Sparks."

"No, the boys didn't admit to anything. They didn't have to. I know my cousins. I know their kind. My father was one of them. They're what I came from."

Without hesitating, without thinking, Deborah touched his hand. Comforting. Caring. So much like the Deborah he'd known and liked.

"You were never anything like those people. You didn't get into any real trouble when you were a teenager. Everything you did, you did to improve your life, to get away from your roots."

He laid his open palm atop her small hand, trapping it between his big, hard hands. "You never looked down on me, never thought you were better than I was, like so many people did. Even though you were just a kid, you seemed to understand what I wanted, what I needed."

Deborah shivered, her stomach quivering, warmth spreading through her like the morning sunshine slowly bathing the horizon with its life-giving light. She couldn't bear feeling this way, longing to put her arms around Ashe, to tell him that she had loved him so dearly, had wanted nothing more than for him to return her love. She'd been a foolish girl; he'd been in love with her cousin.

She pulled her hand out of his gentle clasp. "So, your...
you..." Her voice cracked. She cleared her throat. "...your visit
to your cousins didn't accomplish anything."

Dear God, how he wanted to kiss her. Here in the feminine
confines of her sitting room, surrounded by all her frills and
lace. The smell of her fresh and lightly scented from her bath.
Her skin glowing. Soft. Begging for his touch.

"No, you're wrong," he said. "The visit did accomplish a few
things. I made contact with the enemy camp. I found out Lee
Roy and I still have a connection. And I sent a warning to Buck
Stansell." He reached out; she retreated. He reached out farther
and touched her cheek. She trembled, but didn't pull away from
him. "I laid claim to you. I told them that Buck should know
you are my woman, and if he harms you, I'll seek revenge."

"You...you...*claimed* me?" She widened her eyes, staring
at him in disbelief.

He ran the tips of his fingers down her cheek, caressing her
throat, then circled her neck, urging her forward. "I know Buck
and his type. They're wild, they're ruthless, but they aren't
stupid. The one thing they respect and understand is brute force.
Another man's strength. They know who I am, the life I've
lived. And they know that if I say I'll come after them if they
harm you, I mean it."

"But Ashe, I don't—"

"For as long as I'm your bodyguard, we will pretend to be
a couple. We're old friends who have become lovers. As far as
Buck Stansell and the whole state of Alabama is concerned,
you're my woman, and this isn't a job anymore. This is personal.
In taking care of you, I'm simply defending my own against
any harm. Do you understand what I'm saying?"

Yes, she understood. She understood only too well. Not only
would she have to endure constant threats on her life and Ashe's
daily presence in her life, but she would have to put on an act,
playing the part of Ashe's lover.

"I can't do it," she said, trying to pull away from him.

He held her in his gentle yet firm grip, raking his thumb up and down the side of her neck. "Why can't you?"

"I can't lie about something that important. I can't pretend with Mother and with Allen."

"Tell your Mother the truth, and I don't think Allen will care if you have a boyfriend. He seems to think you need one." Ashe continued stroking the side of her neck.

"You had no right to tell anyone that I'm your woman! I'm not. I never have been and I never will be."

He jerked her up against him, his lips a whisper away from hers. "This pretense just might save your life or at least make Buck think twice about harming you. I don't give a damn about your objections—I'm more concerned about saving your life. From this moment on, for all intents and purposes, you're mine. Do I make myself clear?"

Deborah swallowed hard, then closed her eyes to block out the sight of Ashe's face. She couldn't pretend to be his woman. Dear Lord, didn't he understand anything about her? Years ago she had lived in a fantasy world where she dreamed Ashe would leave Whitney and come to her, claiming her, making her his. And on that one night, the night she conceived Allen, she had given herself to the man she loved, and afterward he had told her he didn't want her.

"You can't order me around. You can't make me do something I don't want to do." She clenched her teeth and stared him straight in the eye.

"You're so damned stubborn."

His lips covered hers with hot, demanding urgency, the need to override her objections forefront in his mind. But his body's needs overcame his intention to bend her to his will. He didn't want to force her to do anything; he wanted her compliance.

Deborah fought the kiss for a few brief seconds, then succumbed to the power of his possession, giving herself over to the feel of his arm around her, pulling her closer and closer, his fingers threading through her hair, capturing her head in the palm of his hand.

Her breasts pressed against his hard chest. His tongue delved into her mouth. Slipping her arms around inside his shirt, she clung to him, her nails biting into the muscles of his naked back. Deborah and Ashe sought to appease the hunger gnawing inside them, their lips tasting the sweetness, their tongues seeking, their hands laying claim to the feast of their aroused bodies.

Ashe felt hard and hot as Deborah ran her hands over his chest, across his tiny, pebble-hard nipples, lacing her fingers through his dark chest hair.

Ashe reached between their bodies, separating the folds of her silk robe, feeling for her breast. He eased the robe off her shoulder, then the thin strap of her gown, exposing her left breast, lifting it in his hand.

When he rubbed his fingers across her jutting nipple, she cried out. He took the sound into his mouth, deepening their kiss. She curled against him. He dragged her onto his lap, lowered his head and covered her nipple with his mouth, sucking greedily. All the while he stroked a fiery path down her back, stopping to caress her hip.

The taste of her filled him, urging him to sample more and more of her soft, sweet flesh. He hadn't meant for things to get so out of hand, but once he'd touched her, he couldn't stop himself, couldn't seem to control his desire.

Deborah's breath came in strong, fast pants as she clung to his shoulder with one hand and held his head to her breast with the other.

They wriggled and squirmed, arms embracing, hands caressing, lips savoring, legs entwined. Losing their balance in the fury of their passion, they toppled off the window bench and onto the floor. Ashe's leg rammed against the mahogany tea table, knocking it over, sending the tea service crashing onto the Oriental carpet.

Breathing erratically, Deborah glanced away from Ashe to the wreckage on the floor beside them. Reality intruded on the erotic dream. She shoved against Ashe's chest.

He wanted her to ignore everything around them, to concentrate on recapturing the raw, wild need that had claimed them, but he saw the hazy look of longing clear from her eyes.

She pulled up her gown to cover her breast and lifted herself into a sitting position on the floor. Ashe rose to his feet, offered her his hand and lifted her, pulling her back into his arms.

"You're Ashe McLaughlin's woman. I think we just proved that it won't be difficult for us to carry off the masquerade for as long as it's necessary."

He brushed her lips with his, then released her. Deborah staggered on her feet, but found her footing quickly, determined not to give in to the desire to scratch Ashe's eyes out.

Damn the man! He had gotten his way. He had proved that she was just as vulnerable to him as she'd been at seventeen.

"I'd like for you to go now," she said. "I'll explain things to Mother and I'll tell Allen what I think will pacify his curiosity."

"There's less than two weeks until the trial. I think we can pretend for that long. Then for another week or so, if Buck Stansell decides to retaliate for your testifying against Lon Sparks."

"I suppose there's always that possibility, isn't there? If that happens, then this nightmare could go on forever."

"Let's take it one day at a time. We'll get you through the trial, then worry about what might or might not happen afterward."

Deborah nodded. Ashe glanced down at the overturned table, the scattered tea service, the spilled tea.

"I'll clean up this mess," he said.

"No, please." She looked at him and wished she hadn't. His gaze said he still wanted her. "I'll take care of it. I'd like for you to leave. Now."

He walked out of her bedroom. She stood there trembling with unshed tears choking her. *I will not cry. I will not cry.* She knelt down on the floor, righted the tea table and picked up the silver service. A dark stain marred the blue-and-cream perfection of the rug. She jumped up and ran into the bathroom, wet a frayed hand towel and glanced into the mirror above the sink.

Dear Lord. Her hair was in disarray, the long strands fanned out around her face. Her cheeks were flushed, her eyes overly bright. Her lips were swollen. A pink rash covered her neck and the top of her left breast, a result of Ashe's beard stubble. She looked like a woman who'd been ravished. Suddenly she felt like a woman who'd been ravished.

Tears gathered in her eyes. She laid her head against the mirror and cried.

IN THE WEEK since they had begun their pretense, Ashe hadn't kissed her again, indeed he'd barely touched her, except in front of others—a part of their performance as lovers. In another week Lon Sparks's trial would begin. But when it ended, would the threats end, too, or would they turn deadly? Ashe screened all of Deborah's calls and her mail. The daily threats continued, meaningless threats since Deborah never heard the messages or read the letters. Two more little *gifts* had arrived, both of these delivered by unknown messenger to her home. One, a green garden snake, Ashe had taken outside and released. The other had been more ominous, one he'd made sure neither Deborah nor Miss Carol saw. A newspaper photograph of Deborah, singed around the edges, a book of matches laid on top and the words "Your house might catch on fire" scrawled in red ink across the newspaper.

Nerve-racking threats to be sure, harassment to say the least, but not once had Deborah's life actually been in jeopardy. Was Buck Stansell playing some sort of sick game or was he trying to throw them off guard, waiting to act at the last moment?

"It's been a long time since you've been in the country club." Carol Vaughn slipped her arm through Ashe's. He looked away from the living room window where he'd been staring sightlessly outside while he waited for Deborah. He smiled at Miss Carol. "Eleven years."

"The night Whitney announced her engagement to George." Carol patted Ashe on his forearm. "She was such a selfish girl, but always so bubbly. Now she's a very sad, selfish woman."

"Are you trying to warn me about something, Miss Carol?"

"Do I need to warn you?"

"I haven't been carrying a torch for Whitney all these years, if that's what's troubling you."

"No, I didn't think you had. You wouldn't look at my daughter as if she were your favorite meal and you hadn't eaten in a long time, if you were in love with another woman."

Had he been that obvious? So apparent in his desire for Deborah that even her own mother had noticed? "Why, Miss Carol, what big eyes you have."

"And sharp teeth, too. If for one minute I thought you'd hurt Deborah again, I'd have no qualms about chewing you up into little pieces."

"And you could do it, too." Taking her hand in his, he walked her across the room and seated her on the sofa. "I never meant to hurt Deborah. I made a mistake, but I tried to keep from making an even bigger mistake. I was honest with her, and I paid dearly for that honesty."

"My husband adored Deborah. She was our only child. I didn't agree with what he did to you, and I told him so at the time. But Wallace could not be reasoned with on any subject, and certainly not when he felt Deborah had been wronged."

"I never made Deborah any promises eleven years ago, and I won't make any to her now. None that I can't keep." Ashe heard Deborah's and Allen's voices coming from the upstairs landing. "I'm attracted to Deborah and she's attracted to me.

We're both adults now. If things become complicated, we'll deal with them."

Carol nodded meekly. Ashe couldn't understand the wary look in her blue eyes, that sad expression on her face. What was Miss Carol so afraid would happen?

Allen rushed down the stairs and into the living room. "Come see," he said. "Deborah's beautiful. She looks like one of those models on TV."

Ashe helped Miss Carol to her feet and they followed Allen into the hallway. All three of them looked up to the top of the stairs where Deborah stood.

For one split second Ashe couldn't breathe. He didn't think he'd ever seen anything as lovely as the woman who walked slowly down the stairs, the diamonds in her ears and around her throat dimmed by her radiance.

Allen glanced up at Ashe, then punched him in the side. "See, what'd I tell you?"

"You're right, pal. She's beautiful."

Deborah descended the staircase, butterflies wild in her stomach. How many times had she dreamed of a real date with Ashe McLaughlin? Now, it was a reality. Now, eleven years too late.

He stood at the bottom of the stairs, Allen to his left. The sight of her son at his father's side tugged at Deborah's heart. What would Ashe say if she told him the truth about Allen? Would he be glad? Or would he be sorry?

Ashe looked at Deborah, seeing her as if for the first time, all sparkling and vibrant, beautiful beyond description. How could any man see her and not want her?

The royal blue satin draped across her shoulders in a shawl collar, narrowing to her tiny waist and flaring into a full, gathered skirt, ankle-length gown. Her satin shoes matched the dress to perfection, and when she stopped at the foot of the stairs, Ashe noticed that the deep rich color she wore turned her blue eyes to sapphires.

"You look lovely, my dear." Carol Vaughn kissed her daughter's cheek. "Please give my regrets to Whitney. I'm sure she'll understand that I'm not quite up to these late-night social affairs."

Deborah hugged her mother close. Her beautiful, brave mother, whose bout with cancer had taken its toll on all of them. "I dread going," Deborah whispered so low that only Carol heard her words. "I have no idea what Whitney will do. She's bound to make a play for Ashe."

Pulling out of Deborah's arms, Carol smiled. "You two run along now and have a wonderful time." Carol glanced at Ashe who hadn't taken his eyes off Deborah. "And don't feel that you need to come home early."

Allen rushed out of the hallway and into the library, returning quickly with a gold foil–wrapped gift. "Don't forget George's birthday present." Allen shook the small package. "What is it anyway?"

"It's a fourteen-karat gold money clip." Deborah took the gift. "Whitney mentioned that George had misplaced his money clip."

"Hocked it, no doubt." Carol nudged Ashe in the center of his back. "I do believe you've taken Ashe's breath away with your loveliness."

"Yeah, he looks like somebody hit him in the head." Allen laughed. "Hey, man, have you got it bad or what?"

Ashe jabbed Allen playfully in the ribs, lifted him up off the floor with one arm and rubbed his fist across the top of the boy's head before placing him back on his feet. "You wouldn't make fun of a guy for mooning over his girl, would you?"

"Naw, as long as you don't kiss her in front of me." Putting his hand on his hip, Allen stood up straight and gave Ashe a hard look. "If I catch you kissing her, then, as the man of the house, I'd have to ask you what your intentions are, wouldn't I?"

"Yes, Allen, I suppose you would," Ashe said. "So, I'll tell you what, I'll try to make sure I kiss Deborah when you're not around."

"Will you two stop this." Deborah tried to hug Allen, but he wriggled away from her. "What's the matter? Have you gotten too big to give me a hug and a kiss?"

"No, that's not it." Grinning, Allen swiped his hand in front of him in a negative gesture. "I'm just afraid your boyfriend will get jealous and sock me."

Allen broke into peals of boyish laughter. Ashe chuckled. Carol covered her mouth to hide her giggle. Deborah shook her head in mock disgust.

"Let's go now, Ashe, before I wind up socking Allen," Deborah said.

Taking the long satin jacket from where Deborah carried it across her arm, Ashe wrapped it around her shoulders. He slipped his arm about her waist and escorted her out to her repaired and newly painted Cadillac waiting in the drive.

When he opened the door, he turned and lifted her hand to his lips. "You're the most beautiful thing I've ever seen."

He kissed her wrist. Chills shivered through her. She looked into his eyes. "Thank you."

He helped her into the car, rounded the Caddy and got behind the wheel. "No matter what happens tonight, there are a few things I want you to keep in mind."

"Such as?" Deborah smoothed the gathers in her skirt, her fingers gliding nervously over the heavy satin. She didn't look at Ashe.

"Such as I didn't come back to Sheffield to protect Whitney. I wouldn't have, for any amount of money. And I'm not staying in town because of her or issuing threats to dangerous men because of her."

"Did she hurt you so badly back then that you hate her now? You know they say there's only a fine line between love and hate. Maybe you still care about her more than you'd like to admit. After all, she was your first love and—"

Ashe grabbed Deborah so quickly that she didn't have time to think of resisting. His kiss came so hard and fast that it obliterated every thought from her mind, filling her with the heat of his anger, the determination of his desire. His mouth devoured hers, the kiss turning from bold strength to gentle power. Her hands crept up around his neck. He stroked her waist. The satin jacket fell from her shoulders leaving them bare. Ashe allowed his lips to retreat from hers, as he nibbled at her bottom lip and tasted her chin. He lowered his head to her shoulder, his mouth closing over her soft flesh.

Shutting her eyes and tossing back her head, Deborah moaned. "Ashe…"

"Don't ever try to tell me how I feel." Lifting his head, he stared into her blue eyes. "Whitney wasn't my first anything. I'd had a dozen girls before her. You should remember all the girls I dated. And as far as my being in love with her, I wasn't. I was infatuated with what she represented. She represented a dream. That night at the country club when she announced her engagement, I saw my dream come to an end."

"Neither of us has ever been able to forget that night, have we? But for different reasons."

He gripped her chin between his thumb and forefinger. "If you think I've ever forgotten what it was like making love to you, then you're wrong."

"I suppose you remember all of them, don't you? Whitney, the dozen before her, and God only knows how many since."

Ashe fell backward against the soft leather of the seat, shook his head and laughed. "You're jealous! You are honest-to-goodness jealous."

"I am not!" Deborah jerked the satin jacket up around her shoulders.

"Somewhere deep down inside, Deborah Vaughn, you're the one who still cares. I still mean something to you, don't I?"

Yes, she wanted to scream. Yes, you mean something to me. You are my first and only lover. You are the father of my child, the child I can never claim as my own. Oh, yes, Ashe McLaughlin, you most definitely still mean something to me.

"I think you're taking the part of playing my lover far too seriously." Deborah turned around in the seat, focusing her attention on the front porch lights. "We are pretending to care about each other. That's all."

"That's not all," Ashe said. "You asked me if I remember all the women I've had sex with. Well, yes, I do remember. Some more than others. But I didn't have sex with you, Deborah." There in the darkness his voice sounded deeper and darker and more sensuous than ever. "I made love to you. I took all that sweet, innocent passion you offered and I drowned myself in your love. I had never been in so much pain, and I had never needed a woman's unselfish love the way I needed yours that night. Don't you think I know that I did all the taking and you did all the giving."

"Please, Ashe, I don't want—"

"What? You don't want to hear the truth? You don't want to hear how much I wanted to keep on taking what you offered? How much guts it took for me to reject you? Hell, I knew I couldn't give a girl like you what you should have. I knew the best thing I could do for you was to get out of your life and stay out."

"And that's exactly what you did." Deborah cringed at the accusatory tone of her own voice. "You couldn't even stay in the same town with me, could you? You couldn't hang around long enough to find—"

Dear God, she'd been about to say *find out if you'd gotten me pregnant!*

"None of this matters now, does it?" Pulling the shoulder harness across her, she snapped the seat belt in place. "If we don't leave for the country club right now, we're going to be more than fashionably late."

"Sooner or later we'll have to finish this conversation," Ashe said. "I think we both have quite a lot to get off our chests."

"It'll have to be later."

"Fine." He turned on the overhead lights. "You might want to check your makeup. I think most of your lipstick is on my mouth." Pulling a handkerchief from his pocket, he wiped his face.

Deborah opened her evening bag, took out her lipstick and glanced in the mirror to see how much repair was needed. She worked quickly, trying not to notice that she looked like a woman who'd just been thoroughly kissed.

"I'm ready," she said.

Ashe backed the Cadillac out of the drive and headed toward the country club.

"ASHE MCLAUGHLIN, you old dog. I never thought I'd see you back in Sheffield."

Keeping his arm firmly around Deborah's waist, Ashe jerked his head around, seeking the familiar voice. "Peanut Haygood?"

The skinny teenage boy who'd lived down the street from Ashe's grandmother had turned into a heavyset, bearded man wearing a uniform and carrying a gun. By the looks of old Peanut, Ashe figured he was part of the private security for George Jamison's big birthday bash.

"Peanut? Man, you've changed since the last time I saw you."

"Yeah, well, a guy grows up and fills out," Peanut said. "I heard you were in town." He nodded politely to Deborah. "Nice to see you, Ms. Vaughn. Sorry to hear about all your problems. One of these days we're going to get the goods on Buck Stansell and put him away for life."

"Are you on the police force?" Deborah asked.

"Yes, ma'am. Over in Muscle Shoals." Peanut slapped Ashe on the back. "Looks like you and me wound up in the same business, huh? You a Green Beret and me a policeman. Now you're a private security agent and I moonlight as a guard for these fancy shindigs at the country club."

"Ashe, if you'll excuse me, I need to go to the ladies' room and then check my wrap." Forcing a smile, Deborah nodded toward the rest room.

"I'll be waiting right outside." Ashe followed her down the corridor, Peanut right behind him keeping up a steady stream of conversation.

From where he stood, Ashe could see the entrance to the ballroom. He spotted Whitney immediately. Her loud laughter echoed out into the hallway. She had her arm draped around a young man who seemed utterly fascinated by her.

"Who'd ever thought Deborah Vaughn would turn into such a looker, huh?" Peanut jabbed Ashe in the ribs. "You two were always friends, weren't you? Rumor was her daddy had you run out of town."

"Rumors aren't always reliable," Ashe said.

"Well, Ms. Vaughn sure got herself into a mess with ol' Buck and his bunch of roughnecks. It's too bad she come up on Lon Sparks shooting Looney. Neither one of those boys was worth a cuss."

"Do you think Buck would kill to protect Sparks or seek revenge if he goes to the pen?"

"I'd say Buck would be more likely to have Lon Sparks killed to keep him from talking than he would to kill Ms. Vaughn. Sparks is a liability to them now. Me and some of the boys at work have got us a theory." Peanut stretched his five feet nine inches and placed his hand atop the gun holster resting on his hip.

"What's your theory?"

"We think Buck is putting on an act of trying to scare Ms. Vaughn, trying to make Lon Sparks think he's protecting him. You get my drift?"

"Yeah, I get it. Buck always was one for playing games." Ashe knew he should be comforted at the thought that it was possible Buck Stansell had no intention of killing Deborah, but Ashe's gut instincts told him that he should take nothing for granted. No matter what Buck's intentions were, the man was dangerous, a highly explosive bad boy, who was capable of anything.

Ashe caught a glimpse of Whitney coming his way. She swayed her narrow hips, encased in silver lamé, as she sauntered out of the ballroom.

"Now there's a real piece of work," Peanut said. "Sexy as hell and so gorgeous she gives a man ideas. But not worth the cost of the lead it'd take to shoot her."

"You seem to know an awful lot about Whitney Jamison." Ashe watched his old lover flirting outrageously with every man in her path as she made her way through the influx of late arrivals congested in the hallway.

"Hey, I've been moonlighting on this job for a good many years and I've seen quite a bit of Mrs. Jamison. She really works these social occasions, and I've rarely seen her leave with her husband, if you know what I mean."

Ashe grinned. "Not the faithful type?"

"Can't say I blame her, married to a loser like George Jamison. The man hasn't held a job in years. They live off her inheritance, you know. Her shares in that real estate firm Ms. Vaughn runs. And Georgie Porgie likes to gamble. They're always flying off to Vegas and Atlantic City and down to Biloxi."

Whitney walked up to Ashe, slipped her arms around his neck and kissed him soundly on the mouth. Still draped around him, she smiled. "Come dance with me, darling. If I remember correctly, you were a marvelous dancer."

"You were the marvelous dancer," Ashe said. "I just followed your lead."

Whitney's throaty laughter rumbled from her chest. Her almost naked chest, Ashe noted. Her strapless silver lamé dress crisscrossed over her full breasts, just covering her tight nipples.

"It's been a long time, hasn't it?" Whitney sighed. "Come on, let's see if we're still good together." She rubbed herself intimately against Ashe.

Peanut cleared his throat. Ashe stared at him. The guard gave his head a few sharp jerks in the direction of the ladies' room. Glancing over his shoulder, Ashe saw Deborah watching him.

Grasping Whitney's arms, he pulled them from around his neck and stepped backward, putting some distance between them. Whitney's gaze followed Ashe's. She laughed again, an almost hysterical giggle.

"You'll have to find yourself another partner," Ashe said. "I'm afraid my dance card is filled."

Whitney leaned over and whispered in Ashe's ear, "If you think my little cousin is going to give you what you need, then you'd better think again. She doesn't know the first thing about men, and most certainly nothing about a man like you."

"That's where you're wrong, Mrs. Jamison." Ashe walked over to Deborah, slipped his arm around her rigid body and pulled her up against his side. "Would you like to dance, honey?" he asked Deborah.

Unsmiling, every nerve in her body tense, Deborah glared at Ashe. "Perhaps, after I've wished George a happy birthday and given him his present." She held up the shiny golden gift.

When Ashe guided Deborah past Whitney, Deborah paused. "You look lovely tonight, Whitney. But then I'm sure you already know that. No doubt every man at the party has told you at least once."

Whitney grinned, a rather shaky grin, one that didn't reach her eyes, one that didn't begin to compare with the smile spreading across Deborah's face.

"And you look adorable," Whitney said, giving Deborah a quick hug. "And aren't you the lucky one, having Ashe McLaughlin as your escort. But then, I suppose Aunt Carol is paying him extra, isn't she?"

"And he's worth every cent." Deborah tugged on Ashe's arm. She led him away from her cousin, down the hallway and into the ballroom.

Ashe and Deborah heard Peanut Haygood's hardy chuckle, but neither turned around to see Whitney's reaction.

"When did you learn to play hardball?" Ashe asked.

"When my father died and I had to take responsibility for his business as well as my mother and Allen."

"Let's find George and give him his present." Ashe ran his hand up and down Deborah's arm. "I want to dance with you."

Deborah wasn't quite sure what she thought or how she felt. A mixture of anger and exhilaration rioted along her nerve endings. All the old jealousies she'd felt for her cousin had come racing to the forefront when she'd walked out of the ladies' room and seen Whitney wrapped around Ashe. But when she had won their verbal sparring match, she'd felt as if she were walking on air.

She couldn't help wondering what would happen if she spent the night in Ashe's arms, dancing with him here at the country club. Perhaps the safest course of action would be to give George his present, stay long enough to appease her social set's curiosity and make a quiet, discreet exit. If Whitney indulged in her usual weakness for champagne, there was a chance she might make a scene later on. And Deborah wanted to avoid a real confrontation that would put her in the spotlight.

The whole town knew she was the prosecution's star witness, and that her life was in danger. And she had no doubt that Ashe McLaughlin's constant presence at her side had set tongues wagging. What would they say once Ashe had shown everyone that their relationship was intimate?

She didn't give a damn what *they* would say. She never had. She'd always been a lot like her mother. Carol Allen Vaughn had known who she was—an Allen—and had never considered herself subject to the rules and regulations of the society biddies. And no one had ever dared question Carol's judgment or suggest her actions were inappropriate. In that respect, Deborah was her mother's daughter.

But Carol had given in to Wallace Vaughn's authority, always the dutiful wife. If only her mother had gone against her father's wishes. If only—

"Deborah, such a smashing dress!" George Jamison III smiled his widemouthed, white-toothed smile and gave his cousin-in-law a peck on the cheek. "For me?" George eyed the gold foil-wrapped gift.

"Oh, yes. This is for you." Deborah hadn't realized that while she'd been thinking, Ashe had led her straight to the birthday boy. Although boy was hardly the appropriate word for a balding man of forty. Then again, perhaps boy was the correct word to describe George, who, in many ways, was far more immature than Allen.

"I'll just put it here with my other goodies." George laid the gift on top of a stack of presents arranged on the table behind him. "I suppose Whitney greeted y'all at the door. She's such a marvelous hostess. And she does love a good party."

"Yes, she met us in the hallway, actually," Deborah said.

Ashe tightened his hold around Deborah's waist. "Happy birthday, George."

George glanced at Ashe, his long, thin nose slightly tilted upward. He made no move to offer Ashe his hand. "McLaughlin." George's pale gray eyes met Ashe's vibrant hazel glare. "I was surprised to hear you'd come back to Sheffield to act as Deborah's bodyguard. Of course, we're all pleased that someone is looking out for her. I understand that you're highly qualified to handle brutes like Buck Stansell. Then, of course, it must be a help that you've had ties to those people all your life."

"Yes, it is a help." Ashe lifted the corners of his mouth just enough to hint at a smile, but he knew George Jamison would recognize the look in his eyes for what it was. Contempt. Dislike. Disgust.

"We can't stay too long," Deborah said. "I don't like to leave Mother alone."

"I quite understand." Glancing across the room, George waved at someone. "Do enjoy yourselves. I'm sure this is a bit of a treat for you, McLaughlin. Finally getting to come to the country club through the front door. Rather different from the last time you were here, isn't it?"

"George, you're being—" Deborah said.

"You're right." Catching sight of Whitney dancing with the young man she had cornered earlier, Ashe nodded in her direction. "Eleven years ago you and I were the only two guys Whitney was seeing."

"How dare you!" George's thin, white cheeks flushed pink.

Ashe led Deborah away from George, quickly ushering her through the crowd and onto the dance floor.

"That was a horrible thing to say to George," Deborah said.

"I was justified, don't you think?" Ashe pulled her close, leaning over to nuzzle her neck with his nose.

She gulped in a deep breath of air. "Yes, you were most definitely justified. George always has been a little snot! He's so immature."

"A little snot?" Ashe chuckled. "I guess that does aptly describe George, doesn't it?"

Deborah loved the feel of Ashe's arms around her, the security of his strength, the sensuality of his nearness. She didn't know what she had expected to happen tonight. Between Ashe and Whitney. Between Ashe and George. But she certainly hadn't expected to feel so light and free and thoroughly amused.

It suddenly hit her that neither she nor Ashe were the same two people who had left this country club eleven years ago. They had both grown up.

Ashe was no longer in awe of the wealthy social set that ruled the county. His dreams weren't wrapped up in a sexy package called Whitney Vaughn. He wasn't an angry, outraged, spurned lover.

And Deborah no longer saw herself as a wallflower beside her exquisite cousin. Any residue of leftover jealousy she might have once felt disappeared completely. She was strong. She was successful. She was attractive.

And Ashe McLaughlin wanted her!

They moved to the music, giving themselves over to the bluesy rendition of an old Glenn Miller song. They spent nearly an hour on the dance floor, wrapped in each other's arms. Occasionally Deborah noticed some curious stares and heard a few whispered innuendoes. None of it mattered, she told herself. She and Ashe were presenting themselves to the world as lovers. She could not allow herself to think otherwise. When the danger to her life ended, Ashe would be gone.

But during the duration of his stay, they could become lovers. She didn't doubt for one minute that Ashe wanted her. He had made that abundantly clear. The question was did she dare risk giving herself to him? Did she dare risk falling in love with him all over again? How could she become his lover and continue lying to him about Allen?

"Are you about ready to leave?" Ashe whispered, then kissed her ear.

Deborah shivered. "Yes. I think everyone has seen us and drawn their own conclusions."

"We don't have to go back to your house." Ashe ran his hand up and down her back. "We could find some place to be alone."

"No. I'm not… Just take me home. I can't handle a repeat performance of that night eleven years ago when we left the country club together."

"It wouldn't be the same. We aren't the same," he said. "We'd both know what we were getting into this time."

"That's the problem, isn't it? At least for me."

The music came to a end. Couples left the dance floor, while others waited for the next set to begin. Deborah pulled away from Ashe, intending to make a quick exit. Ashe jerked her into his arms, grasped the back of her head with his hand and kissed her, long, hard and devouring. Every rational thought went out of her head.

When she was weak and breathless, he ended the kiss, draped his arm around her shoulders and escorted her off the dance floor, past a glaring Whitney and her openmouthed guests.

"Every person in this room knows you're mine," he whispered as they walked out into the hall. "And since they're aware of my reputation, no one will doubt that I'm the kind of man who'd kill to defend his own."

CHAPTER SEVEN

DEBORAH FOLDED THE blueprints and laid them aside. She couldn't seem to concentrate on the plans for Cotton Lane Estates, although she had promised Vaughn & Posey's backers a detailed report on their present subdivision project.

She lifted the cup of warm coffee to her lips and downed the sweet liquid. Clutching the coffee mug in her hands, she closed her eyes. In a few days, Lon Sparks's trial would begin and she'd be called on to testify. The waiting had been almost unbearable, not knowing what might or might not happen. She couldn't give in to her fears and allow the likes of Buck Stansell to frighten her into backing down from doing what she knew was right. But sometimes she wondered what her mother and Allen would do if anything happened to her. Her mother's health was so precarious, and Allen was still so young. What if he lost both her and her mother?

Ashe McLaughlin had a right to know he had a son. That's what her mother had told Deborah's father years ago and that's what she kept telling Deborah now. If anything were to happen to the two women in Allen's life, he would still have his father.

But how could she tell Ashe the truth? She and her mother had kept the true circumstances of Allen's birth a secret for ten years. What would Allen do if he suddenly discovered that the two people he loved and trusted most in the world had been lying to him his whole life?

No, she didn't dare risk losing Allen's love by telling Ashe the truth. She had no way of knowing how Ashe would react and whether or not he'd tell Allen everything.

Her mother had warned her that sooner or later Ashe would have to be told. Deborah had decided that it must be later, much later. She had to be strong. Just a little while longer. Ashe wouldn't stay in Sheffield if she wasn't in danger. He would walk out of their lives and never look back, the way he'd done eleven years ago. She could trust him with her life, but not with her heart—and not with Allen's future.

When she heard a soft knock at the door, Deborah opened her eyes. "Yes?"

Annie Laurie eased the door open. "Mr. Shipman's on the phone. He says it's urgent he speak to you."

"Mr. Shipman? The principal at Allen's school?"

"Yes, that Mr. Shipman."

"Okay. Thanks, Annie Laurie." Deborah picked up the telephone and punched the Incoming Call button. "Hello, Mr. Shipman, this is Deborah Vaughn. Is something wrong?"

Ashe slipped by Annie Laurie and into Deborah's private office, closing the door behind him. Deborah glanced at him.

"Ms. Vaughn, you need to come to school and pick up Allen," Mr. Shipman said. "I'm afraid there's been a problem on the playground during PE class."

"Has Allen been in a fight?" Deborah asked.

Ashe lifted his eyebrows and shrugged his shoulders as if saying "Boys will be boys."

"Oh, no Ms. Vaughn, I didn't mean to imply that Allen had gotten himself into any trouble. Quite the contrary. It seems that when the fifth graders were playing softball during PE, a stranger approached Allen. Your brother won't tell us what the man said to him, but Allen seems terribly upset. I thought it best to phone you immediately."

"Yes, yes, you did the right thing, Mr. Shipman. I'll be right over." Deborah's heartbeat throbbed loudly in her ears, obliterating every other sound, even Ashe's voice. "Please, don't leave

Allen alone. Make sure someone is with him until I pick him up." Deborah returned the phone to its cradle.

When Deborah didn't respond to his questions, Ashe grabbed her by the shoulders, shaking her gently. "What's going on? Has something happened to Allen?"

"A strange man approached Allen on the playground during PE. Mr. Shipman said the man upset Allen." Deborah clutched the lapels of Ashe's jacket. "What if— Oh, God, Ashe, what if Buck Stansell sent someone to hurt Allen?"

"Did anyone besides Allen get a good look at this man? Did they see whether he was on foot or driving?"

"I didn't think to ask, dammit." Releasing her hold on Ashe, Deborah walked around to the front of her desk. Yanking open the bottom drawer, she lifted out her leather bag and threw the straps over her shoulder. "I have to pick up Allen and take him home. I have to make sure he's all right. If anyone dares harm him, I'll—"

"I'll take care of anyone who threatens Allen, in the same way I'll handle anyone who threatens you." Ashe held out his hand. "Give me the keys to your Caddy. I'll drive. On the way over to the school, pull yourself together. Allen doesn't need to see how upset you are."

Deborah took a deep breath. "You're right. It's just that, in the back of my mind, I kept wondering if and when Buck Stansell would target Mother or Allen. Oh, Ashe, I can't let anything happen to Allen."

"Nothing is going to happen to Allen." He took her hand in his. "I promise."

Within five minutes they marched side by side into Richard Shipman's office where Allen sat, silent and unmoving, in a corner chair. The minute he saw Deborah, he ran into her open arms.

"Give us a few minutes alone with Allen," Ashe said to the principal, who immediately nodded agreement and exited his office.

"What happened, sweetheart?" Deborah asked, bending on her knees, hugging her child close, stroking his thick blond hair. "Tell us everything."

Allen clung to Deborah for several moments, then glanced over at Ashe. "You can't let them do anything to hurt her."

"Allen, will you tell me what happened?" Ashe reached down and patted Allen on the back.

Allen shook his head, released his tenacious hold on Deborah, but still clung to her hand as she stood. "He walked up to me on the playground. I was waiting my turn at bat. He said he knew my sister and that he wanted me to give her a message."

"Oh, Ashe!" Deborah clenched her teeth tightly together in an effort not to cry in front of Allen.

Laying his hand on Deborah's shoulder, Ashe gave her a reassuring squeeze. "Had you ever seen this man before?"

"No," Allen said.

"Come on, let's go sit down over here on the sofa." Deborah led Allen across the room to the small, leather sofa situated against the back wall between two oak filing cabinets. "I want you to answer all of Ashe's questions. He's here to help us. Do you understand?"

"What—what do you want to know?" Allen looked at Ashe.

"Would you recognize the man if you ever saw him again? Can you tell me what he looked like?"

"Yeah, I'd recognize him, all right. He was big and ugly and he smelled bad."

"Sounds like somebody Buck would sent around to frighten a child," Ashe said.

"He didn't scare me." Allen tightened his hold on Deborah's hand. "I told him off. If you don't believe me, just ask Tripper Smith. He heard me telling that guy he'd better leave my sister alone."

Ashe knelt down in front of Allen. "I know you're brave and that you'd fight for your sister."

Deborah forced a smile when she looked at Allen's pale little face. "Did the man try to hurt you?"

"Naw, he just said to give my sister a message. He said to tell you that if you show up in court Monday, you'll be very sorry. And I told him that nothing he said or did would keep you from testifying against that murderer. And he said if you did, you were stupid. That's when I tried to hit him, but he just laughed and walked away."

"Did your teacher see the man, or any of the other kids beside this Tripper Smith?" Ashe asked.

"My teacher didn't see nothing, but several of the kids saw him. Tripper's the one who went and told Coach Watkins what had happened."

"Okay, Allen, why don't you and Deborah go do whatever is necessary to get you checked out of school for the day. I'll make a couple of phone calls and then we'll be ready to leave." Ashe wished he had the big, bad-smelling stranger in front of him right now. He'd teach Buck Stansell's messenger that it wasn't nice to go around frightening little boys, especially not a child under his protection.

"Are we going home?" Allen asked. "Do we have to tell Mother what happened? She'll just worry."

"We aren't going home," Ashe said. "I think you and Deborah and I should go somewhere for burgers and fries and then do something fun together this afternoon. How does that sound to you, Allen?"

"Sounds great to me." Allen looked at Deborah. "Can I really play hooky for the rest of the day?"

"You bet you can." Deborah stood. Allen jumped up beside her. "We'll go get Allen checked out of school and wait for you in the office."

"I'll only be a few minutes." Ashe picked up the telephone and dialed the police department. "Allen, I know you don't want to worry your mother, but we'll have to tell her what happened when we go home."

Allen nodded. Deborah ushered him out of the principal's office, thankful that Ashe McLaughlin was taking charge of the situation, thankful that she hadn't had to face this alone. The thought that they had come together like a family—a mother, a father and their child—flashed through Deborah's mind. She couldn't allow herself the indulgence of such thoughts. Thinking of the three of them as a family could be dangerous.

"I CAN'T EAT another bite." Ashe shoved a French fry into Deborah's mouth. She slapped his hand away.

"I want one of those sundaes, don't you, Ashe?" Allen read the list of desserts off the wall sign behind the counter. "I want caramel with nuts."

"That's my favorite, too." Ashe slid out from behind the booth. "I'll order us both one. What do you want, Deborah?"

"Nothing! I've eaten enough for a couple of meals."

"Ah, she's just worried she'll get fat," Allen said. "She used to be sort of plump a long time ago. Hey, you already know that. You knew Deborah even before I did."

"So I did." Ashe sauntered off to order their desserts, coming back with two caramel sundaes and a small chocolate ice-cream cone, which he handed to Deborah.

"Chocolate used to be your favorite," he said.

"It still is," she admitted, taking the cone and napkin he handed her. During the last months of her pregnancy, she had craved chocolate ice cream. Maybe that was the reason Allen hated the stuff. She'd gorged him on it before he'd been born.

She didn't realize she'd been sitting there smiling, a dazed look in her eyes until Ashe waved his hand in front of her face.

"Where did you go?" he asked. "You're a million miles away."

"Just thinking about chocolate ice cream," she said.

"Well, you'd better eat it before it melts." Allen lifted a spoonful of his sundae to his mouth. "Thanks for getting extra nuts, Ashe."

"Nothing's too good for us, pal." Ashe didn't think he'd ever felt about a kid the way he felt about Allen. He didn't understand it, couldn't explain it, but he felt connected to Allen Vaughn. Maybe it was because of his past history with the family, his respect for Miss Carol, his friendship with Deborah. Whatever the cause, he found himself wondering what it would be like to have a child of his own, a boy like Allen.

"Now who's gathering moss?" Deborah wondered what Ashe was thinking. The man was such a mystery to her. Once she'd thought she knew him, but she'd been wrong. He'd never been the man she thought he was.

"What can folks do on a weekday afternoon around here for fun?" Ashe asked. "How about a movie?"

"No matinees except on the weekend," Deborah said.

"What about miniature golf?" Allen wiped his mouth with his paper napkin. "I think it's still open every afternoon until Thanksgiving."

"How about it, Deborah, are you game for a round of golf?" Ashe smiled at her and she returned his smile. "You should do that more often, you know."

"What?" she asked.

"Smile like that. A guy would agree to anything you wanted if you smiled at him like that." The warmth of her smile brought back memories of the way she'd smiled at him, lying in his arms in the moonlight, down by the river. He had never forgotten that beautiful smile or the way it had made him feel just looking at her.

"Aw, are you getting all mushy?" Allen shook his head. "Save all that love talk for when you're alone with her. I'm too young to hear stuff like that."

"Allen!" Deborah rolled her eyes heavenward.

"Eat your sundae," Ashe said. "And I'll keep in mind that

you aren't old enough to learn from a master just yet. But in a few more years, you'll be begging me to share my secrets of seduction with you."

"Ashe! Of all things to say to a ten-year-old."

"Ah, lay off Ashe." Allen spoke with his mouth half full of sundae. He swallowed. "You just don't understand guy stuff."

"Oh, well, excuse me." Grinning, Deborah licked the dripping ice cream from around the edge of her cone. She glanced over at Ashe, who watched her intently, his vision focused on her mouth. She licked a circle around the chocolate ice cream, all the while watching Ashe watch her. This was a grown-up game she was playing, a subtle sexual game that Allen wouldn't notice. But Ashe noticed. He knew precisely what she was doing and why.

His jaw tightened. His eyes shone with the intensity of their gaze, fixed on her mouth, on her tongue. He gripped the edge of the table with one hand and laid his tightly clenched fist beside his half-eaten sundae.

She was arousing him and she knew it. She liked the sense of power he gave her by his display of desire. If they were alone, instead of sitting in a fast-food restaurant with Allen, she wasn't sure she'd have the nerve to tempt Ashe.

"Are you any good at playing miniature golf?" Allen tossed his plastic spoon into his empty sundae bowl. "Hey, Ashe, are you listening to me?"

"What did you say, pal?"

"Are you good at playing miniature golf?" Allen repeated. "Deborah and Mother play real golf and they take me along. They're teaching me how to play. But right now, I still like miniature golf better."

"I can't say I've ever played miniature golf before," Ashe said. "Today you'll have to be my teacher."

"I like that idea. I don't think I've ever taught anybody anything before." Allen beamed with pleasure.

Deborah relaxed and finished off her ice-cream cone,

thinking how easily a child can adapt, how quickly Allen had gone from a frightened, worried little boy into a secure, happy kid looking forward to a new experience.

Would he adapt so easily if someday she told him the truth—that she was his mother and Ashe was his father?

"STRAIGHT UPSTAIRS AND into the bathtub for you, young man." Deborah gave Allen a gentle push up the stairs, then dropped down on the bottom step. When Allen dashed off, galloping up the stairs and down the hall, Ashe propped his foot on the step beside Deborah and leaned over, kissing the tip of her nose.

She stared up at him, bewilderment in her eyes. "What was that for?"

"For being so cute. Your hair is an absolute mess." He twirled a loose strand around his index finger. "Your shoes are ruined and you've got chocolate stains on your blouse."

They both glanced down to the dark circle on the silk that lay over the rise of her left breast. "I need to get out of this blouse and soak it before the stain sets in any worse than it already has."

Ashe released her hair, ran his finger down the side of her neck and over into the V of her blouse. "Need any help?"

Carol Vaughn cleared her throat. Ashe straightened. Deborah looked up at her mother who walked from the living room into the hallway.

"Is Allen all right?" Carol asked. "He didn't seem upset."

"He's practically forgotten about what happened," Deborah said. "Thanks to Ashe. We've eaten hamburgers and fries twice today, played God only knows how many rounds of miniature golf, went to see that ridiculous dog movie and bought Allen a brand-new computer game."

"Should we take Allen out of school until the trial is over?" Carol asked.

"No, that would only make matters worse for him." Getting

up, Deborah walked over to her mother and placed her arm around her frail shoulders. "I think Ashe should act as Allen's bodyguard from now on instead of mine."

"Oh, Deborah, no. Do you think Allen really is in danger?"

"Miss Carol, there's no way to know whether Allen is in real danger, but we don't dare take any chances," Ashe said. "I called the police, and Chief Burton has assured me that they'll send a patrol car around every day during Allen's PE time. And I spoke to Sheriff Blaylock, gave him a description of the man who confronted Allen on the playground."

"Do you think there's any chance of catching the man?" Carol slipped her thin arm around her daughter's waist.

"I doubt it," Ashe said. "My bet is that Buck got somebody from out of town and the guy's long gone by now."

"I didn't want to think that Allen might be in danger," Carol said. "But it did cross my mind that these people might try to get to Deborah through her...her brother."

"You could also be in danger, Miss Carol, especially when you're outside the house. With the security system we have in place now, it would be difficult for anyone to break in." Anyone who wasn't a highly trained professional, Ashe thought. He doubted any of Buck's local boys had the know-how to get past a sophisticated system, but it was possible.

"I'm not worried about myself, only my children. You must keep Deborah and Allen protected no matter what."

"Mother, don't fret this way. It isn't good for you."

"With your permission, Miss Carol, I'd like to bring in another man to guard Allen," Ashe said.

"Someone else from Dundee Security?" Carol asked.

"Yes, ma'am."

"Do you think that's necessary?" Carol looked to Deborah, who nodded and squeezed her mother's hand.

"All right, you do what you think best." Carol allowed Deborah to help her up the stairs. Pausing on the landing, she looked down at Ashe. "You have no idea how reassured I am by your presence here, Ashe McLaughlin, knowing that you have taken responsibility for Deborah and Allen."

Deborah's gaze met Ashe's. Looking away quickly, she assisted her mother to her room. Ashe couldn't quite figure out that strange look in Deborah's eyes, almost pleading. And sad. And even afraid. This wasn't the first time he'd sensed Deborah feared him, but he couldn't understand why. Not unless she still loved him. Dear God, was it possible? Of course not, no one kept loving someone eleven years after they'd been rejected.

Ashe went into the library, closed the door and dialed Simon Roarke's private number. Dundee himself would have been Ashe's first choice, but Sam seldom took on private cases any more. His other top choices were J.T. Blackwood, who was already involved in another case, and Simon Roarke.

He'd known Simon for nearly a year, had met him when he'd first hired on with Dundee Security. The two had liked each other immediately, finding they had enough in common to form a friendship. A couple of former career soldiers who'd been born and raised in Southern poverty.

"Roarke here." His voice sounded like gravel being dumped onto sheet metal.

"This is McLaughlin. I need you on the first plane out of Atlanta. Tonight if possible."

"What's up?"

"The woman I'm protecting has a ten-year-old brother. Today a stranger approached him on the school playground and gave him a message for his sister."

"The bastard!" Roarke said, the sound possessing the depth of a rottweiler's bark. "He didn't hurt the kid, did he?"

"Allen's fine. I just want to make sure he stays that way." Ashe knew that if Simon Roarke had one weakness, it was children. His only child had died years ago, and Simon had never fully recovered, had never escaped the demons of pain.

"I'll let Sam know where I'll be. He can fax me all the

information on your case," Roarke said. "And I'll see you first thing in the morning."

Ashe stayed in the den for nearly thirty minutes after he finished talking to Roarke. He stood by the window, looking out into the darkness, not seeing what lay before him, only envisioning Deborah's smile. He wanted her to smile at him again the way she'd smiled at him that night so long ago. He hadn't realized how much he needed someone to love him.

Hell! He was a fool. Deborah didn't love him. She might desire him the way he desired her, but she wasn't a seventeen-year-old girl anymore. She didn't look at him through the eyes of love and see her Prince Charming. And he had no one to blame but himself. He had been the one to destroy her fairy-tale dreams.

She had offered him everything. And he'd been too young and stupid to realize what he was rejecting.

He made his way upstairs, turning off lights as he went. Allen's bedroom door stood open. The sound of his and Deborah's voices floated down the hall. Strange, how quickly he'd come to feel at home in the Vaughn household, how quickly he had come to think of Miss Carol and Allen, and yes, dammit, Deborah, as his own family.

He stood several feet away from Allen's room, looking through the open door. Deborah, fresh from a bath and wearing a navy blue silk robe, sat on the edge of Allen's bed. She pulled the covers up around his chest, then patted the edges into place. Lifting her hand, she reached out and touched Allen's face, the gesture so filled with love that it hit Ashe in the pit of his stomach with knockout force.

"We're going to be just fine, you know," Deborah said, cradling Allen's cheek with her hand. "I've been taking care of us for a long time now and haven't done such a bad job. Now Ashe is here, and he won't let anything happen to you or me or Mother."

"I like Ashe a lot, don't you? He's the kind of man any guy

would like for a father." Allen threw his arms around Deborah, giving her a bear hug.

Deborah hugged him fiercely. Ashe noticed her shoulders trembling. He wanted to go to them, put his arms around Deborah and Allen and become a part of the love they shared. He wanted to tell them that he'd die to protect them.

Allen fell back into the bed, his eyes drooping as he yawned. "Since Ashe is too young for Mother, you could marry him. He'd make a pretty great brother-in-law."

"I'll keep that in mind, but don't expect anything. Ashe is our friend, but he has a life in Atlanta. Once the trial is over and things gets back to normal, Ashe will be leaving."

"I wish he would stay forever." Allen yawned, then closed his eyes. "Don't you wish he'd stay forever?"

Deborah kissed Allen on the forehead, turned out the lamp on the bedside table and walked out of Allen's room, leaving the door partially open. She saw Ashe standing in the hallway, staring directly at her, the oddest expression on his face.

"You didn't answer him," Ashe said. "Do you wish I'd stay forever?"

"Is anything forever, Ashe?" She walked toward him, then lowered her eyes and passed him, turning to go into her room.

Reaching out, Ashe grabbed her by the wrist. She halted. "I didn't use to think so. Now, I'm not so sure."

Deborah pulled her wrist out of his loose grasp. "Let me know when you're sure, Ashe." She went into her bedroom and closed the door.

CHAPTER EIGHT

COMPLETING THE JURY selection had taken all morning, so Deborah had remained at work until noon, then gone home for lunch with her mother. Ashe had told her there was no need for her to make an appearance in court until she was called on to testify, but she had insisted on going.

Now she wished she hadn't. Local and state newspaper and television reporters swarmed around her like agitated bees, each person trying their best to zero in on the prosecution's eye witness. Ashe shielded her with his body, practically carrying her past the horde of reporters and crowd of spectators. She clung to her protector, closing her eyes against the sight of clamoring people, the din of voices rising higher and higher.

Seating her near the back of the courtroom, Ashe stood at her side, like a guardian angel wielding a flaming sword to keep danger at bay and the unwanted from trespassing on her private space. When Judge Williams entered the courtroom, Deborah stood, taking Ashe's hand in hers. She sought and found comfort in his presence. His power and strength nourished her own, helping her face what lay ahead.

There had been no question in her mind that she would attend this first day of Lon Sparks's trial. She thought it necessary to show the world, by her presence, that she would not be intimidated by Buck Stansell and his gang of hoodlums. Of course, none of them were in attendance. They would stay away, keeping up the pretense that they were not involved, when the whole county knew they were.

One by one, the prosecution called their witnesses. First, the

Leighton police, then Charlie Blaylock and two of his deputies. The day's proceedings moved along quickly, Deborah sitting tensely, Ashe at her side. At five o'clock, the court session ended, the judge announcing a recess until the following morning. Would they get to her that soon? Deborah wondered. Would the trial actually come to an end in a week's time? Unless the defense dragged things out, Deborah couldn't imagine the trial lasting much longer.

When Ashe touched her, she jumped. Standing, he offered her his hand. "I'll get you to the car as quickly as possible. Just stay right by my side. Don't look at or respond to the reporters."

"Some of them kept watching me during the trial proceedings." She accepted Ashe's assistance. "I saw them looking at me during the testimony. Especially when Jerry Don Lansdell told how I came running into the Leighton police station that day. The defense lawyer, that Mr. Prater, had Jerry Don practically admitting that I was too hysterical to know what I was talking about, that I was a raving lunatic."

"Don't worry about it. The jurors aren't stupid. They saw through what Sparks's lawyer was trying to do." Ashe slipped his arm around her. "When you're on the stand, you'll convince the jurors that you saw Lon Sparks murder Corey Looney. These people are not going to doubt your word, Deborah. You're a respected citizen with nothing to gain by lying."

Deborah glanced at her diamond-studded wristwatch. "It's too late to make Allen's soccer game. It should be ending about now."

"Then let's go home and let him tell us all about the game." Ashe led Deborah out of the crowded courtroom.

In the hallway, the same horde of insistent reporters swarmed around her. Deborah squared her shoulders. Ashe kept her protected, holding her close to his side.

"Ms. Vaughn, are you disturbed by the defense's accusation that you were too traumatized by the murder you witnessed to make a proper identification of the killer?" A lanky young reporter stuck a microphone into Deborah's face.

Ashe pierced the man with a sharp look, then shoved his way through the semicircle of inquisitors. They followed in hot pursuit. When Ashe and Deborah reached the stairs, he halted, turning around sharply.

"Ms. Vaughn has no comment, ladies and gentlemen, other than she will be in court to testify when called upon."

Ashe hurried her down the stairs, the reporters following, bombarding them with questions—everything from "Is it true Ms. Vaughn's ten-year-old brother had been attacked by a stranger on the school playground?" to "Is she romantically involved with her bodyguard?"

By the time Ashe and Deborah made their way to her Cadillac, parked across the street in the adjacent parking lot, Deborah wanted to scream. How on earth did celebrities endure their every move being a media event?

Ashe drove the Caddy out of the parking lot and headed up Water Street, making a right turn onto Main Street. Laying her head against the back of the leather seat, Deborah closed her eyes and let out a deep breath. Her face would be spread across the morning newspapers and appear on the evening newscasts. Right then and there, she decided not to turn on the television or even look at the paper.

A train caught them before they entered Sheffield. Ashe shifted the car into Park and glanced at Deborah. She looked like she was ready to scream or cry, maybe both. If only she had taken his advice and not gone to court today. Maybe now she would wait until time for her testimony before returning. She was so damn stubborn, so determined to show him and the rest of the world what a strong woman she was.

"When is Allen's next soccer game?" he asked.

"What?" She opened her eyes. "Oh. Day after tomorrow."

"If you're not on the witness stand, I think we should go to Allen's game."

"I try to make it to as many of his games as I possibly can. Except when she was very sick, Mother's never missed one. She's Allen biggest supporter."

"You haven't been worrying about Allen, have you?" Ashe noticed the last train car pass and the guard rails lifting. "I can assure you that Simon Roarke will guard him and your mother with his life. He's a good man, and highly trained."

"I'm sure you're right." Deborah rubbed her forehead with her fingertips. "But even good men who are highly trained can be taken out. No one, not even you, Ashe, is invincible."

Shifting the gears into Drive, Ashe followed the line of backed-up traffic over the railroad tracks and up Montgomery Avenue. "It's all right, you know, if you want to cry or scream or hit something. I won't think you're weak if you do."

"Thanks for your permission, but I don't need to do anything except get home and show my mother and my...my brother that I'm fine."

"Hey, they already know you're strong and capable and in control. You don't have to try to be a paragon for them. My God, Deborah, what are you trying to prove by this woman of steel routine? And to whom?"

To you, she wanted to scream. To you, Ashe McLaughlin. I want you to know that I'm not the same silly little girl who threw herself at your feet. I want you to see me for the woman I am now. The woman your rejection helped create. A woman in charge of her own life. A woman capable of caring for others, without any help from a man.

Ashe turned into the Vaughn driveway and saw Simon Roarke pulling Carol Vaughn's silver Mercedes in right beside them. He parked in the three-car garage behind the house. The moment Deborah emerged from her Cadillac, Allen, in his gold-and-blue soccer uniform, raced around the cars and directly toward Deborah and Ashe.

"We won. I scored the winning goal." Allen jumped up and down in a boyish frenzy of triumph. "Tell them, Mr. Roarke.

Tell them, Mother. I was awesome, wasn't I? You should have been there."

"Yes, I should have been," Deborah said. "Ashe and I will be at Wednesday's game if I don't have to testify that day."

Deborah caught the quick exchange of glances between Ashe and Simon Roarke. She wanted to ask them what was going on, but didn't dare in front of her mother and son. Besides, it might have meant nothing more than a coded recognition that all was well.

"Allen is quite an athlete," Roarke said in his gravelly voice. "They wouldn't have won the game without him."

"See. See." Full of youthful exuberance, Allen bounced around in the driveway. "Boy, Ashe, I wish you could have seen me make that goal."

A twinge of guilt tugged on Deborah's heartstrings. How was she going to handle Allen's growing dependency on Ashe? How would she be able to keep Ashe from disappointing their son? And that's the way she thought of Allen—as their son.

"Miss Carol should have videotaped it for us." Ashe winked at Carol, who stood near the entrance to the side patio.

"Oh, I could never watch the game and videotape it at the same time. I get too excited at these games," Carol said. "I'd end up dropping the videocamera and breaking it."

"Hey, what's Mazie fixing for supper tonight?" Allen asked, running around the side of the garage, Roarke following him. "I'm starving."

"Pork chops, I think," Carol said, opening the gate to the side patio.

"I gotta go get Huckleberry out of the backyard now that we're home. I'll bet he's hungry, too." Allen bounded out of sight, Roarke on his heels.

Ashe and Deborah followed Carol through the gate and onto the side patio. A cool evening breeze swirled around them. Carol shivered.

"I think autumn weather is here to stay," she said.

"Yes, it seems—" Deborah said.

A loud scream pierced the evening stillness. Allen's scream!

"Allen!" Deborah cried, gripping Ashe by the sleeve, then breaking into a run.

Ashe grabbed her by the arm, stopping her. "You and Miss Carol go into the house and lock the patio door. I'll see what's wrong."

Deborah nodded agreement, then led her mother inside, locking the door behind them. "Sit down in here and rest, Mother. I'll go see what's happened."

Once she had seated her mother on the sofa, Deborah raced through the house, meeting Mazie coming down the stairs.

"What was that screaming all about?" Mazie asked. "It sounded like Allen."

"It was," Deborah said. "Go see about Mother. She's in the living room."

Deborah rushed through the kitchen, flung open the back door and ran into the fenced backyard. Roarke stood facing Deborah, but his attention was riveted to the boy and man and dog on the ground. Deborah's heart stopped, her lungs filling with air as she sucked in a terrified breath.

Huckleberry lay on the ground, Allen on his knees beside him, trying to hug the big dog in his arms. Ashe hovered over Allen, his hand on Allen's shoulder as he talked in a low voice.

In the throes of a spasm, Huckleberry jerked. His spine arched, his head leaned backward, his legs twitched.

"What—what happened?" Deborah walked forward slowly.

"Looks like the dog's been poisoned," Roarke said.

"He's vomited," Ashe said, nodding toward the foul-smelling evidence. "If he has been poisoned, vomiting is a good sign. There's hope a vet might save him."

Tears streamed down Allen's face. He glanced up at Deborah. "Why would anybody want to hurt Huckleberry?"

Why indeed? Ashe looked at Deborah and she knew. This was another warning from Buck Stansell.

"Come on, Allen." Ashe pried the boy's arms from around his dog, lifting him to his feet. "Go inside and get a quilt to wrap Huckleberry in. He's still alive. If we hurry we might be able to help him."

Allen nodded in numb silence, then flew through the open back door.

"Roarke, get the vet's phone number from Miss Carol and call and tell him to meet us." Kneeling, Ashe hoisted the big, stiff-legged Lab into his arms. "Deborah, go get the car started. Allen and I will bring Huckleberry around."

Deborah had the car ready when Allen opened the door and helped Ashe place Huckleberry on the backseat. Father and son leaped into the backseat beside the dog, Ashe pulling Allen onto his lap.

"Let's go," he said.

Deborah drove like a madman, running several red lights as she flew down Second Street. She prayed that nothing would prevent them from making it to Dr. Carradine's Pet Hospital in Muscle Shoals. She heard Ashe talking to Allen, reassuring him without giving him false hope.

"Talk to Huckleberry, son. Tell him we're taking care of him. Tell him he's a fine dog."

Tears gathered in Deborah's eyes. She swatted them away with the back of her left hand while she kept her right hand on the steering wheel. It was so unfair for this to happen to Huckleberry. He was an innocent animal, a child's pet. The rage inside her boiled. If she could have gotten her hands around Buck Stansell's neck, she didn't doubt that, at this precise moment, she had the strength to strangle the man.

When she swerved into Carradine's Pet Hospital, Dr. Carradine rushed out the front door and over to the car. Ashe got out, pulling Allen with him. Dr. Carradine leaned over inside the car.

"I'd say from the looks of Huckleberry that he has been poisoned. My guess is strychnine." Dr. Carradine lifted

Huckleberry, straining himself in the process, his small, slender arms barely able to manage the dog's weight.

Ashe took Huckleberry from the vet the moment he emerged from the car.

"Bring him inside quickly. I'll anesthetize him. It'll stop the spasms."

Deborah took Allen's hand and they followed Ashe into the veterinary clinic. When they entered the lobby, Ashe turned to Deborah.

"You and Allen stay out here."

"No, I want to go with Huckleberry," Allen cried.

"You can help Huckleberry by letting me take care of him," Dr. Carradine said.

Allen clung to Deborah, tears pouring from his eyes, streaking his face, falling in huge drops from his nose and chin.

Ashe laid the big Lab on the examining table. Huckleberry panted wildly, then went into another spasm. Ashe watched while the doctor filled a syringe and plunged it deep into the dog's body. Poor animal. The veterinarian refilled the syringe and administered a second injection.

"What now?" Ashe wondered if there was any hope of saving Allen's pet.

"Wait and pray," Dr. Carradine said. "I've given him enough anesthesia to put him in a deep sleep. If we can keep him this way, he has a slight chance of pulling through. But I have to be honest with you. It doesn't look good."

"Huckleberry had been vomiting when we found him." Ashe looked down at the short, slender young veterinarian. "It's possible he didn't completely digest all the poison."

"Good. It's the best possible sign, and that's what we'll tell Allen. There's nothing to do now but wait. If Allen and Deborah want to come on back here and be with him, it'll be all right."

The moment they saw Ashe in the doorway leading to the examining room, Deborah and Allen hurried toward him.

"Huckleberry is resting," Ashe said. "He's sound asleep. Dr. Carradine says that since Huckleberry vomited, there's a good chance his body hasn't absorbed enough poison to kill him. We have hope he'll pull through."

Allen flung his arms around Ashe's waist. Ashe laid his hand on Allen's head, then leaned down and picked him up into his arms and carried him into the examining room. Deborah followed behind them, tears blurring her vision.

"Huckleberry needs to rest," Dr. Carradine said. "I'll continue to give him injections to keep him peaceful. We'll hope for the best."

Ashe set Allen on his feet beside the examining table, keeping his hand on the boy's shoulder. Allen reached out, stroking his pet's back.

"Y'all can go on home and I'll call if there's any change," the vet said.

"No, I can't leave Huckleberry. What if he wakes up and I'm not here?" Allen threw his arms around the comatose animal.

Ashe pulled Allen away from the dog, turned the child to face him and knelt down on one knee. "We aren't going anywhere until Huckleberry wakes up. You and Deborah and I will keep watch over him."

Deborah gulped down the sobs when she saw the tentative little smile trembling on Allen's lips as he nodded his head.

Ashe glanced over at Dr. Carradine. "I'll bring in some chairs from the waiting room."

The doctor smiled. "I'll help you."

For what seemed like endless hours to Deborah, she and Ashe and Allen waited at Huckleberry's side, rising in fear each time the dog showed signs of going into another spasm. Dr. Carradine kept him medicated, and as the hours wore on, Deborah almost wished she, too, could be given an injection that would ease her pain. Watching the way Allen suffered tore at her heart the way nothing ever had. To watch her child hurting and know she could do nothing to ease his pain became unbearable.

Standing quickly, Deborah paced the floor. Allen had fallen asleep, his head resting in Ashe's lap. Deborah walked into the waiting room and looked out the windows. Evening had turned to night. The bright lights along Woodward Avenue sparkled like Christmas tree decorations. She glanced down at her watch. Ten-thirty.

Turning around, she walked back to the examining room, stopping in the doorway. Ashe was in the process of removing his jacket. He raised his leg just a fraction to give Allen's head a slight incline, then draped his jacket over the sleeping child. Covering her face with one hand, Deborah closed her eyes and said a silent prayer, asking God to save Huckleberry.

Ashe felt a hot fury rising inside him. A killing rage. Buck Stansell had no respect for animal life and little for human life. Buck's kind thought of animals as unfeeling, worthless creatures. Killing a dog would mean no more to him than flicking ashes off his cigarette.

Ashe adjusted his jacket around Allen, amazed how much he'd grown to care about Deborah's young brother. He had never been around children, had never allowed himself to think much about what it would be like to be a father. But he couldn't help wondering about how it would feel to have a son like Allen. The boy was intelligent and inquisitive and filled with a joy for life. He was sensitive and caring. In so many ways, Allen reminded Ashe of the young Deborah he had known and loved. Perhaps that was the reason he felt so close to Allen, so connected. Because he was so very much like Deborah.

Odd thing was, the boy reminded him of himself, too. Tall and lanky, with hands and feet almost too big for his body. He'd been the same as a kid. And cursed with being left-handed himself, he understood the adjustments Allen had had to make.

Ashe felt a twinge of sadness. Eleven years ago, he'd been thankful he hadn't gotten Deborah pregnant, but being around

Allen so much these days had made him wonder if a child of theirs wouldn't have been a lot like Deborah's little brother.

For a couple of months after their passionate night down by the river, Ashe had worried about not having used any protection. But it had been an unfounded worry. By the time Wallace Vaughn had had him run out of town, Deborah would have known whether or not she was pregnant. And if she'd been carrying his child, she would have told him. Deborah had loved him, and she would have known that a child could have bound them together forever.

Deborah came in and sat down beside Ashe. Reaching out, he draped her shoulders with his arm and drew her close. She sighed.

"It's going to be all right, honey," Ashe said. "No way is God going to let that dog die and break Allen's heart."

She couldn't reply; instead she nodded and tried to smile. Closing her eyes, she relaxed against him.

Ashe sat there in the veterinarian's examining room, one arm holding Deborah possessively, the other laid protectively over Allen. As the hours passed, his leg fell asleep and his arms became stiff, but he didn't readjust his position. Both Allen and Deborah slept, as did Huckleberry.

Ashe closed his eyes for a few minutes, resting, then reopened them quickly when he heard movement from the examining table. Huckleberry opened his eyes and raised his head. No longer was his big body grossly contorted, but lay relaxed on the table.

Ashe gave Deborah a gentle shake. Opening her eyes, she glanced up at him. "Huckleberry's awake. Take a look."

"Oh, my God!" She jumped up out of the chair and ran toward the dog, taking his huge face in her hands. "Hey, there, big boy. You sure had us worried."

Ashe shook Allen, who groaned in his sleep. Ashe shook him again.

"What?"

"Wake up, son. Huckleberry wants to see you." Ashe lifted Allen in his arms and carried the boy across the room, sitting him down on the examining table beside his dog. "Go get Dr. Carradine," Ashe told Deborah.

She rushed out of the room. Allen hugged Huckleberry, who, though still groggy, raised his head and tried to sit up. "He's going to be all right!" Allen repeated the words several times, as if to convince himself.

Deborah returned with Dr. Carradine, who took a good look at Huckleberry and smiled. "Looks like we got lucky. I think Huckleberry will soon be as good as new."

The dog struggled to get up. Ashe lifted him off the table and set him on the floor. He staggered around slowly, like a drunken sailor. Sitting on the floor, Allen called his pet to him. The Lab padded over to the boy, who threw his arms around the big dog and hugged him.

"Why don't you folks go on home and get some rest," Dr. Carradine said. "Leave Huckleberry here until—" he glanced down at his watch "—it's after midnight. Well, I was going to say until tomorrow afternoon. Pick him up anytime after 2:00 p.m. today."

"If he's all right, why can't I take him home now?" Allen asked.

"Because Huckleberry needs some rest and so do you, young man." Dr. Carradine glanced at Deborah. "And so does your sister and Mr. McLaughlin. I have a feeling that if you take Huckleberry home now, all three of you would stay up the rest of the night with him."

"Come on, pal." Ashe leaned down to give Huckleberry a pat on the head. "Let's go home. Huckleberry is in good hands with Dr. Carradine. And I promise we'll pick him up at two o'clock."

Allen agreed reluctantly, giving Huckleberry a farewell hug before leaving.

ASHE CARRIED ALLEN, who'd gone to sleep on the drive home, from the car into the house. The boy roused from his sleep and smiled at Ashe.

Allen yawned. "I'm not a baby. I can walk."

"Sure you can, pal," Ashe said.

He set Allen on his feet, then he and Deborah followed the child upstairs and into his room. Deborah spread back the covers. Allen's eyelids drooped. Curling up in the middle of the bed, he made no objections when Deborah removed his shoes, jeans and shirt. By the time she had stripped him down to his white cotton briefs, he had fallen fast asleep.

"He's all tired out," Ashe said. "He's been through almost as much as Huckleberry."

Deborah pulled up the covers, then sat down on the side of the bed. Allen was the dearest, most precious thing in her life. There wasn't a day that passed when she didn't want to tell him she was his mother, to claim him as her own. But she had agreed to this charade when she'd been eighteen and not strong enough to stand up to her father. He had told her she had two choices, either give Allen up for adoption or allow him to be raised as her brother.

If only she'd had the strength to tell her father to go to hell. If only she'd taken her child and found Ashe McLaughlin and forced him to face his responsibility as a father. But she'd done what was expected of her. She'd taken what others would consider the easy way out.

Deborah smoothed the loose strands of Allen's thick blond hair away from his face. Leaning over, she kissed his forehead, then stood.

Ashe watched her, the way she looked at Allen, the way she touched him. No one could doubt the depth of her love for the boy. If he didn't know better, he'd swear she was his mother instead of his sister. But then motherly love was not limited to mothers. Indeed his grandmother had loved and cared for him in a way his own mother never had.

But what if Deborah was Allen's mother? Was it possible? No, don't even consider the possibility, he warned himself. Idiotic thoughts like that could be dangerous to his sanity. He was letting his imagination run away with him.

Allen was Deborah's brother, Miss Carol's change-of-life baby. Any other explanation was out of the question. There was no way Deborah could have been pregnant and not told him. She wouldn't have kept something that important a secret.

Deborah, although lovely beyond words, looked tired. Drained. Sad. On the verge of renewed tears.

"Come on, honey, you need to get some rest." Turning off the light, he guided her out of Allen's room and down the hall.

"I need a bath before I go to bed," she said. "I'm filthy."

He walked her into her sitting room and gently shoved her down in the rocking chair. "Sit still and rest. I'll get your bath ready for you."

When she started to protest, Ashe laid his index finger over her lips, silencing her. She stared up at him, her eyes filled with such deep emotion that Ashe wanted to lift her into his arms. But he didn't. Instead he entered her bathroom and turned on the gold taps, letting the warm water flow into her claw-foot bathtub. Rummaging around in the antique chest beside the vanity, he found some perfumed bath oil and splashed it into the water flow. He laid out two huge, fluffy, blue towels and a crochet-edged wash cloth.

In Deborah's bedroom, he turned down her bed and then found her gown, neatly folded in a top dresser drawer. Pale pink silk, spaghetti straps, heavy white lace across the bodice and hem. After spreading the gown out across the foot of her bed, he flung the matching robe over his arm.

When he returned to the sitting room, she was rocking back and forth slowly, her eyes opening and closing, her chin nodding farther and farther toward her chest.

Before she could protest, he lifted her out of the rocker and into his arms. Her eyes flew open. She grabbed him around the neck to balance herself.

"What are you doing?" She stared at him, wide-eyed.

"Taking you to the bathroom."

"I'm perfectly capable of walking, you know."

"I like carrying you," he said. "It gives me an excuse to hold you in my arms."

She relaxed, allowing him to carry her. She felt completely safe and secure wrapped in Ashe's strong arms. When they passed through her bedroom, she noticed he had turned down her bed and laid out her gown. The gesture touched her, making her feel cherished and cared for in a way she couldn't remember being cared for since she was a child.

"Ashe?"

"Hmm?"

"Thank you for being so wonderful with Allen."

"It was easy. Allen is a great kid. He reminds me so much of you, Deborah. The way you were at his age."

And he reminds me of you, she wanted to say. Every time I look at him, I see you. The way he smiles. The way he rests the side of his face in his hand when he's pondering something. The expression on his face when he's trying to talk me into allowing him to do something he knows is against the rules.

Once in the bathroom, Ashe lowered Deborah to her feet, sliding her slowly down his body, his big hands holding her hips in place against him.

She felt his arousal, knew he wanted her. And heaven help her, she wanted him.

She pulled away, turning her back to him. "Thank you for everything." Bending over the tub, she turned off the faucet. "I can handle things from here on out. Good night, Ashe."

He whirled her around. She gasped when she saw the look of longing in his eyes. "Are you sending me away?"

"Yes, please, Ashe. Go."

"All right. If you're sure that's what you want."

"Yes, I'm sure." She really didn't want him to leave. She wanted him to stay, to undress her, to bathe her, to dry her damp skin and carry her to her bed.

Ashe ran the tip of his index finger down her cheek, then stepped back. "If you need me, you know where I'll be." He laid her pink silk robe on the vanity stool.

Looking down at the bathtub, she nodded. Ashe turned and left her alone. She closed the door behind him, and took a deep breath. She undressed quickly, throwing her clothes into a heap on the floor, then stepped into the bathtub and buried herself in the soft, scented water. Leaning her head back against the wall behind the tub, she closed her eyes and picked up the washcloth. Soaping the cloth, she ran it over her face, then rinsed by splashing water in her face. She slid the cloth down one arm and then the other. Lowering the soapy cloth to her breasts, her hand froze when the material made contact with her nipple, which jutted out to a peak.

She was aroused and aching. Aching to be with Ashe. Aching to open her arms and her body and take him in. But she didn't dare. For if she opened her heart to him, she would be lost.

Hurriedly, she bathed, washed her hair and dried off, praying she would be able to find forgetfulness in sleep.

CHAPTER NINE

ASHE STOOD AT the window of his bedroom that looked down over the patio. The moonlight illuminated the autumn flowers and shrubs so lovingly cared for by the Vaughns' weekly gardener. Ashe sloshed around the brandy in his glass, took a sip and set the liquor down on the ornate antique table to the left of the window. He scratched his naked chest, then ran his hand across his stomach.

He couldn't remember the last time he'd ached so badly for a woman, and certainly not for one particular woman. Deborah Vaughn had insinuated herself into his mind so firmly that he couldn't shake her. She had become his first thought in the morning and his last thought at night. Not Deborah Vaughn his client, but Deborah the woman.

He'd made a mistake coming back to Sheffield, seeing Deborah again. He had walked away from her once, rejected her because he hadn't loved her the way she'd loved him. Now he wanted her as he had never wanted another woman. He burned with the need to possess her.

Ashe slipped on his leather loafers. Buttoning his open shirt, he walked out into the hall. He'd tried for nearly an hour to relax, to stop thinking about Deborah, to quit remembering how she'd felt in his arms when he'd carried her to her bath. But he couldn't forget.

He walked down the hallway, stopping at Allen's open door. Looking inside, he saw the boy sleeping soundly, his upper body uncovered. Ashe crept silently into the room and pulled the sheet and blanket up to cover Allen's shoulders. The little fellow had been through quite an ordeal. Ashe balled his hands into fists. Buck Stansell didn't deserve to live. But his kind always landed on their feet, always found a way to slip through the cracks in the legal system.

After leaving Allen's room, Ashe eased the door to Miss Carol's room ajar and peered inside. She slept peacefully. Deborah had told him that often her mother had to rely on sleeping pills in order to rest.

He opened Deborah's bedroom door. More than anything he wanted to find her awake, waiting for him, her arms open, imploring him to come to her. What he found was an empty bed, Deborah nowhere in sight. Where the hell was she?

He made his way down the stairs, checking each room, one by one, until he entered the library. A table lamp burned softly, casting gentle shadows over the woman sitting alone on the leather sofa, her feet curled beneath her. When he stepped inside the room, she turned her head and looked at him.

"Couldn't you sleep, either?" she asked.

"No."

Did she have any idea how beautiful she was, how irresistible she looked? Like a porcelain figure, all flawless creamy skin and pink silk clinging to her round curves, her long blond hair cascading down her back and over her shoulders.

He grew hard just looking at her, just smelling the scent of her bath oil clinging to her skin. He stood inside the open door. Waiting. Wanting. Needing.

"I can't believe I'm still wide awake." She looked at him with hunger in her eyes, and wondered if he realized how much she wanted him. "I'm exhausted and yet I feel as if I've had an extra dose of adrenaline."

"Yeah, me, too."

She stretched her back, leaning into the sofa. Ashe caught his breath, the sight of her almost more than he could bear. Her firm breasts strained against the silk of her gown. Her full hips pressed into the soft leather cushions.

"I fixed myself a drink." She nodded to the partially full glass on the end table. "It didn't help."

"I did the same thing," he said. "I came down about thirty minutes ago and swiped some of your brandy."

"Obviously it didn't help you go to sleep." She clenched her hands, then unclenched them, repeating the process several times. She wished he hadn't come downstairs and found her alone and restless. He'd know she couldn't stop thinking about him, couldn't make herself forget the feel of his arms around her, the strength of his arousal pressing against her.

"Since neither of us can sleep, how about taking a ride?" Holding his breath, he waited for her reply.

"A ride?" She scooted to the edge of the sofa, knowing there was more at stake than just a moonlight drive. "That sounds like a great idea." Standing, she smiled at him, then rushed past him and out into the hallway. "Give me a minute to put on some clothes," she said softly, then ran up the stairs.

He checked his back pocket for his wallet, then thought about his gun and holster lying on his nightstand. He hurried upstairs, retrieved his gun and put on his jacket, then walked down the hall to Simon Roarke's bedroom. He knocked softly. Within seconds Roarke cracked the door and peered out at him.

"What's up?"

"Deborah and I are going for a ride," Ashe said. "I wanted you to know I'd be out of the house for a while."

"Yeah, sure. No problem." Simon grinned, something the man didn't do often.

"Don't go reading anything into this." Ashe turned to leave.

Opening the door, Roarke laid his hand on Ashe's shoulder, gripping him firmly. "She's the one, isn't she?"

Ashe stiffened at his friend's words. "The one what?"

"The one you told me about that night six months ago when we both got stinking drunk and wound up crying all over each other."

Ashe didn't like to remember that night; he'd thought Roarke would never remind him. "Yeah, she's the one."

Pulling away, Ashe ran his hand through his hair, straightened his jacket and headed downstairs. He paced the marble-floored entrance hall until Deborah descended the stairs wearing a pair of olive green cotton twill pants and a baggy cotton sweater in an olive-and-cream stripe.

"Let's go," she said, her chest rising and falling with quick, panting little breaths.

"You want to take your Caddy or my rental car?"

She tossed him a set of keys. "The Caddy."

He slipped his arm around her waist and they rushed outside, the cool night air assaulting them the minute they opened the door.

"I should get you a set of keys to the Caddy," she said as he helped her inside.

He leaned down, giving her a quick kiss, then closed the passenger door and raced around to the other side of the car.

He knew where he was going to take her; he'd known the minute he'd suggested the ride. It hadn't been a premeditated idea, just something that hit him in a flash. In the dark confines of the car, he could hear her breathing, could smell that heady scent of flowery bath oil mixed with the musty scent of woman. He started the Caddy and backed out of the drive.

She waited for him to ask her where she wanted to go. He didn't ask. It didn't take her long to realize the direction in which he was headed. Dear God, no! Surely he wasn't taking her there. Was he that insensitive? Didn't he realize she'd never been back since that night?

The road leading down to the river was dark, lonesome and flanked on both sides by heavily wooded areas. Deborah closed her eyes, shutting out the sight, clenching her teeth in an effort not to scream. How could he do this to her!

"Please take me home." Her voice wavered slightly.

"I thought you wanted to take a ride." He kept his gaze focused on the view ahead of him.

"I don't want to go down to the river."

"Why not?"

"You know damn well why not."

"I want you to tell me." He glanced at her and wished he hadn't. Her face was barely visible in the moonlight, but he could feel the tension in her body and make out the anger etched on her features.

"Take me home, Ashe. Now!"

He continued driving toward the river. "It's time we talked. Really talked. We need to clear up a few things before we make love."

"Before we make… Why, you arrogant bastard! You think you're going to take me down to the river and screw me again and then walk out of my life and never look back. Well, you'd better think again. I'm not some lovesick teenager who believes in fairy tales."

"No, you're not." He pulled the Cadillac off the road and onto a narrow dirt lane surrounded by trees. "You're a woman who wants to be made love to very badly, and I'm the man who is dying to love you."

When he reached out to touch her, she jerked away from him. "Don't. I don't want you. Do you hear me? I *do not* want you."

"Honey, stop lying to yourself. Do you think I like knowing I'm so hung up on you I can't think about anything else? Do you honestly think you're the only one with bad memories about that night?"

"Oh, I know all about your bad memories!" Whipping around in the seat, she faced him. "You let your anger with Whitney and your need for a woman overcome your better judgment, and you screwed me. Then afterward you were filled with regret."

He jerked her into his arms, lowered his head and whispered

against her lips, "Stop saying I screwed you, dammit! It wasn't like that and you know it. I made love to you, Deborah."

Struggling to free herself, she laughed in his face. "You didn't make love to me, you sc—"

He kissed her hard and fast, adeptly silencing her. She pulled away as much as he would allow and glared at him.

"Maybe I wasn't in love with you," he admitted. "But I did love you. I'd loved you since we were kids. You were one of my best friends."

The tears welled up inside her; her chest ached from restraint. This was what she didn't want—what she couldn't bear. "All right. We made love. But you regretted it. You said it could never happen again."

"I cared too much about you to hurt you by pretending there could be more for us. I felt like a heel, but I did what I thought was best for you."

She took a deep breath. "I hated you after that night, you know. But all the while I swore to myself I despised you, I kept praying you'd come and tell me you loved me. I was such a fool."

"And when two months went by and I didn't come to you, you decided to get revenge. All that love turned to hate so quickly."

"What are you talking about? I admit I thought about how I'd like to toss you into a pool of piranhas, but that's as far as my seeking revenge went." She scooted away from him when he loosened his hold on her. "Besides, you didn't stick around long enough for me to plot any elaborate revenge schemes."

"You don't call siccing your daddy on me revenge?"

Her eyes widened. She opened her mouth on a silent gasp, then shook her head. "What—what do you mean, siccing my daddy on you?"

"Are you pretending you've forgotten or are you trying to tell me you honestly don't know what I'm talking about?"

"I have no idea what you're talking about," she said.

"Then let me refresh your memory." Turning sideways, Ashe leaned his back against the door, crossed his arms over his chest and rested his head on the side window. "About two months after our night down here—" moving his head from side to side, he glanced out at the starlit sky, the dark waters of the Tennessee River and the towering trees tipped with moonlight "—the police chief hauled my rear end downtown. And who do you think was waiting for us when we got to the police station?"

Deborah's stomach did a nervous flip-flop. "Daddy?"

"Bingo! Wallace Vaughn himself, fit to be tied and ready to string me up for raping his little girl."

"Raping!" The blood soared through Deborah, her heartbeat wild, the pounding beat deafening to her own ears.

"Yeah, that was my reaction," Ashe said, uncertain whether to accept Deborah's shock at face value or remain suspicious. "But the D.A. was there with your daddy and he assured me that they weren't kidding. They were accusing me of rape, and when I told them that the charge would never stick, they both laughed in my face."

"I had no idea Daddy could have done anything so—"

"You didn't go crying to your Daddy?" All these years he had been so sure Deborah had lied to her father, that she had made him believe that, at the very least, Ashe had seduced her, and at the worst, had taken her by brute force.

"I didn't tell my father anything." Deborah scooted to the far side of the car, her back up against the door, she and Ashe glaring at each other in the semidarkness.

"Why the hell lie to me now?" He wanted to shake her until her teeth rattled. God, help him, he never thought he would feel such bitter anger again, that confronting her with what she'd done would resurrect the hatred he'd felt—for Wallace Vaughn, for the whole town of Sheffield, and, yes, for Deborah herself.

Deborah lifted her feet up on tiptoes, tensing her legs as she ran her hands up and down the tops of her thighs. "I never told

Daddy about our…about our making love that night. I told my mother." *I had to tell her. I was seventeen and pregnant by a man who didn't love me or want me. I didn't know what else to do.*

"You told Miss Carol?"

"I needed someone to talk to about what had happened." *About the fact that I was carrying your child.* "Who else would I have gone to other than my own mother?"

"Did you tell your mother that I'd forced you?" Cold shivers covered Ashe like a blanket of frost spreading across the earth on a winter night.

"No. I told my mother the truth, all of it. She'd known, of course, that I'd left the country club with you that night and she knew why."

"I'm surprised your father didn't hunt us down."

"He didn't know I was with you. He didn't see me leave," Deborah said. "Mother told him I was spending the night with a girlfriend after the engagement party."

"I know Miss Carol often kept the complete truth from your father in order to maintain peace, so why did she feel it necessary to tell him about what had happened between you and me that night?"

Because I was pregnant! "I was very upset, very unhappy. Mother thought she was doing the right thing by telling Daddy. She couldn't have known what he'd do. And I never knew anything about what he did. Obviously, Daddy realized what a mistake he'd made. You were never arrested. If you had been, I would have told the truth. I would have made them understand that what happened that night was my fault, not yours."

"Deborah?"

"Well, it was, wasn't it? I mean, I did throw myself at you and practically beg you to make love to me, didn't I?"

"If I'd been more of a man and less a boy that night, I'd have turned you down and saved us both a lot of misery."

"And that's what the memory of that night has been for you,

hasn't it, a misery?" Deborah shut her eyes, capturing her tears beneath closed lids.

Dear God, no! The results had been a misery, but not that night. Never that night! "No, honey, that's not true. The memory of that night is bittersweet for me."

"More bitter than sweet." Swallowing her tears, she lowered her head, wrapped one arm across her stomach and cupped the side of her face in her other hand. "That's why you left town, wasn't it? To get away from me?"

"I left town because your father and the D.A. gave me no other choice." Ashe slid across the seat, grabbed Deborah by the shoulders and shook her gently several times. "Look at me, dammit." With her head still bowed, she raised her eyes to meet his. "Your father told me that if I didn't leave town and never come back, he'd make sure I did time for rape. He wanted me out of your life for good."

"No, he wouldn't have... He knew. Oh, Ashe, he knew."

"He knew what?" Ashe gripped her shoulders, tightening his hold when she didn't immediately respond.

"He knew I was—" She'd almost said *pregnant with your baby.* "He knew I loved you, that I would never have testified against you, that I would have made a fool of myself to protect you."

A searing pain ripped through Ashe, the hot, cauterizing pain of truth, killing the festering infection of lies and suspicions, preventing him from clinging to past resentments.

"Dear God, Deborah. All these years I've thought..." He pulled her into his arms. She trembled, and he knew she was on the verge of tears, that she was holding them in check, being strong. He stroked her back; she laid her head on his chest.

She had not betrayed him. She hadn't even told her father, only her mother. She had never accused him of forcing her or seducing her. Lies. All lies. Wallace Vaughn's lies to force Ashe out of Deborah's life. Had the old man been that afraid that sooner or later Ashe would destroy Deborah's life?

Ashe found himself kissing the side of her face, along her hairline, one hand continuing to stroke her back while he threaded the fingers of his other hand through her hair, caressing her tenderly.

"Have you hated me all these years, Ashe?" she asked, her voice a whisper against his chest.

"I've hated you. I've hated myself. Hell, I've hated just about everyone and everything associated with my past." When she gazed up at him, he dotted her forehead with kisses. "But I never hated what we shared that night, the feelings inside me when we made love. It had never been like that for me before." He swallowed hard. "And it's never been that way for me again. Not ever."

"Oh, Ashe." She slipped her arms around him, burrowing her body into his, seeking and finding a closer joining.

He took her mouth like a dying man clinging to life, as if without the taste of her he could not go on. She accepted the kiss, returning it full measure, her hands clawing at his back, inching their way up beneath his jacket, yanking his shirt from his slacks, making contact with his naked flesh. Ashe thrust his tongue deeper into her mouth, their tongues mating furiously.

Breathless, their lips separated, but they clung to each other, Deborah unbuttoning Ashe's shirt, Ashe lifting Deborah's sweater up and under her arms.

"I've wanted you since that first day I came back to town." He nuzzled her neck with his nose as he lifted his hand to her lace-covered breast. "I've called myself every kind of fool, but nothing's eased this ache inside me."

She curled her index finger around a swirl of dark chest hair, then leaned over to kiss one tiny nipple. Ashe groaned. "I hated you for making me want you again," she said. "I swore no one would ever hurt me the way you did, and here I am throwing myself at you again as if I were seventeen."

"No, honey, no." He took her face in both his hands, looking deep into her eyes, smiling his irresistible smile. "This works both ways. I want you and you want me. Neither of us are kids. We're two responsible adults who are as frustrated as hell."

She laughed. "Ashe, I don't know if I can handle this, what I'm feeling. It scares me. It scares me more now than it did when I was seventeen." She circled his neck with her arms, pressing her cheek against his. "When I was seventeen I was so in love with you that nothing we did seemed wrong. I didn't know the first thing about sex. Now…well, now I'm aching with wanting you. It's different now. It's—"

"It's right this time, honey," he said against her lips. "No fairy tales, no declarations of undying love, just a man and a woman who want each other desperately. Mutual desire."

"Yes." She nodded. "Mutual desire." *You're wrong,* she wanted to shout. *It isn't all that different now. I'm still in love with you and you still don't return that love.*

"Let's vanquish all those bad memories," he said. "Let's lay the past to rest. Tonight."

His kiss was less frantic this time, more tender and giving, yet as hot and needy as the one before. There was no way to make him understand that she could never lay the past to rest, that Allen was the embodiment of that night so long ago when a young and foolish girl had given herself to a man who didn't love her.

Ashe held her in his arms, burying his face in her neck, breathing in the sweet fragrance of her hair. "We can't make love back at your house and I know you don't want to make love here, in the car, the way we did that night. Where can we go, honey? A motel room seems cheap and I want this night to be special for you—for us."

"You're wrong about my not wanting to make love here and now, in the car," she said. "I do."

"Why would you want to—"

"I'm not sure I can explain how I feel, but… Well, it would somehow validate that first time. I know it sounds crazy, but… I need for us to make love here, now, in the car, the way we did that night when… Please, Ashe, make love to me."

"That's exactly what you said to me that night." And damn his rotten soul, he hadn't been able to resist her. She had been the sweetest temptation he'd ever known—and she still was.

"I guess I'm still begging." A lone tear escaped her eye and trickled down her cheek.

Ashe kissed the teardrop. "No, Deborah, I'm the one doing the begging this time. I'm the one who'll die if I can't have you. I'm the one willing to do anything to make you happy, to see you smile, to make your forget."

He actually remembered every word she'd said to him that night when she'd told him she wanted to make him happy, wanted to make him forget Whitney, wanted to make him smile again. She had pleaded with him to make love to her, saying she'd die if he didn't.

"You remember what I said."

"Every word." He lifted her sweater up and off, tossing it into the back seat, then unhooked her bra and eased it off her shoulders. "And I remember how you looked and how you felt." He covered both breasts with his hands and planted a row of kisses from her collarbone to her shoulder. "And the smell of you. My sweet, innocent Deborah."

He licked the tip of her breast; she moaned. He unsnapped and unzipped her slacks; she shoved his jacket off his shoulders. Ashe removed his shoulder holster, laying it on the dashboard before removing his shirt.

She kissed his chest, tiny, loving nicks. He tugged her slacks down and off her legs, throwing them on top of her sweater. She shivered when he dipped his hand beneath the elastic of her silky panties and cupped her buttocks, lifting her up and over him as he slid down onto the seat, his head braced against the armrest on the door.

While he suckled at her breasts, his fingers delved between the delicate folds of her body, finding the sensitive, hidden peak. She unzipped his trousers and reached inside to cover his arousal with the palm of her hand. Their kisses grew hotter, harder, longer, as they moved to the rhythm of nature's mating music, their bodies straining for closer and closer contact.

Lifting his hips, Ashe removed his wallet, then tugged his trousers downward and kicked them into the floorboard. "I'm dying," he groaned. "I wanted to wait, to take more time, to—"

Leaning over him, she covered his mouth, silencing him with the fury of her kiss. He ran his hands up and down, over her shoulders, down her back, pulling at her panties until she helped him remove them. He eased her over and onto her back, drawing her body beneath his as he ripped off his briefs, sheathed himself and positioned her for his possession.

"Now, honey? Now!" He was fast losing control.

"Yes, now!"

He plunged into her, lifting her hips, delving deep and hard. She gripped his shoulders, rising to meet his demands. Sliding her legs up his until she reached his hips, she whispered his name over and over, telling him with the tone of her voice and little moans of pleasure that she was near the brink. He didn't want this to end, wanted it to go on forever, but knew he couldn't last much longer. The pleasure was too great, too intense to slow the upward spiral toward completion.

"It's too good, honey. Too good."

He felt her tightening around him. She clasped him like a tight fist. Crying out, she quivered in his arms as spasm after spasm of fulfillment racked her body. His release came hard and fast, shaking him to the core of his being.

He cried out, losing himself in her, kissing her as they shivered from the aftershocks of such a powerful loving.

Lifting himself, Ashe pulled Deborah up off the seat and into his arms, holding her against him, listening to her rapid breathing.

"I want to make love to you again," he told her. "Tonight. Tomorrow. The day after tomorrow."

She didn't say anything; she couldn't. She knew he was telling her that, this time, there would be no rejection and no regrets. She lifted her face to him, glorying in the feel of his arms around her, the passion in his consuming kiss.

DAWN SPREAD A honeyed pink glow across the horizon. When Ashe parked the Caddy in the driveway, Deborah awoke. Lifting her head from his shoulder, she smiled.

"It's 5:40," he said. "Mazie is going to be up and about any time now."

"Think she'll catch us sneaking in?"

"Would you care if she does?" Ashe opened the car door and assisted Deborah. Wrapping his arm around her, he led her to the front door.

"She'd probably be shocked. She's not used to me sneaking into the house at all hours."

Ashe unlocked the door. They walked into the entrance hall, arm in arm. "What do you usually do, stay overnight at your lover's house?"

Shadowy morning light coming through the windows illuminated the stairs. Deborah stopped dead still in the middle of the staircase.

"I haven't had any lovers," she said, then pulled out of Ashe's arms and ran up to the landing.

He caught her just as she flung open her sitting room door, whirling her around to face him, pulling her into his arms. "What do you mean you haven't had any lovers?"

"There's never been anyone else. Only you." Lowering her head, she looked down at the floor.

He lifted her chin in the curve of his thumb and forefinger. "Honey, I—"

"I never fell in love again, that's all. I hoped that sooner or later the right guy would come along and I'd be ready, but it just didn't happen."

"Just Mr. Wrong again, huh?"

"No, Ashe, not Mr. Wrong. Just not Mr. Right." She slipped her arms around his neck and kissed him, then stepped back and smiled. "This time we're lovers. Remember? Mutual desire?"

"You'd better get in your room and lock me out or we'll be right in the middle of some mutual desire any minute now."

"Good night, then." She laughed. "Or should I say good morning."

"Next time, we're going to have to find someplace else to make love." He rubbed the small of his back. "I'm too old to do it in a car, even a big Caddy."

"Next time," she whispered to herself. Next time. She knew she would never be able to resist him and that for him this was only an affair. But not for her. She was already so in love with Ashe McLaughlin she couldn't bear for him to leave her.

He kissed her with a passion that told her that even if he wasn't in love with her, leaving her was as difficult for him as it was for her. Releasing her, he shoved her into her room and closed the door. She took a deep breath, turned and raced into her bedroom, falling in a heap on her bed. Hugging herself, she rolled into a ball and closed her eyes.

This was what she had dreaded since the moment she'd walked in and seen Ashe talking to her mother in the living room. And, if she was honest with herself, this was what she had wanted to happen. No matter how hard she had tried to deny it, she still loved Ashe McLaughlin. She had never truly stopped loving him.

What on earth was she going to do now? She had rushed headlong into an affair with her son's father. How could she continue lying to Ashe, keeping the truth about his child from him? The longer she waited to tell him, the more difficult it would be—for both of them. But did she dare tell him? Would he understand? Or would he hate her for keeping his son from him all these years?

CHAPTER TEN

"Please, tell us, Ms. Vaughn, what happened when you took that wrong turn off Cotton Lane?" the district attorney asked.

"I realized I'd gotten off on the wrong road and was looking for a place to turn around." Deborah sat straight, her hands folded in her lap. "I noticed a truck pulled off the road. One man jumped out of the truck, but I couldn't see his face. There were two other men behind the truck, one holding a gun to the other's head."

Deborah's stomach tightened into a knot; she gripped her damp hands together. Glancing out into the courtroom she sought Ashe. Their gazes met and held. She took a deep breath.

"Are you all right, Ms. Vaughn?" District Attorney Jim Bitterman spoke softly, his voice a light tenor, a distinct contrast to his rugged, almost ugly face and wiry, muscular body.

"Yes." Deborah kept her vision focused on Ashe for several seconds longer, gaining strength from his presence.

"Will you continue, please?"

"The man holding the gun was Lon Sparks."

"Objection, your honor," the defense attorney, Leland Prater shouted, rising from his seat and moving his short, rotund body around the desk. "Ms. Vaughn was not acquainted with Mr. Sparks and therefore could hardly have recognized him."

"Ms. Vaughn later identified Mr. Sparks from a photograph, your honor," Jim Bitterman said.

"Overruled," Judge Heath said.

"Please continue." District Attorney Bitterman stood directly in front of Deborah. "Tell the jury what you saw."

"Lon Sparks shot the man in the head." Deborah closed her eyes momentarily, the memory of that dreadful sight closing in around her, filling her with the sense of fear she'd known in those horrific seconds when she'd witnessed the murder.

Jim Bitterman allowed her to continue recalling the events at her own pace. Leland Prater, long known as an old bag of wind and one of the most crooked lawyers in the area, objected every chance he got, deliberately unnerving Deborah as much as possible. But she did not waver in her testimony, not even when Prater cross-examined her.

She'd been warned, by Jim and by Ashe, that Prater's strategy would be to bring her to tears, show her to be a highly emotional, hysterical woman, who had allowed her hysteria and fear to wrongly identify Lon Sparks.

Not one tear fell from her eyes. Not one shrill word escaped her lips. When her nerves rioted, she took deep breaths and looked to Ashe, seeking and finding the strength she needed to do the job she and she alone could do.

When she was dismissed, Deborah stepped down and walked slowly toward Ashe, who stood and waited for her. He slipped his arm around her and led her out of the courtroom. Even the bevy of reporters flinging questions at her did not disturb the serenity she felt as Ashe led her downstairs and out of the courthouse.

Neither of them said a word until they were safely inside Deborah's car. Ashe buckled her seat belt, kissed her on the nose and smiled at her.

"It's over." She sighed. "It's really over."

"Yeah, honey, it's over." But Ashe wasn't sure. Not one incident of harassment had occurred since Huckleberry's poisoning two days ago, and that made Ashe all the more suspicious. Buck Stansell should have escalated his threats the closer the day

came for Deborah to testify. But he hadn't. He hadn't done anything. Did that mean he was waiting to take revenge? Hell!

Deborah checked her watch. "We have time to make the last
half of Allen's soccer game, don't we?"

"That's where I'm headed." Ashe maneuvered the Caddy
out of the parking lot and onto Water Street.

Leaning against the cushioned headrest, Deborah closed her
eyes. Ashe reached out and took her hand, squeezing it tightly.
She smiled, but didn't open her eyes or speak. She felt such a
great sense of relief.

She had done the right thing, despite being afraid. She had
faced the devil—and won! Now, all she had to face were her
own personal demons, the biggest lie in her life. She'd had the
courage to stand up against Buck Stansell and his gang, but
did she have the guts to tell Ashe the truth about Allen? She
knew now that she'd been wrong to keep his son's existence a
secret from him all these years. Despite her own feelings, her
deep sense of betrayal and rejection, she should have contacted
Ashe long ago. Mama Mattie would have given her his phone
number or address if only she'd asked.

But what would telling Ashe the truth now do to their new
relationship? Although he had promised her nothing permanent,
had made no commitment to her, she knew he truly cared about
her. She, and she alone, was the woman he wanted. Would it
be so wrong to wait, to take what time she had left with Ashe
and savor the joy she felt, the mutual passion and desire?

"Are you sure you're up to this?" Ashe parked the Cadillac
behind a row of cars lined up along the shoulder of Avalon
Avenue, west of the railroad tracks that separated Muscle Shoals
from Tuscumbia and Sheffield.

"The worst is over. Right? There's no reason why I can't
resume my normal activities, is there?"

"Deborah…" Dear God, he didn't want to tell her that he

thought the worst might not be over, that the worst might be yet to come. But he would not lie to her. "We can't be sure what Buck Stansell might do if Lon Sparks is convicted."

"You're saying it isn't over." She clutched her shoulder bag to her stomach. "You think he might try to kill me after the trial ends, don't you?"

"There's no way to know." Ashe grasped her shoulder, urging her to turn to him. "But my guess is that you're safe until the jury reaches a verdict."

She leaned toward him, wanting to fall into his arms, wanting and needing his comfort and reassurance. But this was hardly the time or the place. "Then I'm going to try not to think about it, for now. I don't know how much more Mother and Allen can take. I can't bear to think what it would have done to Allen if Huckleberry had died."

"Don't think about it. Huckleberry is as good as new," Ashe said. "Come on, let's go cheer for the home team."

Deborah and Ashe joined Carol Vaughn and Simon Roarke on the sidelines of a tense soccer game between two sets of ten- to twelve-year-olds. Carol had built herself a comfortable nest around her folding lawn chair. She sat with a plaid blanket wrapped about her legs, a thermos of hot coffee at her side. Roarke stood directly behind her chair, his gaze moving around the crowd, then back to the soccer game where Allen Vaughn raced down the field, his long, strong legs moving with agile grace.

Roarke stepped aside when Deborah laid her hand on her mother's shoulder. Ashe nodded, motioning to Roarke.

"How's the game going?" Deborah asked.

"We're ahead," Carol said. "Two to one."

Deborah glanced at the sky. "It's getting cloudy and the wind's up. I hope it doesn't start raining."

"Where's your coat?" Carol asked.

"I didn't wear one today. Just my suit. But don't worry, I'm fine."

"Mothers worry."

"I'm okay. Really. Everything is going to be all right."

Ashe and Roarke moved away from the crowd, close enough to keep an eye on everyone and yet far enough away to have a private discussion.

"We're going to be staying for at least another couple of weeks," Ashe said. "If we're lucky, this will be over when the trail ends, but my gut instincts tell me not to count on it."

"A man could do a lot worse than living around here, spending the rest of his life in a small town." Roarke's dark gaze came to a halt on Allen Vaughn as the boy kicked the ball past the goalie and scored a point for his team.

Ashe slapped Roarke on the back. "Did you see that? Damn that boy's good. He's big and fast and strong and a real fighter. Look at his face. Good God, how I know that feeling. He's lightheaded from the victory."

"He reminds me of you," Roarke said.

"What?"

"Allen Vaughn reminds me of you."

"Hell, he's just like Deborah. They could be twins."

"I know he looks like Deborah, but the more I'm around the kid, the more he reminds me of you."

"What the hell are you talking about?" Ashe watched Allen, seeing nothing except his blond hair, his blue eyes, his strong physical resemblance to Deborah.

"When did you leave Sheffield and join the army?"

"When did I… Eleven years ago."

"When exactly?"

"In July."

Grunting, Roarke nodded. "Allen Vaughn was born in February. Seven months after you left town."

"So?"

"Has it never once crossed your mind that you might have gotten Deborah pregnant, that Allen could be your son?"

Ashe's body rebelled, tensing every muscle, bringing every

nerve to full alert, knotting his stomach painfully. "She would have told me. Deborah never would have kept something like that from me. She was in love with me. If she'd been pregnant with my child, she would have come running to me."

"Are you sure?"

"Yes, dammit, I'm sure!"

"Then forget I said anything."

"I sure as hell will." Ashe glared at his friend, a man he had come to like and respect since their first meeting over a year ago. Roarke stood eye to eye with Ashe, the two equal in height and size, broad-shouldered, long-legged. Roarke, like Ashe himself, a former warrior, still in his prime.

"You want me to give Sam a call tonight and let him know we'll be staying…indefinitely?" Roarke asked.

"No. This is my case. I'll call Sam." Ashe watched Allen, inspecting his every move with an analytical eye, searching for evidence to substantiate Roarke's suspicion. "I'll let him know we could be here for a few more weeks. Once I know Deborah is safe, we'll head back to Atlanta."

Dammit! Why couldn't Roarke have kept his suspicions to himself? They were totally unfounded. They had to be! Not getting Deborah pregnant that long-ago night was the one and only thing Ashe hadn't had to feel guilty about all these years. Allen Vaughn was Deborah's brother, not her son. Most certainly not *his* son. No way in hell!

DINNER HAD BEEN a double celebration. Deborah's court appearance was over and Allen Vaughn had once again scored the winning goal that led his team to victory.

Deborah and Ashe had allowed her family to believe the danger was over; indeed, Deborah convinced herself that there was hope all the threats and harassment had come to an end.

She had sensed a tension in Ashe she hadn't noticed before tonight. He kept watching Allen and his close scrutiny unnerved her. Did he suspect something? Or was he simply worrying that Buck Stansell still posed a threat to her family, that Allen might be the target of the man's revenge?

But then Ashe would look at her and his eyes would warm, his expression telling her plainly that he was remembering their lovemaking in the early morning hours. Yesterday. Less than forty-eight hours ago.

"I'm afraid I must say good-night." Carol rose from her chair in the library. "Come along, Allen. It's a half hour past your bedtime."

"How about coming up with me, Ashe?" Allen asked. "You said you wanted to see my science test."

"You bet I do. I want to see what you did to get 105% on that test instead of just a plain old 100%." Ashe laid his hand on Allen's shoulder and the two followed Miss Carol.

"Are you staying down here for a while?" Carol asked her daughter.

"Yes, I think I'll fix myself a drink and relax a bit before I come up."

"Don't forget to say good-night," Allen called out from the hallway.

"I won't forget."

Alone in the library, Deborah kicked off her shoes and tucked her feet up on the sofa. Suddenly she felt the man's presence before she heard him clear his throat. Jerking her head around, she saw Simon Roarke standing in the doorway.

"Come on in, Mr. Roarke," Deborah said. "Would you care for a drink?"

"No, thanks." He walked over to the liquor cart. "May I fix something for you?"

"Just a little brandy."

Roarke poured the liquor and handed it to Deborah. "This about right?"

"Perfect." Deborah looked up at Simon Roarke, thinking, and not for the first time, that there was a hint of sadness in his eyes. "Please, sit down and talk to me."

"What do you want to talk about, Ms. Vaughn?"

"Call me Deborah. And I'd like to ask you about your friend-ship with Ashe."

Roarke sat in the wing chair to Deborah's left. "We've known each other a year. We have similar backgrounds and found we worked well together and enjoyed spending some of our off time together."

"You were in the army, too?"

"Yeah."

"How long have you worked for the Dundee Agency?"

"Over two years."

"You aren't married?"

"No."

"Girlfriend?" Deborah asked.

"Neither Ashe nor I are in a committed relationship, if that's what you're asking. I'm sure he's told you that."

Deborah smiled. "I'm not very good at this, am I? Cross-examining you to get information about Ashe isn't something I'd ordinarily do, but—"

"But you're curious about Ashe. Why don't you just ask him what you want to know?"

"Yes, that would be the logical thing to do, wouldn't it?" Deborah slid her feet off the sofa and back into her shoes. "Did he tell you that we knew each other, years ago?"

"Yes."

"You aren't making this easy for me, Mr. Roarke."

"Just Roarke," he said. "I'm afraid I can't tell you what you want to know. I'm not sure Ashe can tell you. He probably doesn't even know himself."

"Is it that obvious?" Deborah clasped her knees with her fingertips. "I made a mistake about the way Ashe felt about me once, and I don't want to make another mistake."

"You're talking to the wrong man. I can't speak for Ashe." Roarke grunted, then chuckled softly. "Hell, I'm a failure when it comes to figuring out the way other people feel and think. I'm thirty-five. I'm alone, and I'll be alone the rest of my life.

Ashe is different. He's not so far gone, the right woman couldn't save him."

Deborah took a sip of the brandy, then set the glass aside. "I like you, Roarke. I—"

"Allen is waiting for you to come up." Ashe stood in the doorway, a rather comical look of jealousy on his face.

Deborah couldn't suppress a gurgle of laughter from escaping.

Standing, Roarke took a couple of steps, leaned over, lifted Deborah's hand and kissed it. "I like you, too, Deborah." He walked past Ashe without glancing his way.

"What the hell was that all about?" Ashe asked.

"I was pumping Roarke for information about you."

"That's not what it sounded like when I walked in. Sounded more like a mutual admiration society."

Deborah stood and walked over to Ashe, slipped her arm around his neck and pressed her body into his. "I like your friend Roarke." She rubbed herself against Ashe. "But not the same way I like you."

Ashe jerked her up against him and his lips covered hers, claiming her with demanding possession. Breathing hard, they ended the kiss, but held each other close.

"I want to make love to you," he said. "Is there any way we can slip off somewhere? Anywhere?"

"Let me go up and say good-night to Allen, then I'll meet you in the pool house in thirty minutes."

"The pool house? Out back?"

"Yes. We'll have all the privacy we want out there."

Ashe laughed. "I don't know if I can wait thirty minutes."

"Let's make it twenty minutes," she said, pulling out of his arms.

"You aren't afraid someone will find us out, using the pool house as a rendezvous?"

"I really don't care, do you?"

"No, honey, I don't give a damn who knows we're lovers."

DEBORAH SAW THE light in the pool house from where she stood on the back patio. Soft, shimmering light. Candles? Had Ashe found the candles left over from the last pool party they'd given back in the summer, the one for her mother's garden club friends?

She straightened her green satin robe, readjusted the quilted lapels and tightened the sash belt. She told herself not to be nervous, that she had no reason to be. After all, it wasn't as if she were a seventeen-year-old virgin.

Who was she kidding? She might not be a totally inexperienced teenager, but she was hardly accustomed to late-night rendezvous in the pool house with a virile, amorous lover. She couldn't believe she was actually going to do this. But then she had never dreamed that she and Ashe would become lovers. Truly lovers.

She walked slowly toward the pool house, her heart hammering, her nerves quivering, her body filled with anticipation. Music met her as she hesitated in the doorway. An instrumental version of "The Shadow of Your Smile" surrounded her. Apparently he'd found the tape player and the stack of her mother's favorite tunes on cassettes. He stood inside waiting for her, two glasses of wine in his hand. He held out one to her when she entered the small octagon-shaped shelter, centered directly behind the swimming pool.

Ashe had changed into a pair of faded jeans and a zippered fleece jacket. He looked incredible. All muscle and firm flesh, tanned and lean and waiting for her.

She accepted the wine. He nodded toward the padded poolside chaise longue that had been stored for the winter. Seating herself, she glanced around inside the twelve-by-twelve-foot room. A dozen fat pink and yellow candles, half consumed on a previous occasion, circled the inner perimeter, casting a mellow, romantic glow over the room.

"To the most beautiful woman in the world." Ashe saluted her with his glass.

Her smile wavered, but she managed to keep it in place after she took a sip of the white wine. "You're beautiful, too, you know. You always were. The most beautiful boy, the most beautiful man. I never could see anyone else except you."

Hurriedly she downed the remainder of the wine. The tune changed to "What Are You Doing for the Rest of Your Life?" She'd heard her mother hum these old tunes for as long as she could remember. They were such romantic songs, meant to be shared by lovers.

Ashe took her empty glass. "Want a refill?"

"No." She looked up at him. "I don't dare drink any more. I'm already drunk from just looking at you."

He set their glasses on a small round glass and metal table, then took Deborah's hands and lifted her to her feet. Drawing her into his arms, he rubbed his cheek against hers and danced her slowly around the room.

"You don't have any idea what your honesty does to me, do you?" He caught her open mouth before she could reply, thrusting his tongue inside, loving the taste of the wine that lingered in her mouth.

When he ended the kiss, he smiled when he saw her face. Eyes closed, face flushed, she was so beautiful it tore at his heart to look at her. "I can't believe how much I want you."

"Oh, Ashe, I never dreamed this could happen, that you and I… But it's real, isn't it? We're here, together. Lovers."

"Lovers, in every sense of the word." Reaching down, he loosened her sash belt until her robe fell open. Seeing that she was naked beneath the green satin, he swallowed hard. "My God, Deborah!"

Her shaky fingers grasped the metal pull on his jacket zipper and opened the hooded blue sweatshirt. She laid her hand on his chest. He covered her hand with his.

"I don't really know anything about this. I don't have any experience. Teach me, Ashe. Show me what you want."

"Take off my jacket," he said.

She obeyed, sliding it off his shoulders and tossing it on the floor. "Now what?"

"Remove my jeans."

Without hesitation, she unsnapped, unzipped and tugged off his jeans. He kicked his shoes off and to one side, then spread the satin robe away from her body, allowing it to fall to her feet.

They stood, only inches separating them, naked and unashamed, passion wild within them both. He took her hands in his, lifted them for a kiss, then placed them on his chest before lifting her in his arms.

Ashe was magnificent. Big, tall and lean. He carried her back to the chaise, but set her on her feet.

"Night before last we were so hungry for each other, we didn't take the time to savor the moment. Not the first time nor the second time. Tonight, I want to learn every inch of your body, and I want you to know every inch of mine."

"Whatever you want, Ashe." She moved closer, her breasts brushing against his hair-rough chest. She gulped down a sigh as shivers of pleasure shimmied through her.

"No, honey. Whatever you want." He cupped her buttocks, bringing her completely up against him, letting her feel his arousal, telling her, even without words, how much he wanted her.

"I just want you, Ashe." She slid her hands up his chest and around his neck. "I just want you."

He kissed her until she was breathless, then he painted a trail of warm, moist kisses across her shoulder and down to one breast. All the while he caressed her hip with his other hand. She quivered, then cried out when he suckled her breast. Her knees weakened. He stayed at her breast long enough to have her panting, then knelt on bended knee and delved his tongue into her navel at the precise moment his fingers found the soft inner folds of her body. Her knees gave way and she would have fallen if she hadn't caught Ashe by the shoulders, bracing herself.

He covered her stomach in kisses, then moved back and forth from one thigh to the other, kissing, licking, nipping her tender flesh. She moaned with the pleasure, shivering as she dug her nails into his shoulders.

Lifting her, he laid her on the chaise and came down over her, one knee resting on the side of the cushion, his other foot on the floor.

"Touch me, Deborah. Feel me."

She sucked in a deep breath, then began a timid exploration of his chest and belly. Garnering her courage and enticed by his glorious body, she ran her fingers over his hardness. He groaned, but she knew the sound was one of pleasure and not pain. She circled him. He covered her hand, teaching her the movements that pleased him. But as quickly as he'd instructed her, he pulled her hand away and laid it on his hip.

"I can't take much of that, honey."

Lowering his head, he captured her nipple in his mouth, teasing it, then sucking greedily. She arched her back up off the chaise. He delved his fingers between her satiny folds, finding her most sensitive spot. She writhed beneath him as he fondled her. Within minutes she shuddered and he swallowed her cries of completion in a tongue-thrusting kiss. As the last wave of pleasure shook her, Ashe lifted her hips and entered her. One sure, swift move that joined their bodies and began the mating dance.

Slowly. Precisely. In and out. Hands roamed. Lips kissed. Bodies united in pleasure. Soon the rhythm changed, the waltz became a wild fandango. Slow. Quick. Slow. Quick. Deborah clung to Ashe as the tension in her body mounted. He thrust into her harder and faster, sweat forming on his body.

She called his name over and over again as her pleasure climbed upward, closer and closer to the apex. Ashe's movements became frantic, his need for this woman growing hotter and hotter.

She cried out in the moment of release, spiraling out of control and into oblivion. Ashe thrust once, twice more, and followed her over the precipice. His own hardy male cry blended with her feminine ones, their breaths ragged, their bodies coated with perspiration.

Ashe maneuvered Deborah so that they fit together on the chaise, their bodies stuck together with the moisture of their lovemaking.

"We're going to stay here all night," he told her.

"Yes. I know." She kissed him, taking the initiative, smothering him with all the passion she'd buried deep within her eleven years ago when he had walked out of her life.

But he was back and for however long Ashe McLaughlin stayed in her life, she planned to be his lover. Maybe nothing lasted forever. Maybe they didn't have a future. But for tonight, she would pretend. Tomorrow was a million miles away. Nothing mattered tonight, nothing except loving and being loved by Ashe.

DEBORAH OPENED THE door to her bedroom. Ashe circled her waist with his arm, pulling her back against his chest, nuzzling her neck with his nose.

"Get in your room. It's nearly six. Mother will be up and about soon," Deborah said, but turned in his arms, kissing him.

He shoved her away, turned her around and swatted her behind. "See you downstairs for breakfast in about an hour."

Deborah stood in the open doorway, watching until Ashe disappeared down the hall and into his room. Smiling, she walked into her sitting room, humming "Goin' Out of My Head," the tune that had been playing on the cassette when she and Ashe had made love right before returning to the house.

"Good morning," Carol Vaughn said.

Deborah came fully alert, stared across the room and saw her mother perched on the edge of the window seat. "Mother!"

"Come in and close the door. I think we need to have a little talk, don't you?"

"How long have you been waiting in here?" Deborah closed the door and walked across the room, sitting down beside her mother.

"Only a few minutes." Carol took Deborah's hand. "I awoke early. I'd had a difficult time sleeping all night. The sedatives don't last very long. I walked around and just happened to stop by the windows and saw light coming from the pool house. I checked your room and found it empty, then I knocked on Ashe's door. Mr. Roarke heard me and came out to see what was going on."

"Did you tell Roarke that Ashe and I were missing?"

"I told him that y'all had obviously spent the night in the pool house," Carol said. "I rather think I embarrassed the man."

"Oh, Mother, really."

"I was awake and heard the two of you on the stairs, so I came over here to wait for you."

"I'm a big girl now. I don't need your approval to spend the night with a man."

"No, of course you don't." Carol patted Deborah's hand, then released it. "But if you and Ashe have begun an affair, then I can't help being concerned. For you and for Allen."

"Mother, I—"

"Shh. I deliberately brought Ashe back here because I knew you'd never gotten over him, that there had been no one else." Glancing down at her hands, Carol twisted her diamond ring and her gold wedding band about on her finger. "I admit I played God in your life, but I want you to be happy."

"I'm glad Ashe came back into my life. We've cleared up several misconceptions we had concerning each other."

"He told you what your father did, didn't he?"

"Yes, he told me."

"Deborah, your father thought he was doing the best thing for you. I disagreed, but you know how your father was. He wouldn't listen to me."

"I don't blame you, Mother. I don't even blame Daddy." Deborah hugged Carol. "It's all right. Really it is. We can't change what happened. Besides, I'm the one who has kept Allen's parentage a secret. I could have gotten in touch with Ashe at any time and we both know it."

No, Deborah blamed no one except herself. If she had been a little older and less dependent on her parents, she never would have agreed to her father's plan to send her and her mother away to Europe for the last few months of Deborah's pregnancy. A chubby girl who had been able to disguise her pregnant state with loose, baggy clothes, even at six months, Deborah hadn't had a problem keeping her pregnancy a secret. And once they had returned to Sheffield with Allen, no one had dared to openly question his parentage.

"I lied to Mattie," Carol said. "She asked me once, when Allen was just a baby, if he was your child. Yours and Ashe's."

"You never told me that she suspected Allen wasn't yours and Daddy's."

"I lied to her. I convinced her that her suspicions were wrong. She never questioned me again."

"If she'd known, she would have told Ashe."

"She does know, Deborah." Carol kept her eyes downcast. "I told her the truth when I asked her for Ashe's telephone number in Atlanta."

"Mother!"

Carol's chin quivered as she looked directly at her daughter. "She has promised not to tell Ashe, to give you time to tell him the truth." Carol clutched Deborah's hand. "You must tell Ashe. You can't keep putting it off, not now the two of you are lovers."

"Mother, I'm not sure telling Ashe would be the best thing to do, under the circumstances."

"What circumstances?"

"Ashe and I have made each other no promises. He hasn't committed himself to me for any longer than his business here will take. Once I'm no longer in danger, he's going back to Atlanta."

"I see."

"If I tell him about Allen, I have no idea what he might do. He could tell Allen. He could demand joint custody. Or he could make a commitment to me because of Allen and not because he loves me." Jumping up off the window seat, Deborah walked around the room. She stopped abruptly, then turned to face her mother. "I'm afraid to tell him. I'm afraid I'll lose him all over again."

"Deborah, dear child, you musn't—"

"I know. I know. I'm not fooling myself. It's just that I want whatever time we have together to go on being as wonderful as it was tonight."

"You must tell the man he has a son." Carol shook her head. "You can't lie to Ashe if you love him."

"I didn't say I loved him."

"You didn't have to. I see it in your eyes. I hear it in your voice."

"I can't tell him. Not yet."

"I go back to the doctor for a checkup and more tests soon," Carol said. "If you haven't told Ashe by then—"

"No, Mother, you musn't tell him."

"Then you tell him. We should have told him long ago. Besides, if you don't tell him before he leaves Sheffield, Mattie will tell him."

"But what if he tells Allen?"

Carol stood, walked across the room and laid her hand on Deborah's shoulder. "Ashe isn't going to do anything to hurt Allen. Don't you know him any better than that?"

"Give me some time, Mother. Please, just let me do this my way and in my own good time."

"Don't wait too long. My heart tells me that you'll be sorry if you do."

ASHE CAME OUT of the shower, dried off and stepped into a pair of clean briefs. He didn't know when he'd ever felt so good, so glad to be alive.

Deborah. Sweet, beautiful Deborah.

She was, in so many ways, the same innocent, loving girl she'd been eleven years ago; but then she was also a woman of strength and courage and incredible passion.

Whoever she was, part innocent girl, part bewitching woman, Deborah Vaughn was honest and trustworthy. She would never lie to him. Never!

He had tried to put Roarke's suspicions out of his mind, and for those magic hours he'd spent with Deborah he'd been able to do just that. But now he had to face them again.

There was no way Allen Vaughn could be his son. Deborah would have told him if she'd been pregnant. She'd have come running to him. She'd been so crazy in love with him that she would have...

She would have come to him after he'd rejected her, after he'd told her that he didn't love her the way she loved him?

Allen isn't your son, he told himself. He looks just like Deborah. He's her brother, dammit. Her brother!

Besides, Mama Mattie would have told him if she'd thought Allen was his child.

Don't do this to yourself! Don't look for similarities between you and Allen. Don't let Roarke's outrageous suspicions spoil what you and Deborah have found together this time.

Miss Carol never would have dared you to come back to Sheffield and face the past if Allen was your son.

Ashe dressed hurriedly, then rushed downstairs, eager to see

Deborah again. He would not look at Allen Vaughn and search for a truth that didn't exist. He trusted Deborah. His heart told him she wouldn't lie to him. And just this once, he intended to listen to his heart.

CHAPTER ELEVEN

THE TRIAL HAD lasted eight days, everyone saying the case was pretty well cut and dried since the prosecution had a reliable eyewitness to the murder. After three and a half hours of deliberation, the jury had rendered a guilty verdict, surprising no one. Five days later, the judge had sentenced Lon Sparks to life in prison, and Deborah Vaughn had been free from threats and harassment for nearly two weeks.

Ashe had been waiting for Buck Stansell to strike, but nothing had happened, not even a wrong-number telephone call. He'd thought about paying Buck a visit, but decided against it. Why take a chance on stirring a hornet's nest? He had talked to his cousin Lee Roy, who'd said little, except that *people* weren't overly concerned with an insignificant guy like Lon Sparks, that the man wasn't worth enough to cause trouble over.

Roarke had suggested it might be time to think about returning to Atlanta, but Ashe kept putting him off. How could he take a chance on leaving Deborah undefended? She'd come to mean far more to him than she should. He had allowed himself to become too involved with her, with Allen and Miss Carol. This was a job, but not like any other. These were people he cared about, a family he'd started thinking of as his.

Maybe he had reached the age when he needed to settle down, to start considering marriage and children. He wasn't sure. He and Deborah were attracted to each other, always had been, although he'd fought that attraction when they'd been younger. Maybe somewhere deep down inside him, he'd always thought he wasn't quite good enough for Deborah. Not just because her parents were wealthy and socially prominent and he'd come from white-trash hoodlums, but because he'd never been innocent or pure or good, and Deborah had been all those things. Even now, at twenty-eight, she still personified everything right with the world.

And he still wasn't good enough for her.

Ashe paced the floor in the doctor's office, waiting for Deborah and Miss Carol. He'd told himself that he would hang around Sheffield until they knew the test results. It was as good an excuse as any. This way he could justify his reluctance to leave, to Deborah and her family, as well as to himself.

Sitting, he flipped through several magazines, then stood and paced the floor again. He glanced at the wall clock, checking it against his watch. Nearly an hour. Dammit, how long did it take for a doctor to explain test results?

Just when his patience came to an end, Deborah and Miss Carol emerged from the office, solemn expressions on their faces. Deborah's arm draped her mother's slender shoulders.

"We're ready to go home, now, Ashe," Deborah said.

Ashe didn't ask any questions, didn't say a word, simply nodded his head and led the ladies outside and assisted them into the car.

Miss Carol, sitting in the front seat beside Ashe, reached over and touched his arm lightly. "Can you stay awhile longer?"

"Yes, ma'am, of course I can stay." He pulled the car out of the parking lot and onto the main thoroughfare.

"Deborah and Allen will need you," Carol said.

"Mother, please don't—" Deborah said.

"Hush up." Carol swatted her hand in the air. "Ashe is like family and I want him here. Even if you think you can handle this alone, I believe you'll need a strong man at your side."

"I take it the tests results weren't good." Ashe kept his gaze fixed straight ahead.

"The cancer has returned and Dr. Mason has scheduled surgery for the first of next week." Carol opened her purse, took out a lace handkerchief and wiped her hands, then returned the handkerchief to her purse.

"I'm sorry, Miss Carol."

"No need for all this gloom and doom." Carol sat up straight, squaring her shoulders as if preparing herself to do battle. "I licked this thing once and I can do it again. But I'll rest easier knowing Deborah won't be alone, that you'll be at her side."

"You hired me, Miss Carol. I won't leave Sheffield as long as you need me."

"Thank you, Ashe." She patted him on the arm.

Little more was said on the short drive home. Indeed, what more could be said? Ashe wondered. Life certainly didn't play fair. Not when it heaped more trouble on one family than it could bear. But then, Deborah and Miss Carol were both strong women. They were fighters despite their genteel backgrounds.

Sirens blasted, shrill and menacing in the quite, lazy atmosphere of Sheffield's main street.

"Oh, my." Carol shivered. "I do so hate the sound of those things. Sirens always mean bad news."

"Look at that black smoke," Deborah said. "It's coming straight up Montgomery Avenue."

"My goodness, you don't suppose it's one of our neighbors' homes, do you?" Miss Carol leaned toward the windshield, her gaze riveted to the billowing smoke filling the blue sky.

The closer they came to home, the darker the smoke, the louder the sirens. A sudden sick feeling hit Ashe in the pit of his stomach. Allen was still at school. Roarke would be with him. Ashe blew out a breath.

Before they reached the Vaughn driveway, they saw one fire truck parked at the back of the house and another just turning in behind it. "It's our garage!" Deborah gripped the back of her mother's seat. "It's on fire!"

Ashe pulled the Cadillac up to the curb, stopped and jumped out. "Stay here." He ran across the front yard.

"Stay in the car, Mother. I'll come back and check on you in just a few minutes."

"But Ashe said for both of us to stay here," Carol said.

"Ashe isn't my boss."

Deborah jumped out of the car, catching up with Ashe at the back corner of the house, where he stood watching the firemen do their job. He grabbed her around the waist, pulling her to his side.

"It's just the garage," he said. "And it looks like they're getting the fire under control."

"Mazie? Where's Mazie? Is she all right?"

"She's at the grocery store. Remember? This is Wednesday morning, her midweek trip to pick up supplies."

"Oh, yes, of course."

Deborah leaned against Ashe, watching while the firefighters extinguished the blaze, leaving a charred three-car garage, a blackened Mercedes, a soot-covered BMW and swirling clouds of gray smoke spiraling heavenward.

Fire Chief Greg Wilbanks nodded, removed his hat and wiped his face with the back of his hand. "Damn curious blaze. Whoever set this baby didn't try to hide the fact that it was out-and-out arson."

"What do you mean?" Deborah asked.

"The place was doused with gasoline and torched. We found two empty gas cans at the back of the house." Greg looked at Ashe. "I've called Chief Burton. I'd say your job isn't finished, Mr. McLaughlin. Looks like somebody's out to get himself a little revenge."

"Ashe?" Deborah grabbed his arm. "Do you think that—"

"I don't think anything," he said.

"But Greg said—"

"I know what he said. There's no point jumping to conclusions. We'll take every precaution, but we're not going to panic." He grasped her by the shoulders. "Go tell Miss Carol that everything's all right. The fire's out. Tell her the truth, but play it down. There's no need to worry her any more than can be helped."

"You're right." She slipped her arms around Ashe's waist and sighed when he hugged her close. Pulling away, she tried to smile. "I'll take Mother in the front door. There's no need for her to see this until later."

"Don't read anything into this," Ashe said. "Not yet. Let me handle things. I'm not going anywhere, not until you're completely out of danger. Trust me, honey."

"I do trust you. With all my heart."

Ashe watched her walk away, a tight knot forming in the pit of his stomach. She expected a great deal from him. Was it more than he could deliver? Would he let her down again, or could he be the man Deborah wanted and needed?

Ashe approached Greg Wilbanks. "When Chief Burton arrives, tell him I'd prefer he not bother Miss Carol or Deborah. I'll talk to him. And once you've filed your report on this fire, I'd like a copy."

"As Miss Carol's representative?" Greg asked.

"Yeah, as Miss Carol's representative."

"No problem."

Going in the back door, Ashe met Carol and Deborah in the hallway.

"I'm taking Mother upstairs to rest," Deborah told him, then turned to assist her mother. "I'll fix you some tea and bring it up in just a little while."

"Tea would be nice." Halting on the landing, Carol grabbed Deborah's arm. "Let him do whatever he has to do to put an end to this."

"Mother, what are saying?"

"I'm saying that Ashe knows how to deal with those people. However he chooses to handle the situation, I don't want you trying to persuade him otherwise."

"Ashe is not a hired assassin, Mother. He's not going to kill Buck Stansell."

"You two go on," Ashe called out from the downstairs hall-way. "I'll fix you both some tea and bring it up."

"Thank you," Miss Carol smiled.

"Mother!" Deborah glared at Carol. "Do you honestly think Ashe would murder someone?"

"Not murder, my dear, kill. There is a difference. And Ashe McLaughlin has been trained to kill. There is no doubt in my mind that he would kill anyone who'd harm you."

"I don't want him to have to kill to protect me, but... Perhaps Buck Stansell wasn't responsible for the fire. Besides, no one was harmed."

Downstairs, Ashe put on the water to boil, set two cups on a tray and laid two Earl Grey tea bags in each cup. Lifting the phone out of the wall cradle, he dialed Roarke's cellular phone number.

"Roarke, here."

"Keep a very close eye on Allen."

"What's wrong?"

"We've had a fire here," Ashe said. "Someone doused the garage with gasoline. They left the cans for the firemen to find."

"Looks like we'll be hanging around Sheffield for a while longer than we thought."

"Yeah. I'd say Buck Stansell is back to playing games with us. The question is just how deadly will his games become."

DEBORAH TOOK CARE of her morning phone calls, dictated several letters and closed a deal on the old Hartman farm before her ten-thirty coffee break. She had wanted to stay home with her mother, whom she worried would fret the day away there at the house with only Mazie, the eternal pessimist, as company. But her mother had insisted she didn't need a baby-sitter, so Deborah had found an alternative plan.

She glanced in the outer office where Ashe sat with his long legs stretched out, his big feet propped up on a desk in the corner, situated where he could see directly into Deborah's office. He had begun work on his second crossword puzzle book since his arrival in Sheffield.

Deborah dialed the telephone, hoping her plan for keeping her mother occupied would work out.

"Hello."

"Mama Mattie," Deborah said. "I have a favor to ask of you."

"What is it, child?"

"Mother's at the house all alone with Mazie, and I'm afraid, after the doctor's news and the fire in the garage yesterday, she'll spend the day fretting."

"You need say no more. I've just baked an apple cinnamon coffee cake. I'll take it over and spend the rest of the day with Miss Carol."

"Thanks so much, Mama Mattie."

"It'll be my pleasure." Deborah hung up the phone and glanced back at Ashe, who looked up from his puzzle and grinned at her. She lifted her hand to her mouth in a drinking gesture. Ashe nodded agreement. They met at the coffeepot, one of three set up on a table in a small, open room directly across from the office rest room.

"Good morning." Holding a mug of hot coffee in one hand, he cupped her hip with the other and brought her close enough for him to kiss.

She returned the kiss, then pulled away, turning to pour her coffee. "Get your hand off my hip, Mr. McLaughlin. This is an office, not a bedroom," she teased.

"I'm glad you told me," he said. "I was planning on backing you up against the wall over there and ravishing you. But since this is an office, I don't suppose ravishing the boss lady is allowed."

"Most definitely not."

"You've had a busy morning."

"I've accomplished a great deal."

They carried their coffee back into the outer office, pausing just outside Deborah's private domain.

"Ashe, have there been any threatening phone calls or a letter today?" she asked.

"No, honey, not a one."

"I'd thought that since…well since the fire yesterday, the harassment might start all over again."

He nudged her through her office door. "There may not be a connection. But…" He didn't want to alarm her.

"But what?"

"If Buck Stansell was behind yesterday's fire, I'd say phone calls and letters are a thing of the past. Simple harassment will no longer be the order of the day."

"I see. You're saying things will get nasty."

"They could."

"Do you think Allen and Mother are in danger?"

"Possibly."

"Oh, Ashe." The coffee sloshed over the edge of her mug. Quickly holding the mug outward so the liquid could run down the sides, she averted being burned.

Just as Ashe started to close the door to Deborah's office, a string of loud, piercing blasts sounded. The front office windows shattered. Glass blew across the room. The office staff screamed and dived for cover under their desks. Ashe knocked Deborah to the floor, covering her body with his as he drew his gun.

"Crawl to the left," he told her.

She obeyed silently, not questioning Ashe's order for one minute. Standing, he lifted her to her knees and sat her in the corner behind a row of metal file cabinets.

"Stay put."

She nodded. He made his way to the outer office where he found the staff in hiding. The front of the office wall consisted of a line of long windows, all of which had been destroyed by a barrage of bullets.

Annie Laurie looked up from beneath her desk, her eyes wide with fright. "Ashe? Oh, my God, what happened?"

"Everyone stay put," Ashe said.

Cracking his office door a fraction, Neil Posey peered outside. "Is everyone all right?" he asked. "Is Annie Laurie okay? Was Deborah hurt?"

"As far as I know the only damage is to the windows," Ashe said as he made his way to the bullet-riddled front door. He walked out onto the sidewalk. People were staring at him and at the Vaughn & Posey building. In the distance he heard a police siren and knew, the police station being only a few blocks away, the authorities would arrive at any moment. Returning inside, he made his way toward Deborah's office.

"It's all right," Ashe said. "Whoever did all this damage is long gone."

One by one the staff of Vaughn & Posey emerged from under their desks.

Neil opened his office door. "Annie Laurie, are you sure you're all right?"

"I'm fine, Mr. Posey. Just scared to death."

Ashe found Deborah still sitting in the corner behind the filing cabinets. She stared up at him, her eyes dry, her face pale.

"It's okay, honey." Reaching down, he lifted her to her feet. She shook uncontrollably. "Deborah?"

She clung to him, her trembling growing worse. "Was anyone hurt?"

"Everybody's fine. Nothing's hurt but the building."

"I can't let the people who work for me be at risk because of me."

Ashe stroked her back, trying to soothe her. "You can't blame yourself for this."

"Yes, I can. And I do. I'm Buck Stansell's target. If I hadn't been here at the office, then he wouldn't have sent someone *here* to shoot up the place."

"Don't start blaming yourself for something that isn't your fault." Dammit, she was shaking like a leaf. He wasn't getting through to her.

He grabbed her by the shoulders and shook her soundly. She glared at him, then nodded her head. Ashe pulled her back into his arms, and that's how the police chief found them.

"Deborah, Chief Burton is here," Annie Laurie called out from the doorway.

Deborah turned in Ashe's arms, but made no move away from him. He kept his arms tightly around her.

"They sure as hell made a mess of things," Chief Burton said. "A couple of witnesses across the street said they saw one man drive by real slow, coming to a stop right out front before he pulled out what they thought looked like some sort of automatic weapon. Of course, they can't identify the weapon. Said it happened too fast. He was driving a new Chevy."

"The car was probably stolen," Ashe said.

"Could've been. Anyway, I just wanted to ask if either of you saw anything that could help us."

"No," Ashe said. "We didn't see anything."

"Nobody in the office seemed to have seen a thing. Just heard the shooting." The police chief looked directly at Deborah. "Ms. Vaughn, you might want to think about staying at home for a few days, that is, unless you plan on closing down the business."

"No, I do not plan on closing Vaughn & Posey." She stiffened her spine. Sliding his hand up and around, Ashe caressed her back, then placed his arm around her shoulders. "However, I will consider staying at home. I don't want to put my employees' lives at risk."

"I'm taking Ms. Vaughn home, now," Ashe said. "If you need to question us further, you'll know where to find us."

"Fine," Chief Burton said. "I don't think we'll need either of you any more today."

"I need to make arrangements to have the building cleaned

and repair work started immediately." Deborah allowed Ashe to lead her across the shattered glass and splintered wood covering the outer office floor.

She stopped at Annie Laurie's desk; the two women hugged each other. Deborah turned to face her employees. "I'm sorry this had to happen. I'm so relieved no one was injured." She glanced over at Neil, whose normally pink face was a pale gray. "Let everyone go home for the rest of the day. I'll have someone come in and clean up. Rearrange things so work can continue tomorrow. Make use of my office. I'll be working at home. Temporarily."

"Certainly, Deborah. We'll carry on," Neil said.

Ashe hurried her outside and into her car. "Just hang on, honey. I'll take you home."

"I dread telling Mother, but I have no choice. You know someone may have already called her."

"Miss Carol will handle this okay. She's a strong woman, just like her daughter."

When they arrived at the Vaughn home, they found Mattie Trotter waiting on the front porch. The minute Deborah approached her, she opened her arms.

Going into Mattie's arms, Deborah sighed. "Oh, Mama Mattie, this has become a nightmare. I thought it was over, that the worst had been Huckleberry's poisoning."

"It'll be all right," Mattie said, glancing over Deborah's shoulder at Ashe. "Ashe isn't going to let anything happen to you."

"Someone called already, didn't they?" Deborah asked. "Mother knows."

"Miss Carol is fine. She's lying down in the library, taking a little nap." Mattie winked at Deborah as she slipped her arm around her waist and led her inside. "I put a few drops of brandy in her tea."

"Where's Mazie?" Deborah looked around in the hallway. "I

can't believe she's not out here foretelling the end of the world for us all."

"I sent that silly woman to town on an errand," Mattie said. "I had to get her out of the house. She was driving me crazy and upsetting Miss Carol. She should be gone a couple of hours. And Allen won't be home from school until after three."

"Thanks." Deborah swayed, her head spinning. Mama Mattie motioned to Ashe, who lifted Deborah in his arms.

"Put me down!"

"Take her on upstairs and tend to her." Mattie pointed to the closed library door. "I'll go sit with Miss Carol and finish reading that new Grisham book. If we need y'all, I'll let you know."

Ashe carried Deborah up the stairs and into her sitting room, but didn't put her down. With her arms around his neck, she stared into his eyes and knew he was going to kiss her. She didn't resist, indeed she welcomed the kiss, needing it desperately. Quick. Hard. And possessive. Deborah sighed.

He carried her over to the window bench and sat down, placing her in his lap. She laid her head on his shoulder.

"Do you want a drink?" he asked. She shook her head from side to side. "A bath?" Another negative shake. "A nap?"

"All I want is for you to hold me," she said, clinging to him.

He hugged her fiercely. "Nobody was hurt."

"This time. But what about the next time or the time after that? You can't guarantee me that some innocent person won't be harmed because of me."

"Not because of you, honey! Dammit, why do you insist on blaming yourself?"

"Maybe I should go away. Far away. That way the people I love would be safe."

"Not necessarily," Ashe said. "Running away isn't the answer if Buck Stansell is out for revenge. If you leave town, he might target Miss Carol or Allen."

"Oh, God, Ashe, Mother has enough to deal with already."
Deborah grasped the lapels of Ashe's jacket. "Promise me that
you won't let anything happen to Allen."

"I won't let anything happen to Allen." He kissed her forehead, then smoothed the loose strands of her hair away from
her face. "You love Allen a great deal, don't you?"

"He's the most important person in the world to me. I—I…
He's just a little boy."

Ashe caressed Deborah's face, cupping her cheek in his
palm. "I'll take care of you and Allen. And Miss Carol."

Gulping in air, Deborah looked at Ashe pleadingly. She
needed him, needed his tender loving care, needed his strength,
his power.

He stood with her in his arms and carried her into the bedroom, laying her on her bed. He came down over her, turning
her to one side as he eased his body onto the bed. Facing her,
he removed her jacket, then unbuttoned her blouse. Slowly,
carefully, stroking and caressing her as he uncovered more and
more of her body, Ashe undressed her completely.

She was a bundle of nerves, her emotions raw. She needed
soothing, needed to forget, at least for a few hours, the nightmare her life had become. He hated the feeling of helplessness,
knowing he hadn't been able to prevent the drive-by shooting at
her office. But he could give her the reassurance and care she
needed now. And soon, very soon, he would have to confront
her enemy.

Ashe made love to her with his hands and mouth, whispering endearing words of comfort and admiration. Never before
had he felt so totally possessive about a woman, wanting her
and her alone in a way that bordered on obsession. How had
this happened? When had Deborah become the focal point of
his existence?

Every touch, every word was meant for her pleasure, but
with each touch, each kiss, each heated word, he became lost
in the fury of a passion over which he was fast losing control.

He caressed her breasts, loving the way her tight nipples felt beneath his fingertips, loving her hot little cries. He kissed her inner thighs. She sighed, squirming when his tongue turned inward for further exploration.

She moaned and writhed, her body straining for release as Ashe pleasured her, his lips and fingers masterful in their ministrations, bringing her to the very brink, then pausing, only to return her to that moment just before satisfaction.

She cried out, begging him not to prolong the agony, clinging to him, pleading for fulfillment. His words grew more erotic, more suggestive, as he carried her to the edge. With one final stroke of his tongue, he flung her into ecstasy.

Covering her mouth in a heated kiss, he devoured her cries of pleasure. Pulling her close, he reached down and lifted the hand-crocheted afghan and covered her. He lay there holding her while she dozed off to sleep and the noonday sun began its western descent.

His heart beat like a racing stallion. Sweat coated his body. He ached with the need for release. But this time had been for Deborah, not for him. She had needed the powerful fulfillment, and what Deborah needed was far more important to him than what he needed.

When Ashe had sent Buck Stansell a warning, declaring Deborah Vaughn his personal property, it had been a ruse. Now it was a fact. If he had to destroy Buck Stansell to keep Deborah safe, he'd do it. No one was going to harm his woman.

CHAPTER TWELVE

DEBORAH SET UP a temporary office in the library, moving in a computer and borrowing Annie Laurie for the first day. She would do whatever was necessary to protect her employees. That might mean staying away from Vaughn & Posey for a few weeks, but it also meant business as usual. Too many people depended upon the real estate firm for their livelihoods, including Deborah's family. She had no idea whether or not Whitney had any money left in her trust fund, but she doubted it. Not after nearly eleven years of marriage to George Jamison. That meant Whitney, too, depended upon revenue from Vaughn & Posey to keep her and her worthless husband from bankruptcy.

Ashe McLaughlin's return to Sheffield was a mixed blessing. He and Roarke guarded the family night and day. Anyone wanting to harm her or Allen or her mother would have to go through two highly trained professionals. But her personal relationship with Ashe had her confused and uncertain.

She could not deny that she was in love with him. Always had been. Always would be. But the lie about Allen stood between them as surely as Ashe's inability to make a commitment. If she knew Ashe loved her, if she knew he wanted to spend the rest of his life with her, telling Ashe the truth about Allen would not be as difficult. But he hadn't said he loved her and certainly had made her no promises beyond defending her with his life.

"Where do these go?" Ashe stood in the doorway, a stack of file folders in his arms.

"What are those?" she asked.

"They're printouts of all your current files on your present listings." Annie Laurie scurried past Ashe, dragging a swivel desk chair behind her.

Deborah smiled at Ashe; he returned her smile. She couldn't stop looking at him, couldn't stop remembering how it felt when they made love. She was as giddy and light-headed as a teenager in love for the first time. And the crazy thing was she honestly thought Ashe was acting the same way.

He looked incredible this afternoon, but then he always did. Tall, muscular and lean. Gray slacks. Navy blue jacket. Light blue shirt, worn unbuttoned and without a tie. She could see the top curls of dark hair above his open shirt.

They hadn't made love since yesterday and she ached to be with him.

Annie Laurie cleared her throat. "We could take a break. It's after one and we haven't stopped for lunch."

"Good idea." Ashe laid the file folders to the left of the computer atop the antique mahogany desk. "Why don't you two do whatever it is you need to do and I'll tell Mazie we're ready for some of her famous chili. I've been smelling the stuff for hours now."

"Check on Mother, will you?" Deborah asked. "She's been busy all morning working on that cross-stitch piece she wants to finish before she goes in the hospital."

"I'll see if she wants to join us for lunch or have something in her room," Ashe said.

Deborah looked around the library and wondered if it would ever return to normal once she went back to Vaughn & Posey's downtown office. Together she and Annie Laurie had managed to keep everything fairly neat, but office clutter had certainly changed the charming old room's atmosphere.

Deborah fell into the huge, tufted leather chair behind the desk. Her father's desk. Her grandfather's desk.

"So, Neil finally came to his senses and asked you out." Folding her arms behind her, Deborah placed her hands at the back of her head and stretched. "You'll need to leave here early enough to go home and change and—"

"It really isn't a date, Deborah. We're just having dinner and Neil is going to help me study. If I can't pass the test, I'll never become a Realtor. There is no need for me to leave early. Neil's picking me up here after work."

"Neil could have helped you study without taking you out for dinner," Deborah said. "My goodness, Annie Laurie, give the man a little encouragement. I think everyone, except Neil, knows how you feel about him."

"I can hardly throw myself at Neil when he's in love with you." Annie Laurie plopped herself down in the swivel chair she'd placed at the edge of the desk.

"Neil is not in love with me. It's just that he's had a sort of crush on me for years. I've made it perfectly clear that we can never be more than friends."

"I guess none of us can help who we love, can we? I'm in love with Neil, he's in love with you and you're in love with Ashe."

"I see you have this all figured out." In Annie Laurie's version of their love lives, they were beginning to sound like a modern day Southern version of *A Midsummer Night's Dream*. "But if actions speak louder than words, as Mama Mattie says, then I'd say you're the woman Neil cares for the most. After all, I'm not the one he checked on first yesterday after the gunman's drive-by attack."

"He couldn't have gotten to you without going through Ashe and Neil certainly would never try to confront Ashe."

"I'm telling you that if you want Neil, you're going to have to let him know. And I mean in no uncertain terms. Seduce the man."

Annie Laurie gasped. "Why Deborah Luellen Vaughn, what

sort of advice is that? Are you saying that if I sleep with Neil, he'll fall madly in love with me?"

"No. I'm saying he's already in love with you, but just doesn't know it. Besides, a man Neil's age isn't going to be seduced unless he wants to be. And I'm telling you, he's ready for you."

"You and Ashe are having an affair, aren't you?" Annie Laurie kept her head bowed, but risked a quick glance in Deborah's direction. "I know it's none of my business, but you've been a good friend to me and I don't want to see you get hurt."

Deborah sighed, then smacked her lips lightly. "Yes, Ashe and I are having an affair. And I know only too well that I could wind up getting hurt again. But I've been in love with him for as long as I can remember. I've never wanted anyone else."

"I know exactly how you feel."

"Then don't wait around. Go get what you want. Neil isn't going anywhere, and take my word for it, you're exactly what Neil needs and what he wants, whether he knows it or not."

Ashe knocked on the doorpost, announcing his presence. "Chili is served in the kitchen. Coffee? Tea? Cola?"

"Tea," Deborah said.

"I'll go wash up and help Mazie get everything on the table." Annie Laurie stood. "Is Miss Carol joining us?"

"Yes, she said for me to come up and get her when we're ready to eat," Ashe said.

"I'll bring her down after I help Mazie." Annie Laurie rushed out of the library.

"What's wrong with her?" Ashe asked.

"I think my advice on her love life upset her."

"What kind of advice did you give her?"

"I told her to seduce Neil."

Ashe bellowed with laughter. "Good God, woman! I'd say you're sending two virgins into uncharted waters. How the hell will they know what to do?"

"I think they'll figure it out." When Ashe walked around the desk, Deborah slipped her arms around his neck.

"Annie Laurie and Neil? How long has this been going on? I thought the guy had a thing for you." Ashe pulled her up against him.

"He thinks he has a thing for me. But given the right encouragement, he'll realize Annie Laurie is the only woman for him." Deborah nuzzled the side of Ashe's neck with her nose. "Besides, Annie Laurie's so in love with Neil she can't see straight. A man would have to be a complete fool to reject that kind of love."

The moment she said the words, she wished them back. She tensed in Ashe's arms.

Taking her chin in one hand, he tilted her face. "It's all right, honey. I know you were talking about Neil, but the shoe certainly fit me once, too, didn't it?" He kissed her. Quick. Hard. Passionate. With his forehead resting on hers, he held her close. "I know what a fool I was eleven years ago. I didn't appreciate what I had. I was too young to know what I wanted or needed."

And now? she wanted to ask. Did he know what he wanted and needed now? "We can't change the past. Either of us."

"We aren't a couple of kids anymore, are we, Deborah? We can handle a love affair without either of us getting hurt this time."

"Yes, of course, we can." She nudged him with her hip. "I'm starving. Let's go eat."

NEIL ARRIVED AT six-thirty, late and haggard, fuming about the workmen Deborah had hired to clear away the rubble from the office and fussing at the price their contractor was charging them to repair the damage.

Deborah tried to soothe his ruffled tail feathers, but he calmed very little, even after Deborah assured him their insurance would cover most of the costs.

She finally shooed Neil and Annie Laurie out of the house, suggesting the perfect restaurant for their dinner. When she and Ashe turned to close the front door, they realized Neil couldn't get his car started.

Getting out of his car, Neil walked back toward the house, leaving Annie Laurie waiting patiently in the car.

"I've been having trouble with the darn thing for weeks now, but haven't had time to take it in for a check-up."

"Leave it here." Deborah and Ashe met Neil on the porch steps. "Take my Caddy and you two go on for dinner. Keep it for the night. We'll call the garage in the morning and have them come get your car."

"I couldn't possible take your Cadillac."

"I insist. I'll go get the keys."

When she turned to go inside, Ashe grabbed her by the wrist. "I've got the extra set of keys you gave me." He pulled the keys out of his pocket and tossed them to Neil, who caught them, then almost dropped them from his shaky hand.

"I appreciate this," Neil said. "I'll drive safely."

Ashe and Deborah waved goodbye. Arm in arm, they returned inside to spend the evening with Allen, Miss Carol and Roarke, both of them counting the minutes until bedtime when they could meet at the pool house and make love.

Although the company was pleasant, Ashe wished the time would pass more quickly. He had wanted to drag Deborah off to some secluded spot all day. As the minutes ticked away, he grew more and more restless.

Deborah only partially heard most of what was said during and after dinner, her mind was so completely consumed with Ashe. All she could think about was being alone with him, loving and being loved.

There was no other man like Ashe—not for her. She had always been fascinated by him, even when she'd been a young girl. Indeed, she wondered if his years as a Green Beret hadn't enhanced the very basic male drives that had been born a part of him.

They watched each other, their eyes speaking the words they dared not utter in the presence of others. Deborah had no idea a man could make love to a woman without touching her. Ashe McLaughlin could. And did.

She felt herself growing moist and hot, her body responding to his every glance. She checked her watch for the hundredth time, wishing her mother and Allen would go to bed early. Roarke had excused himself thirty minutes earlier to take a walk around the block as he did each night.

The phone call came three hours after dinner. Ashe took the call, saying very little, but Deborah immediately knew something was terribly wrong.

Ashe replaced the receiver, a solemn expression on his face. His gaze met Deborah's; terror seized her.

"What happened?" she asked.

"There's been an accident," he said.

"What sort of accident?" Carol Vaughn glanced at Allen, who had stopped watching television and looked straight at Ashe.

"A car accident. Neil and Annie Laurie. They've been taken to the hospital in Florence." Ashe's gut instincts told him the car wreck had been no accident. Neil had been driving Deborah's car.

"Oh, dear Lord, no!" Miss Carol clutched her hands together.

"They're both alive. That's all I know." Ashe looked at Deborah. "I think we should go to the hospital immediately."

"Yes, of course we should," she said.

"I'll let Roarke know we're leaving." He turned to Carol. "We'll go by and get Mama Mattie. Pray for them, Miss Carol. Pray for all of us."

Carol nodded, then placed her arm around Allen's shoulders when he started after Ashe and Deborah. "Did somebody do something to Deborah's car? Were they trying to hurt her?" Allen asked.

Ashe halted in the doorway. Deborah rushed over to Allen, pulling him into her arms.

"No, darling, of course not," Deborah kissed Allen's cheek. "Please don't worry about me."

"We don't know what happened," Ashe said. "I'll talk to the police and find out. But Deborah's right. Don't worry about her. I'll take care of her."

Allen hugged Deborah, then released her, waving goodbye as she and Ashe left.

No one, not even Ashe McLaughlin, could make Neil Posey leave Annie Laurie's side, and the doctors allowed him to stay when he told them he was Annie Laurie's fiancé.

When Deborah, Ashe and Mattie Trotter had first arrived at the hospital, Neil had been incoherent, his eyes glazed with tears as he sat holding Annie Laurie's hand. Neil had suffered a few cuts and bruises, but nothing serious. Annie Laurie was unconscious. A concussion, they'd been told. If she came around soon, there should be nothing to worry about; however, if she remained unconscious…

Hour after hour passed without any change in Annie Laurie. Mattie Trotter dozed in the big chair in the corner of the room. Still holding Annie Laurie's hand in his, Neil had laid his head on the side of her bed.

Easing open the door, Ashe glanced around the room, saw his grandmother and Neil sleeping and Deborah looking out the window, watching the sunrise. He set the cardboard carton containing disposable coffee cups on the meal tray, removed the lids from two cups, picked them up and walked over to Deborah.

"Thanks." Deborah took the coffee. "A few more minutes and you would have found me in the other chair over there asleep, too."

"Why the hell doesn't she wake up?" Ashe squeezed the cup he held, pressing a bit of the dark liquid over the edge and onto his hand. "Damn! Good thing this stuff isn't very hot."

"I wish we knew exactly what caused the wreck. I can't believe a careful driver like Neil would have simply lost control of the car." Deborah sipped her coffee.

"Thank God they were both wearing their seat belts. If that pole hadn't crashed through the windshield and sideswiped Annie Laurie on the side of her head, she'd be okay." Ashe drank half his cup of coffee, then set the container down on the windowsill.

"I keep wondering what caused the accident. Neil is such a careful driver. He said the brakes didn't work, that coming off the hill on Court Street, he realized he couldn't slow down, couldn't stop."

"I think he probably panicked," Ashe said. "He realized he was going to slam into the back end of the car in front of him and possibly cause a pileup, so he tried to take the car off the road."

"I have my car serviced often. There's no reason the brakes shouldn't have worked." Deborah clutched her coffee cup in both hands.

"We both know there's a good chance someone tampered with your Caddy." Ashe balled his hands into fists. All night he had fought the desire to smash heads together, to run out of the hospital and hunt down Buck Stansell. But he would wait. Wait until he knew for sure.

A tall, skinny nurse walked into the room. Covering her lips with her index finger, she signaled Deborah and Ashe to be quiet. Silently she went about her business, checking on Annie Laurie, then nodding goodbye as she left.

"Are you hungry?" Ashe asked. "We could go down for breakfast soon."

"Let's wait awhile, until Mama Mattie wakes up. She needs some rest."

A soft knock sounded at the door. Ashe walked over and opened the door a fraction. Detective Morrow, from the Florence police, stood in the hallway.

"Could I speak to you, Mr. McLaughlin? The chief said to let you know what we've found out. He's talked to Chief Burton over in Sheffield and also to Sheriff Blaylock. They both said to fill you in."

Ashe stepped into the hallway, closing the door behind him. "Let's have it."

"The wreck wasn't an accident. Ms. Vaughn's Cadillac had been tampered with. There was no brake fluid. It had all leaked out. Looks like somebody intended for Ms. Vaughn to wreck her car."

Deborah stood with the door cracked enough to overhear what the detective said. Biting down on her bottom lip, she closed her eyes and said a silent prayer. A prayer to end this madness, to keep those she loved safe.

Ashe thanked Detective Morrow. "I'd like to see a copy of your mechanic's complete report as soon as possible." He shook hands with the policeman, then glanced at Deborah.

She opened the door, walked over to Ashe and tilted her chin defiantly. "So now we know for sure."

"Yeah, we know Buck isn't through playing games, and the games are getting more and more deadly." Ashe looked at her, his eyes hard, his face tense. "I think it's time ol' Buck and I have a little talk. Face-to-face."

"No, Ashe. Please." Deborah grabbed him by the arm. "You can't go off alone and confront a man like Buck Stansell. He could have you murdered on the spot."

"Yeah, he could, but he won't." Ashe put his arm around Deborah, hugging her to his side. "You forget that I know Buck and his kind. He's had me checked out thoroughly and he isn't about to bring down any more investigations on him and his boys right now. Lon Sparks has kept his mouth shut, but there isn't any doubt who was behind Looney's murder."

"But Ashe, you should let the police handle Buck Stansell. Talk to Charlie Blaylock. Let him talk to Buck."

"Honey, you don't understand. There is nothing to link your car's brake failure to Buck Stansell. Sheriff Blaylock has no legal reason to question Buck." He kissed Deborah quickly, then gave her a gentle shove away from him. "I don't need a legal reason. Your safety is the only reason I need. If I don't hunt Buck down after what happened with your car last night, he'll be wondering why."

Mama Mattie rushed out the door, waving her hands and laughing. "She's awake. She's talking to Neil. Come see. Oh, thank you Lord, she's all right!"

Deborah and Ashe went inside, stopping at the foot of Annie Laurie's bed. Sitting on the side of the bed, Neil held Annie Laurie in his arms, tears streaming down his face.

"Guess what?" Annie Laurie smiled, her bruised face beaming. "Neil just told me that he and I are going to get married."

Everyone laughed. Mama Mattie fluffed Annie Laurie's pillow, then went around the room hugging everyone.

Neil glanced at Deborah and smiled. "Funny how it takes something like this to make a man realize who he loves and how much he loves her."

"I think this is wonderful," Deborah said. "As soon as Annie Laurie is out of this dreadful place, we'll start planning an engagement party."

"Well, I think first we need to let the nurses know that Annie Laurie has regained consciousness," Ashe said. "The doctors will want to examine her."

"I'll go with you." Deborah gave Annie Laurie and Neil loving hugs, then put her arm around Mama Mattie's waist. "Why don't we leave these two alone until the doctors storm in here? We could go have breakfast."

"Sounds good to me."

Mattie followed Ashe and Deborah out into the hallway. After stopping by the nurses' station to alert the staff that Annie Laurie was conscious, the three headed for the elevators. The elevator doors opened and Roarke stepped out, Carol and Allen at his side.

"Mother! Allen! What are y'all doing here?"

Ashe eyed Roarke, who nodded toward Allen, but didn't say anything.

"Allen has been frantic," Carol said. "None of us got any rest last night. He's convinced himself that someone tampered with your car, that you aren't safe."

Deborah drew Allen into her arms, hugging him with fierce motherly protectiveness. "Oh, darling, Ashe isn't going to let anybody hurt me."

Pulling out of Deborah's arms, Allen turned to Ashe. "They think I'm nothing but a baby. They won't tell me the truth. But you will, won't you, Ashe?"

Everyone moved away from the elevators and into the hallway. Deborah held her breath. Ashe knelt on one knee and put his hand on Allen's shoulder.

"Somebody tampered with the brakes on Deborah's car. They wanted to hurt her. But she's okay. And so is Neil and Annie Laurie."

"But what if Deborah had been driving the car, what if—" Allen beat his fists against Ashe's chest. "I hate Buck Stansell. I'd like to tell him what I think of him. I'd tell him if he hurts Deborah, I'll kill him!"

Ashe drew Allen into his arms. Deborah's eyes glazed with tears, but she saw the look in her mother's eyes, the look that said *He's his father's son. End this lie. Tell Ashe the truth.*

"That's exactly what I'm going to do, go see Buck Stansell." Ashe patted Allen on the back, then stood and looked at Roarke. "You take care of things for me. I have to go talk to a man about revenge."

"No, Ashe!" Deborah reached for Ashe, but Roarke grabbed her, physically restraining her while Ashe entered the elevator and punched the Down button.

ASHE CAUGHT LEE ROY and Johnny Joe just as they were leaving. He pulled his car up in the drive, blocking their departure. Both men stayed in their vehicle when Ashe got out and walked over to them. Lee Roy stepped out of his car and faced Ashe.

"You're out bright and early, cousin." Lee Roy grinned, the look on his face as innocent as a newborn baby's.

"I've been up all night." Ashe stood several feet away, his gaze focused on Lee Roy.

"I'm surprised you'd leave your woman alone, even to pay a visit on your relatives."

"This isn't a social call."

"Yeah, I figured as much."

"I want to see Buck. I don't think sending him another message can get my point across like a personal visit."

Johnny Joe opened the passenger-side door, got out and placed his elbows on top of the car. "We heard about that wreck last night. Sure was a shame. Guess Miss Deborah Vaughn was lucky she loaned her car out to somebody else."

"Annie Laurie is family." Ashe didn't move a muscle, didn't even glance Johnny Joe's way. "Lucky for everyone involved, she's going to be all right."

"We wouldn't want to see Annie Laurie come to no harm." Lee Roy grunted. "Hell, we've always been fond of that girl, even though she's no blood kin to us, her being on your mama's side of the family and all."

"I want to see Buck," Ashe repeated. "Today."

"Well, Buck's a busy man," Lee Roy said. "It'll take time to arrange things. You understand."

"Then you get things arranged."

"Buck'll be agreeable to seeing you. He ain't got nothing but the best to say about you, you know. He respects you. And he wouldn't have allowed nothing really bad to happen to your woman."

"Bad things *are* happening. If he's seeking revenge against Deborah for testifying, then he'd better think again. Revenge works both ways."

"Hellfire, Ashe, Buck ain't no fool. He might have given orders to throw a scare into Deborah Vaughn, just for the principle of it, you know. But Lon Sparks ain't nothing but a speck of dirt on Buck's shoe. Not worth the trouble. Buck don't want to cross you."

"I need to hear Buck say that." Ashe turned, walked over to his rental car and opened the door. His gaze focused on the ground, Ashe laid one hand against the side window. "I'll be back this evening, around six. Tell Buck I won't wait any longer than that."

Johnny Joe jerked a .38 revolver out of the back of his belt, aimed it just to the left of Ashe and fired, hitting a nearby tree limb. Ashe didn't blink an eye.

"God a'mighty," Johnny Joe said. "Did you see that? He didn't move!"

"You damned fool." Lee Roy shook his head. "Sorry about that, Ashe. You know Johnny Joe ain't never had a lick of sense."

Ashe looked up and grinned. "Being foolhardy runs in the family, doesn't it? Remind Buck of that inherited trait. Tell him that when it comes to defending my own, I'm not much concerned with the consequences, just the results."

"Ain't nobody in our gang been behind what's happened to your woman since the trial ended," Lee Roy said. "I know you ain't going to believe me, but I'll warn you that you'd better start looking elsewhere. There's somebody else wanting to see Deborah Vaughn dead. It ain't none of us. You'd better start checking out some of her highfalutin friends and relatives. See who's got something to gain if she dies."

"I'll keep that in mind." Ashe slid behind the wheel of his rented car. "I'll be back at six."

CHAPTER THIRTEEN

ASHE PARKED OUTSIDE the Sweet Nothings club, a huge blue metal building. From where he sat inside his car, he heard the loud, lonely wail of a guitar. So this was Evie Lovelady's place, huh? Ashe's old teenage girlfriend was now Buck Stansell's private property.

Lee Roy had told Ashe that meeting with Buck would clear up everything and show Ashe that none of *their* bunch was responsible for Deborah's most recent misfortunes. Ashe hadn't mentioned anything to Deborah about Lee Roy's insinuations that someone other than Buck Stansell might have reasons for wanting her dead. She'd been through enough in the last couple of months to last a lifetime, and now Miss Carol faced a second surgery for cancer. There was no point in worrying Deborah with something until he was absolutely sure.

Ashe got out, locked his car and entered the nightspot. Typical Southern honky-tonk. Nothing more. Nothing less. Loud music. Smoky air. Fun-loving rednecks and good old girls ready for a hot time on the town. A country band belted out the latest heartbreaking tunes.

Ashe glanced around, looking for the right person to ask about Buck Stansell. A tall, willowy brunette approached him.

"Long time no see, stranger." Evie slid her arm around Ashe's waist, dropping one hand to cup his buttock. She gave him a quick little squeeze, released him and laughed. "Tight as ever."

"You're looking good, Evie. How've you been?" Ashe

grinned at his old girlfriend, one he and Lee Roy had both dated. The scent of her expensive perfume overwhelmed him. Damn, had she taken a bath in the stuff?

"I've been just fine, sugar. Got my own business now, and I hooked me the top dog in these parts." She held up her left hand, showing Ashe the three-carat diamond on her finger. "Of course, I haven't forgotten old friends and our good times together."

"Yeah, we had some good times, didn't we," Ashe said. "But we were just kids fooling around. We're grown up now and life's not fun and games anymore."

"Come on, sugar." Keeping her arm around Ashe's waist, Evie nudged him with her hip. "Let me get you a drink."

"I didn't come here to drink. I came to see Buck."

"Yeah, I know. He's waiting in back for you. I just wanted to be friendly and make you feel welcome, let you know I hadn't forgotten what good friends we used to be."

Ashe followed Evie around the edges of the enormous room, past the dance floor and down a narrow corridor. "You were friends with a lot of guys, before me and after me."

"You're right about that," she said. "I used to be a real good-time girl. Now I'm a one-man woman. And Buck's that man."

"Lucky Buck."

Evie smiled. She was almost pretty, Ashe thought. Her eyes were too big, her lips too thin and her cheeks scarred by teen acne, scars she covered with heavy layers of makeup.

"He's waiting on you." Evie opened the last door on the left. "Just remember that Buck thinks of you as family. Your old man and his were tight." She crossed her index and middle fingers. "He's not going to lie to you. If your woman was marked, he'd tell you."

Ashe looked straight into Evie's eyes and knew she believed what she'd told him. Hell, maybe she was right. These men, men like his father and uncle and cousins, might be thieves, drug dealers and murderers, but they did adhere to a certain code of behavior when it came to their own people. And it was possible that they still considered Ashe one of their own.

"Take care of yourself, Evie." Ashe kissed her on the cheek.

She punched him playfully on the arm, stuck her head inside the office and waved at her husband. "Ashe is here, sugar."

Ashe entered Buck's private domain. Evie closed the door, leaving Ashe alone with the man he'd come to question. The man he'd come to warn. The man he would have to kill if all else failed.

"Come on in, Ashe." Buck Stansell pushed back his big black velvet chair and stood. Tall and husky, with a thick mustache and the beginnings of a beer belly, Buck looked every inch the successful no-class gentleman with money that he was. "You haven't got a drink. Didn't Evie offer you something?"

"She offered," Ashe said.

"Evie's still looking good, isn't she? She's held up well. You know she's thirty-five and had three kids. Two of 'em mine." Buck's loud, hardy laughter filled the room.

"Yeah, Evie looks good."

"She's having herself the time of her life running this place. Named it herself. Sweet Nothings. I try to keep her happy. We do that, don't we, Ashe, try to keep our women happy?"

"And safe." Ashe glanced around the office. Expensive bad taste. Money could buy just about everything except good breeding and an innate sense of style.

"That goes without saying." Buck walked around the huge, ornate desk and sat down on the edge. "I had to put a scare into Deborah Vaughn before Lon was convicted. Had to keep up appearances and let Lon think I was doing what I could for him."

"You never meant to harm Deborah or her family?" Ashe asked.

"To be honest with you, I did consider having her taken care of, but once you showed up, I had second thoughts. Lon Sparks is small potatoes. An idiot who made the mistake of doing his business in front of a witness. Guess I should have just gotten rid of him. It might have been easier, but I have a reputation for taking care of my own. You understand how it is?"

"You want me to believe that you're not after Deborah for revenge."

"Why should I need revenge? Lon hasn't got the guts to double-cross me. Besides, he trusts me more than he does the law. He knows I'll keep my promises, one way or the other. He'd rather do time in the pen than spend the rest of his life looking over his shoulder, wondering what day might be his last. As long as he's in prison and keeps his mouth shut, he stays alive. He knows how things work. And he understands I've done all I intend to do on his behalf."

"Since the trial ended, the Vaughns' garage was set on fire, a gunman destroyed the front of Vaughn & Posey Realty and somebody tampered with the brakes on Deborah's Cadillac." Ashe stood, his legs slightly apart, his arms at his sides, his jacket hanging open. "If you want me to believe you had nothing to do with these incidents, then you're going to have to prove it to me."

"Look, old friend, I've given you some leeway because of who your daddy was, because of the man you've become, but I can be pushed only so far."

"I haven't even begun to push you, Buck, if you have any plans to kill Deborah. There are only a few things in this world worth killing for and even fewer worth dying for. To me, Deborah Vaughn is both. Do you understand?"

"I understood just fine when Lee Roy told me that she was your woman." Buck rose off the edge of his desk, straightened the jacket of his three-piece gray pinstriped suit, and ran his hand across the top of his head, smoothing the strands of his slick, brown hair.

"All right, let's say I believe you. If you're telling the truth, then someone else has put out a contract on Deborah. Who?"

"I don't know anything about a contract, but…for a friend, I could find out."

"For a friend?" Ashe wasn't sure what to believe, but his gut instincts told him that he just might have to trust Buck Stansell. "Okay, Buck, old friend. Although the local and state authorities may be interested in your illegal dealings, my only concern is Deborah Vaughn. As long as she's safe, I have no reason to cause you any grief."

"You give me your word and I'll give you mine." Buck stuck out his broad, square hand, each finger sporting an expensive ring.

"As long as Deborah and her family are safe, you have nothing to fear from me," Ashe said.

"You stay out of my business and, as proof of my innocence and a show of my friendship, I'll make some inquiries and find out who's behind Deborah Vaughn's recent problems."

Ashe took Buck's hand, exchanging a powerful, macho shake, sealing a deal with the devil, a deal to keep Deborah safe. Ashe knew only too well the kind of man Buck Stansell was, the kind of man his own father had been. Among these redneck hooligans there was a certain code of honor, so Ashe was willing to give Buck the benefit of the doubt. For the time being.

He knew better than to trust Buck completely, knew he'd better watch his back. If Buck thought Ashe posed a threat to his organization, his old friend would have no qualms about killing him. A guy like Buck might even ask Lee Roy to do the job for him, and get some sort of perverse pleasure from seeing which cousin would come out alive.

No, Ashe trusted Buck Stansell only so far. Now wasn't the time to bring the man down. He'd leave that to the authorities. Unless Buck lied to him. Then he'd take care of Buck himself.

ASHE MADE SEVERAL calls after he left the Sweet Nothings club, one to Sam Dundee to ask him to initiate an investigation of the people in Deborah's life, those who might benefit from her death. Buck Stansell could be lying about his innocence in the garage fire, the drive-by shooting, and the brakes tampering. If he was telling the truth, then someone else had a motive; someone else wanted Deborah out of the way. But who? And why?

He spoke with the Florence police again, then met with Sheriff Blaylock and Sheffield police chief Ed Burton. He couldn't fault the local authorities. They'd done their jobs the best they could. Ashe especially liked Burton. He respected the man. The two of them had spent the past few hours going over all the leads, all the possibilities.

Ashe had expected the entire Vaughn household to be in bed when he arrived; after all, it was nearly eleven. Tapping in the numbers for the security alarm at the back of the house, Ashe unlocked and opened the door. Only the tiny night-light on the refrigerator's ice and water dispenser burned, creating a dim glow in the room.

Wearing a floor-length maroon red robe, Deborah stood in his path, blocking him from entering. Dear God, she looked good enough to eat, all soft and silky, lush and delicious. His first instinct was to reach out and grab her.

"I thought you'd be in bed." He took a step inside the kitchen. Deborah stood right in front of him, not moving an inch. "You didn't get any sleep last night. You should be resting, honey."

"How am I supposed to rest with you out till nearly midnight? Allen asked about you at supper and Mother's been worried."

What was this? She was fit to be tied. What was her problem? He didn't want to argue; he wanted to make love.

"Before I left, I told you I wouldn't be in until late." When he reached out to take her by the shoulders and draw her into his arms, she backed away from him, her blue eyes cold, their expression daring him to touch her.

"I had business to take care of," he said. "The business of keeping you safe, of making sure nothing happens to you or Allen or Miss Carol."

"Roarke was protecting us. Just what were you doing?"

"What the hell's wrong with you, Deborah? Why are you so angry?"

"I'm not angry." He took several steps toward her; she backed farther and farther away. "I was worried. You left here to go see Buck Stansell. You told us you'd be late, but you've been gone nearly five hours. For all I knew, you'd been killed or—"

Ashe charged across the room, drew her into his arms and held her close. "I'm fine, honey. You shouldn't have worried about me. I told you that I know how to handle Buck Stansell and his type."

Hell, she'd been worried about him. He should have called to let her know he was all right. But he wasn't used to having anyone worry about him.

Deborah clung to Ashe, running her hands up and down his arms, clutching him as she laid her head on his chest. She knew she was acting irrationally, but she couldn't help herself. With each passing minute that she had waited for Ashe, she'd grown more tense, more worried, more concerned that Buck Stansell might have killed him.

Smelling his jacket, she jerked her head up and looked at him, then pulled out of his arms. He'd been with a woman, someone who bathed in her perfume.

Deborah glared at him, her small hands tightening into fists. She'd been worried sick about him and he'd been with another woman! Damn him! She'd been a fool to trust Ashe McLaughlin, to believe she was the only woman in his life.

"You smell like a very expensive French whore!"

Ashe laughed. "Actually, I smell like a fairly cheap Alabama whore."

He had left the house hours ago, on a mission to confront Buck Stansell. She'd been half out of her mind with worry. When hours passed and he didn't return, didn't call, she had imagined all sorts of terrible things, but she certainly hadn't thought that he was with another woman.

"I've spent the last two hours crazy with worry, scared to death that something had happened to you, and you've been with some woman!"

Ashe covered his mouth to conceal his chuckle. He'd never seen Deborah this jealous, not even over Whitney. Did she honestly think that he'd been fooling around with someone else? Didn't she realize that he couldn't see anyone except her, that she was the only woman he wanted, that thoughts of her filled his every waking moment?

"Don't you dare stand there and laugh about it!"

"Your life is in danger," Ashe said. "There could be a contract out on you and what are you worried about? You're worried about whether or not I've been out messing around with another woman."

Dammit, he couldn't believe this! She honestly thought he'd touch another woman when he could have her.

"I don't care who you…you…mess around with!"

Ashe came toward her, taking slow, determined steps. He shoved Deborah against the kitchen wall, then braced his hands on each side of her head. "I'm only going to say this once, so listen very carefully. I have not been having sex with another woman. I don't want or need another woman. There has been no one else in my life since the day I came back to Sheffield."

Deborah's breasts rose and fell with her labored breathing. She stared Ashe right in the eye, her gaze hard, her lips trembling, her cheeks flushed. "Then I suppose what I smell on you is some sort of new aftershave."

Ashe leaned down, touching her lips with his. When she turned her head, he reached out and grabbed her chin in his hand, forcing her to face him. "What you smell is Evie

Lovelady's perfume. She wrapped herself around me when I arrived at the Sweet Nothings club tonight to meet with Buck."

"Evie Lovelady?" Deborah spat the woman's name out between clenched teeth. "You and she used to be quite an item if I recall correctly."

"Evie and most of the guys I hung out with used to be an item. Now she's a happily married woman with three kids. She's Buck's wife."

"So you had to get reacquainted with Evie before your meeting with Buck Stansell." Deborah tried to pull out of Ashe's grip. He leaned forward, trapping her against the wall with his body. "Let me go. I've had enough!"

Ashe rubbed his body against Deborah's, then released his hold on her chin, only to pull her into his arms. "I had no idea I'd come home to this. A jealous woman ready to scratch out my eyes."

"I'm not jealous. I have no reason to be, do I? We haven't made a commitment to each other. We haven't promised each other anything." She couldn't bear having him this close, his hard body pressed intimately against her, his arms holding her tightly. "Just let me go, Ashe. I'm tired and I need some rest. Unless Buck Stansell confessed to trying to kill me and has promised to leave me alone, I think any discussion about your visit with him can wait till morning."

Her jealousy aroused him as much as it irritated and amused him. He had no intention of letting her go to bed angry and hurt and filled with jealous rage.

Ashe lowered his hands to her buttocks, lifting her up and against his arousal. "I've been with Ed Burton for the last couple of hours, discussing my visit with Buck and going over the best way to end this nightmare for you and your family."

"You've been with the police?" She gasped when he began inching her robe and gown upward, gathering more and more of the material in his hands.

He hadn't been in bed with Evie Lovelady. He hadn't been

enjoying himself with another woman while she sat at home worrying about him. She should have trusted Ashe. She should have known he wouldn't betray her.

"Buck claims he ended his harassment of you when Lon Sparks was convicted. He says someone else is after you." Ashe buried his face against her neck, nibbling, licking, kissing.

She squirmed in his arms. "You—you don't believe him, do—do you?" She could hardly breathe. The blood rushed to her head, her knees weakened, her body moistened.

"I'm not sure."

He reached under the bunched material he held against her buttocks and stroked her tenderly, then ran his hand up her back, loosening the tie belt of her robe. Nuzzling her soft flesh with his nose, he parted the robe in front, uncovering the rise of her breasts exposed by the low-cut nightgown. He took her tight nipple in his mouth, biting her gently through the maroon silk and ecru lace bodice. Deborah moaned with sweet pleasure.

He wanted her. Wanted her bad. He hurt with the need to take her. Here. Now. Hard and fast.

"We'll discuss this tomorrow," he said, his breath ragged. If he didn't take her soon, he'd die.

"Tomorrow," she agreed, reaching for his jacket, tugging it off his shoulders.

He covered her mouth, thrusting his tongue inside. She clung to his arms, holding onto his jacket sleeves, which she'd managed to bring down to his elbows. He shrugged out of the jacket, letting it fall to the floor. Deborah unbuttoned his shirt, quickly, ripping off the last two buttons in her haste. Ashe removed her silk robe, then pulled her gown down to her waist. He teased her aching nipples with the tips of his fingers. Closing her eyes, she threw her head back and sighed, deep in her throat.

"Deborah," he moaned her name. "Honey…how I want you."

She reached out to touch his chest, moving her hand back and forth from one pebble-hard nipple to the other, curling her fingers in his hair. Lowering her head, she licked one nipple and then the other. She stroked his shoulder holster, then reached around and under his shirt to caress his back, her nails biting into his flesh as she urged him to take her.

Clutching the sides of her gown, he eased it down her hips. It fell into a dark red circle at her feet. He lifted her breasts in his hands, as if testing their weight, then put his mouth on her, suckling her while she unbuckled his belt and lowered his zipper.

Deborah clung to his shoulder, her body aching with desperate need. Her breasts felt heavy, almost painful. Her body clenched and released, dampening, throbbing, ready for the ultimate pleasure.

When Ashe touched her most sensitive spot, she cried out, then covered her mouth with her hand, realizing she should be quiet. Somewhere in the back of her desire-crazed mind, she knew they were not alone in the house, that they were insane for taking such a risk.

He took her hand and placed it around him, telling her without words what he wanted. They stroked and petted each other, then Ashe removed her sheathing hand and whipped her around to face the wall. She shivered. He lifted her hair off her neck and kissed her, then covered her shoulders and back with kisses and stinging little nips which he followed with moist tongue caresses.

When he dropped to his knees behind her, Deborah squirmed and tried to turn around. He held her in place, his hand parting her thighs, his fingers seeking and finding the secret heart of her femininity. All the while he fondled her, he lavished attention on her buttocks, kissing every inch of her sweet, womanly flesh.

Deborah became wild with her need, pleading in soft, almost incoherent words for him to end the torture and take her. When he turned her to face him, she grasped his shoulders and urged him to stand. Instead, he buried his face against her stomach, then nuzzled her intimately and spread her thighs farther apart. While his mouth brought her to the brink of fulfillment, his hands tormented her nipples.

The moment she fell apart, shattering her into a thousand pieces as if she'd been a glass doll, Ashe lifted her in his arms, carried her a few steps over to the kitchen table and set her down. Before she had a chance to catch her breath, he parted her thighs and plunged into her. He filled her completely. The aftershocks of her first release surged within her, gripping him as he invaded her hard and fast, with a fury born of a desire he could not control. The tension built again, higher and higher, and Deborah clung to him. He groaned, then shook from head to toe as he thrust into her one last time, emptying himself as unbearable pleasure claimed them both.

They kissed, again and again. He left her on the table while he picked up their scattered clothes. Her gown and robe. His jacket. Tossing the items over his arm, he lifted her and carried her out of the kitchen, down the hall and up the stairs.

He deposited her in her bed, kissed her on the tip of her nose and looked into her blue, blue eyes.

"Stay the night with me." She clung to him, her arms still draped around his neck.

"And what if Miss Carol or Allen find me in here in the morning?"

"Lock the door."

He smiled and nodded his head. "I'll go back to my room before daylight."

He tossed their clothes on the foot of the bed, pulled out of her embrace and locked the bedroom door. Returning to her side, Ashe lay down and took her into his arms. Tomorrow he would tell her about his meeting with Buck Stansell. Tomorrow they would discuss the possibility that someone else might have a reason to want her dead. But tonight they would keep the rest of the world at bay, they would forget everything and everyone except each other.

He could think of nothing but making love to her all night long, taking her again and again, hearing her wild little cries of pleasure and the way she repeated his name.

For now, this heady, wild passion would be enough. And now was all that mattered.

CHAPTER FOURTEEN

DEBORAH SAT IN the hospital waiting room, her head resting on Ashe's shoulder, her eyes closed as she ended a prayer pleading with God to spare her mother's life and keep them all safe and well. The doctors had warned them after the first surgery that, although they had every reason to believe all the malignant tissue had been removed, there was always a chance the cancer could return. Now they faced a second cancer, a second surgery.

As if her mother's life hanging in the balance wasn't enough to worry about, Deborah now had to face the possibility that someone other than Buck Stansell was behind the recent threats on her life. Ashe had told her that he had considered waiting until after her mother's surgery before burdening her with Buck's denials and accusations. But with her life, and possibly Allen's, in danger from an unknown source, Ashe felt it necessary she be informed.

Ashe. Ashe. He was like a tower of strength, an endless source of comfort and protection. She could not imagine her life without him. She loved him more now than she ever had, and he had become such an integral part of her life, of all their lives, especially Allen's.

Allen hero-worshiped Ashe, adored him the way so many ten-year-olds adored their fathers. But neither Ashe nor Allen knew their true relationship, and Deborah's guilt at keeping the truth from them ate away at her conscience and broke her heart by slow degrees.

"Ms. Vaughn?" Missy Jenkins, a young LPN for whom

Deborah had found a house a few months earlier, stood in the waiting-room doorway.

"May we see Mother now?" Deborah asked.

"Yes. She'll be going in to surgery in about thirty-five minutes, if the doctor's schedule doesn't change." Missy's smile made her rather homely face brighten to a certain degree of cuteness. "She'll be getting groggy soon, so you'd better go on in."

Ashe stood, assisted Deborah to her feet and kept his arm around her waist as they walked down the hall. Deborah eased open the door to Carol's private room. Her mother looked so thin and pale lying there on pristine white sheets, an IV connected to her arm.

Carol opened her eyes and smiled. "Good morning, my dears. Come in. They've given me something and I'll be a babbling idiot soon."

Ashe stood beside Deborah, who leaned down and hugged her mother gently, kissing her forehead. "Roarke is bringing Allen by before he takes him to school. I expect they'll be here any minute."

"Such a precious child," Carol said. "So much like you, Deborah."

"Yes, Mother."

"Ashe, thank you for coming back to Sheffield, for keeping watch over us, for bringing Roarke here to help you." Carol closed her eyes, then reopened them, focusing her gaze on Deborah. "I want to talk to you while I still can. I want you to promise me that—"

"Mother, this can wait until you're feeling better." Deborah patted Carol's hand.

"Ashe, would you mind leaving us alone for a few minutes." Carol glanced over her daughter's shoulder at the big man standing guard. "Mother-daughter talk. You understand?"

Ashe squeezed Deborah's shoulder. "I'll be in the waiting room. As soon as Allen arrives, I'll bring him down here."

The moment Ashe closed the door behind him, Carol Vaughn looked up at Deborah. "I may not live through this surgery, and if I don't—"

"Mother, please, you mustn't talk this way."

Carol held up a hand in restraint. "Hush up. We both know there's a chance that the cancer has spread this time."

"We have to be optimistic, to think only positive thoughts."

"And we shall do just that, but…I want you to promise me you'll tell Ashe the truth about Allen."

"Mother, please…please, don't ask that of me. Not now. Not this way."

Carol gripped Deborah's hand with an amazing amount of strength. "Must I beg you to do this? I begged your father, years ago, not to make us all live a lie. If I had been stronger and stood up to him, none of us would be faced with this dilemma now."

"I'm in love with Ashe. We're lovers. I keep telling myself that he won't leave me this time, that he cares enough to stay. But I'm not sure how he really feels about me, so how can I tell him that I gave birth to his child over ten years ago and have kept that child from him? What if Ashe hates me?"

"Ashe cares deeply for you. He always did." Carol motioned for Deborah to come into her arms.

Deborah cuddled close to her mother's comforting body, careful not to bear her weight on Carol's thin frame. "What if I tell Ashe the truth and he tells Allen?"

"I don't think Ashe will tell Allen. Not now." Carol stroked Deborah's hair, petting her in a loving, motherly fashion. "But you must tell Ashe. Tell him now. Don't wait. Do this for me. Consider it a last request."

"Mother!" Deborah jerked away from Carol, tears filling her eyes. "Please, don't ask this of me."

"I am asking," Carol said. "Tell Ashe that he is Allen's father. Tell him today."

"I can't!" Deborah turned away from her mother, tears trickling down her cheeks. She swatted them away with the tips of her fingers.

"You must tell him, Deborah. If you don't, Mattie will. She won't continue keeping our secret. And someday, you and Ashe must tell Allen the truth. He has a right to know."

Deborah swallowed her tears. Her mother was right. The lie had gone on long enough. It was one thing to keep the truth from Ashe when he wasn't a part of their lives, but now that he had come to mean so much to Allen, now that she had fallen in love with him all over again, it was wrong to keep the truth from him.

"I promise I'll tell him," Deborah said.

"Today?"

"Yes. Today."

At that precise moment Ashe knocked twice, opened the door and escorted Allen into Carol's room. Ashe glanced at Miss Carol, then at Deborah's tear-stained face. His eyes questioned her silently. She shook her head, saying "Not now," and went over to stand by Allen at her mother's bedside.

ASHE WASN'T A man who prayed often, and most people wouldn't call his supplications to a higher power prayers. He wasn't a religious man, wasn't a churchgoer, but he'd been in enough tight situations to know that even the unbelievers called on God for help when all else failed.

Ashe felt a bit out of place in this small hospital chapel. He could remember the last time he'd been in a house of worship. It was a funeral. Another soldier who hadn't made it back to the U.S. alive. A friend whose body had been shipped home.

He knew Deborah was having a difficult time dealing with her mother's surgery and the threats on her own life. It infuriated him that he could do so little to make things easier for her. At the moment, he felt helpless. He might be able to stand between her and danger, to protect her physically, but he hated being unable to defend her against her own fear and sadness.

Miss Carol's condition was in God's hands; all any of them could do was pray and hope for the best. But the continued threats on Deborah's life were another matter. It shouldn't take Sam long to get the information he needed—who besides Buck Stansell had reason to threaten Deborah? Who had something to gain from her death?

Neil Posey was her partner, owning less than forty percent of the business. But what would he have to gain from Deborah's death? And what about Whitney? Did she stand to inherit anything from Deborah? Deborah had told him that Allen and her mother were her beneficiaries.

Maybe Buck had been lying, covering his tracks, knowing Ashe would have no qualms about coming after him if he thought Buck was responsible for harming Deborah.

Ashe looked at her, sitting several feet away from where he stood. Her shoulders trembled. He knew she was crying. They had come into the chapel nearly fifteen minutes ago, and Deborah didn't seem ready to leave yet. Maybe she found some sort of solace here. He hoped she did. He'd do anything, bear any burden, pay any price, to ease her pain.

When she stood, her head still bowed, Ashe walked up behind her, draping his arms around her. She leaned back onto his chest, bracing her head against him, folding her arms over his where they crossed her body.

She smelled so sweet, so fresh and feminine, such a contrast to the medicinal odors that mixed with the strong cleaning solutions in the hospital corridors.

"Miss Carol is going to be all right, honey. You've got to hang on to your faith." Ashe kissed her cheek.

"You can't imagine how close Mother and I are. How much we've shared. How we've depended on each other completely since Daddy died." Closing her eyes, Deborah bit down on her lower lip. She could not put off telling Ashe the truth about Allen any longer. She had promised her mother.

"We're all going to come out of this just fine. Miss Carol is a fighter. She's not going to let the cancer win. And I'm going to make sure y'all are safe." Ashe hugged her fiercely, as if holding her securely in his arms could keep the evil away. "I'm going to find out who's behind the threats and end this nightmare you've been living. After that, you and I have some decisions to make."

Deborah's heart skipped a beat. This was the first time Ashe had even hinted at the possibility they might have a future together. Would he feel differently about her, about their future, once she told him Allen was his son?

"Ashe?"

"Hmm-hmm?"

She pulled away from him enough to turn around in his arms and face him. He placed his hands on both sides of her waist. She looked into his warm hazel eyes, seeing plainly the care and concern he felt.

"Let's go to the back of the room and sit. Please. I have something to tell you. Something to explain."

"What is it, honey?" The pleading tone of her voice unnerved him. He sensed her withdrawal from him even though they were still physically connected. The emotional fear he noted on her face scared the hell out of him. "Deborah?"

She took his hand and led him to chairs in the back of the small chapel. They sat side by side. She wanted to continue holding his hand, to keep the physical contact unbroken, but she wasn't sure she could even look at him when she told him the truth.

Her heartbeat grew louder and louder; she was surprised he couldn't hear its wild thumping. Bracing her back against the chair, she took a deep breath.

"Deborah, are you all right?" She had turned pale, her eyes darkening with what he sensed was fear.

"This isn't easy for me, so please bear with me. Let me tell you what I must without your questioning me. Not until I've said it all. All right?"

Ashe reached for her. Shuddering, she cringed, holding both hands before her in a warning not to touch her. "Deborah, what's going on? I'm totally confused."

"Please remember that I didn't know what Daddy did to you eleven years ago." She took another deep breath. "I thought you'd left town on your own, that you washed your hands of me and..."

"We've been over this already," Ashe said. "I don't see any need to rehash it."

Under different circumstances, there would be no need. If she hadn't gotten pregnant the night they'd made love eleven years ago. If she hadn't given birth to his son. If she hadn't kept Allen's identity a secret.

Dear God, did she have the courage to tell him? Could she make him understand? Ashe McLaughlin was a possessive, protective male, one who would proclaim his fatherhood to the world. If she had ever doubted the deep, primeval urges within him, she knew now, only too well, that the man she loved was a man to be reckoned with, a man whose strength was feared and respected by others.

If only she knew how he truly felt about her. If he loved her, if...

"Please, Ashe, listen to me. A couple of months after that night...our one night together...I—I..."

A tight knot of fear twisted in his gut. "You what?"

"I discovered that I was—" she died a little inside "—pregnant."

God, no! No! He did not want to hear this. He couldn't handle the truth. He didn't want to know that Deborah had lied to him. The one woman on earth he'd thought he could trust.

"What did you do when you found out you were pregnant?" he asked, a deadly numb spreading through his body.

Already his voice had grown cold. How distant would he become when he'd heard the complete truth? "I went to Mother. That's the reason she told Daddy. After you left town, Daddy said that I was better off without you, that he and Mother would take care of me and the baby."

"Your father ran me out of town, knowing you were carrying my child?" Nausea rose in Ashe's throat. Hot, boiling anger churned inside him.

"Daddy arranged for Mother to announce that she was pregnant, but due to her age, she was having problems. He told everyone that Mother needed to be under a specialist's care." Twining her fingers together, Deborah alternated rubbing her thumbs up one palm and then the other. "When I was six months pregnant, we went away, then returned to Sheffield several weeks after Allen was born."

Anger, confusion and hurt swirled inside Ashe's mind and body. The truth had been there all along, staring him in the face. Even Roarke had tried to tell him. But he'd been too blind to see, too sure Deborah wouldn't lie to him, too afraid to accept the possibility that Allen could be his son. He hadn't wanted to admit that he was partially responsible for not having been a part of the boy's life for the past ten years.

"Allen." Ashe spoke the one word.

Allen Vaughn was his son. His and Deborah's. Their one passion-filled sexual encounter eleven years ago had created a child. Why had he never considered the possibility? Despite his rather promiscuous teen years, Ashe had been fairly cautious, using a condom most of the time. But he hadn't taken any precautions that night. He'd been so out of his head, needing and wanting Deborah, that he'd been careless—careless with an innocent girl who had deserved far better treatment.

Deborah looked at Ashe then and saw the mixed emotions bombarding him. "Daddy gave me two choices. I could give my child up for adoption or I could allow him to be raised as my brother."

You could have come to me! he wanted to shout. She should have come to him and told him. He would have taken care of her and their child. "You had a third choice," Ashe said.

"No, I didn't. You left town. You never called or wrote. You didn't give a damn what happened to me. You never asked yourself whether or not you might have gotten me pregnant."

Ashe grabbed her by the shoulders, jerking her up out of her chair as he stood. "Maybe you didn't feel that you could come to me when you first discovered you were pregnant. I guess I halfway understand your reasoning. But later… Mama Mattie always knew how to get in touch with me. All you had to do was ask her for my phone number, my address. Ten years, Deborah. Ten years!"

"I didn't know how you'd feel about being a father, about our child. You didn't love me. You'd made that perfectly clear." She sucked in her cheeks in a effort not to cry, not to fall apart in his arms. Somehow she knew he was in no frame of mind to comfort her. Not now. Not when he was in so much pain himself.

He shook her once, twice, then stopped abruptly and dropped his hands from her shoulders. Glaring at her, he knotted his hands into fists. God, how he wanted to smash his fist against the wall. He wanted to shout his anger, vent his rage.

"Is that why you kept Allen a secret from me?" He ached with the bitterness building inside him. "You were trying to punish me because I'd told you I didn't love you?"

"Of course not!" Seeing the hatred and distrust in his eyes, Deborah knew her worst fears were coming true. "Allen has a good life, surrounded by people who love him."

"Allen's life is a lie," Ashe said, his eyes wild with the hot fury burning inside him. "He thinks Miss Carol is his mother. Hell, he thinks Wallace Vaughn was his father."

"I did what I thought was best." Deborah wanted to touch Ashe, to lay her hand on his chest, to plead for his understanding. But she didn't dare. "I was seventeen years old. My father gave me two choices. Telling you wasn't an option. If I'd thought it was, then I might have—"

"What about later? After your father died? I know Miss Carol wouldn't have tried to prevent you from contacting me."

"After Daddy died, bringing you back into my life was not a consideration. I had to take over my father's business. I had to support Mother and Allen. Besides, you were halfway around the world most of the time."

"Miss Carol wanted me to know, didn't she? Allen was one of the reasons she hired me to protect you."

"Mother has the foolish idea that you once actually cared about me and that if she could get you back into our lives, you wouldn't leave us this time."

Ashe lifted his clenched fists into the air, willing himself to control his rage. He glared at Deborah, at the one woman he thought he could trust. Suddenly, he grabbed her again, barely suppressing the desire to shake her. "I did not *leave* you eleven years ago. Your father ran me out of town. Do you honestly think that anything or anyone could have forced me to leave you if I'd known you were pregnant?"

"Are you saying that you'd have married me for the baby's sake?" Deborah pulled away from him, tears swelling in her eyes. "I didn't want you under those conditions then and I don't want you under those conditions now. I wanted you to love me. Me!" She slapped her hand against her chest. "I wanted you to want me, not marry me because of Allen."

"You've kept my son away from me all his life because of what you wanted? Didn't you ever think about what Allen might want or need? Or even what I wanted or needed?"

Ashe clenched his fists so tightly that his nails bit into the palms of his hands. Pain shot through his head. He couldn't think straight. He needed to escape, to get away from Deborah before he said or did something he would regret. But he couldn't leave her. He was her bodyguard.

"You mustn't tell Allen," she said. "Not now. He's not old

enough to understand. That's one of the reasons—the main reason—I haven't told you the truth before now. I was afraid you'd want Allen to know you're his father. I just don't think he could handle the truth as young as he is."

"I won't do anything to hurt Allen." *My son.* Allen Vaughn was his child. He'd looked at the boy and all he'd seen was Deborah. That blond hair, those blue eyes. But Roarke had seen what Ashe had been too blind to see.

"He's a wonderful boy," Deborah said. "The joy of my life."

"Do you know me so little that you think I'd do anything to jeopardize Allen's happiness, his security? I thought you and I had something special between us years ago. I thought you were my best friend. But you didn't trust me enough to come to me and tell me you were pregnant. And now, when I thought we might have a future together, you still couldn't trust me enough to put Allen's life in my hands."

"I do trust you, Ashe. I've put all our lives in your hands. I know I should have told you weeks ago, but... I was afraid."

"How am I going to be able to face Allen and not want to pull him into my arms and tell him I'm his father? God, Deborah do you have any idea how I feel?"

Someone just outside the chapel door cleared their throat. Ashe and Deborah glanced toward the white uniformed young woman.

"Ms. Vaughn, I thought you'd want to know that your mother is out of surgery and the doctor is ready to speak to you."

"How is Mother?"

"She's in recovery. She came through the surgery just fine, but I'm afraid that's all I can tell you," the nurse said.

THE NEXT FEW hours seemed endless to Deborah. She alternated between the desire to scream and the desire to cry. Silent and brooding, Ashe stayed by her side. The barrier of tension between them grew stronger with each passing minute.

Now, when she needed him most, he was as remote, as far removed from her as if he were a million miles away. He would not leave her unguarded, his sense of honor would never allow him to desert her and put her life at risk. But he could not bring himself to look at her or speak to her.

Ashe was afraid of his feelings, of allowing the bitter anger free rein. More than anything, he needed to get away from Deborah, to go off by himself and think.

The doctor's news had been good. In his opinion, they had been lucky once again. They would have to wait a few days on the final test results, but the preliminary findings were positive, giving them every hope that Carol Vaughn would fully recover.

Neither Deborah nor Ashe had gone for lunch. They had paced around the waiting room, avoiding each other, not speaking, not even looking at each other. Their being together had become an agony for her and she had no doubt it had been as difficult for Ashe. She knew he wanted to get away from her, but he couldn't. He was bound by his honor to protect her.

When Miss Carol was returned to her private room, Ashe went in and said a brief hello. Not wanting to say or do anything that might upset Deborah's mother, he made a quick exit, telling Deborah he would remain outside in the hallway and that she should stay with her mother for as long as she wanted to.

"Did you tell him?" Carol Vaughn asked.

"Yes, Mother, I told him."

"And?"

"And everything is going to be all right," Deborah lied. "He understands."

Carol Vaughn smiled. "I knew he would. He'll take good care of you and Allen."

When her mother fell asleep shortly before five in the afternoon, Deborah kissed her pale cheek and walked out into the hallway.

Ashe stood, leaning against the wall, his hands in his pockets. "Is she all right?" he asked.

"She's sleeping." Deborah glanced at Ashe, but when she saw the coldness in his eyes, she looked away. "I'd like to go home now."

He escorted her downstairs to the parking lot, not touching her, not saying another word. The drive home was an exercise in torture. For Deborah. And for Ashe.

Suddenly her life seemed void of hope. Where she had felt the joy of being in love, the resurgence of dreams she'd thought long dead, now she felt only loss. Had she lost Ashe again? Or as in the past, had he never truly been hers?

Deborah glanced out the side window of Ashe's rental car, knowing that nothing she could say or do at this point would change the way he felt. When she heard him dialing his cellular phone, she glanced at him.

Quickly he returned his gaze to the road ahead. "Roarke?"

"How's Miss Carol?" Roarke asked. "Ever since Deborah called Allen with the good news, he's been wanting to talk to his mother."

"Miss Carol is doing real good. We left her sleeping." Ashe paused for a second. "I'm bringing Deborah home, but something's come up and I need to go out. Alone."

"No problem. Want to tell me what's wrong?"

"You were right about Allen."

"How'd you find out?" Roarke asked.

"Deborah told me. Today. While Miss Carol was in surgery."

"What are you going to do?"

"I don't know." Ashe clutched the steering wheel. "I can't see Allen right now. Keep him inside until I drop Deborah off. Okay?"

"Yeah, sure."

Ashe closed his cellular phone and slipped it back into his coat pocket. "Roarke will take care of you."

"Where are you going?" Deborah wished he'd look at her, but he didn't.

"I need to get away by myself for a few hours and do some serious thinking."

"Ashe, please… You may not believe this now, but…I love you."

Without replying, he drove up Montgomery Avenue, turned into the Vaughn driveway and waited for Deborah to get out. She hesitated for just a moment, hoping he would say something. He didn't. She jumped out of the car, slammed the car door and rushed up on the front porch where Roarke stood waiting. Ashe roared away, leaving Deborah alone, uncertain and miserable.

Ashe McLaughlin was good at that, she thought. Leaving. Maybe she had made a mistake, eleven years ago and more recently, too. But everything wasn't her fault. Surely when his temper cooled and he had time to think reasonably, he would see that he wasn't the only injured party in this situation.

She wasn't sure exactly what she had expected when she told him the truth, but somewhere deep inside her, she had hoped he would understand, that he would forgive her.

"Are you all right?" Roarke asked.

"I've been better," she said.

"Allen's helping Mazie set the table for dinner. He's going to want to know why Ashe isn't with you."

"I gather you suspected that Allen was Ashe's son."

"I saw the similarities. I knew your and Ashe's background. He told me about you, one night when we'd both had a little too much to drink."

"Ashe told you about me?"

"That surprises you?" Roarke opened the front door, placed his hand in the small of Deborah's back and followed her into the entrance hall.

"Why would Ashe tell you about me, about our... Ashe didn't love me. I don't understand."

"Maybe he didn't love you," Roarke said. "But he sure as hell never forgot you. He never got over the way he felt about you."

"I was in love with him then, you know. I'm even more in love with him now."

"Give him time to sort out his feelings." Roarke laid his big hand on Deborah's shoulder. "He has a son he never knew about and he's found out that a woman he'd just learned to trust again has kept a secret from him for eleven years."

Allen ran into the entrance hall, Huckleberry loping behind him. "How's Mother? When can I go see her?" Allen glanced around, then stared at the door. "Where's Ashe? Parking the car?"

Deborah took a deep breath. "Ashe had some business to take care of immediately. Mother is doing beautifully, and you can see her tomorrow after school."

"Great. May I call her tonight?"

"Right after dinner," Deborah said.

"Will Ashe be home in time to help me with my math homework?"

"I'm not sure how long his business will take." She wanted to wrap Allen in her arms and keep him safe. For the millionth time in ten years, she wished she could tell him she was his mother. Dear God, how Ashe must feel. But he had no idea the price she had paid pretending to be Allen's sister. Both of them had lost so much not having the chance to be Allen's parents. Maybe it really was all her fault. Maybe Ashe had every right to hate her. If she'd had the strength to stand up to her father or the courage to have gone to Ashe with the truth long ago, things would be different now.

Deborah checked her watch as she followed Allen into the kitchen. Would Ashe return tonight? Tomorrow? Or would he leave town and never return? Oh, he would return, all right. He might leave her again, but he would never leave his son.

CHAPTER FIFTEEN

ASHE SAT IN his car, the window down, the crisp night air chilling him. He had to go home, home to Deborah. For the past several hours he had thought of nothing except what she'd told him about Allen. His son. Their son.

He'd stopped by a local lounge for a couple of drinks, then come down here by the river and parked. He hadn't wanted to be around anybody. He'd needed time alone to lick his wounds, to resolve his feelings for Deborah.

The fact that he cared deeply for her complicated his life considerably. If she hadn't come to mean so much to him, he could hate her. But he didn't hate her; and he didn't even blame her for what she'd done. How could he? Eleven years ago he'd taken her innocence and broken her heart. He'd tried to reject her gently, telling himself he was doing what was best for her. If he'd been a man instead of a thoughtless boy, he would have made sure he hadn't gotten her pregnant. That had been his fault. He'd been the one with experience, not her. And she'd loved him. He hadn't appreciated how much the love of a girl like Deborah meant. Now he did.

Why hadn't he, just once, considered the possibility that he'd gotten her pregnant and she'd kept it a secret from him? Hell, he knew the answer only too well. He couldn't have handled the guilt. He didn't blame her for not coming to him, after the way he'd treated her. Back then she hadn't known her father had run him out of town; she'd thought he'd deserted her.

He couldn't justify her keeping Allen's existence a secret after her father died, but he understood her reasoning. He had hurt her badly. She had been afraid to trust her life and Allen's to him.

Things were different now. She did trust him. And she still loved him. That was the greatest miracle of all. Somehow, he'd find a way to make up all the lost years to Allen and to Deborah.

They needed to talk, to come to an agreement on the best way to handle the situation. He wanted Allen in his life, whether or not they ever told the boy he was his father. And he didn't want to lose Deborah, not again. All these years she had stayed alive inside him, her gentle beauty, her unconditional love.

He didn't know exactly how they'd work things, but they would find a way. He'd make Deborah see that no obstacle was too great for them to overcome—together. He wasn't going to lose his son or his son's mother.

Ashe started the car, turned around and headed toward Sheffield, all the while thinking about what he wanted to say to Deborah. When he turned into the driveway, he noticed every downstairs light was on. In the distance he heard sirens. A police siren and an ambulance siren. His heart raced, his nerves rioted. What if something had happened while he'd been off licking his wounds?

He flew to the front door and through the house, calling for Deborah, then he bellowed out Roarke's name. When he entered the kitchen he ran into Allen, who trembled and cried and spoke in incoherent phrases. Huckleberry stood at Allen's side, licking the child's hand.

Ashe grabbed his son by the shoulders. "Allen, what's wrong? What's happened? Where's Deborah? Where's Roarke?"

"Deborah's gone." Allen sobbed, his big blue eyes wide with fear. "I don't know what happened. I heard Deborah scream."

"When did you hear her scream?"

"Just a little while ago. Her scream woke—woke me and—and Huckleberry."

"Where's Roarke?"

"Outside. In the—the backyard. I think he's dead!" Allen threw his arms around Ashe's waist, hugging him fiercely.

Ashe lifted his son in his arms, sat him down on top of the kitchen table and wiped the tears from his face with his fingers. "Are you all right, Allen?"

"Yes. But I can't find Deborah. Where is she? Did they get her?"

"Show me where Roarke is," Ashe said.

"I called 911. Roarke told me to call, then he passed out."

Ashe lifted Allen down from the table. Holding his son's hand, he followed the boy and his dog outside. Roarke's big body rested in a fallen heap on the patio. Huckleberry sniffed Roarke's semiautomatic, which he'd obviously dropped when he'd passed out. The gun now lay in a pool of fresh blood that had formed on the bricks.

Ashe leaned down, turning Roarke slightly. The man groaned, then opened his eyes.

"Hang in there. An ambulance is on its way," Ashe said. "Can you tell me what happened?"

"She was restless." Roarke spoke slowly, his breath ragged. "Worried about you. Thought she…heard your car parking in the back."

"Where is she?"

"He took her." Roarke tried to lift his head. "Told her not to go outside. Couldn't catch her. Couldn't stop her. She thought it was you."

Ashe inspected Roarke's body and discovered he'd been shot several times. Dear God, why didn't that ambulance hurry? If Roarke lost much more blood, he'd be dead before the medics arrived.

"Take it easy," Ashe said.

"I walked out—out the door." Roarke coughed several times. Blood trickled from the corner of his mouth. "The minute I stepped out… Shot me. Kept shooting."

"Did you get a look at him?"

"Big guy. Ugly. Sandy hair. Jeans. Leather jacket." Roarke lifted his hand, but the effort exerted too much of his strength and his hand fell to his side. "Failed. Sorry."

"I'll find her," Ashe said. "You just hang in there until—" Ashe realized Roarke had passed out again.

Four Sheffield policeman stormed the backyard, their guns drawn. Standing, Ashe placed his arm around Allen's shoulders. His son leaned against him.

"Come on, Allen. After we talk to the police and see Roarke off to the hospital, I'm taking you over to Mama Mattie's. I'll get Chief Burton to send one of his officers to stay with you until I find Deborah."

"You'll find her, won't you, Ashe? You won't let anybody hurt her, will you? You love her, just like I do."

"Yeah, son, you're right. I'll find her, and I'll never let anybody hurt her because I love her, too."

Ashe barely contained the rage inside him, and the fear. Dear God, the nauseating fear! If anything happened to Deborah, it would be his fault. If he hadn't left her, deserted her again, then she wouldn't have been in such a tormented state of mind. She never would have rushed outside without thinking, disobeying Roarke's orders. If anything happened to her or if Roarke died, Ashe would have to face the fact that he could have prevented tonight's disastrous events.

ASHE MARCHED INTO the Sweet Nothings club like a storm trooper. Evie tried to grab his arm, but he threw her off and swept past the bouncer, making his way to Buck Stansell's office. If the man was responsible for Deborah's kidnapping, he'd kill him with his bare hands—after he found out where Deborah's abductor had taken her.

Ashe flung open the office door. Buck jumped up from behind his desk, like a scared rabbit dodging a hunter's bullet.

"Where is she?" Ashe demanded, as he advanced on Buck, not heeding Buck's bodyguard's warning.

Buck motioned for his bodyguard. Ashe turned on the burly man and, using several expedient thrusts with his hands and feet, brought the big man to his knees.

"Why are you here?" Buck asked.

Evie rushed into the office, bringing two bouncers with her. Ashe pulled his gun from the shoulder holster and aimed it at Buck.

"Call off your goons," Ashe said.

"Take them back inside the club," Buck ordered. "Go with them, sweetie. I can handle things in here."

"Where is Deborah?" Ashe asked again.

"If she's missing, I don't have her," Buck said. "I've been trying to tell you that I'm not behind the recent threats. I thought you were checking into other suspects."

"I'm still checking." With gun in hand, Ashe walked across the room, motioning for the bodyguard to sit. "Someone shot my partner at the Vaughns' home tonight and kidnapped Deborah. What do you know about it?"

Buck eased down in his big velvet chair behind his desk. "I didn't put a contract out on Deborah, but I know who did."

"Keep your hands where I can see them." Ashe stood in front of Buck's desk. "Tell me what you know."

"I checked into the situation for you, just like I said I would." Buck laid his hands flat atop his desk. "I found out that a prominent Sheffield citizen hired one of my former employees—Randy Perry—to kill Deborah. Randy just got out of the pen a couple of months ago and I didn't see fit to rehire him. He's a bad apple, that one."

"Who hired him?"

"A relative of Deborah Vaughn's, one who had a twofold purpose in wanting her dead."

"Who?"

"The man wanted revenge on his wife's former lover, the

one he's cried in his beer about here at Sweet Nothings on more than one occasion. Seems his wife has always compared him to this guy and he's always come up lacking."

"Whitney's husband?" Ashe asked.

"Of course, getting back at you isn't his main reason. The inheritance is. Seems Jamison thinks that old Mrs. Vaughn hasn't got much longer to live, and with Deborah out of the way, his wife would be the logical one to oversee Deborah's estate and take custody of Allen."

"My God! Is Whitney involved in this scheme?"

"Don't know. Wouldn't know what I do if Randy hadn't stayed buddies with some of my boys and if he wasn't the type to brag to the ladies."

"Do you have any idea where he's taken Deborah?"

"I didn't even know he'd taken her tonight until you stormed in here. Why don't you pay a visit on Mr. Jamison?"

"That's exactly what I intend to do." Slipping his gun back into the holster, Ashe nodded to the door. "Why don't you walk me out, Buck, old friend?"

Buck chuckled. "Still don't trust me completely? I don't blame you."

Buck walked Ashe all the way outside to his car, then put his hand on Ashe's shoulder. "I'll find out what I can about where Randy's taken your woman. If I learn anything that can help you, I'll send Lee Roy to find you."

Ashe didn't say anything, only nodded, got in his car and headed back to Sheffield, straight to the Jamison house on River Bluff.

THE JAMISON HOME sat on the bluff overlooking the Tennessee River. Ashe parked his rental car behind George Jamison's Jaguar. The fury inside him had built to the "kill" stage. His common sense urged him to stay calm, telling him that he must remain in control in order to find Deborah before her kidnapper killed her.

The very thought of Deborah being harmed angered Ashe, and created a pain deep inside him. The hired assassin had been waiting for his chance to get Deborah, and Ashe had given him the perfect opportunity. If anything happened to her, he'd never forgive himself.

He rang the doorbell and waited, checking his gun. After endless minutes of keeping his finger pressed against the buzzer, Whitney Vaughn swung open the double doors and stood in the foyer smiling.

"Why, Ashe McLaughlin, whatever brings you to my house in the middle of the night?"

Ashe noticed she wore nothing but a thin, lavender nightgown, sheer and revealing. "Where's your husband?"

"Not in my bed." She draped her arm around Ashe's neck. He pulled free, walking farther into the foyer. She closed the doors and followed him.

"You want to see George?" she asked. "At this time of night?"

"Where is he?" Ashe went from room to room, turning on lights as he went. "If he's not here, tell me where he is!"

"What the devil's the matter with you, Ashe?" Whitney planted her hand on her slender hip.

"Deborah's been kidnapped," Ashe said. "And I have reason to believe that your husband put out a contract on her life."

"George?" Whitney's large brown eyes widened, giving her an owlish look. "But George would never... What reason would he have?"

"You tell me. For all I know you could be in on it with him."

"I'd never do anything to hurt Deborah. She's my cousin. I care deeply for her."

"Where's your husband?" Grabbing Whitney by the shoulders, Ashe shook her soundly.

"He—he's upstairs in his room."

"Show me." Ashe jerked Whitney around, grasping her wrist. "I don't have any time to lose."

Whitney ran up the stairs, Ashe beside her. Halting, she pointed to a closed door. "That's George's room."

Ashe crashed through the door. George Jamison had one leg in his trousers, the other on the floor. Ashe grabbed him around the neck. When George swayed, Ashe steadied him by slamming him up against the wall. Whitney stepped inside, but stayed by the open door.

"Where did Randy Perry take Deborah?" Ashe tightened his hold on George's neck.

"I—I don't know what you're—you're talking about." George pawed at Ashe's hand, trying unsuccessfully to loosen his hold around his neck.

"Don't play games with me, Jamison. You tell me what I want to know or I'll break your neck. Do you understand me?"

"For pity's sake, Whitney, call the police," George said.

"I'm not doing anything." Whitney glared at her husband. "If you hired someone to kill Deborah, you'd better tell Ashe what he wants to know."

"Please, believe me. I don't know what he's talking about."

With his right hand still pressed against George's windpipe, Ashe reached inside his jacket and retrieved his gun from the shoulder holster. He pointed his 9 mm directly at George's temple.

"If you have any doubts that I'd kill you, then you don't know me at all. Deborah Vaughn is the most important thing in this world to me. I'd lay down my life for her. Do you understand what I'm saying, Jamison?"

"Don't kill me," George pleaded.

Ashe despised the weakness in this man. He pressed the 9 mm against George's head. "Where has Perry taken Deborah?"

"I don't know!" When Ashe glared at him, fury in his eyes,

George cried out. "I paid him 5,000 and promised him 5,000 more to do the job."

"You hired someone to kill Deborah!" Whitney screamed, tears forming in her eyes. "I knew you weren't much of a man, but I never realized what a monster you are. How could you do it? Deborah has taken care of us for years. I don't know what we would have done without her."

"But don't you see, my darling, I did it for us." George tried to turn his head so he could look at his wife, but Ashe kept him trapped against the wall, the 9 mm at his temple, Ashe's big hand at his throat.

"With Deborah out of the way and Miss Carol dying soon, then who but to you would the courts award custody of Allen?" George said. "Who but you would be in control of Allen's inheritance?"

"I can't believe this." Whitney slumped against the doorpost, as if her slender weight was more than she could bear. "You're out of your mind!"

"I'd have never thought of killing Deborah. But once the threats started, I thought how lucky for us if Buck Stansell had her killed." George trembled. "Look, Ashe, killing me won't save Deborah. I hired Perry. Yes, I admit it. Once the trial ended and I realized that Buck Stansell wasn't going to continue with his threats, I decided I could hire someone to kill Deborah and everyone would think Stansell and his gang were responsible."

"You sorry son of a bitch," Ashe growled, then returned his gun to its holster. He grabbed George around the neck with both hands, lifting him off the floor.

George gasped for air, his feet dangling, his arms flying about, trying to catch hold of Ashe.

Whitney screamed. "You're killing him, Ashe!"

Not one rational, reasonable thought entered Ashe's head. He worked on instincts alone. His hands tightened around George's neck. With one swift move, he could break the man's neck.

This stupid fool was responsible for whatever might happen to Deborah before Ashe could find her. He didn't deserve to live.

"Ashe, think what you're doing," Whitney cried out, beating against Ashe's back with her tight little fists. "He's not worth it. Do you hear me? George isn't worth it!"

"Put him down, cousin," Lee Roy Brennan said from where he stood in the doorway. "She's right. He's not worth it."

Without loosening his hold on George, Ashe glanced at Lee Roy. "Did Buck send you?"

"We found out where Randy might have taken Deborah."

"A reliable source?" Ashe asked.

"A friend of Evie's," Lee Roy said. "A gal Randy's sleeping with. He shared his plans with her, telling her he'd be coming into another 5,000 after the job was done."

"Where did she say he planned to take Deborah?" Ashe set George down on his feet, but kept his hands around his throat.

"Somewhere close to Deborah's house in downtown Sheffield. Some deserted warehouse."

"What deserted warehouse?"

"My guess is the old streetcar warehouse."

Ashe released George, allowing him to fall to his knees. With expert ease, Ashe snapped the purple top sheet from George's bed and ripped off two long strips. Using his foot, he pressed George over against the bed, jerked his hands behind his back and hogtied the man with the scraps of his own bed sheet.

"Whitney, don't let your husband out of your sight until the police arrive."

"Don't worry," she said. "I'll kill him myself if he even tries to move."

"Come on." Ashe motioned to Lee Roy, who followed him out into the hall and down the stairs.

Lee Roy grabbed Ashe at the front door. "When we find her, she might not be alive."

"She'll be alive! She has to be."

"Even if she is, it could be bad. Randy was in the pen for rape."

"Whatever happens, he's a dead man," Ashe said.

ASHE CALLED THE Sheffield police on his cellular phone, telling them where he was going and asking them to send some officers over to George Jamison's home. Lee Roy followed in his truck, the two cousins speeding along Jackson Highway, racing toward downtown Sheffield. Ashe prayed, begging God to keep Deborah safe, offering his own life in place of hers.

SHE COULDN'T BEAR his touch, rough and clammy. She'd screamed the first time he'd squeezed her breast, but he'd slapped her so hard she'd fallen to her knees in pain.

He was going to rape her before he killed her. He'd told her what to expect.

This was all her fault. Her own stupidity had cost Roarke his life and now would cost her hers. How could she have been so stupid, rushing out to meet Ashe, when in fact she'd run headlong into her kidnapper?

Did Ashe know what had happened? Was he searching for her? *Please, God, please let him find me in time.*

"I ain't never had me no society lady before." Randy Perry snickered as he ripped open Deborah's blouse, exposing her lace-covered breasts.

Deborah tried to back away from him, but he grabbed her, dragged her up against him and thrust his sour tongue into her mouth. Gagging, she fought him, hitting him repeatedly as she kicked at his legs.

He threw her to the floor and came down on top of her, crushing the breath out of her. "You like it rough, huh, society lady? Well, ol' randy Randy can give it to you rough."

He ran his hand up her leg and under her skirt, fondling her hip. When he lowered his head to kiss her again, she spat in his face. He laughed. Then he slapped her.

Deborah closed her eyes against the reality of what was happening to her. She retreated into a silent, constant prayer for Ashe to rescue her before it was too late.

CHAPTER SIXTEEN

THE OLD STREETCAR warehouse stood in darkness, the moonlight casting shadows across the window panes. Ashe could hear nothing except the loud pounding of his heart. He couldn't ever remembering being so scared, not even in battle. But then Deborah's life had not been in jeopardy, only his.

He drove down the street slowly, looking for any sign that someone had broken into the empty building. He circled the block. An older model Pontiac Grand Prix was parked directly across from the warehouse. Ashe eased his Buick up behind it, got out and checked the license plate. A Colbert County tag.

Lee Roy pulled his truck up behind Ashe, getting out and following his cousin across the street.

"It's Randy's car," Lee Roy said. "He got it off a fellow who brings stolen cars in from Mississippi."

"That means they're here." Ashe removed his gun from the holster before crossing the street. "Look, you may not want to get involved in this. I've phoned for the police. They should be here any time now."

"All I'm doing is helping my cousin rescue his woman. Right? I don't know nothing about nothing. We made a lucky guess as to who had kidnapped Deborah and about where he'd taken her."

"Yeah, right." Ashe nodded toward the building. "You check that side and I'll check this side. If you find them, don't act on your own. Randy Perry is mine."

"Got you." Lee Roy rounded the side of the warehouse.

Ashe crept along the wall, checking for an unlocked door,

looking for any sign of forced entry. Then he saw it. Toward the back of the building, a dim light flickered.

Ashe found a jimmied lock, the door standing partially open. Taking every precaution not to alert Randy Perry to his presence inside the warehouse, Ashe followed the light source, keeping his body pressed close to the wall as he made his way inside, searching for any sign of Deborah.

A lone lantern rested on the floor, spreading a circle of light around it. Deborah lay at Randy Perry's feet, her blouse in shreds, her skirt bunched up around her hips, half covering the gleaming white of her lace underwear. Ashe garnered all his willpower, resisting the urge to let out a masculine cry of rage. He wanted to kill the big, bearded slob of a man who gazed down at a half-naked Deborah as he unzipped his jeans.

Ashe whirled away from the wall, aiming his gun at Deborah's kidnapper. In a split second, before Ashe could fire his 9 mm, Perry fell to the floor, grabbing Deborah into his arms. Lifting her along with himself, he rose to his knees, holding Deborah in front of him, his thick arm around her neck.

"I'll break her neck like a twig," Perry warned Ashe. "And that would be a pity. She's got such a pretty little neck."

"You're a dead man, Perry!"

Randy Perry stood, jerking Deborah to her feet, using her body as a shield. Walking himself and Deborah backward, he kicked the lantern across the floor, extinguishing the flame and sending the room into darkness. The lantern rolled into a corner, crashing into the wall.

Ashe swore aloud. His breathing quickened. It would take a few minutes for his eyes to adjust to the darkness, but then it would take just as long for Perry to be able to maneuver without any light.

Sirens blared like the thunder of an attacking elephant herd. Tires screeched. Doors slammed. Chief Burton's voice rang out loud and clear, telling Randy Perry that the warehouse was surrounded.

"Don't look like I got nothing to lose by finishing this job, does it?" Perry called out, taunting Ashe.

"Be careful, Ashe." Deborah's voice sounded shaky but strong.

"Deborah!" Ashe couldn't see her now, but he could make out the direction in which Perry was moving from the sound of their voices.

"Don't hurt her," Ashe said. "If you do, I'll kill you before the police come through the door."

"He has a gun, Ashe. Don't—"

Randy Perry held Deborah in front of him as he walked backward, directly past a row of windows. Moonlight created enough illumination for Ashe to see the gun Perry held to the side of Deborah's face, his other meaty hand covering her mouth.

"Let her go." Ashe issued one final warning.

Randy Perry laughed. "No way in hell!"

Ashe aimed and fired. Deborah screamed. Randy Perry slumped, knocking Deborah down as he dropped to the floor. Blood spurted from the lone bullet wound in his head. Deborah looked over at the man's still body, then crawled away from him. Standing hurriedly, she ran toward Ashe.

He grabbed her, pulling her into his arms, encompassing her in his tight embrace. She gulped for air, her body racked with heavy, dry sobs. Ashe rubbed her back, petting her tenderly.

"It's all right, honey. You're safe now. You're safe."

The police stormed into the warehouse after hearing the gunshot. They found Randy Perry lying on the floor in a pool of his own blood and a partially undressed Deborah Vaughn clinging to Ashe McLaughlin.

"Is she all right?" Ed Burton walked over to Ashe. "Did he hurt her?"

"She'll be all right." Ashe slipped his gun into the holster, then removed his jacket and placed it around Deborah's shoulders. "I'm taking her home."

"Maybe you should take her to the hospital. If she's been raped—"

"No!" Deborah cried. "He—he didn't—didn't rape me. He would have, but Ashe—Ashe—"

Ashe lifted her into his arms, carried her past a row of gawking police officers and out onto the sidewalk. She laid her head on his chest. He kissed the top of her head.

Standing by the side of Ashe's car, Lee Roy opened the door. Ashe deposited Deborah inside, got in and looked up at his cousin.

"Thanks," Ashe said. "Pass it along. Okay?"

"Yeah. Sure thing. Glad we made it in time." Lee Roy grinned. "Guess I'll be seeing you from time to time. I figure you'll be staying around these parts to keep an eye on your woman."

Lee Roy walked over to his truck, got in and drove off. Ashe removed his jacket and draped it around Deborah's shoulders, then pulled her close to his side, started his car and headed southwest.

"Where are we going?" she asked.

"Allen is with Mama Mattie. Chief Burton has an officer keeping an eye on them."

"I can't let Allen see me like this, with my clothes—" She swallowed hard, biting the insides of her cheeks in an effort not to cry.

"He'll be asleep when we get there. I'm sure Annie Laurie can find you something of hers to put on." Ashe hugged Deborah, leaning the side of his head against the top of hers. "It's all over, honey. Go ahead and cry. Let it all out."

"I can't cry," she said. "I hurt too much to cry."

"Did you tell Ed Burton the truth? Randy Perry didn't rape you, did he?"

"No, he didn't. He slapped me around. He scared me to death. Oh, Ashe, how can you say it's over? Buck Stansell will just hire someone else to come after me."

Ashe pulled the car off Shop Pike and into the parking lot of the old converted train depot. Killing the motor, he turned to Deborah. She looked so pale, there in the moonlight, her eyes overly bright and slightly glazed with tears. But she hadn't cried, hadn't gone into hysterics. His strong, brave Deborah. Taking her face in both hands, he lowered his lips to hers and kissed her tenderly.

Still holding her face, he shook his head. "It's over, honey. Believe me. Buck Stansell didn't put out a contract on you. George Jamison did."

Deborah gasped. "George!"

Ashe slipped one arm behind her and crossed the other over her body, bringing her into the comfort of his embrace. "Buck was telling me the truth. Lon Sparks wasn't an important enough cog in their wheel for Buck to make an example out of you. Especially when he found out he'd have to contend with me."

"But George? I can't believe he would… Ashe, are you sure? How did you find out?"

"I got a confession out of George, tonight."

"But—but why would George want to kill me? I don't understand."

"The man has a sick, devious, greedy mind. He thought Miss Carol would die, then if you were out of the way, Whitney would be given custody of Allen and the entire Vaughn estate."

Deborah gripped Ashe's arms. "What about Whitney? Does she know what he did? Oh, dear Lord, is she all right?"

That was his Deborah, kindhearted and loving to the bitter end. "Yeah, she knows. And she's all right. When she found out, she was ready to kill George herself."

"So, it really is over, isn't it?" Deborah sighed, her body relaxing in Ashe's embrace. "Oh, Ashe, I was so afraid. I didn't know if you'd find me in time."

Ashe kissed the top of her head, the side of her face, his arms tightening around her. "I had to find you, didn't you know that? I couldn't let anything happen to you. Not now when we've just found each other again. Not when I've realized exactly how much you mean to me."

The tears she'd been holding at bay rose in her throat, choking her. She swallowed hard. "I didn't want to die. And I was scared, so scared. I didn't want to leave Allen and Mother and… you."

"We have a lot to talk about," Ashe said. "But not now. You've been through hell these last few hours. We've both been through hell!"

"I want to see Allen. I want to take him home. Once we're all safe and together, then you and I can talk and work things out." She would have to share Allen with his father in the future. Would that mean trips to Atlanta for Allen, or was there a possibility that Ashe would return to Sheffield permanently? "We can work things out, can't we, Ashe?"

"Yeah, honey, we most certainly can work everything out."

Keeping one arm around Deborah, Ashe started the car and drove them straight to Mama Mattie's. The moment they pulled into the driveway, Annie Laurie rushed outside. The fading bruises on the side of her face were the only physical reminder of the accident four days ago. After a two-day hospital stay and countless tests, the doctors had sent her home with a caution to take it easy for a while.

Opening the passenger door, Annie Laurie grabbed Deborah when she stepped out of the Buick Regal.

A young police officer followed Annie Laurie. "I see you found Ms. Vaughn."

"You're all right." Annie Laurie glanced at Ashe. "You're both all right." She looked at Deborah's tattered clothing and gasped. "Oh, God, did he—"

"No," Deborah said. "Ashe found us before he really hurt

me." She ran a hand down across her torn skirt. "I need something to put on before Allen sees me."

"Allen's asleep. Finally. He's lying on the couch with his head in Mama Mattie's lap. That's the reason she didn't come out here with me. She didn't want to wake him up. Poor baby has been worried sick and we thought he'd never rest."

"Thank you for keeping watch over Allen." Ashe got out of the car and shook hands with the officer. "The man who kidnapped Ms. Vaughn is dead."

"Yeah, Chief Burton just called. He said to tell you that George Jamison has been arrested and is in jail."

"Tell the chief that Ms. Vaughn and I will be glad to answer any questions tomorrow." Ashe placed his arm around Deborah's shoulders. "We'll go around to the back door. Annie Laurie, I hope you find Deborah something to wear before we wake Allen and take him home."

Deborah and Ashe walked around the house to the back porch, while Annie Laurie went in the front and met them at the kitchen door. Annie Laurie ushered Deborah into her bedroom. Ashe walked through the kitchen and the small dining area adjacent to the living room and stood in the arched opening, looking across the room at his grandmother and his son. His son!

Mattie Trotter placed her index finger over her lips, cautioning Ashe to be quiet. He nodded and smiled. Ashe noticed his grandmother's old photo album in Allen's arms.

More than anything, Ashe wanted to lift Allen in his arms and hold him. His child. His son. Ten years of the boy's life had already passed. Would they ever be able to make up the lost time? Would Allen ever accept him as a father?

When Deborah and Annie Laurie emerged from the bedroom, Deborah walked over to Ashe and handed him his jacket. He slipped it on, then put his arm around her waist. She took his hand in hers. He thought she looked beautiful in Annie

Laurie's little burgundy-checked shirtwaist dress, her long hair disheveled and her face void of any makeup.

"Let's go get our son and take him home," she said.

Mama Mattie's eyes widened, her mouth gaping as she looked at Deborah and Ashe, then down at the sleeping child.

"What?" Annie Laurie said. "Allen is—"

"Allen is Deborah's child," Ashe whispered. "Deborah's and mine."

"But—but… Oh, my goodness."

With Ashe at her side, Deborah walked across the living room, knelt beside the sofa and kissed Allen on the cheek. He stirred, the photo album dropping to the floor. The boy opened his eyes, saw Deborah and jumped up into her open arms.

"You're all right!" He squealed with happiness. "I knew Ashe would find you. I knew he wouldn't let anything bad happen to you."

"And you were so right," Deborah said. "Ashe is my hero." She looked up at him with all the love in her heart showing plainly on her face.

Reaching down on the floor beside the sofa, Allen picked up the photo album. "Mama Mattie's been showing me pictures of Ashe when he was just a kid and then when he was a teenager. He was big for his age, just like I am. How about that?"

"Yeah, how about that?" Mama Mattie said, glancing at Ashe.

Deborah sat down on the sofa beside Allen. He laid the photo album in her lap. "Look at the pictures of you and Ashe together. You two must have spent a lot of time together. Mama Mattie has a ton of pictures of you two."

"They were the best of friends." Mattie's eyes glazed with tears.

"Hey, they told me they weren't an item, you know, that they didn't go together, but I think they had a thing for each other." Allen looked up at Ashe. "Come on, Ashe, fess up, you and Deborah were more than friends."

"Back then we were friends, but we should have been sweethearts," Ashe said. "You know what, pal? I've just realized, very recently, that I've always loved Deborah."

Deborah raised her eyes, looking at Ashe with disbelief. Had she heard him correctly? Had he just confessed his love? Here, in front of his grandmother and cousin. In front of their son.

"A lot has happened tonight," Ashe said. "Deborah and I haven't had a chance to talk about the future, but I was wondering if I could have your permission to ask Deborah to marry me?"

"Wow-wee!" Allen jumped up off the sofa, threw himself against Ashe and hugged him, then turned to Deborah. "Are you going to say yes? It'd be neat to have Ashe for a brother-in-law."

"Don't I have any say in this matter?" Deborah asked, not sure she liked being bulldozed by her two men.

Ashe kept his hand on Allen's shoulder when he spoke to Deborah. "Doesn't look like you get a vote. Allen and I are a two-thirds majority."

"Is that right?" The look on Allen's face broke Deborah's heart. She couldn't remember a time when her son had been so happy. He adored Ashe. That was plain to see.

Ashe pulled Deborah up off the sofa and slipped his arm around her waist. Allen grinned from ear to ear.

"Once I was too big a fool to realize what I had," Ashe said. "But now I know, and I'll never let you go, Deborah. Never."

"Isn't this great!" Allen hugged Ashe and Deborah, then spun around to bring Mattie and Annie Laurie into the celebration. "Just think, when Deborah and Ashe get married, they'll sort of be like parents to me. Deborah's always been a second mother to me. Now, I'll have a dad, won't I?"

"Yes, son, you will." Ashe could barely speak, the emotions erupting inside him overwhelming in their intensity.

"I like this just fine," Allen said. "Everything is working out great. I sure am glad Mother hired Ashe to protect Deborah."

"So am I," Ashe said.

"Well, it's time we go home, don't you think?" Deborah patted Allen on the back.

"Could I stay here with Mama Mattie?" Allen asked. "We've already made plans for tomorrow. She said I didn't have to go to school. We're going to the hospital to see Mother and Roarke."

"Roarke!" Ashe and Deborah said simultaneously.

"He's going to be fine," Mattie said. "We've called the hospital several times. He came through surgery with flying colors. Looks like he'll be laid up for a spell, but he's going to live."

"Thank God." Deborah leaned against Ashe. "What happened to him was my fault."

"Can I stay with Mama Mattie?" Allen repeated his request. "She's going to make biscuits and chocolate sauce for breakfast, then we're going to bake tea cakes and take Mother and Roarke some. Please, Deborah, let me stay."

"Allen, I don't know. I—"

"Please. Besides, you and Ashe probably want to be alone anyway."

"He's right," Ashe said. "Let him stay. We can pick him up tomorrow."

Fighting her motherly reluctance, Deborah agreed. "Oh, all right." She hugged Allen. "I love you, you know."

"Yeah, I know." Allen glanced over at Ashe. "You'd better always love her and be good to her or you'll have to answer to me."

Everyone in the room laughed, Deborah thinking how much like Ashe Allen was.

"You have my word, son," Ashe vowed.

DEBORAH LAY IN Ashe's arms as dawn spread its pink glow across the eastern horizon. They'd come home, showered together and fallen into bed, making love like two wild animals. They had fallen asleep without talking. They hadn't discussed the kidnapping or the fact that Ashe had killed Randy Perry, nor had they mentioned Allen and their future.

Ashe stroked her naked hip. "What are you thinking about?"

"About how we need to talk."

"Yeah, I guess we kind of got distracted by other things." He grinned, then kissed her.

"I was too exhausted to think straight and I guess you were, too." She laid her hand on his chest, directly over his heart. "What are you going to do about Allen?"

"I'm going to marry his mother—" Ashe pulled Deborah into his arms "—and be a father to him."

"Are you going to tell him the truth?"

"Someday I think we should. In a few years, when he's a little older and can understand." Ashe nuzzled Deborah's neck with his nose. "We need some time to become a family, for the three of us to bond."

"What about your job? Are you willing to move back to Sheffield? I can't leave Mother, and Allen wouldn't want to live anywhere else. This is his home."

"I can find a job around here. Who knows, ol' Buck might offer me a position as his bodyguard."

Deborah slapped Ashe on the chest. "That isn't a joking matter."

"Let it all go, honey. It's over. Let's don't look back, let's look forward. What's done is done. We've all lived through a pretty rough time, but it *is* over."

Deborah knew she had to face the truth and had to confront Ashe with her fears. She couldn't marry him if he confirmed her doubts.

"I can't marry you." She pulled away from Ashe, but he jerked her up against him.

"What do you mean you can't marry me?"

"I told you that I didn't want you to marry me because of Allen. That was true eleven years ago and it's true now."

"I'm not marrying you because of Allen. Didn't you hear me tell you and Allen and Mama Mattie and Annie Laurie that I'd been a fool to ever let you go, that I realize I've always loved you?" Ashe tilted her chin with one hand while he held her close with the other.

"There are all kinds of love, Ashe. As much as I love you, I can't spend the rest of my life married to a man who doesn't feel the same way about me."

"You're confusing me, honey. What the hell are we talking about here? I've said I love you."

"Not the way I want to be loved."

"What does that mean?"

"It means that…" Pulling out of his arms, she got out of bed, picked up her robe off the floor and put it on.

"Deborah?" Ashe stood, totally naked, and followed her over to the windows.

"I came close to dying tonight," she said, her back to him. "I realized how very much I want to live. I've been in love with you for as long as I can remember, but you didn't feel the same way about me. You still don't."

He eased his arms around her, leaning her back against his chest, enfolding her in his embrace. "If a man ever loved a woman, I love you. Nothing and no one is more important to me."

She trembled. He soothed her, caressing her arms, kissing the side of her face.

"You've been a part of me forever," he said. "Maybe I didn't have sense enough to know I loved you eleven years ago, but you've stayed alive inside me for all these years. I've never been able to forget you. Now I know why."

She turned in his arms, her eyes filled with tears. "Why?"

"Because I'm in love with you, Deborah. Deeply, passionately, completely in love with you."

"Oh, Ashe."

Lifting her in his arms, he carried her back to bed. Laying

her down, he eased off her robe, then braced himself above her. "Marry me. Let me spend the rest of my life proving to you how much I love you."

"Yes. Yes."

He buried himself within the welcoming folds of her body, telling her again and again that he loved her. She accepted him and his proclamations of love. Giving and taking, sharing in equal measure, they reached fulfillment together. Resting in the aftermath, they accepted the beautiful reality of their life, knowing in their hearts that love and happiness was truly theirs.

EPILOGUE

THE WHOLE FAMILY gathered around the shiny, new, black Mitsubishi 3000 GT. Mattie Trotter clicked snapshot after snapshot, while Carol Vaughn zoomed in on Allen's beaming face with her camcorder.

"We couldn't wait until after graduation tonight," Deborah said. "We thought you might want to drive it to your class party afterward."

"Wow! I hoped for something like this, but I wasn't sure. Thanks, Mom!" Tall, lanky, handsome eighteen-year-old Allen hugged Deborah. "I'll bet you picked her out for me, didn't you, Dad?"

Ashe grinned. "Yeah. Your mother wanted to get you something a little more practical."

"I helped, too," seven-year-old Martha McLaughlin said, tugging on her big brother's pants leg. "I wanted to get the red one, but Daddy said no, that you'd like the black one better."

"He was right, squirt." Allen lifted his little sister up in his arms. "I think I'll take this baby for a spin around the block. Want to go with me, Martha?"

"You bet I do."

"Don't be gone too long," Deborah said. "You'll want time to go over your valedictory speech one more time. I know you want it to be perfect."

Allen deposited his sister in the car, jumped in and revved the motor. "Listen to her purr."

"Don't drive too fast!" Deborah cautioned.

"Hey, if I get a speeding ticket, my dad will take care of it for me," Allen said jokingly. "He's the sheriff, you know."

Ashe reached out and took two-year-old Jamie McLaughlin off his mother's hip, then turned to watch his older son spin out of the driveway in his high school graduation present.

"Don't worry, honey. They'll be all right. Allen won't take any chances with Martha in the car with him. Besides, he drives like I do."

"I know. That's what worries me."

Everyone laughed. Ashe kissed his wife, saying a silent prayer of thanks to the powers that be for his many blessings.

All the dreams of his youth had come true. He had married his beautiful society wife and she'd given him three perfect children. Having been elected sheriff of Colbert County when Charlie Blaylock retired, Ashe had acquired the respect and admiration of the community, especially after he'd helped the Feds put Buck Stansell behind bars and break up the local crime ring.

Ashe didn't know whether he deserved his wonderful life, his three great kids and a wife like Deborah, but he spent every day trying to be the best husband and father in the world. And not a day went by without him thanking God for giving him a second chance with the only woman he'd ever truly loved.

* * * * *

GUARDING JEANNIE

PROLOGUE

THE MAN LAY facedown in the sand, the water lapping at his feet. From where Jeannie stood on the knoll above the beach, she could make out very little in the moonlight, only that he was quite large and he wasn't moving.

Who was he? From where had he come? A boat hadn't docked at Le Bijou Bleu in over a week. Had the man fallen overboard out there somewhere in the Gulf and his body washed ashore?

Leaning heavily on the simple wooden cane she relied on in order to walk, Jeannie made her way down the hill, slowly, carefully. If the man was dead, there was no hurry; if he was alive, she would be of little help to him if she fell and injured herself.

Maneuvering on the sand wasn't easy for Jeannie. Her heavy limp hampered her movements. As she neared the prone figure, her hands trembled. If he was alive, what would she do? Did she dare touch him, a stranger whose injuries she might not be able to discern?

Sticking her cane in the sand, she lowered herself onto her knees, all the while saying a silent prayer for assistance. *Help me do the right thing.*

Reaching out, she held her hand over the man's head. The moonlight revealed the width of his huge shoulders. His wet white shirt stuck to his muscular back. His thick blond hair lay plastered to his head and neck. With every ounce of willpower she possessed, Jeannie forced herself to touch him. The heat from his body seared her. She moaned softly. Threading her fingers through his damp hair, she closed her eyes and allowed the energy from his body to begin its journey into hers.

He was alive! Dear Lord, he was alive—but just barely. She could save him. She knew in her heart that she could.

He groaned, the sound a deep growl in his throat. When he moved his head to one side, Jeannie caressed his face, her hand cradling his cheek and jaw. For one incredible moment, she couldn't breathe, so intense was the power emanating from his big body.

She jerked her hand away, but could not stop looking at his face. Pale, haggard, and yet devastatingly handsome. Fresh blood dripped from a wound at his temple.

Did she have the strength to save him? Could she keep him alive until they got him to the mainland, to a hospital? Was he too powerful, his pain too great? She had learned from past experiences that her body and mind could accept only so much pain before the transference endangered her own life.

But she couldn't let him die, could she? Jeannie had no idea who he was, but one thing she knew—fate had ordained that he wash up on her beach, placing him in her care. This man had been sent to her. She believed that as surely as she believed the sun would rise in the morning.

With her heart beating rapidly and her stomach twisted into knots, Jeannie released her cane, which she had been holding on to with one hand, and sat down in the sand.

The man groaned again, louder, harsher, and moved his body slightly, as if he were trying to turn over. Jeannie ran her hand down his arms, soothing him, comforting him. He rolled over onto his side, opened his eyes for a split second, then passed out again.

"You're going to be all right," she told him as she lifted his head onto her lap and took his face in her hands.

She felt the first faint trickling of energy again leaving his body, the pain a delicate fluttering. Now, before the pain overwhelmed her, Jeannie surveyed what she could see of his body, searching for any other injures besides the gash on his forehead. An enormous scarlet blot stained his shirt from armpit to waist. Had he been shot? Stabbed?

"Oh!" Jeannie cried out when the pain increased. Hot, searing pain, doubling her over. She clutched at the man's shirt, holding on, trying to make her hands lie flat against the surface of his chest.

He groaned loudly, opened his eyes and cried out, rending the night air with the sound of his agony.

Help me, Jeannie pleaded. His pain was so great. She screamed when the fullness of his torment filled her. Sweat broke out on her face. Rivulets of perspiration trickled down her neck, dripping inside her blouse, leaving a moist trail between her breasts.

He manacled her wrist with his big hand, but she did not feel the pressure of his grip. All she felt was the pain she had taken from him, the torturous physical agony.

"Where...am...I?" His deep, husky voice huffed out the words, each syllable a strained effort. "Who...are...you? An angel...?"

Although she heard his questions, Jeannie could not answer him, could respond only with a wild look of helplessness in her eyes.

Now his mental and emotional pain entered her, and she screamed from the sheer misery of his thoughts. He blamed himself for someone's death. *All my fault. I was a fool. I should have been the one to die.* Oh, dear Lord, the guilt, the sad, bitter guilt. And the anger. The anger could destroy her quicker than the pain. She had to hold on, absorb it and release it. Negative energy was so destructive. It could kill her.

"What...what are you...doing?" He tried to lift his head, but the effort was too great. "I feel... I don't hurt..."

Releasing him, she fell down beside him, her face only inches from his. She was weak, so very, very weak. But she always was afterward—after she had absorbed another's pain, taken it into herself and shared an agony too great to be borne alone.

But this man would still die if they didn't get him to the hospital soon. She would have to go with him. When the pain returned, he would need to share it with her.

She had to summon Manton. The stranger was a big man, but Manton was far bigger. He would be able to carry the man to the boat, and if they hurried, they could get him to the mainland before he died.

With the remnants of the stranger's pain still radiating through her, Jeannie focused her mind on the task of summoning Manton. He was one of the few people with whom she was able to connect mentally.

Lying there in the sand, waiting for Manton to respond, Jeannie lifted her hand, then reached out and took the stranger's hand into hers. She looked into his eyes. They were a steely blue-gray in the moonlight.

"You're going to live," she said. "I won't let you die."

He didn't seem to have the strength to respond. He gazed at her for endless moments, then closed his eyes.

Jeannie didn't know how long she lay there. She, too, had closed her eyes and slept. But now Manton stood towering above her, his round bronze face and bald head shining in the faint glow of the moon.

He helped her to her feet, then glanced down at the man still lying on the beach.

"We have to get him to the hospital in Biloxi as quickly as possible." Jeannie spoke slowly, so that Manton could read her lips. She was too exhausted to speak to him telepathically, having used so much of her energy in saving the stranger. "Do you think you can carry him to the dock?"

Manton nodded, then bent down on one knee and lifted the big, unconscious man. Grasping her cane, Jeannie jerked it out of the sand and followed Manton up the beach and toward the dock where their boat was anchored.

She cradled the man's head in her lap on the journey from the island of Le Bijou Bleu to Biloxi. Each time he started to bleed again, she stopped it. Each time his pain returned, she removed it, taking it into herself, suffering it for him.

CHAPTER ONE

WHIPPING HER TAN Lexus around the corner, Jeannie raced up the driveway and came to a screeching halt at the side entrance of the antebellum home she shared with her foster father. She hoped Julian was still at the hospital board meeting. If he saw how upset she was, he would worry. Not that he wasn't already worried enough to give himself another heart attack.

Checking in the rearview mirror, she sighed with relief. Somehow she had lost the reporter who'd been following her since she left the Howell School. Tory Gaines had been waiting for her when she walked out the door. The aggravating man was bound to show up on her doorstep anytime now. After all, he knew where she lived. It seemed everyone in Biloxi, Gulfport and the surrounding towns knew where Jeannie Alverson lived, thanks to Gaines's eavesdropping and subsequent snooping into her past.

Jeannie opened the door, set the tip of her wooden walking cane down on the paved drive and eased out of the car. Leaning on her cane, she retrieved her briefcase from the front seat, then shoved the door closed with her hip. Oh, what she'd give for a cup of tea and a few moments of utter quiet.

For the past five days, ever since the story about her performing a miracle and saving a student's life had hit the newsstands, and Tory Gaines had revealed the ugly truth about her past, Jeannie's world had been turned upside down. Newspaper and magazine reporters from coast to coast called, wanting interviews. Television reporters from every network offered her the chance to tell her story to the world. And letters from across the country were pouring in, from people pleading with her to heal them from a thousand and one different ailments.

This couldn't be happening. Not again. Not after all these years of being so careful to use her extraordinary talents selectively and to keep her past life as a child healer on the revival circuit a secret.

Jeannie made her way around the hood of the Lexus, her briefcase tucked under her arm. A thin, sallow-faced middle-aged man walked out from behind the row of six-foot-high, neatly trimmed shrubbery that separated the Howell property from that of their next-door neighbor. Jeannie gasped. Who was this man? What did he want? He certainly didn't look like a reporter.

"Jeannie." His high-pitched voice sounded shrill to her ears.

"What do you want?" Remain calm, she told herself. He isn't going to harm you.

"I'm dying." He held out both hands to her, gesturing for her to come to him. "I—I have an inoperable brain tumor. You're my only hope."

"I'm sorry," Jeannie said. "I'm so very sorry. What's your name?"

"Jeremy Thornton." He grabbed Jeannie's free hand. "Please heal me. I'll give you everything I own, if you'll heal me."

Jeannie clutched her walking cane tightly. Her briefcase slipped down to her hip. She tried to catch it with her elbow, but Jeremy Thornton tugged her forward, and the briefcase fell to the ground.

"Mr. Thornton, if I could heal you, I would, but I can't. I'm not God. I don't have the power to do what you're asking."

The wild, deranged look of disbelief in Jeremy's eyes said he thought she was lying.

Jeannie squeezed his hand. "I can ease your pain… temporarily." She looked into his gaunt face, and her heart ached for him.

"I don't want you to just ease the pain," he said. "I want you to heal me. Make the tumor disappear."

"I can't do that."

"But you must." Tears welled up in his eyes. He gripped her by the shoulders, shaking her. "I don't want to die."

She focused her attention on the man's face for a brief moment, then closed her eyes. She felt the humming inside her head, the tingling current passing through her body. It would be so simple to ease his pain. All she had to do was accept it into her own body, drain it slowly away from him and experience the pain herself. So simple, and yet so devastating for her.

He shook her again, harder this time. "Help me! Everyone claims you're a healer, a miracle worker. Heal me, damn you, heal me!"

His hands tightened painfully on her shoulders, his bony fingers biting into her flesh. What could she say to reason with him? How could she make him understand the limits of her abilities?

"Ollie!" Jeannie cried the housekeeper's name at the top of her lungs, praying Ollie could hear her.

"No, don't call out for help. They're not going to take you away from me until you've healed me."

Just as Jeremy placed his hands around Jeannie's throat, she saw a lanky, sandy-haired man walking up her driveway. She didn't know or care who he was. She didn't even care if he was another reporter.

"Please, whoever you are, help me make this man understand that I can't heal him."

Jeremy's grasp around her neck loosened slowly as he turned around to face the man, who carried a white Bible under his arm.

"Brother," the man said, "you do not wish to harm this woman, do you? Her fate should be in the Lord's hands."

Jeremy slowly released Jeannie. Taking a deep breath, she stepped away. Her hands trembled. Her heart pounded.

"I want her to heal me," Jeremy said. "I can't—can't go until she heals me."

"I'm afraid you must leave. You heard her say that she cannot heal you. If you do not leave, we will have to call the police. You don't want that, do you?"

The sandy-haired man placed his hand on Jeremy's shoulder. "The Lord will heal you, if it is his will." He then turned to Jeannie, "I'm the Reverend Maynard Reeves, pastor of the Righteous Light Church. I have important business to discuss with you, Miss Alverson—the Lord's business."

The Reverend Reeves knelt down, picked up Jeannie's briefcase, then extended his arm to her. "May I escort you inside your home?"

Relief washed over Jeannie. Jeremy Thornton seemed to have calmed somewhat. Now was her chance to escape into the safety of her house, with the Reverend Reeves as an escort.

"Thank you, Reverend." She took her briefcase, accepted his arm and allowed him to lead her away from Jeremy, who stood in the driveway, dazed and unmoving, until they entered the house. "Please come down the hall and into the library with me. I'll have Ollie fix us some tea."

"Tea isn't necessary," Reeves said. "All I require is a few moments of your time."

"I suppose that's the least I can do to repay you for your assistance." Jeannie shuddered at the thought of poor, pitiful Jeremy Thornton's wild-eyed anger.

The inadequacy of her healing gave her the greatest grief. If only she could truly heal. If only she had the power to annihilate pain and suffering permanently, to put an end to all illnesses. People like Jeremy would not believe the truth, preferring to believe that she *could* heal them and was withholding that precious gift from them.

Jeannie laid her briefcase on the enormous oak desk that sat directly in front of the two floor-to-ceiling windows. "Please, sit down."

She relaxed in a tufted leather chair beside the empty fireplace. Reverend Reeves took the matching chair to her left.

"What is this important business you have to discuss with me?" Jeannie asked.

"I've driven in from New Orleans. That's where our church's headquarters are. But the Righteous Light Church has a faithful following here along the Mississippi Gulf Coast." Maynard Reeves smiled, showing a set of perfect white teeth—sparkling purity against a golden-tanned face covered with freckles. "We are greatly concerned about the gambling curse that has invaded this state."

"I don't understand." Jeannie slid her body forward, sitting on the edge of her chair. "What possible connection can I have to legalized gambling in Biloxi?"

Reeves laughed; the sound was hearty and jubilant. "I digressed. Forgive me. I simply wanted you to know that I am a man doing the Lord's work."

Where had she heard that before? All the years her stepfather dragged her from one revival meeting to another, forcing her to use her empathic abilities, he had told her they were doing the Lord's work.

"How does your work involve me?" Balling her hands into fists, she clutched them at the sides of her hips.

"I am here to offer you the opportunity to prove to me and to the world that you derive your powers from the Almighty and not from Satan." Reeves jumped to his feet. The loose jacket of his black suit swung open, revealing the gleaming silver cross hanging from his neck. "If your powers are from God, join me in my ministry, and together we will heal the sick and spread the holy message to the world."

Maynard Reeves was offering her the life she'd once known, the life that had destroyed her childhood and kept her in continual pain from the age of six until she was thirteen, when her mother's and stepfather's deaths had freed her.

"Am I to understand that you are inviting me to become a

part of your ministry, to use my abilities to further the cause of your Righteous Light Church?"

"Indeed I am." Kneeling in front of her, Reeves stared at Jeannie, his eyes glowing, his face flushed with zealous eagerness. "Powers such as yours, psychic powers, empathic powers, have a supernatural source. Those who possess power from Satan must be destroyed, and those who possess power from God must use it in his service."

"I was born with my special talent, Reverend Reeves. I have been an empath since childhood." Being able to draw the pain from others and experience it herself had seldom been a blessing to Jeannie. In fact, most often it had been a curse. But she knew her talents had no sinister, evil source, and she did not need to join forces with some hellfire-and-brimstone fanatic to prove the goodness of her heart.

"Join me, sister. I offer you the chance to acquire glory and fame and wealth, all in the name of God."

When he reached out to touch her, Jeannie leaned back in her chair, not wanting any physical contact with this man. He rose to his feet, then held out his hand to her. She shook her head.

"I don't want fame and glory," she said. "And I am already a wealthy woman. All I want is to be left alone, to continue the life I've chosen for myself."

"You're refusing to join me?" The smile vanished from his all-American-boy face. "I did not want to believe you were a child of the devil."

"I am not a child of the devil." Lifting her cane into position, Jeannie stood. "I appreciate your helping me with that poor man outside, Reverend Reeves, but I'm afraid I must ask you to leave. I'm not interested in joining your ministry. The last thing I want is to have my empathic powers exploited again, the way they were when I was a child."

"You are either with me or against me!" Reeves raised his

voice to a thundering bellow. "If you are my enemy, I will destroy you!"

Jeannie stood, bracing herself with her cane. "Reverend Reeves, I must ask you to leave. I'm not interested in joining your ministry. I have nothing to offer you."

Grabbing Jeannie by the arm, Reeves jerked her toward the window. "Come see what awaits you as Satan's daughter."

Dear God, by accepting the reverend's assistance, had she simply exchanged one danger for another? If this man didn't agree to leave, Jeannie thought, she would scream. Surely Ollie was in the house somewhere.

Lifting the edge of the sheer curtain, Reeves shoved her in front of the window and pointed outside. Jeannie gasped. A small crowd lined the sidewalk in front of the house, every person carrying a sign, each message a threat, ranging in tone from Refuse Evil, Choose God to Death to the Devil's Seed.

"I am not alone," Reeves said. "My disciples are prepared to do my bidding. Join us, Jeannie, and live life to its fullest. Refuse me, and prepare yourself to be a sacrifice to a vengeful God who will not abide your black magic."

"You're crazy." Jeannie tried to pull away from him, but he tightened his hold about her arm. "Let me go. *Now.* I'm not alone in the house."

"Choose, Jeannie Alverson. Choose the path of righteousness." Reeves's voice rose higher and higher with each word. "I offer you life or death! The choice is yours!"

"Just what's going on here?" Julian Howell, tall, slender, and regally commanding, stood in the open doorway. "Who are you, sir? And how dare you speak to Jeannie in such a manner?"

Releasing Jeannie, Reeves spun around, his captivating smile returning. "I am the Reverend Maynard Reeves, a servant of the Lord. Put on this earth to save the wicked and destroy those who will not repent."

"How the hell did you get into my house?" Julian's brown eyes turned black with indignation.

"Julian, please don't upset yourself," Jeannie said. "Reverend Reeves was just leaving." She glared at Reeves.

"You have not seen or heard the last of me," Reeves said. "I shall tell the world the truth about you. You are the devil's daughter. The Righteous Light brethren will help me destroy your evil."

"Get out of my house at once, sir, or I shall telephone the police!" Julian shook a long, slender finger at the reverend.

Reeves glowered at Jeannie. "You had your chance." He walked quickly by Julian, who followed their unwanted visitor to the front door and out onto the veranda. Jeannie waited in the foyer until Julian returned.

"This has gone too far." Julian ran a shaky hand through his thick mane of white hair. "Reporters hounding you day and night. Sick, dying people pleading for your healing touch. And now, some lunatic threatening to destroy you because he believes you're the devil's child."

Jeannie slipped her arm around Julian's waist. She loved him dearly. He had been a father to her since she was thirteen, and he was the dearest, kindest man in the world. "Calm yourself. He's gone."

"But we haven't heard the last from him." Julian shook his head. "I'm afraid for you, my dearest girl. Reporters we can deal with somehow. But there is no telling when some terribly ill soul in pain may turn on you. And Maynard Reeves is a man to fear. I saw the insanity in his eyes."

"I know you're right." Jeannie led Julian down the hall and into the library, then rang for Ollie, asking her to bring them a pot of tea.

"I've heard of this Reeves fellow," Julian said. "He and his followers have a reputation for being dangerous fanatics. His threats aren't idle threats."

"He frightens me, too." Jeannie squeezed Julian's hand. "I sensed his hatred when I refused to join him."

"You need protection," Julian said as he sat down on the oxblood-leather sofa. "I want to hire a bodyguard for you."

"A bodyguard? Surely that's not necessary. Perhaps the police—"

"The police won't provide you with twenty-four-hour-a-day protection, and that's what you need."

"Julian, do you realize what hiring a bodyguard would mean?" Jeannie asked. "We would have no privacy. This man would live in our house, share our meals, go with me everywhere I went."

"Exactly." Julian slapped his hands down atop his thighs. "And I know just the man for the job."

"You do?"

"Yes, I do. That fellow you and Manton brought in from Le Bijou Bleu a few years back. That big blond DEA agent who came by here to see you after he was released from the hospital. I can't remember his name." Clicking his tongue, Julian frowned. "What was his name?"

"Sam. Sam Dundee." Intense memories flashed through Jeannie's mind at the mere mention of his name.

Sam Dundee. In the six years since she'd found him lying on her beach at Le Bijou Bleu, she hadn't forgotten the man whose pain she had endured, whose emotional agony she had shared—the man whose very soul had joined with hers for a fleeting moment.

No, Sam Dundee would never return to Biloxi, not even for her. He might have promised that if she ever needed him, he would help her, but how could she hold him to that promise?

"I'm sure Mr. Dundee is far too busy to be bothered with coming to Biloxi," Jeannie said.

"Nonsense. The man sent you his business card when he opened his private security business, didn't he? He wouldn't have done that if he hadn't wanted you to be able to reach him if you needed his assistance."

"Why don't you call Mr. Deaton? Our lawyer should be able to line us up with a reputable security firm."

"I don't understand your reluctance to call this Dundee fellow. After all, he does owe you his life. I'm sure the man will want to repay his debt to you."

Jeannie had thought she'd never seen Sam Dundee again. There had been no legitimate reason to contact him. Over the years, she had come to realize that the link she'd made with Sam had not been severed, that in some strange way they remained connected. He was still a part of her soul. Such a joining had never happened to her, before or since, and admitting the strength of their bond, even to herself, unnerved Jeannie.

"Mr. Dundee won't come to Biloxi himself." She had known the day he came by the house to thank her and say goodbye that he had no intention of ever returning to the Gulf. What had happened to him on his last DEA assignment had changed his life forever and put him on the run from guilt and remorse. The day she found him on her beach, she had felt his emotional agony, as well as his physical pain.

"I'll call him all the same." Julian patted Jeannie's hand. "I'm sure he'll want to repay his debt to you. And if he can't come personally, I'm sure he'll send one of his associates."

"I wish you wouldn't insist on—"

"What's wrong, my dear? Is there something about Mr. Dundee I don't know? Some reason I shouldn't call him?"

"No, of course not. It's just that…" Jeannie groaned, then took Julian's hand into hers, instantly sensing his unease and his great fear for her. She shouldn't be arguing with Julian. He was an old man with a weak heart. If calling Sam Dundee would put his mind at ease, then she'd make the phone call.

"I'll call Mr. Dundee," Jeannie said.

Julian smiled. "Yes, yes, by all means, call the man. Ask him to fly down as soon as possible. Tonight, or tomorrow at the latest. We should have him here before your press conference tomorrow."

Jeannie hugged Julian, then kissed his weathered cheek. "I still have the business card Mr. Dundee sent me. It's upstairs in my address book. After we have our tea, I'll call him in Atlanta and let him know I need his help."

"Your Mr. Dundee is the answer to my prayers," Julian said. "You know I'd give my life to protect you, but I'm an old man, and do well to take care of myself. As a surgeon, I've spent my whole life helping other people, and now I can't help the person I love most in this world."

"You *can* help me, and you do, just by loving me."

And Sam Dundee could help her. He could provide what Julian could not, the protection she so desperately needed. Now, after six long years, she would see him again—the man who haunted her dreams and possessed a part of her soul, the man whose power over her she feared far more than she feared Maynard Reeves.

SAM DUNDEE LOOSENED his black-and-gray silk tie, then flipped through the stack of newspaper articles piled on top of his desk. Jeannie Alverson stared up at him from the black-and-white photograph some determined reporter had snapped of her as she was leaving her home several days ago. Hell! The woman had become front-page news across the country.

They were calling her a miracle worker. A healer. A psychic. An empath with unlimited powers.

A tremor shook Sam's shoulders. For six years he'd told himself that he had imagined what happened on that beach, when an angel of mercy held him in her arms. He had pretended he'd been delusional, that she had not drawn his pain from him. He had not wanted to believe she had delved into his mind and eased the torment he had felt—still felt—knowing he'd been responsible for the deaths of others. But here the truth was—in print. Or was it the truth? Hell, it couldn't be. No one possessed those kinds of powers.

Sam picked up the remote control, switching on the videotape of the newscasts from the past several days—the ones dealing with the Mississippi empath who had once been touted throughout the south as a child healer.

He froze the picture the moment the camera zoomed in for a close-up shot of Jeannie. Jeannie. She was as hauntingly lovely as her name. Even though Sam knew the woman's strength, had experienced it firsthand, he saw the sadness in her eyes, the vulnerability in that soft, endearing face.

Jeannie Alverson had somehow bewitched him six years ago, leaving him unable to forget her. He owed her his life. There was no doubt about it. He had felt compelled to see her after his release from the hospital, to find out if what he remembered had really happened. But once he looked into her hypnotic brown eyes, all he'd wanted was to get away from her before it was too late. His gut instincts had warned him that if he ever became involved with Jeannie, he would never be able to escape.

Sam stopped the VCR tape. Damn, what was he doing to himself? Jeannie was a part of his past, a part of that dark, devastating misery he had endured in Biloxi. He could not remember Jeannie without remembering all the rest. Perhaps that was his punishment, never being able to put the past behind him.

Several quick taps on his closed office door brought Sam's head up and focused his vision on the opening door. His secretary peeped in.

"I'm leaving early, Sam." Gertie Saunders waved her ring-clad fingers at her boss. "Everybody's out except J.T. He said to tell you he'll bring in some sandwiches for the two of you in about five minutes."

"Thanks, Gert. Have a nice dinner."

"I will," the attractive grandmother of three said, a flirtatious smile on her face. "My gentleman friend is taking me somewhere special."

"Well, in that case, feel free to come in late tomorrow morning."

Gertie had worked for Sam since he'd opened his Atlanta office, nearly six years ago. A recent widow, with two sons in college, she hadn't worked outside the home in twenty-five years, but hiring her was the smartest thing Sam had ever done. She ran his office like a well-oiled machine, and she knew how to keep him and his partners in line. No one intimidated Gertie Saunders, not even J. T. Blackwood, and J.T. could intimidate the devil.

The telephone rang just as Gertie was closing the door. "You want me to get that?" she asked.

"No, I'll get it," Sam said. "You don't want to keep your gentleman friend waiting."

Sam picked up the receiver. "Dundee Private Security. Dundee speaking. How may I help you?"

"Sam?"

Every nerve in his body froze instantly. He hadn't heard that voice in over six years, but he would never forget it. He heard it in his dreams, whispering his name, comforting him, reassuring him.

"Jeannie? Jeannie Alverson?"

"I suppose you've read about me in the newspapers and seen the stories on television."

"You're headline news."

"My whole world is topsy-turvy. My life's a mess. I can't go anywhere or do anything without being followed by reporters, and people begging me to heal them, and now…"

"And now what?" She wasn't calling him to discuss the details of her life that he'd seen on television for the past few days. No, there had to be something wrong, terribly wrong, for Jeannie Alverson to contact him.

"There's a man named Maynard Reeves. He's the minister of a group who call themselves the Righteous Light Church."

"Never heard of him."

"He's based in New Orleans, but he has a congregation in Biloxi," Jeannie said. "He's claiming I received my powers from Satan, and he's threatened to destroy me. I believe he's fanatical enough to kill me if he has to."

"Are you calling to ask for my help?" *No, don't ask me to come back to Biloxi. Don't ask me to face the demons that have haunted me for six years. Don't ask me to become personally involved in your life.*

"Yes. Julian and I agree that I need a bodyguard until all this hullabaloo dies down and we are certain Reverend Reeves isn't a real threat to me."

"Who's Julian?" Sam asked before he even thought, then suddenly remembered what he'd read about Jeannie having been raised by foster parents—Dr. and Mrs. Julian Howell.

"Julian is my father. My foster father."

"So you and your father think you need a bodyguard." *But not me,* Sam thought. *I'll send you my best man. I'll make sure you're safe, but I will not come back to Biloxi.*

"Of course, we'll pay you your regular fee. It isn't a question of money."

Sam swallowed hard. It wasn't a question of money for him, either. It was a matter of preserving his sanity. If he went to Biloxi to guard Jeannie, he would have to come to terms with his past. Jeannie Alverson would probably want to help him. He didn't want to be helped. He had become accustomed to living with the anger and guilt, had accepted it as his punishment.

"I'll send J. T. Blackwood to Biloxi tomorrow. He's one of my partners and the best at what he does." Sam heard the indrawn breath, then the silence on the other end of the line. "I don't take bodyguard assignments myself. Not anymore."

"Oh, of course, I understand. By sending your best man here to guard me, you'll still be keeping your promise to me."

Why had he ever made that stupid promise? *If you ever need me, all you have to do is ask.* He supposed he'd thought she'd never need him. Hell, he'd prayed she'd never need him, that he'd never have to deal with what had happened between them.

"What difference does it make whether I come myself or I send someone just as capable?"

"It doesn't make any difference," she said. "I understand. Believe me, I do."

"Ms. Alverson, I owe you my life." Blowing out an aggravated breath, Sam clutched the telephone fiercely. "I want to repay you, but…Biloxi holds a lot of really bad memories for me."

"You still haven't forgiven yourself, have you?"

"I don't know what you're talking about."

"I need help, Sam Dundee. My life could be in danger. If you feel you can't return to Biloxi, that you don't have the strength to face your ghosts, then send Mr. Blackwood. But ask yourself one thing. Do you really want to put my life in another man's hands?"

Bull's-eye. She'd hit the mark. Jeannie Alverson knew that for any other man the assignment would be nothing more than a job, but for Sam it would be personal.

"When do you need me?"

"Now," she said. "By tomorrow at the latest. I'm holding a press conference at the Howell School tomorrow, and I really need—"

"You're doing what? Where?" Sam hollered at her.

"I'm holding a press conference at the Howell School, in the gymnasium."

"What's this Howell School and why the hell would you agree to hold a press conference there?"

"The Howell School was founded by Julian's wife, Miriam, to help children with physical and mental challenges that make it difficult for them to receive the help they need in regular schools. I work at the school as a counselor. My degree is in psychology." Pausing, Jeannie took a deep breath. "Julian and I decided to hold a press conference where I'll have the opportunity to explain to everyone the exact limitations of my powers. We think it's a wise course of action."

"You're crazy if you hold a press conference anywhere," Sam said. "But especially in a school gymnasium. You'll be too confined. It's a stupid idea. Don't do it."

"I disagree," Jeannie said. "The press conference is already set for ten tomorrow morning. Can you be here by then?"

What the hell was the matter with her reasoning? And with Julian Howell's? Didn't they realize that the press would eat her alive? "I'll fly my Cessna down first thing in the morning and meet y'all at the Howell School."

"Thank you, Mr. Dundee. I knew I could count on you."

"Goodbye, Ms. Alverson." Sam slammed down the telephone. "Dammit!"

J. T. BLACKWOOD stood in the doorway, holding two roast beef sandwiches in his hands. It looked like Sam was in rare form this evening.

His partner of over four years had become his best friend. Oddly enough, the two men had found they had a lot in common, despite the vast differences in their backgrounds and present lifestyles. J.T. admired Sam Dundee more than anyone he knew. Sam was a man you could trust with your life, a man you could count on to be a tower of strength.

Like J.T. himself, Sam didn't make friends easily. Of course, he could be a mean bastard at times, but that was part of his charm. And one more thing the two of them had in common. In any fight, J.T. would want Sam on his side.

A lot of men disliked Sam, but J.T. didn't know one smart man who wasn't just a little bit afraid of Sam Dundee.

"Got a problem?" He walked into the office, laid the sandwiches on top of the stack of newspaper clippings and sat down on the edge of the desk.

"Nothing I can't handle." Sam glanced at the sandwiches. "Roast beef?"

"What else?" J.T. eyed the coffee machine on the low shelf in the corner. "I take mine black."

"What?"

"My coffee," J.T. said. "I brought the sandwiches. I figured you'd fix the coffee."

"That stuff's been sitting there for a couple of hours. It'll probably grow hair on your chest."

"I'll take my chances."

Sam scooted back his chair, walked across the room and poured two cups of strong, well-aged coffee. "Here." He handed J.T. a bright red mug.

"So, are you going to tell me or not?" J.T. asked.

"I've got to fly to Biloxi in the morning. I don't know how long I'll be gone. A week, two, maybe more."

"Biloxi, huh?"

"Yeah, I know. I said I'd never go back there."

"What changed your mind?" J.T. unwrapped his sandwich, took a bite, then washed it down with the coffee.

"Jeannie Alverson."

"Who's Jeannie—? Hey, you mean the woman on the news, the healer who saved some kid's life after she'd been wounded in a drive-by shooting?"

"Yeah, that Jeannie Alverson."

"You're taking a bodyguard assignment? You haven't done that in years. Why now?"

Sam lifted his mug to his lips, tasted the bitter coffee and frowned. "I should have made us a fresh pot."

"Is there something personal between you and this Jeannie Alverson?"

"Yeah, you could say that. She's the woman who saved my life six years ago, when the DEA sting I was involved in went sour."

"So you owe her."

"Yeah, I owe her. I promised her that she could demand payment in full anytime she needed me."

"And she's called in your marker."

"Something like that."

There was more going on here, something Sam wasn't telling. J.T. had known the man for nearly five years, he considered him his best friend, but there was a lot the two of them had never discussed. Oh, they shared old war stories… Sam's days in the marines and the DEA… J.T.'s own stint in the army and his life as a Secret Service agent. He had explained to Sam why he wore the black eyepatch, had told him all about how he'd lost the vision in his left eye when an assassin's bullet lodged in his head. But he'd never told Sam about his childhood, had never told him about his Navaho mother. J.T. twisted the silver-and-turquoise ring on the third finger of his right hand.

A man usually didn't share the demons in his soul, those personal demons that kept him raw and bleeding inside, long after old wounds should have healed.

J.T. had known, when Sam told him the bare-bones details of his last DEA assignment, that something had happened during that time to change Sam's life forever. J.T. wondered if that something had anything to do with Jeannie Alverson.

CHAPTER TWO

SWEAT COATED THE palms of Jeannie's hands, beaded across her forehead and trickled between her breasts. Her heartbeat roared like a runaway train, the sound drumming in her ears, pounding in her chest. Her legs weakened. She gripped the curve of her wooden cane. Nausea rose in her throat, bitterness coating her tongue.

Why wouldn't they leave her alone? She had tried to answer their questions, had tried to make them understand. But they circled her like vultures waiting for the moment of death. They shoved microphones in her face. They bombarded her with questions so personal her cheeks flamed with embarrassment. Flashes of light from their cameras blinded her.

If only she could escape. But there was no escape from the media—from the frenzied crowd of reporters determined to get a story out of Jeannie Alverson. Nor did there seem to be any escape from Maynard Reeves and his followers. At least a dozen of the reverend's disciples were there this Thursday morning, dispersed throughout the crowd, their Die Witch posters held high for everyone to see.

How could this have happened? She'd been so careful for the past fourteen years, revealing the truth to no one, using her abilities to only a limited degree, so that others would not suspect.

The day Cassie Mills was shot, how could Jeannie have known that by helping her, she would doom herself to a living hell? Poor Cassie, in all her childish innocence, had told the police exactly what had happened, and neither she nor the police had realized a snoopy reporter could hear their conversation at the hospital. Tory Gaines had not been content to exploit the present facts. No, he had dug into Jeannie's past—a past she had prayed would never return to haunt her.

"When did you realize you possessed the ability to heal, Ms. Alverson—or should we call you Ms. Foley?"

"Do you claim to work miracles for God?"

"How much money did your mother and stepfather cheat people out of by passing you off as a faith healer?"

"What religion are you, Jeannie?"

"The people we've questioned who were present when you supposedly worked your magic on Cassie Mills claim that you seemed to go into shock, taking away the child's pain and stopping the bleeding from her gunshot wound. Is that true?"

Dr. Julian Howell wrapped his arm around Jeannie's shoulders. She desperately wanted to lean heavily on the man who had been her foster father since she was thirteen, but Julian was a very old man, and his health had been failing these last few years. Jeannie realized she had to be strong as much for him as for herself. But she wasn't sure how much longer she could endure the endless questions, the clamor, the noise, the bodies that pushed closer and closer.

Dear Lord in heaven, help me, she prayed. Agreeing to hold this press conference had been a terrible mistake. She should have listened to Sam Dundee. He'd tried to warn her. Why, of all places, had she chosen the gymnasium of the Howell School as the location for this debacle? There was nowhere to run, and no one to help her and Julian.

Tory Gaines shoved his way through the throng of reporters, his tall, gangly frame towering over the others. His dark eyes focused on Jeannie.

"I understand that since the truth was revealed about you, Jeannie, you've been flooded with requests from terminally ill people begging you to heal them."

"Is it true that a man you refused to help actually attacked you?" a red-haired TV news reporter asked.

"Please, listen to me." Jeannie couldn't bear the way they were looking at her, the way they were treating her. As if she were some freak, some alien creature. "I do not possess the power to heal people. I never have. I have certain... abilities... as an empath. I can feel the pain of others. What I do for people is temporary. That's all—"

"You can't only feel their pain, you can take it away." Tory raked back a long strand of black hair that had fallen over his right eye. "You can remove both physical and psychological pain, can't you, Jeannie?"

"I am not a true healer." Jeannie glanced down at her wooden cane. "If I could heal others, why wouldn't I heal myself?"

Julian's arm, clasping her shoulder, trembled. Jeannie sensed her foster father's frustration at not being able to protect her.

"I'm all right, Julian," she whispered. "Please don't worry. All this stress isn't good for your heart."

"We have answered every question we can," Julian said, facing the crowd, his voice strong and authoritarian. "Jeannie has told you everything. There is no more. Please, allow us to leave."

When Julian, aided by Marta McCorkle, the supervisor of the Howell School, tried to assist Jeannie through the crowd, the media closed in around them, pushing and shoving. Julian and Marta flanked Jeannie, slowing their pace to accommodate Jeannie's hampered gait.

"I had hoped he would be here by now." Julian leaned down, directing his conversation to Jeannie. "When you spoke to him again early this morning, he promised he would arrive in time for the press conference, didn't he?"

"He'll be here soon." Jeannie saw the microphone as it came toward her face. She stopped dead, aware that the young female reporter for the local television station was not going to move aside.

"Is it true, Ms. Alverson, that the deacons from the Righteous Light Church here in Biloxi have condemned you as a fraud, and their minister, Reverend Maynard Reeves, has gone so far as to claim you are a witch, a devil worshipper?" The reporter glanced meaningfully at the Die Witch signs held high in the air by Reeves's avid disciples.

Jeannie tried to turn her head, wanting to avoid answering the question. But the reporter was persistent, stepping closer, inserting one of her feet between Jeannie's feet, pressing the microphone a hairsbreadth from Jeannie's mouth.

"Let us pass," Julian commanded, unaccustomed to people disregarding his orders.

"I've called the police." Marta pointed her index finger at the persistent reporter.

"Are you a fraud, Jeannie? Or are you a witch?" the reporter asked.

"I'm neither."

The reporter's foot slid into the side of Jeannie's walking stick. Jeannie gripped her cane, but to no avail. The cane tumbled from her hand. Her knees gave way. She clutched at Julian's sleeve, but her clammy hands slipped off the soft material of his jacket. Marta cried out, reaching for Jeannie, her fingers just touching her hair as she toppled over, landing roughly on her knees.

SAM DUNDEE SAW Jeannie Alverson fall, accidentally tripped by the overzealous redhead harassing her. Sam cut through the media horde like a machete slicing through untamed jungle. The reporters stared at him, whispers rising from the mass, questioning the big man's identity.

"Who the hell do you think you are?" a bearded middle-aged tabloid photographer asked.

"I'm the cavalry to the rescue," Sam proclaimed, the deadly curve of his mouth an easily understood warning to others.

Sam reached out, grabbing the red-haired reporter who had

tripped Jeannie Alverson. Manacling her arm, he glared at her, noting the shock in her green eyes. When he released her, she backed away, the surrounding swarm following her lead.

Sam stared down at the woman whose face had been plastered on the front page of newspapers and across every television screen in the country for the past few days. Jeannie looked even more delicate, more fragile, in person. Bending on one knee, Sam gently shoved Julian Howell aside and lifted Jeannie into his arms. She gazed into his eyes, and a hard knot of fear formed in the pit of Sam Dundee's stomach. He remembered those compassionate eyes. Those warm, compelling brown eyes.

Jeannie clung to Sam, draping her arm around his neck, resting her head on his shoulder.

"Everything will be all right, Ms. Alverson. I'm here now. I'll take you to safety. I had a limousine pick me up at the airport. It's waiting outside."

The crowd watched in stunned silence while Sam Dundee carried Jeannie Alverson through their midst. Once the pair had exited the building, the reporters followed, taking little note of Dr. Julian Howell or Marta McCorkle.

Sam told himself not to look at Jeannie Alverson again, to simply carry her out to the waiting limousine. Her fingers touched the nape of his neck. A soft, tender touch. Sam's nerves screamed. His body tensed.

"I prayed for your help." Her voice was sweet, and unintentionally sultry. A slow, honey-coated southern drawl. "Thank you, Mr. Dundee. I appreciate your coming in person."

Against his better judgment, Sam looked at her then. She smiled—a closed-mouth, half-formed smile. Jeannie was not classically beautiful. Her features were too large—her big eyes a gentle, faded brown, her full lips a pale pink, her round cheeks flushed with emotion. Despite the frailty of her appearance, she felt sturdy and solid in his arms. And at that moment, Sam knew without a doubt that her fragile facade was an illusion, that behind her delicate feminine softness existed an incredibly strong woman. Jeannie Alverson was a survivor. And yet she possessed a quality so totally feminine, so genuinely genteel, that Sam wanted nothing more than to protect her, to keep her safe from all hurt and harm.

He forced his gaze away from her face.

The chauffeur held open the limousine's door. Sam slipped inside, depositing Jeannie on the seat.

"Where's Julian?" she asked, tugging her billowing skirt over her legs.

"I'm sure he's fine. The reporters aren't interested in him. Only in you," Sam said, then turned to the driver. "Take the route I mapped out for you. That should take care of some of our followers."

"Where are we going?" Jeannie took a long, hard look at her rescuer, and her breath caught in her throat. This big, strong man, who had carried her through the crowd as if she weighed nothing, was the man she had found dying on the beach at Le Bijou Bleu six years ago. She had saved his life then; now he was here to protect her and repay the debt he thought he owed.

"I'm taking you home." Sam sat back in the seat, his gaze focused out the side window. He was not going to be suckered by this woman, despite her aura of sweet innocence. She was a job, and nothing more. *Liar!* His conscience screamed at him. He should have sent Blackwood or Roarke. *But this was Jeannie Alverson.* He had no choice but to handle the job personally.

He owed her his life. If she hadn't found him six years ago, he would have died. And nothing she asked of him would be too great a price to repay her for his life.

Jeannie didn't mean to stare at Sam, but she couldn't stop herself. She had dated several men over the years, but hadn't allowed herself to become close to any of them. She knew she never could give herself to a man without first being honest with him about her past, about who and what she was. And she had been able to control her sexuality all her life. So why couldn't she handle the attraction she felt for Sam Dundee?

She wanted to reach out and touch his hard, lean face. She wanted to say or do something that would make him smile. He looked as if he seldom smiled. His face had set into a sensually beautiful aloofness, every feature blatantly, irresistibly male.

His thick, wavy blond hair was styled short in the back and sides, with more length left on the top. His heavy brown eyebrows hooded a set of intense blue-gray eyes.

Sitting at his side, Jeannie could feel the power and strength of the man. She felt safe and protected, and at the same time she was vividly aware of the danger Sam Dundee posed to her.

In six years, she had not been able to forget him. He had remained a vivid image in her mind, a smoldering passion in her heart.

They sat alone in the back of the limousine, neither of them speaking. Sam continued gazing out the window. Jeannie closed her eyes in silent meditation, praying for the strength to live through this ordeal, to be able to resume her normal life and find a way to bring peace to Sam Dundee's tortured soul.

When they arrived at Julian's home, the limousine slowed to a snail's pace as the chauffeur turned into the driveway. Crowds of people—reporters, curiosity seekers, true believers and accusers—lined the driveway, filled the front yard and spilled over into the street.

"Damn!" Sam cursed under his breath.

"What's wrong?" Jeannie peered out the tinted side window. "Oh, dear Lord!" There were more people surrounding her home than had overrun the Howell School.

"Don't worry. I'll try to get things under control before I take you inside." Sam glared at her, his look a warning in itself. "Stay here. I'll come back for you in just a minute."

Jeannie nodded her head. She clutched her hands together in a prayerlike gesture, trying not to think about anything—not the past, not the present, not the future. Summoning all her willpower, she forced herself not to look out the window, not to check on what was happening. If she and Julian were going to survive this ordeal, they would have to allow Sam Dundee to do his job. After all, he was a trained professional who was ready to lay his life on the line to protect her.

She heard voices outside, a mixture of questions, shouts and pleas. Closing her eyes, she tried to concentrate on emptying her mind, on blocking out everything except the serenity within her own soul. Someone threw a brick at the limousine, shattering a side window. The loud crash jarred her from the moment of peace she sought.

The door flew open. Sam Dundee reached inside, dragged Jeannie across the seat and lifted her into his arms. "We're going in the side entrance. The housekeeper will open the door the minute we approach."

"What about all these people?" Jeannie asked, holding on to Sam's neck as he carried her up the sidewalk, the crowd closing in around them. "Why won't they leave me alone?"

Sam knew that he couldn't hold back so many people for long without using his 9 mm Ruger. He had to get Jeannie inside as quickly as possible.

"Just hang on tight." Sam broke into a slow run, carrying Jeannie directly to the side porch.

The housekeeper flung open the door the moment Sam's feet hit the porch. When they were safely inside, he didn't turn, but continued down the narrow hallway. Ollie Tyner shut and locked the side door.

"Bring her on in here to the back parlor." Ollie, a short, plump, gray-haired woman, darted in front of Sam, sliding back the panel doors. "She can't walk without her cane, so don't put her on her feet."

Sam looked directly into Jeannie's faded brown eyes and wished he hadn't. He couldn't shake the feeling that his very life depended on protecting this woman, this gentle, helpless woman. No, not helpless. Even if she couldn't walk without her cane, she would never be helpless. Her eyes told him that she was strong, that she would endure whatever came her way. And her eyes told him that she knew he would help her.

Sam eased Jeannie down onto a red velvet settee in front of an empty fireplace. She slipped her arms from around his neck slowly, never taking her eyes off his face.

"Thank you, Mr. Dundee."

"You're welcome, Ms. Alverson. I was just doing my job."

"Won't you sit down?" Without waiting for his reply, she turned to Ollie. "I would very much like some tea. Mr. Dundee, would you care for anything?"

He shook his head, indicating that he didn't. Ollie exited the room quickly.

"I'm worried about Julian," Jeannie said. "He has a heart condition, and all this excitement isn't good for him."

"I'm sure Dr. Howell is fine. He probably left right after we did. I don't think he was in any danger. You were the reporters' target. They aren't interested in anyone except you at this point."

Sam glanced around the room, looking up at the high ceilings and the elaborate moldings, then down at the antique furniture. "Where's the telephone?"

"On the desk. There." Jeannie pointed to the gold-and-white mock-antique telephone perched atop the small cherry desk.

"The police need to clear out this crowd around the house," Sam said. "We've got a near-riot situation on our hands."

"The emergency numbers are listed there by the phone." Jeannie rubbed her forehead with her fingertips, massaging the ache in her temples. "Thank you, Mr. Dundee. I appreciate your arriving when you did. I don't know how I would have gotten away from the school without your help."

Sam glared at her. "Why the hell did you agree to a press conference? You should have known what would happen. I tried to warn you. Why didn't you listen to me?"

Jeannie sat up straight, stiffening her spine. She wasn't used to being spoken to so harshly. "We…Julian and I thought that if we met with the press, we might be able to reason with them."

Sam grunted. "Lady, nobody is that naive. You're news, big news, and those vultures aren't going away for a long, long time. Not until something or someone else comes along that is bigger news."

He scanned the pad on the desk, dialed the police department and demanded to be put through to a senior officer. After explaining the situation and being assured that the police would disperse the crowd, Sam hung up the phone and paced the room. Glancing at Jeannie, he noticed the strained look on her pale face and wondered if she was in pain.

Jeannie rubbed her thigh. Even thirteen years after the car wreck, after several surgeries and endless therapy, the pain never completely left her. But it was a bearable pain, a pain she had become accustomed to, unlike the pain of being exposed to the world as Jeannie Foley, child faith healer. She thought it ironic that she could share the pain of others, vanquish it from their lives temporarily, but had to endure her own pain alone.

"Are you all right?"

"Yes, I'm… I'll be fine. Thanks to you. I feel safe, here at home."

"Well, the safest place for you, for the time being, is going to be inside this house. You don't want a repeat performance of today's events, do you?"

"I can't allow my life to be disrupted this way," she said.

"I'm afraid you have little choice in the matter." Sam took the biggest chair in the room, a floral-tapestry wing chair. "The best I can promise you is to keep you safe, to protect you from the press and anyone else who won't leave you alone, especially this fanatical minister you told me about when you called."

"I will not let my life become the three-ring circus it was when my mother and Randy Foley were alive." Knotting her hands into fists, Jeannie held them in front of her. "From the time I was six years old and Randy persuaded my mother to take me to a revival meeting, until I was thirteen and they were both killed in a car crash, my life was a living hell."

"I've read all the newspaper accounts," Sam said. "The recent ones from the past couple of days, and the old ones from when you were a child. Your parents made a lot of money off of you, didn't they? They must have died millionaires."

Ollie knocked at the door, then entered, carrying a silver tray. She placed it on the marble-topped mahogany table in front of the settee.

"Thank you, Ollie. That will be all for now." Jeannie lifted the silver teapot.

"Ollie," Sam said just as the housekeeper started out the door.

"Yes, sir?"

"Keep watch at the side entrance," Sam told her. "We're expecting Dr. Howell."

"Yes, sir." Ollie left the parlor.

Jeannie added sugar to her tea, then lifted the china cup to her lips, sipping leisurely. She eyed Sam over the rim of her cup. "Randy Foley was my stepfather," she said. "And yes, my mother and Randy did die millionaires."

"Money they fleeced off suckers who believed that little Jeannie Foley possessed a special power from God that could heal them."

"Yes. Money that poor, gullible fools handed over to Randy eagerly, just to have me lay my hands on them and take away their pain, to give them a temporary healing." The cup in Jeannie's trembling hand quivered on the saucer. She set her tea on the silver tray.

Just to have me lay my hands on them and take away their pain. Was that what the woman who'd found Sam on the beach six years ago had done? Had she laid her hands on him and taken away his pain? Sam could remember those hours vaguely, could remember soft, caring brown eyes filled with tears—his tears, tears she had cried for him when she drew his pain out of his body and into hers.

Hell, it hadn't happened that way. It couldn't have. He had imagined the whole thing, hadn't he? He'd been burning up with fever and conscious only part of the time. For a few minutes, he'd thought he had died and that the woman who held him in her arms was an angel. Didn't that show how crazy he'd been? How totally out of his head?

"How long have you lived here in Biloxi?" Sam asked.

"Since I came out of the hospital, when I was thirteen. Julian and his wife, Miriam, became my foster parents."

A door slammed shut. Feet tramped up the hallway. The parlor door opened, and Dr. Julian Howell walked in, followed by Marta McCorkle.

Julian rushed to Jeannie's side. Sitting beside her, he took her hands in his. "My dearest girl, are you all right? There's an enormous crowd hovering around outside."

"I'm fine, Julian. Really I am. With Mr. Dundee acting as my protector, how could I be otherwise? Besides, Mr. Dundee has telephoned the police. They should arrive shortly and take control of that unruly crowd."

Marta McCorkle walked over to Jeannie and handed her a wooden cane. "I was able to pick this up before we left the school. I know it's your favorite, and I was afraid someone would take off with it."

"Thank you, Marta. You're right, it is my favorite cane. Miriam gave it to me."

Turning, Jeannie gazed up at Sam, her lips curving into a warm smile. Sam felt as if he'd been hit in the stomach with a sledgehammer. Dammit, this had to stop, and stop now! He couldn't allow himself to feel anything special for this woman, couldn't allow their relationship to become personal.

Who was he kidding? Their relationship was already personal, about as personal as a relationship could be without sexual intimacy. Sam shuddered, his big shoulders moving only slightly. His guts knotted painfully. When a man owed a woman his life, anything that happened between them was personal.

Standing, Julian offered Sam his hand. "I'm Julian Howell. I can't tell you how glad I am that you agreed to take this assignment yourself. I knew you were the only man for the job."

Every nerve in Sam's body came to full alert. Of course he was the only man for the job. No one else owed Jeannie as much as he did. No one else was as highly trained to protect her as he was, or as prepared to die for her.

"All of us who love Jeannie are grateful for your presence, Mr. Dundee," Marta said.

Turning to Julian, Jeannie squeezed his wrinkled, age-spotted hand. "I've told Mr. Dundee that I would like to continue living my life as normally as possible."

"And I've told Ms. Alverson that what she wants will be impossible," Sam said.

"Oh, my dear, Mr. Dundee is right." Julian shook his head, grunting sadly. "Until this scandal dies down, I believe the safest place for you is Le Bijou Bleu. No one could reach you except by boat or helicopter, and it's doubtful anyone would discover your whereabouts there."

"I will not be run out of Biloxi!" Jeannie jerked her hands out of Julian's grasp, positioned her wooden cane, then stood and confronted Sam. "I have my work at the school. The children need me. They're very special children, with special needs. You're going to have to find a way to protect me. Here in Biloxi. I intend to hold my head high and see this thing through to the end, without running away, without shirking my duties to the students at the Howell School."

Marta, who still stood at the side of the settee, reached out and patted Jeannie on the back. "If continuing to work at the school puts you in any danger, we can make do without you for a while."

Sam stared into Jeannie's eyes, those faded brown eyes that he would never be able to forget. Julian Howell had mentioned

Le Bijou Bleu, the island where Sam had washed ashore. Memories of those hours when Jeannie Alverson had acted as his angel of mercy flooded Sam's mind.

"You're the boss, Ms. Alverson. We'll do things your way," Sam said. "But it won't be easy for you, and the minute things get out of hand, we start playing by my rules, no questions asked. Agreed?"

Jeannie was unaccustomed to men like Sam Dundee. Men who issued orders. Men who put their lives on the line to protect others. Men who carried guns. She had felt Sam's holster when he held her in his arms.

"I agree to your terms," Jeannie said. "We do it my way, and if that doesn't work, then we'll do it your way."

"All right." Sam turned to Julian Howell. "I'll need a room as close to Ms. Alverson as possible. At this point, I think the physical danger to her isn't life-threatening. The reporters will continue to hound her as long as they think the public is interested. My main concern is this Reverend Reeves. Fanatics are unpredictable, especially those who are under the false impression that God is on their side."

"The reporters are a nuisance," Julian said, "and I feel sorry for those poor people who are begging for Jeannie to heal them, but you're quite right—what concerns me most is that this Reverend Reeves has threatened her. He and his congregation have accused Jeannie of being the devil's daughter. Reeves told her that if she didn't join his church, he would destroy her."

"We can handle the threats," Sam said. "As long as these people don't act on them. If that happens, we'll be in for some real trouble."

"Maynard Reeves is the worst of his kind," Marta said. "He uses every opportunity possible to get himself on TV and in the news."

"Mark my words," Julian said, "Reeves will do more than make threats. Jeannie has sensed he wants to kill her."

Dammit, Sam thought, was Jeannie claiming to be telepathic,

as well as empathic? He didn't believe she was a healer, but he might buy her being psychic. His niece Elizabeth was psychic. She'd had the uncanny ability to read people's minds and pick up on their feelings since she'd been a child.

"Are you telepathic, Ms. Alverson? Can you read people's minds, send and receive messages?" Sam asked.

"Only to a limited degree," Jeannie said. "But I am able to feel other people's emotions. When Reverend Reeves touched me, I felt a deep hatred. If I don't join his ministry, I think he plans to kill me."

"It will be my job to make sure that doesn't happen." Sam clasped Jeannie's elbow, uncertain what was true and real about this woman, and what was pure hype. "Why don't you give me a tour of the house, Ms. Alverson? I'll need to know what sort of security system y'all have here. And I'll want a list of the people who would normally visit you or Dr. Howell here at home."

"Fine." Jeannie led Sam to the door, then stopped and turned, smiling at her foster father. "Why don't you go upstairs for a nap before dinner? I'll take care of Mr. Dundee."

"Yes, very well," Julian said. "Put him in the guest room directly across the hall from your room. I'll have Ollie prepare it for him."

"I'll see Julian upstairs," Marta said. "I'm staying for dinner, if that's all right."

Jeannie nodded. "I'm glad you didn't allow what happened today to change your plans to dine with us tonight."

Sam cleared his throat. "Ready to give me that tour, Ms. Alverson?

"Yes, I'm ready."

Nodding goodbye to Julian and Marta, Jeannie leaned heavily on her cane, the stress of the day's upheaval having taken its toll on her. She willed herself to stand as straight as possible. Sam Dundee was watching her closely, and she did not want him to think of her as helpless. He was the kind of man who would respect strength, not weakness, and she very much wanted Sam's respect. She dared not admit, even to herself, that she wanted far more than that from him, more than she'd ever wanted from any other man.

CHAPTER THREE

SAM PULLED BACK the green cotton velvet draperies in the room he had been given. The room's elaborate style wasn't to his taste, but that was of little importance. Over the years, he had discovered that he was equally restless or content, whatever his surroundings. Whether he slept on silk sheets or in a sleeping bag, Sam's state of mind was the only factor dictating his satisfaction.

And tonight he was greatly dissatisfied. His gut instincts told him that this case might well be his undoing. After six years of waiting for the inevitable, Sam was now back in Biloxi, with the one person on earth who knew the depth of his torment and guilt.

Six years ago, Sam had been a DEA agent on an undercover assignment. Foolishly, he had thought he had the upper hand, that the game would be played by his rules. He'd been wrong. Dead wrong.

Sam removed his coat, laying it across the chair where he'd thrown his tie. There was definitely something different about Jeannie Alverson. She didn't claim to be a healer; she professed to have only the power to take away a person's pain. Temporarily. But did he believe her?

His memories of Jeannie were all tangled up in his mind with the memories of his last DEA assignment and the tragedy that had almost ended his life. He wouldn't have met Jeannie, never would have washed ashore on her island, if he hadn't been trying to entrap a big-time drug dealer.

Jeannie was lovely and sweet and certainly the type of

woman who made a man want to protect her. All feminine
and fragile. What man wouldn't be attracted to her? It was only
natural for a man to think about making love to her.

And Sam certainly didn't live a celibate life. But he did
choose his sexual partners with great care. It was a proven fact
that Sam Dundee had a heart of stone, and he always steered
clear of permanent entanglements.

He had learned, the hard way, never to have an affair while
working on a case. Any man who allowed his sexual needs to
overrule his better judgment was a fool. Sam had been a fool
once, but never again! And most certainly not with Jeannie
Alverson. A man with a raging beast inside him didn't have
the right to even think about making love to an angel.

Sam stormed out of the bedroom, slamming the massive
wooden door behind him. Dammit, he hadn't allowed himself
to truly desire a woman in a long time.

He could handle his attraction to Jeannie Alverson, but he
couldn't forget how he felt about the woman who had saved his
life. If he could separate the two in his mind, he didn't have
anything to worry about. But what if he couldn't?

JEANNIE SAT AT the antique secretary in her bedroom. Staring
down at the blank page in her daily journal, she lifted her pen.
She dated the page, then wrote.

Today he came back into my life. Sam Dundee.

Clutching the pen in her hand, Jeannie bit her bottom lip as she
thought about the day's events.

For six long years she'd been unable to forget him, yet certain
she'd never see him again. And now here he was, in her home,
a few yards away, across the hall. He would be at her side,
near her day and night, protecting her from the nightmare her
life had suddenly become, keeping her safe from the outside
world.

Why had this happened? Why had she become front-page news? For thirteen years, her past had lain dormant, and she'd prayed it would never awaken. She could not—would not—allow the painful memories to destroy her, any more than she would allow recent events to take away the life she dearly loved.

A soft knock sounded on Jeannie's door. Surely it wasn't Julian. He had retired shortly after dinner. Perhaps it was Ollie, saying good-night before she went to bed.

Jeannie lifted the pastel floral silk robe off the edge of her bed, slipped into it and, leaning on her cane, walked across the room. She opened the door, smiling, prepared to say good-night to Ollie.

Sam Dundee, all six feet four inches of him, stood in her doorway, the muted hall light turning his blond hair to dark gold.

Jeannie's smile faded as she gasped at the sight of the big man, who had discarded his jacket and tie and removed his gun holster. His shirt was partially unbuttoned, revealing his thick neck and a swirl of brown chest hair.

"I'm sorry to bother you, Ms. Alverson, but I'd like to speak to you for a few minutes."

Sam tried not to look directly at her, focusing his gaze over her shoulder. Her room was even larger than the one he had been given and, if it was possible, even more elaborately decorated. In quick succession, he noted the intricately carved mirrored wardrobe, the massive matching bed, the pale pink quilted bedcover and the light floral-and-striped wallpaper.

"Yes, please come in, Mr. Dundee." Jeannie stepped back, spreading out her arm in a gesture of welcome.

The only man who had ever been in her bedroom was Julian. She had to admit it felt odd having Sam Dundee enter her private feminine sanctuary.

"Won't you sit down?" Jeannie indicated the sitting area by

the floor-to-ceiling windows where the rococo-revival sofa, armchair and marble-topped table had been arranged.

"No. Thanks. This won't take long." Sam felt like a bull in a china shop. Despite the sturdy appearance of the antique furniture, Jeannie's bedroom was totally feminine, as soft and delicate as the woman herself. He had the oddest feeling that if he walked too heavily, he would destroy the beauty of the room.

"What did you want to discuss with me?" Jeannie walked across the room, leaned on the bedpost and rested her cane against her side. Suddenly feeling exposed in her floor-length ivory silk gown and floral robe, she tightened the sash around her waist.

"As you already know, six years ago I was here in Biloxi on an undercover assignment for the DEA." Sam looked directly at her then, searching for some sign to indicate how much she really knew about him. She walked away from him, seating herself on the sofa. "I was shot, then thrown overboard off a barge. Undoubtedly I wasn't far from a small island. I don't have any memory of what happened until I awoke on the beach and found myself in the arms of an…angel."

Jeannie's head lifted, and she gazed into Sam's steely blue-gray eyes. She was indeed his angel of mercy, and at this precise moment she looked like an angel, her long, wavy brown hair cascading down her back like a waterfall of dusty beige silk.

"I only remember bits and pieces about that night. I was unconscious most of the time." Sam sat in the chair beside the sofa. "I'll never forget your gentle brown eyes and your soothing voice. Or the enormous dark-skinned man who carried me to the boat."

"Manton," Jeannie said. "His name is Manton."

She had thought Sam Dundee remembered practically nothing about that night. After his release from the hospital, he had found her and thanked her for saving his life. He'd told her then that he remembered very little of what had happened after he was shot.

Did he know that, for one brief instant when she had borne his pain and cried his tears, their souls had been united? No, of course he didn't.

"Manton, huh?" Spreading his legs apart, Sam leaned forward and placed his hands on his knees. "When I came to in the hospital, after surgery, I was told that some huge bald man had carried me into the emergency room and then disappeared. If it hadn't been for that report from the emergency room staff, I would have thought I'd dreamed the whole thing. The island. The woman. The man.

"Lucky for me one of the emergency room nurses had a child enrolled in the Howell School, or I would have had a tough time finding you. Why didn't you and Manton stick around after he carried me into the emergency room?"

"We had done all we could do for you. There was no need for us to stay."

"Where is Manton now?" Sam asked.

"Manton lives on Le Bijou Bleu. He never leaves the island unless there's an emergency." Jeannie rested her trembling hands in her lap. "When my mother and Randy bought the island, Manton was the caretaker, so they kept him on. Manton is a deaf-mute, but he can read lips." *And he and I can speak to each other telepathically,* Jeannie thought.

"Then Le Bijou Bleu belongs to you?"

"Yes, it's mine. I go there whenever I want to escape from the world."

"Why did you protest so strongly when Dr. Howell suggested you go there now, until things settle down?"

"Because I will not be run off. I will not allow others to dictate my actions." Jeannie lifted her cane from the side of the sofa where she had placed it. "For years, Randy Foley controlled every moment of my life. Once I was no longer at his mercy, I swore that no one would ever again force me to do anything I didn't want to do."

Jeannie stood and walked to the windows. Noticing the way her shoulders quivered, Sam knew she was crying. He couldn't bear to see her hurting. Hell, why did he let her get to him this way? Women's tears usually had little, if any, effect on him.

Walking over to her, Sam placed his hand on her shoulder. She tensed. He draped his arm around her, then turned her slowly to face him, gripping her shoulders in his big hands.

"You saved my life that night."

She did not try to hide her tears from him, but she ignored them, allowing them to fill her eyes and fall onto her cheeks. "I did all that I could to keep you alive until we arrived at the hospital."

Sam let out a deep breath. "For six years I've wondered about you. Wondered if you were as pure and sweet and caring as I'd thought you were. Wondered if you really did take away my pain, or if I'd been delusional and just imagined the whole experience."

"You didn't imagine any of it. What happened between us was real."

"Tell me something."

"What?" Did he remember the moment when they had become one, the moment when she had prayed for his life and for her own, and the tears she had shed were the tears of two?

"Do you have the power to heal?" he asked, taking her chin in his hand and tilting her face.

She shook her head. "No, I'm not a true healer. I can't make the sick well again. Randy passed me off as a faith healer, but I've never had that kind of power."

"But you can take away pain? You draw physical and mental pain out of a person, and bear that pain yourself?"

"Yes. Julian and Miriam said that I was an empath, that I could experience another's pain. Somehow I reach inside people's minds, inside their hearts and their bodies, and feel what they're feeling. I can heal temporarily, but the pain returns, as does the injury or the illness. It usually returns in a few hours. Sometimes the results last for a few days. But that's rare."

He wiped the tears away from her face, their moisture coating his fingertips. "That's what you did for me six years ago on the beach, isn't it? You drew the pain out of me and experienced it for me? Is that why I felt practically no pain, although I was suffering from gunshot wounds and exposure?"

"You were almost dead," Jeannie said. "And you didn't want to live. You felt a tremendous guilt for someone else's death."

"You absorbed that guilt, too, didn't you? You took it away for a while."

"I had no choice. Otherwise you might not have willed yourself to live."

Releasing her abruptly, Sam backed away, his gaze riveted to her gentle face, her warm eyes, her caring smile. She lifted her hand, extending it toward him.

This woman had saved his life. There was no doubt about that fact. He remembered how the pain had left him, not only the physical pain from his wounds, but also the mental and emotional torment he'd suffered. Had she taken the burden of his pain, his guilt and his unspoken wish to die, and suffered for him, freeing him, saving him?

Did he dare believe her? Could he trust his own feverish memories?

Taking a tentative step toward her, Sam accepted her welcoming hand and pulled her into his arms. She gasped when their bodies touched. He released her, then cupped her face in his big hands.

"Jeannie." He said her name with reverence.

"Sam." The man she had dreamed of for six years, the stranger she had been unable to forget, was looking at her with a passionate, possessive hunger he could not disguise.

"I'll take good care of you, Jeannie." Lowering his head, he kissed her tenderly. A gentle, undemanding kiss. A kiss of gratitude. A kiss filled with promise.

Jeannie felt that sweet kiss in every nerve of her body, and for one tiny instant, she was tempted to ask for more. But now was not the time. Sam Dundee was confused about his feelings, about what was happening. She sensed his frustration, his doubts, his fears and the guilt that never left him.

Sam grabbed her by the shoulders, shaking her gently. "Don't misunderstand the reason I'm here. I'm not looking for healing and salvation. So don't go probing into my past. Maybe you really can take away pain. Maybe you took mine away. Hell, I don't know. But I do know I owe you my life. And I always pay my debts. Do we understand each other?"

He rushed out of the room, leaving her standing there staring at his broad back. Leaning on her cane, she made her way to the bed, removed her robe, folded it and draped it around the bedpost. She lay down, drawing the sheet up to her waist.

She willed herself to relax, to erase everything from her mind. Tomorrow she would have to face reality again. Tonight she needed rest, and if she didn't stop thinking about Sam Dundee, she wouldn't get any sleep.

SAM DIDN'T EVEN try to sleep. He had far too much on his mind. The past, the present and the future. He could never escape from the past. Where Jeannie Alverson was concerned, the present kept getting all mixed up with the past. She was a part of that horrible night when everything had exploded in his face and two people had died because of his stupidity.

Sam checked his watch. Almost midnight. He pulled out a chair and sat down at the kitchen table. Everything had been quiet for hours. The local authorities had patrolled the street for several hours after dark, and once the few stragglers still hanging around outside saw the police car, they had disappeared.

Sam entwined his fingers, then laid his hands on top of the

table. He had no idea how long he'd have to stay in Biloxi. He knew he'd be here until Jeannie was no longer in any kind of danger. That could be weeks or even months, depending on how long the press continued making her front-page news, and if and when Maynard Reeves made good on his threats.

Sam owed Jeannie his life. He'd never told anyone except his niece Elizabeth about everything that had happened the night he washed ashore on Le Bijou Bleu. And he'd had no choice but to level with Elizabeth. Since she'd been psychic since childhood, she would have read his mind anyway.

Sam sat at the table in the semidarkness. The only light came from a fluorescent fixture over the sink. He was pretty sure he could handle things here alone, but if necessary, he'd send for J. T. Blackwood, one of his partners, or Hawk or Kane, the new members of his agency.

Sam grunted, the sound containing an element of humor. He recalled a female acquaintance once comparing him to J.T. She'd said that where Sam was Chivas Regal, J.T. was pure white lightning; they were as different as night and day, and yet both possessed the power to kick you on your butt.

WAKING WITH A start, Jeannie lay in the darkness, listening to the sound of her own breathing. She had been dreaming—a sweet dream at first. But it had turned dark and frightening. She had been dancing in Sam Dundee's arms, not needing her cane, her legs strong and sturdy. She felt free and happy and totally safe. Then Sam had been ripped from her arms and she cried out, but no one heard her screams. And then Sam had returned to her, broken and bruised and writhing in pain, but he wouldn't allow her to touch him.

The dream had been so real. Too real. She wiped away the tears that had gathered in the corners of her eyes. Was the dream a premonition, or just the result of a traumatic day? Surely the latter, for she knew she would never dance in Sam's arms. And who could bring such a strong and powerful man to his knees? But then she remembered that Sam had been shot and dumped in the ocean six years ago. Sam was a strong, powerful man, but he was not invincible.

Slipping out of bed, Jeannie felt for her cane. Leaning on the wooden stick, she walked across the room, pulled back the curtains and gazed out at the dawn. Fingers of pale pink light wiggled across the charcoal sky. She glanced down into the courtyard at the back of the house and saw a shadowy figure standing against the wall, near the trailing red rosebush, barren in late summer.

The faint moonlight blended with the first tentative rays of sunlight. Pressing her face against the windowpane she sought a better look at the man. He stepped away from the wall, and she knew instantly that it was Sam Dundee. Few men were as big and tall as he; few possessed his broad shoulders and tawny blond hair. She wondered what he was doing up at this hour. Had he been restless and unable to sleep? Had nightmares kept him awake?

Turning his head, he looked up at her window. Jeannie sucked in her breath. Had he seen her? Yes, she knew he had. He continued staring up at her and she down at him. She laid her hand on the windowpane. He nodded his head.

What would it take, she wondered, to reach his soul, to get inside him and free him from his pain and anger and guilt? He would never willingly allow her to help him.

"Somehow, I'll find a way to save you, Sam Dundee," she vowed.

CHAPTER FOUR

SITTING AT THE mahogany table in the dining room, Sam glanced away from Jeannie Alverson, who was nibbling on a banana muffin and sipping her morning coffee. Sam stared at the ceiling, only half noticing the intricate plaster molding that complemented the graceful plaster detailing in the dado and cartouche panels. He had gotten very little sleep last night, but that didn't bother him. It took days of sleep deprivation before Sam felt the effects. Lack of sleep wasn't what was bothering him, nor the small group of people gathered on the sidewalk across from the Howell home.

What was bothering Sam was Jeannie herself.

He could not allow himself to become involved with Jeannie. A close relationship could be dangerous for both of them. For a woman like Jeannie, a delicate, tenderhearted, spiritual creature, he would mean disaster. Sam knew himself only too well. He was a hard-edged, tough realist who had nothing to give a woman except a brief physical encounter. Jeannie would want more—more than he could ever give her. By keeping his distance, both physically and emotionally, he'd be doing them both a big favor.

"Do you think there will be a problem for Jeannie leaving the house?" Julian Howell asked. "It's not even eight o'clock and already there's a crowd outside."

Sam glanced toward the head of the table, where Dr. Howell sat, his dark eyes filled with concern. "I can control the crowd temporarily. The limo will arrive shortly and I can whisk Ms. Alverson away without incident. Don't worry, Dr. Howell, I know what I'm doing. If I thought I couldn't handle the situation, I'd have already called the police."

"I wasn't questioning your abilities, Mr. Dundee. I was simply voicing my concern." Julian's long, thin fingers gripped his china cup, his hand quivering slightly.

"I understand," Sam said. "But rest assured that nothing is going to happen to Ms. Alverson."

"I spoke with Marta before I came down for breakfast." Jeannie looked at Sam for the first time since she'd walked into the dining room. She had deliberately avoided eye contact, knowing how difficult it would be to stop herself from trying to mentally connect with him, something he would resist. As far as he was concerned, he had come to Biloxi to do a job and repay a debt. She had to respect his desire to be left untouched by her empathic powers.

"What's the situation at the school?" Julian asked.

"Marta said that things are relatively quiet. There are only a few people waiting around outside." Sam's steely gaze surveyed her. She tilted her chin, continuing to stare directly at him. "You think going to the school is a mistake, don't you, Mr. Dundee?"

"I think you're asking for trouble by exposing yourself." Sam picked up his coffee, swallowed the last of the warm liquid and set his cup on the saucer. "My job would be a lot easier if you stayed at home. You would be a lot safer. By the time we arrive at the school, the crowd probably will have doubled."

"There are people counting on me at the school." Could she make him understand how important her job was, how essential helping the children was to her? "I can't allow the frenzy that has taken over my life to deprive the children of the guidance and comfort I give them."

"If you want to go to work today, then I'll take you to work." Sam scooted back his chair and stood. "But if anything goes wrong and I think you're risking your life, you'll take my advice. You'll do what I tell you to do."

Jeannie glared at Sam. She had to stop herself from making a biting retort. She wanted to scream that he wasn't going to tell her what to do, that she wouldn't allow him to order her around. Although Julian and Miriam had guided her gently through her teen years, they had been careful not to try to control her life, well aware of the scars left on her soul by her stepfather's domination.

Jeannie laid her napkin on the table, eased her chair back and stood, lifting her cane from where she had hung it on the chair arm.

"Will you check and see if the limousine has arrived?" she asked Sam, then leaned over and kissed Julian on the cheek. "Don't worry about me. I'm in capable hands."

Jeannie did not see Sam's body tense, but she sensed his reaction. Watching him exit the room, she marveled at the sensations coursing through her, at the pure sensual longing that came over her. These feelings weren't new, but they were unique. She had felt them only twice. Six years ago, with Sam Dundee. And now.

But why? Why, out of all the men in the world, did she respond only to this particular man?

Returning, Sam halted in the doorway. "The limousine is here. We can leave whenever you're ready."

Walking over to Sam, Jeannie took his arm. The moment she touched him, she sensed the anger and pain simmering inside him, just below the very controlled surface of his emotions.

He walked slowly, adjusting his long strides to her shorter, partially unbalanced gait. She curled her fingers around his forearm, tightening her grip when he opened the door and guided her outside.

Shouts from the group on the sidewalk bombarded them the moment they stepped onto the side porch. Cameras clicked, flashes blinded, voices rose higher and higher. In the background, the Righteous Light brethren chanted, "Witch!" as they held their posters high above their heads.

Sam hurried Jeannie into the waiting limousine, got in beside her and slammed the door. She touched his shoulder, then jerked her hand away and stared at him, into those blue-gray eyes that told her she shouldn't be surprised by what she had sensed. Jeannie shivered. Within Sam Dundee there existed a suppressed violence, a deep remorse, a guilt so great that it created a physical ache in him.

Dear Lord, how had he survived for six years with so much pain? If he would let her, she could help him. The emotions buried within Sam were slowly killing him, destroying him as surely as any bullet could.

And now the anger and pain and, yes, even the guilt, extended to her. Because she had helped save his life six years ago, Jeannie was tied to his past, had become a part of his torment. He would never allow her to help him, to reach inside his tortured soul and give him peace. And yet he longed to repay his debt to her, to keep her safe, to protect her from all harm.

The limousine made its way slowly past the milling crowd. Jeannie sat beside Sam, looking neither to the right nor the left, wanting desperately to shut out the intruding world. The silence within the limousine was somehow comforting, as was Sam Dundee's presence. There was something so powerful about the man; he radiated strength and control.

Surely there was some way she could help him, some way she could save him from himself, without running the risk of falling in love with him. Loving Sam Dundee would be disastrous. His inability to return her love would destroy her. If she was smart, she would accept him on his terms, allow him to act as her bodyguard and repay the debt he owed her. She dared not give him more, nor expect more in return.

TWENTY-FIVE MINUTES later, Jeannie opened the door at the side entrance of the Howell house and jerked away from Sam's hold on her arm. "I'll be in the front parlor, if anyone needs me."

"Dammit, there's no need to act this way," Sam said. "I couldn't allow you to go inside the school. The risk would have been far too great. Those idiots were throwing rocks at you, yelling, 'Stone the witch.' I told you before we left here that if anything went wrong, we'd do things my way."

"And that's exactly what we did." Jeannie stopped in the hallway, pivoted quickly and glared at Sam. "No discussion. No compromise. The minute we arrived and a few people threw some pebbles at the limo, you ordered the driver to turn around."

"A few pebbles, hell! I'll bet there are dents all over the limo. Those people meant business. Why do you suppose Marta McCorkle had called in the police?"

Gritting her teeth, Jeannie squinted her eyes and huffed, then turned around and marched down the hallway, the *tap-tap-tap* of her cane echoing in the stillness.

Sam followed her, although what he wanted to do was go to the airport, board his Cessna and fly home to Atlanta. "We need to talk."

"What is there to say?" Jeannie shoved back the panel door and entered the front parlor. "You overstepped your authority. You are my employee. I'm supposed to give the orders."

"You hired me to protect you, didn't you?" Sam stood in the doorway. "If you won't listen to my advice, how the hell am I supposed to save you from your own stupidity?"

"My own stu— Oh! It is not stupid to want to go to work, to want to help the children I love so dearly, to want my life..." Jeannie slumped down on the sofa, clutching her cane in her trembling hands.

Damn, was she going to cry again? He hated it when she cried. Other women used tears like a weapon, wielding them to make a man do their bidding. But Jeannie wasn't like other women. And that was *his* problem. He had to stop thinking of her as special and start remembering that she was just a woman—nothing more, nothing less.

"For the time being, you're going to have to stop worrying about everyone else and concentrate on yourself and your safety." Crossing the room, Sam stood in front of her, neither looking at her nor touching her. "I know you're upset because the media and the miracle seekers and Maynard Reeves have stolen your privacy."

"They've stolen my life!" Jeannie yelled.

Julian Howell rushed into the front parlor. "What happened? What's wrong? I could hear the two of you screaming at each other all the way upstairs."

"We weren't screaming at each other," Jeannie said. "We were having a slight difference of opinion."

Julian turned to Sam. "Why have y'all come back to the house? What happened at the school?"

"Ms. McCorkle had to call in the police," Sam said. "The place was crawling with reporters, and a huge crowd of Righteous Light brethren were marching, chanting and throwing rocks. The grounds outside the school were a madhouse."

"You didn't allow Jeannie to get out of the limousine, did you?"

"No! He most certainly didn't let me get out of the limousine!" Jeannie repeatedly tapped her cane on the floor.

"Oh, I see. So that's what this is all about." Smiling, Julian sat down on the sofa beside Jeannie, then looked up at Sam. "You see, Mr. Dundee, our Jeannie doesn't like to take orders. Give her a little time and she'll see that you did the right thing. She's too busy fuming over being told what to do to see the reason behind your actions."

Jeannie rested her cane against the edge of the sofa, leaned back and crossed her arms over her chest. "What are the children going to think if I don't show up? They won't understand."

"Marta will try to explain things to them, my dear," Julian said. "Until Maynard Reeves can be stopped, you must allow Mr. Dundee to take every precaution."

Jeannie glanced at Sam, who was looking not at her, but at

some point over her head. "I'll allow Mr. Dundee to do his job. But in the future, I would appreciate his discussing his decisions with me, instead of issuing orders."

"If the situation warrants a discussion, we'll discuss it," Sam said. "Otherwise, you'll do what I say, when I say. Your life might depend on your following my orders."

"If you think—" The moment he looked at her, she couldn't speak. His cold, steel gray eyes issued a warning. "We'll discuss this later. I want to call Marta and check on the situation at the school."

The doorbell rang. Ollie, who had been dusting in the foyer, stuck her head just inside the open parlor door. "There's no need to call Marta. That's her at the front door, with some gray-haired man. And there's a couple of policemen with them."

"Let them in, Ollie," Sam said.

"Show them in, please, Ollie," Jeannie said, as if Sam hadn't already spoken.

Sam walked out into the hallway, standing just outside the front parlor and watching while Ollie opened the door. Marta hurried inside, not speaking to Ollie or acknowledging Sam in any way, and went straight to Jeannie.

"Are you all right? I've been so worried," the plump, petite Marta said. "I've never seen anything like it!"

"I'm fine. Just a little shaken. I had no idea it would be so bad," Jeannie said.

The two uniformed policeman stayed in the foyer, by the front door; a heavyset middle-aged man in a lightweight cotton suit walked up to Sam.

"I'm Lieutenant Rufus Painter. We've taken care of things at the Howell School. I left several men there to make sure things are safe for the staff." Painter held out his hand. "Good thing you got Ms. Alverson out of there as quickly as you did. That crowd was getting mean."

Sam shook the lieutenant's hand. "Sam Dundee. We spoke over the phone recently. I'm Ms. Alverson's private bodyguard."

"Well, Dundee, things are going to get worse before they get better. As long as Ms. Alverson is front-page news, people are going to hound her. She'd be better off if she stayed out of sight until things die down a little. And so would the whole town of Biloxi."

"Please come into the parlor, Lieutenant," Jeannie said, her voice a bit louder than usual.

Sam followed Lieutenant Painter, the two men coming to a standstill, side by side, in front of Jeannie. "Glad to see you're all right, ma'am," Painter said.

"How could I be otherwise, with Mr. Dundee taking such good care of me?" Jeannie smiled at Sam, then at the detective. "Would you care for some coffee, Lieutenant?"

"No, thank you, ma'am. I just came by to check on you, and to let you know we arrested several of those Righteous Light people."

"What about Reverend Reeves?" Julian asked.

"I'm afraid not," Painter said. "The reverend was gone by the time we arrived."

"Is there any way you can keep those people from blocking the school entrance?" Jeannie asked. "It's important for me to be able to go to work."

"Ma'am, all we can do is disperse the crowd and arrest anyone who isn't cooperative or is causing any harm." Painter shook his head. "I'm afraid we just don't have enough manpower to keep officers at the school all the time."

"Jeannie?" Reaching down, Marta took Jeannie's hand. "Most of the children didn't come to school today."

"What?" Jeannie stared up at Marta, who squeezed her hand.

"We had numerous parents call to say that they saw WXBB's morning newscast showing the crowd outside the school. They're afraid, Jeannie, and I can't blame them."

"This situation is intolerable!" Rising off the sofa, Jeannie lifted her cane. "Our children are being punished by that swarm of reporters and that picket line of so-called Christians. And it's all my fault. Because of me, the children can't even come to school."

"This isn't your fault," Marta said. "You've done so much good for the children. You've helped them in a way none of us can."

"But now my coming to the school will harm them." Jeannie walked over to Sam. "I thought I was doing the right thing going to school today, but I see now that as long as things stay the way they are, I can't continue my work at the Howell School. My presence would pose a threat for the children and the staff."

"The staff is one hundred percent behind you," Marta said.

Jeannie smiled that warm, gentle smile that tore at Sam's heart. He couldn't let her smile or her tears keep getting to him this way!

"Marta, you and the others will have to carry on without me. Until I have control of my life again, I can't come back. But I would appreciate being kept informed on each child's progress."

"I'll call you every day and fill you in on all the details." Marta gripped Jeannie's free hand tightly.

"Thank you." Jeannie closed her eyes for a brief moment, absorbing Marta McCorkle's fear and concern. "Don't be afraid. Everything will be all right."

"I know it will." Marta bit her bottom lip. Tears gathered in the corners of her hazel eyes. "I'll handle things." Marta glanced at Sam. "Please take care of her. She's very dear to all of us, you know."

Sam swallowed hard. Damn sentimental females! He nodded. What was he supposed to say? Hell, he owed Jeannie Alverson his life, and he was going to do whatever was necessary to keep her safe.

Jeannie looked at Sam. "I'm sorry I overreacted. You were right and I was wrong."

Sam didn't say anything; he simply nodded again. Maybe now she'd follow his orders without question. It sure would make life a lot simpler if she did.

One of the young policemen standing in the foyer called for Lieutenant Painter. "I think you'd better come here, Lieutenant. Take a look outside."

"Stay here," Sam told Jeannie.

"All right." Jeannie held on to Marta's hand.

Sam stood behind Lieutenant Painter, looking over his head, when the man gazed out the panel window on the right side of the front door.

"Damn," Painter said.

A live news team from WXBB had one camera aimed at the Howell house and another at a small group of Righteous Light brethren surrounding their leader. Reeves, his mane of sandy red hair glowing like fire in the morning sunshine, stood atop a folding chair in the midst of his followers, who waved their signs in the air and looked to Reeves for cues. A shout of "Repent, devil's daughter!" rose from the disciples.

"I ran a preliminary check on Reverend Reeves," Sam told Painter. "He talks a good game, and he appears to be a spell-binding speaker. I'd say he sees an opportunity for publicity and intends to use his damnation of Jeannie Alverson as a stepping-stone to national recognition."

"I'd say the man could be dangerous." Painter motioned to the two uniformed policemen. "Go outside and ask the reverend to take his band of merry men and women somewhere else before I have their butts tossed in jail."

"Yes, sir," the two men replied in unison.

Painter opened the door for his men. "Whatever you do, Dundee, keep Ms. Alverson inside."

Sam stood in the open doorway, watching Painter walk out onto the veranda. Suddenly a war cry of "Witch!" rose from the Righteous Light disciples. Reverend Reeves, sweat dripping from his flushed face, pointed a neatly manicured index finger toward the Howell house and demanded that Jeannie end her unholy alliance with the devil. The WXBB newswoman shared with her audience the hoopla surrounding the Howell home, where the Mississippi faith healer lived. The camera zoomed in on Reeves's face, showing plainly the righteous indignation of the evangelist determined to bring Jeannie Alverson to repentance.

Sam realized that Reeves considered himself a power to be reckoned with. His gut instincts warned him that the scripture-quoting evangelist was evil incarnate, a disciple of hate, not of love. And Jeannie was right. The man probably did intend to kill her.

What Sam needed was a complete, detailed report on Reeves's life. Somewhere there was bound to be a well-kept secret, a little flaw in the man's holier-than-thou armor. Sam hoped he could show the police proof that Reeves was a real danger to Jeannie before the man actually tried to harm her.

He had to find a way to stop Reeves. Even if that meant killing him to defend Jeannie. If it came down to that, he'd have no other choice. But what would she think of him then, gentle, tenderhearted Jeannie? Would she be able to understand the savage warrior in Sam, the primitive nature inside him that made him capable not only of dying to protect her, but also capable of killing, if need be, to keep her safe?

Sam shouldn't give a damn what Jeannie thought of him. But, heaven help him, he did.

CHAPTER FIVE

LATER THAT FRIDAY evening, Jeannie decided to face the mounting correspondence piled on her desk. She divided the letters into three separate stacks on top of the pale pink heirloom quilt that covered her bed. Every day, more and more letters poured in from across the United States, and now requests were coming in from Canada, Mexico, South America and Europe. In a week's time, her sane, sensible, orderly life had been completely destroyed. Poor little Cassie Mills, in all her sweet innocence, had opened a Pandora's box of problems for Jeannie.

"Why do you read those things? You should throw them in the trash." Sam Dundee stood just inside the open door, pure masculine beauty in his tailored gray pin-striped suit and coordinating burgundy-and-gray silk tie.

"I divide them into categories." Jeannie patted the stack directly in front of her. "These I throw away—" she pointed to the stack on her left "—and these, too."

"Let me guess." Sam closed the heavy wooden door behind him. "The throwaway letters are from journalists requesting interviews and from crackpots condemning you as a witch."

Jeannie looked up at Sam, standing by her bed, his steely blue-gray eyes piercing in their intensity as he stared at her. Her heart skipped a beat. "These—" she cleared her throat "—are from people asking for my help." Lifting the large stack of letters in her hands, she pressed them to her bosom. "They break my heart. So much misery and suffering, and I can't even offer them hope."

Tears gathered in the corners of her eyes. Sam looked away, not wanting to see her cry. Why the hell did she care so much about people she didn't know? And why weep over the fact that she couldn't permanently heal the whole world of its illnesses? Because Jeannie was that kind of person. She cared too much, and that caring caused her great pain.

He realized there was a lot he didn't know about Jeannie. And he wanted to know everything, yet at the same time he was afraid to find out more.

Sam walked over to the window and looked outside. Early-evening shadows, violet blue and cool, wavered in the August twilight. He kept his back to Jeannie, hoping she wasn't crying and hoping she didn't realize what he was thinking. Sam Dundee was a man who'd seldom been afraid of anything, and yet Jeannie Alverson frightened him in a way nothing and no one ever had.

In some ways, she reminded him of his niece Elizabeth. Both of them were unique women, born with special talents. But there was a vulnerability in Jeannie that Sam had never seen in Elizabeth. A sadness that ran so deep in her that he instinctively knew that only an abundance of love could ever lessen it.

The telephone on the nightstand rang. Jeannie reached out to answer it; Sam grabbed the phone.

She glared at him. "I don't like not being able to answer the phone in my own home."

He thrust the phone at her. "Here, answer it!"

Snatching the telephone out of his hands, she scooted to the center of the bed and turned her back on him. "Hello. Oh, hi, Julian." She cut her eyes in Sam's direction. He looked at her, his expression unreadable. "No, no, you musn't come home for dinner on my account. Ollie's prepared us a nice light chicken salad. You go ahead and take Marta out for dinner."

Sam hated it when Jeannie confronted him with her displeasure over his specific orders. One of his rules was to always let Ollie, Julian or him answer the phone if she chose not to let the answering machine get it. He'd also strongly advised her to allow him to take care of her mail, without her ever having to see it. But she was so damned stubborn. She didn't like having her routine disrupted and seemed to resent his suggested changes, changes meant to protect her.

Jeannie replaced the telephone on the nightstand. "Who did you think it was, Maynard Reeves? I doubt he has our new number, since it's unlisted."

"There are ways to get unlisted numbers." Sam stuffed his hands into the pockets of his trousers, lifting the edges of his jacket, revealing the hip holster that held his Ruger.

Jeannie shivered at the sight of the gun. She hated guns, hated weapons of any sort. But she understood the necessity of Sam carrying a gun. There were bound to be times when a man in his line of work would have to rely on more than brute strength.

How difficult it must be for him, Jeannie thought, to protect others, to carry the burden of their security on his wide shoulders. She could not imagine a man more suited for the job, a man more capable. Despite his cool and aloof attitude, his hard, ironclad exterior, Sam Dundee possessed a golden center of gentle strength and loving compassion. He would deny its existence, perhaps didn't even know of its existence, but Jeannie knew. She knew because she had once tapped into that golden core, had touched the secret heart and soul of this man.

She knew she shouldn't be fighting him at every turn, repeatedly refusing to follow his orders. No, not *orders,* exactly. Perhaps *directions* was a better term. He didn't make suggestions to irritate her, even though they did; no, he made suggestions he thought would protect her.

"You're right about these letters. There's really no need for me to go through them." She mixed together the three piles of correspondence, scooped them up in her hands and placed them in the curve of her left arm. Bracing herself with her cane, she walked into the sitting room and tossed the letters into the brass wastepaper basket near the mahogany writing desk. "From now on, you can handle all the mail. And I won't answer the phone again."

"Such easy compliance, Ms. Alverson." Sam's lips twitched in an almost smile. "What brought about this sudden change of heart?"

"It wasn't sudden," she admitted. "I've been thinking about all the suggestions you've made, and I realize that if I continue being stubborn, I'll make your job more difficult. I don't want to do that."

"I appreciate your cooperation." Dear God, how he wanted to pull her into his arms, kiss those full, sweet lips and hear her sigh.

Jeannie avoided eye contact with Sam, sensing a growing hunger within him. She had never before been confronted with a man's needs—needs that she wanted to fulfill. She knew very little about male-female relationships, had distanced herself from the sensual side of her nature, but Sam Dundee made her want to explore that unknown.

A soft knock on the door came as a welcome relief. Sam opened the door to Ollie, who came bustling in, carrying a cloth-covered silver tray.

"I've brought your supper up here, just as you requested," she said to Jeannie, who willed herself not to blush. "Just leave everything on the tray when you're finished, and I'll take care of it in the morning."

"Thank you." Jeannie smiled at Ollie, then turned her attention to the silver tray that the housekeeper had placed on the Battenburg-lace-covered round table.

Ollie excused herself, leaving Jeannie and Sam alone. Lifting the cloth covering the tray, Sam surveyed the contents of their meal. Chicken salad, croissants, fresh fruit and cheese.

"Sit down, please." Jeannie lifted her eyes and glanced directly at Sam.

"Ladies first." He pulled out her chair and seated her, his hand brushing her shoulder. He sat across from her, watching while she poured hot tea into the delicate Lenox cups. Her hands quivered ever so slightly. Sam glanced down at the china plate containing a mound of freshly prepared chicken salad lying on a bed of crisp lettuce.

He made her nervous. Sam found that realization strangely reassuring. Obviously he wasn't the only one experiencing an unnerving, unwanted attraction. Since arriving in Biloxi yesterday, Sam had felt unbalanced, as if his equilibrium were a bit off center. Jeannie Alverson had that effect on him.

With emotions he usually had no trouble keeping under control gone haywire, Sam had no point of reference in how to deal with what he felt. He was torn between his desire to protect Jeannie at all costs and to repay the debt he owed her for saving his life, and another, equally strong desire. The desire to claim her, body and soul...his primeval masculine need to possess. Heaven help him if he ever acted on his desires—heaven help them both.

"You aren't eating." Jeannie's smile trembled, her brown eyes questioning his silent absorption in his dinner plate.

Picking up his fork, he lifted a small portion of salad to his mouth and ate. He nodded, then glanced at Jeannie. "It's delicious."

But not as delicious as her mouth last night, when he'd taken one tender kiss. Being with her, wanting her so desperately and knowing he was totally wrong for her, only added to Sam's confusion. He had never known a woman like Jeannie, and he'd have bet his last dime that she'd never known a man like him. They were poles apart, opposite ends of a spectrum—a physical man and a spiritual woman.

He had once run away from his past, from the painful memories and the woman who had saved his life. Now he was trapped by a promise he'd made, captured by his own deepest, most primitive needs. Needs that could destroy him if he didn't keep them under control.

They ate in silence, each sneaking occasional glances at the other. The room was utterly, devastatingly quiet, the steady tick-tock of the grandfather clock in the hallway and the clink of silver against china the only sounds.

If the silence continued much longer, Jeannie thought she might scream. How had this happened, this long stretch of tense stillness? They were aware of each other to such a heightened degree that Jeannie began to sense Sam's thoughts. The moment she realized he was fighting the desire to kiss her, she immediately withdrew, ending the connection.

Jeannie's telepathic abilities had always been extremely limited. She and Manton could converse, and in the last days of Miriam's life, they had been able to connect. But Sam was the only other person with whom she had shared this rare joining, and he would not admit it, even to himself.

Scooting back his chair, Sam stood, then tossed his linen napkin down on the table and glared at Jeannie. "You were doing it again, weren't you? Trying to get inside my head."

Tilting her chin defiantly, she looked up at him. "I couldn't have made the connection without your cooperation. You were connecting with me, too. That's why I was able to sense what you were feeling."

He rounded the table so quickly that when he hauled Jeannie to her feet, she cried out in alarm. She clung to his arms, feeling the bulging muscles beneath his jacket and shirt.

"Don't do it again! I don't want any connection, any 'spiritual joining.' Got it?"

"You want to kiss me," she said. "That's why you're so angry. You don't like my knowing how much you'd like to kiss me."

"What?"

"I'd like to kiss you, too."

"Lady, are you out of your mind?"

"Maybe I am, but I've never been truly kissed by a man, and the thought of your kissing me intrigues me."

"You're paying me to be your bodyguard," Sam said. "Not your lover."

She covered his lips with her fingertips. "Shhh. I'm not asking you to make love to me, just to kiss me. What's wrong, Mr. Dundee, are you afraid to kiss me?"

With one hand, he tightened his hold around her waist, and with the other he grasped her chin. "All right, if you're sure it's what you want. Just remember that it doesn't mean anything. I've kissed a hundred women before you, and will probably kiss a hundred more before I die."

"Then I expect you're very good at this, at kissing, aren't you?"

Her eyelids fluttered. She clutched his arms. Drawing her up against him, Sam slipped his hand under the wavy fall of her hair and gripped her neck. His heartbeat roared in his ears like the hum of his Cessna's twin engines.

A steady, throbbing ache spread through him, threatening to overpower his restraint. When he lowered his head, his lips just making contact with hers, she seemed to melt into him, to become a part of him. He felt her surrender, her eager compliance, in every cell of his body.

Of all the women he'd known, all the pretty faces, all the luscious bodies, not one had ever sent him into a panic. But then, he had never wanted anyone the way he wanted Jeannie. And it was that need, that raging, all-consuming need, that frightened the intrepid Sam Dundee.

"I'm no good for you," he warned her. Or was he warning himself? "So don't let this kiss give you any ideas."

Slipping her arms around his neck, she closed her eyes and welcomed his kiss. Her soft, sweet, giving lips met his. Innocent and untutored, she gave herself over completely to his mastery, absorbing the undeniable pleasure he was experiencing, realizing that she felt their shared enjoyment in the kiss.

Opening her mouth on a sigh, Jeannie accepted the tender thrust of his tongue, the sensual probing. Her body tingled with excitement. A slow, steady throb of desire began to build inside her.

Sam deepened the kiss. He cupped her buttocks, shifting her body, lifting her up and into him, so that his arousal pulsated against her femininity. She moaned loudly, then slid her tongue inside his mouth, exploring him the way he had her. He ached. She ached even more. He groaned deep in his throat, the power of Jeannie's nearness rendering him helpless against his own masculine needs.

Jeannie cried out from the hot, pounding hunger and de-manding desire raging inside her. Sam's hunger. Her desire. She felt them both, and felt them simultaneously.

She scratched his back, her short, rounded nails clawing fiercely at his cashmere jacket. Her body undulated against his, feeding his hunger, fanning the flames of her desire. She was on fire with their combined passion, and was no longer in control of her actions. Sam's needs dictated hers. The greater his desire was for her, the more she desired him.

She overpowered him with the fervor of her response, mo-mentarily stunning him. Slowly ending the kiss, he lifted her into his arms and carried her out of the sitting room and directly toward her bed, then lowered her on top of the quilted pink coverlet. Her arms still draped around his neck, she pulled him downward. With his lips almost touching hers, he braced his hands on each side of her.

He had never expected her to go wild in his arms, had never imagined that sweet, innocent Jeannie possessed the power to bring him to his knees with nothing more than a smoldering kiss.

He looked down at her face, flushed with arousal, her lips red, damp and slightly swollen. "Jeannie?" He wanted to take her and make her his. He wanted to remove her clothes and cover her naked body with his own. He wanted to bury himself deep inside her and find the ecstasy he knew awaited them. But he could not, would not, take advantage of her. He sensed that she had never before felt this way, that she was experiencing sexual desire for the first time in her life.

Suddenly the truth hit him, like a bullet between the eyes. This really *was* the first time for her. The first time she'd ever been kissed. The first time she'd ever been aroused.

"Sam? Is it…is it always like this?" Was it possible that what they were feeling was what normally took place when a man and a woman shared a passionate kiss?

"You can feel what I'm feeling, can't you?" Suddenly he pulled away from her, easing her arms from around his neck as he stood up beside the bed. "Your empathic powers obviously include sharing your partner's arousal."

Jeannie sat up on the bed, looking at Sam, a mixture of wonder and uncertainty in her eyes. "Does it bother you that I—"

"That you're not only inside my head, but my body, as well, when I'm making love to you? Yeah, it bothers me. You actually felt everything I felt!" Sam loosened his tie, then ripped it off his neck and clutched it in his big hand.

She had not only known how much he wanted her and how out of control he'd been, but had felt those exact same emotions. But how could that be?

Jeannie Alverson really was an empath, Sam admitted to himself. To what degree, he wasn't sure, but he knew for certain that she'd somehow felt exactly what he had felt.

"You sensed what I was feeling, too, didn't you?" she asked, scooting slowly toward the edge of the bed. "Has that ever happened to you?"

"Hell, no! And it didn't happen this time, either." Sam crammed his silk tie into his pocket. "When I have sex with a woman, the only way I know what she's feeling is in the way she responds. And no woman has ever been able to experience what I'm feeling."

Jeannie slid her legs over the side of the bed. Sam stepped out of her reach. "Then what just happened between us was very special, wasn't it?"

"All we did was kiss!" Sam raked his hand through his hair, disheveling it.

She held out her hand to him, bidding him to come to her. "Yes, all we did was kiss."

He stared at her hand. Small, soft, delicate. Did he have the courage to accept what she was offering? All Sam had ever wanted, all he'd ever expected, from a woman was a mutually satisfying, uncommitted relationship.

Jeannie Alverson was a forever kind of woman, a woman who'd want to know everything about a man, a woman who'd want to save his soul.

"I'm in your life again because I want to repay a debt," Sam said. "I'm not here because I want anything from you. I don't want your healing. I don't want your sympathy. And I sure as hell don't want your love."

"You're afraid of me." Her voice held a breathless tremor. "You don't want to share yourself with anyone. You think you deserve to be unhappy and alone for the rest of your life. You see it as your punishment. And you're afraid I have the power to change all that."

"I told you that I'm no good for you. I am the wrong man for you. You deserve—"

"I deserve a man who will truly love me."

"That man isn't me. Not now. Not ever."

Tilting her chin defiantly, Jeannie looked directly at Sam, her bottom lip quivering slightly. Sam glared at her, wishing he'd never kissed her, wishing he wasn't obligated to stay in Biloxi and guard her.

Several sharp taps on the door snapped Jeannie and Sam out of their silent confrontation. Ollie rushed into the room, oblivious to Jeannie's position on the bed. "You gotta come downstairs right now, Mr. Dundee. And hurry!"

"What's wrong, Ollie? You're white as a sheet," Jeannie said.

"I found a package on the front porch. It's a small brown-paper-wrapped package. I don't know where it came from, but it's addressed to Jeannie."

"No one delivered the package?" Sam asked. "You just found it lying on the porch?"

"It could be a present for her, you know." Ollie wrung her hands together. "But what if it's… I mean, there could be something dangerous inside. A snake, or a—"

"A bomb," Jeannie said.

Ollie gasped.

"Where did you put the package?" Sam asked.

"Where did I—? I didn't put it anywhere. I left the thing on the porch."

"Good girl." Sam patted Ollie on the back. "You stay up here with Jeannie. I'll go take a look at our little gift."

Jeannie called out to him. "Sam?"

Halting in the doorway, he turned and looked at her.

"Please, be careful," she said.

"I always am," he told her, then walked out into the hall.

The minute Sam was out of sight, Jeannie turned to Ollie. "Get my cane for me."

"Why do you need your cane? Mr. Dundee said we were to wait up here."

"Ollie, don't ask questions. Just get me a cane. Please."

Obeying, Ollie handed Jeannie a walking stick, then grabbed her by the arm when Jeannie stood and headed straight out the bedroom door. "He'll be furious if you go downstairs."

"I won't get near the package," Jeannie said. "I promise. But I can't sit up here not knowing what's happening."

"Oh, all right. I'll go with you. But I won't take the blame for this. If Mr. Dundee gets all fired up—"

"I take full responsibility."

THE PACKAGE WAS just as Ollie had described it. Small, brown-paper-wrapped and lying on the front veranda, only a few inches from the steps. Well, it might be nothing more than a gift from an admirer of Jeannie Alverson. But then again, it might be a bomb. No use taking any chances, Sam decided.

He went back into the house and phoned Lieutenant Painter. "I'll keep an eye on the package until your boys get here," Sam said. "Tell them to make it quick. I don't know how long this thing has been out here, and if it's a bomb, it could be timed." Sam replaced the receiver.

"You really do think it's a bomb, don't you?" Jeannie stood in the library doorway, Ollie at her side.

Sam jerked around, glaring at her. "What the hell are you doing down here? Didn't I tell you and Ollie to stay upstairs?"

"I would have gone crazy staying up there, wondering what was happening, not knowing if you were all right or not."

"Ollie, take her out the back door and keep her there, even if you have to sit on her."

"Come on, Jeannie." Ollie tugged on Jeannie's arm. "Mr. Dundee's right. If it's a bomb, it could explode any minute now."

"Sam, please come and tell me the minute you know for sure." Her warm brown eyes pleaded with him. "Be very careful. Let the police handle things."

"That's just what I intend to do," Sam said.

After he'd made certain Jeannie and Ollie were out back, he returned to the front porch to wait on the Biloxi police. The wait was short; Lieutenant Painter arrived with the bomb squad in ten minutes flat.

"You think someone left a little present for Ms. Alverson?" Lieutenant Painter asked, stepping around the square-shaped object lying so innocently on the veranda.

"I have no idea, but my gut instincts are scaring the hell out of me." Sam leaned back against the closed front door, bending his knee and bracing the tip of his left foot on the floor. "If this package is from Reeves, then it's obvious the man means business. But what do you want to bet that there will be no way to trace the package and whatever's inside to the good reverend, or anyone else?"

Sam and Rufus Painter watched from afar while the bomb squad took every precaution unwrapping the package and then opening the box within.

One of the policeman laughed, another grunted and cursed. Sam and Lieutenant Painter walked off the porch and down the sidewalk.

"What have you got there, Ivey?" the lieutenant asked.

"You're not going to believe this one," Ivey said. "Come take a look, Lieutenant. This is a new one on me."

When they approached the policemen hovering around the opened package, Ivey turned around and held out a brand new white Bible.

"What the hell?" Painter shook his head.

"A Bible," Sam said. "A white Bible. Maynard Reeves's trademark. But my guess is there isn't a fingerprint on it, other than your men's."

"Yeah, if it is from Reeves, he's too smart to leave fingerprints," Painter said. "Besides, there's no law against someone sending someone else a Bible, is there?"

"Take a look inside," Ivey said. "Just flip it open where the bookmark is."

Painter eased the pages back. "Hell! Take a look, Dundee."

"I wish I didn't have to show this to Jeannie, but she won't give us any peace until she knows," Sam said. "Any reason why she shouldn't be shown the Bible?"

"No reason I can think of. We can go ahead and show it to her." Lieutenant Painter clasped the Bible in his hand. "I'll go with you and reassure Ms. Alverson that everything's all right. Then we'll take the Bible downtown and have the lab run some tests."

Jeannie met them at the door leading into the kitchen. "Was it a bomb?"

"No bomb," Sam said.

Sam moved out of the way as Jeannie entered the kitchen, Ollie following. "What was it?"

The lieutenant held out the white Bible. "I believe this is yours."

Jeannie stared at the Bible.

"Why, it's the good book," Ollie said. "And you were worried somebody sent Jeannie something to harm her."

"Do you want to see this?" Sam asked Jeannie.

She looked at him, realizing the import of his question. There was more to the gift than the obvious. She nodded. He handed the Bible to her. A white satin ribbon marked a page near the beginning. Jeannie opened the Bible to the specified page and noticed that the white ribbon was dotted with dark red spots. One short verse had been smeared with the same red liquid that dotted the marker.

Jeannie read the verse silently. She swallowed hard, then read it aloud. "Thou shalt not suffer a witch to live."

"Who'd send such a thing?" Ollie jerked her head around in Sam's direction, and when he didn't respond, she looked back at Jeannie.

"It's a warning, isn't it?" Jeannie asked.

"What do you think?" Sam lifted the open Bible out of her unsteady hands. Placing the marker and the page to his nose, he sniffed, and then he scratched at the red spots on the marker with his fingernail.

"What are you doing?" Ollie stared at him, perplexed by his actions.

"The stains are blood, aren't they?" A knot of fear formed in Jeannie's throat, threatening to cut off her breathing.

"Yeah, they're blood," Sam said. "But not necessarily human blood."

"Just what are the police going to do about this?" Ollie

asked. "Folks don't have the right to be sending bloodstained Bibles to other folks and as good as accusing them of being a witch."

"Ollie, there's nothing you can do about this," Jeannie said. "Lieutenant Painter will handle the matter—won't you, Lieutenant?"

"I'll be glad when all this business with the reporters and the sick folks and that crazy preacher comes to an end." Ollie continued mumbling to herself as she walked over to the kitchen cabinet. "I'll fix us all some coffee. I doubt we'll be getting any sleep tonight."

"I'll give y'all a call if we find out anything," Lieutenant Painter said.

"Please let me know if the blood is human or animal," Jeannie said.

Sam grabbed the Bible out of her hands. "There's no way we'll be able to prove Maynard Reeves is the gift-giver, but I don't have a doubt that this—" he snapped the Bible shut "—is the good reverend's handiwork."

"He's doing more than accusing me of being a witch." Jeannie shivered, the reality of the warning hitting her full force. *Thou shalt not suffer a witch to live.*

"He's threatening your life." Sam handed the Bible to Lieutenant Painter. "We have to find some sort of evidence against Reeves and put a stop to him before—"

"I know Maynard Reeves wants me dead," Jeannie said. "He's going to try to kill me."

"We'll do everything we can to help." Painter held the white Bible securely in both hands. "But without some hard evidence, our hands are tied." He nodded, smiling sadly at Jeannie, who returned his smile, then he left the kitchen.

"Coffee is nearly ready," Ollie said. "Dr. Howell will be home soon, and when he finds out what happened tonight, he's going to be terribly upset."

Jeannie sat down at the kitchen table. "There's no need to

worry Julian about this until tomorrow." She looked up at Sam. "Maynard Reeves *is* going to try to kill me, isn't he?"

Sam knelt down in front of Jeannie. Taking her face in his hands, he looked her directly in the eye. "The truth?" he asked.

"Between us, always," she said.

"Since you refused to join his ministry, Reeves has convinced himself that your empathic powers came from the devil. He sees it as his duty to destroy the evil, and the only way he can do that is to kill you."

Jeannie gasped several times, repeatedly sucking in gulps of air. Sam put his arm around her. She laid her head on his shoulder, accepting his comforting caress.

"I won't let him succeed, Jeannie. I promise. I'll keep you safe. I'll guard you with my life."

Jeannie closed her eyes. One tear caught in her eyelashes, another trickled slowly down her cheek. Unconsciously she began absorbing the rage inside Sam. The hatred and anger centered on Maynard Reeves, but spread out in tiny waves toward anyone who meant Jeannie harm.

Sam was prepared to kill to protect her. Jeannie had never felt that type of hatred. Not even when she longed to be free from her stepfather's cruelty had she wished him dead. Jeannie wasn't sure she was capable of killing, even to defend her own life. There was a gentleness in her soul that longed to ease pain and suffering, to eliminate hatred and fear. Could she ever understand the barbaric ability to kill?

Safe in Sam's arms, the cruelties of the world far away, Jeannie delved into her soul, into that minuscule spot where a fragment of Sam's soul remained from their joining six years ago. Such a fragile link, one she knew Sam would sever if he was aware of its existence.

He kissed the side of her face, his lips brushing it tenderly, as he stroked her shoulders and back, soothing her with his touch.

In an instantaneous flash that left her as quickly as it had come, Jeannie knew exactly what Sam was. Sam Dundee, her protector, was a unique creature. He was an elegant savage, a compassionate warrior, and only if she was strong enough to become his equal could they ever truly be united.

CHAPTER SIX

"No. ABSOLUTELY NOT." Crossing his arms over his chest, Sam Dundee gave Jeannie his killer glare, the look that had made many a formidable opponent quake in his boots.

"Yes! Definitely yes." Jeannie didn't glance up from the task at hand, transferring the contents of her shoulder bag to a beige leather purse.

"It's out of the question." What would it take to get through to this woman? Didn't she realize that every time she went out in public, she was exposing herself to danger?

"I have not missed church in years. I'm not asking to attend the regular service the way I usually do. All I'm asking is for you to take me to the early-morning prayer service. There won't be many people at church." Jeannie snapped her purse shut, then smiled at Sam. "Now, I'm ready to go whenever you are."

"I'm not ready."

Jeannie surveyed him from head to toe, leisurely inspecting every inch of his massive body. She drew in a deep breath. Shivers of remembrance rippled through her, memories of a kiss that had rocked the very foundation of her life, memories of being held lovingly, protectively, in those enormous arms.

Sam was devastatingly handsome, and the very picture of a successful businessman in his navy blue double-breasted suit, a gold Rolex his only piece of jewelry.

Any other man Sam's size would look like a muscle-bound gorilla in a suit, but not Sam Dundee. His tailored clothes fit him to perfection, his thick blond hair styled by an expert and his massive hands recently manicured. He possessed an air of unpretentious sophistication, one Jeannie felt certain he had cultivated over the years.

But inside the expensive clothes lay the finely honed body of an athlete. Beneath the polished exterior beat the heart of a primitive male. Chip away his refined facade and you'd find brute strength. Sam Dundee had the soul of a warrior.

"Like what you see?" His mouth curved into a smirk. "Thinking about staking a claim?"

Jeannie willed herself not to blush at his comment. He'd caught her shamelessly assessing his physical attributes. "Actually, I was noticing that you look like you're ready to go to church."

"I advise you not to attend services today."

"I'm going to church," Jeannie said. "Are you going with me, or do I have to go by myself?"

"Doesn't Dr. Howell go to church?"

"Julian is a Catholic. He's going to Mass with Marta before they go out for lunch."

"You're damned and determined to do this, aren't you?" Sam shook his head, frustration boiling inside him, threatening to overflow. He wanted to make Jeannie stay at home, where he knew he could keep her safe and protect her from a threatening world.

"I've looked outside the house, and there's not one reporter or protester in sight." Clutching her purse in her hand, Jeannie laced her arm around Sam's. "And I don't think we have to worry about Reverend Reeves today. After all, this is Sunday, and he'll be preaching to his Righteous Light brethren."

Accepting defeat, Sam eased his arm around Jeannie's waist. "Yeah, he's probably firing them up with a sermon on witches. No doubt quoting from the Old Testament."

"Exodus," Jeannie said, knowing she would never be able to forget the Bible verse marked in blood, blood she prayed the police lab would find to be animal and not human. "You're right, of course, Sam. Just because I'll be safe from Maynard

Reeves at my church, that doesn't mean he isn't inciting his followers to condemn me as a witch."

Sam tightened his hold around Jeannie's waist, wanting to pick her up in his arms, carry her upstairs and lock her away from the evil she could not escape in the outside world.

Jeannie walked slowly, carefully, always aware of her limited abilities to maneuver and her dependency on her cane.

Sam adjusted his gait to Jeannie's step-by-step movements. His gut twisted into knots as he watched her struggle with the simple task of walking. It would be so easy for him to carry her to the car and then carry her into the church when they arrived. But Jeannie would never allow it. She was fiercely, stubbornly proud. Sam marveled at her strength and determination.

The late-August morning held a hint of autumn, especially in the refreshingly cool breeze blowing in off the Gulf waters. The sun's early warmth blended with the wind, creating perfect weather.

Sam seated Jeannie on the passenger side of her Lexus. She had insisted he dismiss the limousine, telling him she felt uncomfortable riding in the big gray Cadillac.

He reached for the shoulder harness at the exact moment Jeannie did. Jerking her head up, she looked into his eyes, and he knew she saw clearly what he was thinking. His hand covered hers; she didn't pull away. With quick precision, he snapped her seat belt in place, stood up straight and closed the door. Jeannie's gaze focused on her clasped hands, placed atop the purse in her lap. Sam got in on the driver's side, fastened his safety belt and started the engine.

Jeannie knew that he would never be able to touch her again without wondering if she was experiencing his emotions, feeling what he felt. Friday night, the moment he realized she had gotten inside him, that she had become a part of him, he had withdrawn from her. Was he so afraid to share himself, to open himself up to another person, even someone who cared for him?

Jeannie sat silent and unmoving, aware that Sam opposed this short trip down Beach Boulevard to the small Congregational church where she'd been a member for a dozen years. Although Julian was Catholic, his wife Miriam had been a Protestant who attended one of the oldest congregations in Mississippi, and she had taken Jeannie to services with her.

Sam headed the Lexus east, up Beach Boulevard, occasionally glancing at Jeannie, who seemed spellbound by the view of the Gulf through her side window. Why did his throat tighten and his heart pound every time he looked at her? He'd known women more beautiful, women more voluptuous. And he'd certainly known women more experienced. But he couldn't remember ever looking at a woman and being so captivated by her loveliness, her gentleness, her compassion.

Jeannie had secured her long brown hair in a soft bun at the nape of her neck. Loose tendrils of silky beige curled about her ears and forehead. The outfit she wore, a cream shirtwaist dress with a pastel flowered scarf tied around her neck, was as understated as her beauty, and suited her fragile facade.

Every time Sam glanced her way, she was tempted to look at him, to confront him, but she didn't. Instead, she gazed at the Gulf, at the murky water and the barrier islands she could barely see in the distance. One huge gambling casino after another—a reproduction of a pirate ship, an old riverboat—lined the coast, and rows of motels flanked Beach Boulevard. The beach was empty, except for the gulls. Jeannie knew that if she rolled down her window she would be able to smell the fishy scent so prevalent along the Gulf shore.

Within a few minutes, Sam caught a glimpse of the small Congregational church in the distance, a white cross positioned prominently above the arched upstairs windows. He turned the Lexus onto the narrow street beside the wooden church, breathing a sigh of relief when he saw only four cars in the parking area and only a woman and a child outside the building.

Not one relevant detail of Jeannie Alverson's life had escaped being printed in the newspapers or broadcast on the television and radio. Everyone in Biloxi, Gulfport, Pass Christian and Ocean Springs knew where Jeannie went to church. Hell, the whole state of Mississippi probably knew. Luckily, no one would be expecting her to arrive at church for early-morning prayers, since this was not her normal routine.

Sam parked the Lexus, rounded the car and helped Jeannie to her feet. With his arm securely planted around Jeannie's waist, he led her up the sidewalk.

Suddenly, the little boy who had been standing beside his mother at the front of the church fell to his knees at Jeannie's feet. She stopped dead still and stared down at the dark-haired child. A thin woman with huge brown eyes stepped forward and lifted the child to his feet.

"Please, Jeannie, help my little boy. I came early, wanting to be first in line to see you. Matthew is only six years old, and he lives with unbearable pain. Touch him and take away his pain." Tears streamed down the woman's pale face and dripped off her nose and chin. "He's such a little thing. It isn't right that he suffers so much."

Sam nudged Jeannie, urging her to move on, not to stop, but she leaned against him and whispered, "She didn't ask me to heal him. All she asked was that I take away his pain. I can do that much for the child."

"No, Jeannie, don't." The bitter, metallic taste of fear coated Sam's tongue. If she took away the child's pain, didn't that mean she would have to endure it?

"What's wrong with Matthew?" Jeannie asked.

"He has a severe form of arthritis that causes him great pain. He's been suffering all night. When I heard on TV that you always attend Sunday services here, I knew what I had to do. I've been here over an hour, waiting, knowing in my heart you'd come today and that you'd help my child."

Jeannie looked at Matthew. Such a pretty little boy, but his eyes told the story of his suffering. "Bring Matthew inside the church with me."

The woman grabbed Jeannie's hand and kissed it. "Thank you." New tears filled her eyes. "God bless you." She lifted her child into her arms.

"Jeannie?" Sam questioned her, yet he knew he couldn't stop her doing what her heart dictated.

"The minister's study is down the hall to the left. When we're inside the vestibule, it'll be the first door," she told him.

Jeannie made certain the woman and her son entered the building first, and then she followed, Sam helping her maneuver the short row of steps. Once inside, Jeannie went directly to the minister, who stood at the doorway to the sanctuary. When she whispered her request, he simply nodded his agreement and glanced forlornly at Jeannie, then smiled at the tormented woman and her sick child.

Once inside the study, Jeannie sat in a sturdy wooden chair directly in front of a bookshelf-lined wall.

"Please, close the door, Sam."

He didn't want anything to do with this. If he couldn't prevent what was going to happen—and he knew couldn't—he'd prefer to step outside and wait.

"You don't have to stay, if you'd rather not," Jeannie said.

Oh, he'd rather not, all right, but he would. Hell would freeze over before he'd leave her alone at a time like this. He closed the door, then blocked the entrance with his massive body. Crossing his arms over his chest, he stood there, a silent sentinel, feeling powerless against Jeannie's determination.

"Bring Matthew to me." Jeannie held open her arms.

The mother placed her child in Jeannie's lap and knelt at her feet. Jeannie encompassed Matthew's skinny little body with her arms. She closed her eyes. Matthew squirmed.

"Don't be afraid, sweetheart. All I'm going to do is hold you, and very soon the pain will go away and you won't hurt for a while."

The wide-eyed mother wiped the tears from her eyes. Jeannie sighed. A soft brightness surrounded her; a sweet, flowing current rippled through her body. The first minute twinges of discomfort ebbed and flowed, coming and going, then returning to stay. Jeannie gasped. Sam flinched. Matthew sobbed.

The minister's opening prayer floated down the hallway from the sanctuary, the words muted by the closed door of the study. Acting as a receptacle, Jeannie allowed Matthew's pain to slowly drain from his body. She was still aware of her surroundings, of the child's mother trembling at her feet, of Sam staring at a spot somewhere over her head, refusing to watch the performance of her task.

Sam gritted his teeth. He focused his vision on the certificates on the wall behind the minister's desk. Matthew breathed so deeply that the sound drew Sam's attention. The boy appeared relaxed, almost asleep, as he lay in Jeannie's arms. All the color had drained from Jeannie's face, leaving her normally rosy cheeks pale. Sam looked away, taking note of every picture on the walls, scanning the bookshelves, tracing the stripes in the wallpaper, searching for stains on the carpet.

Jeannie groaned, low and soft in her throat, the sound gaining Sam's instant attention. She had released her hold on Matthew. Her arms lay at her sides, her hands gripping the edge of the chair. Her body shivered, once, twice, and then she opened her mouth, leaned her head back and sucked in gulps of air. As she continued drawing in deep breaths, she began to moan quietly.

She was experiencing physical pain. Matthew's pain. And there was absolutely nothing Sam could do to help her. Sweat broke out on Sam's forehead. Moisture coated the palms of his big hands.

Time ceased, standing still for the four people in the minister's study. When Matthew slipped out of Jeannie's lap and into his mother's open arms, Sam didn't know for sure whether minutes or hours had passed. The torment he'd felt at watching

Jeannie suffer seemed to have lasted for hours, but when he looked at his Rolex, he realized that less than fifteen minutes had gone by.

When Matthew's mother tried to thank Jeannie, she did not receive a response. Jeannie appeared to be unconscious.

"It doesn't hurt, Mommy," Matthew said, smiling broadly. "I don't hurt at all." The boy pulled free of his mother and walked around the room. "And I can walk, and it still doesn't hurt." Matthew raced around the room in a circle. Grabbing the child by the shoulder, Sam halted his jubilant running.

"Please, take Matthew and go," Sam said. "Jeannie's done all she can for him. She needs her rest now."

"Thank her again for me," the woman said. "Even if the relief lasts only a few hours. Tell her for me."

"I'll tell her."

Sam held open the door for Matthew and his mother. Once out in the hallway, Matthew stopped, turned around and waved at Sam. Sam waved back at the child.

"Mommy said the angel at this church would take away my pain, and she did."

Closing the door, shutting out the world and all its problems, Sam leaned his shoulders and head back against the stained wood surface and closed his eyes for one brief moment. Then he looked at Jeannie, who was lying slumped in the chair, tears sparkling in her dark eyelashes like diamonds on sable. He walked over, bent down on one knee and pried her clenched fists away from the chair's edge.

"Jeannie?"

She moaned. Her eyelids flickered. Sam brought her hands to his lips, opened her palms and anointed them with kisses. Jeannie moaned again.

"Sam." His name was a mere whisper on her lips.

"What can I do to help you? Just tell me, and I'll do it." He had no idea what she needed from him, but he wanted to do something, anything, to help her.

"Hold—hold me."

He enveloped her in his arms, stroking her tense back, trapping her arms between their bodies. She swayed into him, brushing her face over the side of his face, resting her cheek against his. Feeling the dampness on his cheek, Sam looked down and saw that Jeannie was crying.

"Don't cry. Please, don't cry." He lifted her into his arms, not sure it was the right thing to do, but unable to stop himself.

Jeannie tried to lift her arm to his neck, but she didn't have the strength. Sam sat down on the small love seat in the far corner, bringing Jeannie down into his lap. He lifted her arm and placed it around his neck. She laid her head on his shoulder.

"How long will this last? Isn't there anything I can do?" Frustration on an incomparable level clawed at his guts.

"Not long. Just a little while." She opened her eyes, those warm, compassionate brown eyes, and looked at Sam.

The bottom dropped out of his stomach. "Rest, Jeannie. Rest."

"Take care of me, Sam." She closed her eyes and went limp in his arms.

"Jeannie? Jeannie?" He shook her gently. She didn't move. He shook her again. "Jeannie!"

He realized then that she was unconscious. Shudders racked his body. He pulled her close, burying his face against her neck.

They sat there for endless minutes, Sam wishing more than ever that he'd asked J.T. to come to Biloxi to guard Jeannie instead of coming himself. He was prepared to act as her body-guard, but he wasn't suited to playing nursemaid. And he sure as hell hadn't expected to have to watch her perform one of her miracle healings. Seeing her suffer had ripped him apart. He'd known from the beginning that this assignment would be more than a simple business arrangement, but he hadn't counted on just how personal it would become. What man in his right mind would want to become involved with a woman who possessed Jeannie's miraculous abilities? He sure as hell didn't.

Jeannie awoke, weak and pale. "Sam?"

"Are you all right? You scared the hell out of me when you passed out that way."

"We've missed most of the church service, I'm afraid." She touched his face with her fingertips. He flinched. So sensitive—her strong, fearless warrior. "Take me home, Sam. I'll be all right. You musn't worry so. When I was a child, I took all the pain from at least half a dozen people each night."

"Your childhood was a living hell, wasn't it?" Sam had never thought about what it must have been like for her, going from town to town, from one revival meeting to the next, always expected to perform her miracles.

"I suffered every day of my life. I remember feeling very little except pain."

"Other people's pain."

She nodded. "I'm fine, Sam. Really I am."

"You didn't have to take away Matthew's pain."

"Yes, I did." She caressed his cheek. "How could I look at him and not want to help him?" Jeannie sighed. "His mother understood that I couldn't heal him. She knows his pain will return."

Jeannie tried to stand. Sam picked up her cane and handed it to her. Bracing the tip of the walking stick on the floor, Jeannie lifted herself to her feet. Sam stood up beside her. The moment Jeannie took her first step, her knees gave way. Crying out, she grabbed for Sam. He swooped her up in his arms.

"I can't walk," she said. "I suppose it's because I felt all Matthew's arthritic pain in my legs, and they're already weak."

Sam carried Jeannie outside, hoping he could take her away before any reporters or curiosity seekers arrived. Only the minister and three church members remained inside the building, and outside one lone reporter and his photographer waited. Tory

Gaines watched from afar, then started to approach them. Sam glared at the man.

"You come near her, Gaines, and you're a dead man." Sam didn't pause.

Tory Gaines stopped where he stood, not moving a muscle as he watched Sam carry Jeannie to her Lexus.

Traffic wasn't terribly heavy, so Sam drove them home in record time, while Jeannie closed her eyes and rested. Neither of them said a word. He carried her into the house and up the stairs to her bedroom, not once inquiring what she wanted. Easing her down onto her bed, he removed her beige heels, then sat beside her.

"Don't look so worried," she said. "I told you I'm fine."

"You may be, but I'm not." Leaning over her, he positioned his hands at either side of her shoulders. "Guarding you has turned out to be a lot more than I bargained for. How could I protect you from what happened today? I had to stand there and watch you suffer and know there wasn't a damned thing I could do about it! How do you think that made me feel?"

"Helpless?" She twined her arms around his neck.

"I don't ever want to see you suffer like that again. Not for anyone, but especially never again for me. Do you understand what I'm saying?"

"Yes, Sam, I understand."

She understood only too well, but she doubted he did. For the first time, Sam truly accepted the fact that she had taken away his pain the day she saved his life. He hadn't wanted to believe she was a true empath, that her psychic talents were strong enough not only to probe inside his mind, but to actually experience his emotions and share his feelings. Friday night's events, coupled with those at the church today, had forced him to admit the truth. This was a beginning, Jeannie realized, but only a beginning. Sam was not the kind of man who would ever surrender easily. He knew she wanted to help him, but he wasn't ready to accept her help. If she pushed him too hard and too fast, he would balk. As it was, he would fight her every inch of the way. If she was ever to reach his soul and save him, she would have to start by using whatever means were available.

Jeannie smiled. She accepted the inevitable. She was falling in love with Sam Dundee, but she knew he might never love her, might never willingly take what she had to offer him. Was she brave enough to accept him on his terms, share a purely physical relationship, when she so desperately needed more?

Pulling him down to her, she lifted her lips to meet his. She nibbled at his bottom lip, and sighed when he groaned.

"I've never wanted anyone else. You're the first and only man I've ever desired," she told him.

"Don't say things like that to me. I'm having a hard enough time as it is, keeping my hands off you."

"I make you feel helpless. I make you feel afraid. And those aren't emotions you're familiar with, are they, Sam Dundee?" She gave him a quick kiss. He groaned again. "I can get inside you, feel what you feel, experience your pleasure, as well as my own." She licked a circle over his lips.

"Maybe you *are* a witch," he said. "God knows you've bewitched me."

He took her lips completely, with a tender savagery that sent pinpricks of pleasure through her body. He wanted her with a quiet desperation, knowing she wasn't ready to make love, realizing that he needed to progress slowly, allowing both of them to become accustomed to their unique ability to unite on an emotional level.

Deepening the kiss, exploring her mouth with his tongue, encouraging her to reciprocate, Sam unbuttoned her dress. Slipping his hands inside, he caressed her shoulders, easing her dress apart. He ran a loving hand over her collarbone. Clutching his shoulders, she thrust her hips off the bed and rubbed herself against him. He nuzzled her neck, then kissed the swell of each breast rising over the lace cups of her bra. His big hands spanned her waist.

"Sam, I—I'm aching. I need… You need… We want…"

He unsnapped the front closure of her bra, peeled it off her high, round breasts and lowered his mouth to cover one beaded nipple. Jeannie cried out from the pleasure, the sheer sensual delight.

The ache grew more and more intense. The throbbing sensation pulsing through her robbed her of her breath. She gasped for air. Trembling, his own breathing ragged, Sam kissed her on the forehead and sat up, making sure he didn't touch her again.

She caught her breath. "Sam?"

"It was almost too much, wasn't it?" He stood up beside the bed. "You're going to be the death of me, Jeannie Alverson." Sam smiled. "I'm not used to waiting for what I want, but in your case, I have no choice."

"Do you think the wait will be worth it?"

Sam walked over to the door, opened it and paused. "Get some rest. I'll check on you later, and carry you down for lunch whenever you're hungry."

"Thank you for taking care of me."

"That's what I'm here for," he said, and closed the door behind him as he walked out into the hall.

He couldn't stay there, looking at her, wanting her, needing her, when she wasn't physically or emotionally strong enough to make love. She was worried that once they'd made love, he'd think the experience hadn't been worth the wait. Didn't she know, couldn't she sense, that just kissing her turned him inside out?

Oh, she knew, all right. She felt his fear, sensed his helplessness. And she'd said she understood. Did she? Did she really know that the thought of making love to her scared the hell out of him?

CHAPTER SEVEN

JEANNIE WALKED SLOWLY over to where Sam stood looking through the long, narrow windows in the kitchen. Outside, the morning sunshine brightened the small garden and patio, which were surrounded by a privacy fence. She laid her hand on his back; he tensed immediately at her touch and stepped away from her.

Although he guarded her day and night, Sam had kept his distance—an emotional distance. Something had happened to him Sunday, something he didn't like in the least. Jeannie had indeed gotten inside him, had become a part of him. And he hated it!

Seeing her suffer Matthew's pain had hurt him deeply, reaching inside to touch a part of him that he hadn't even known existed. A part of him he didn't want to exist. Then, after they returned home and he kissed her again and caressed her intimately, he'd been forced to admit the truth to himself, the truth Jeannie already knew. She did make him feel helpless and afraid. Not only was Sam unaccustomed to those emotions, he hated them. Except for a few regrettable lapses, Sam was always in control, of himself and those around him. And although he had experienced fear on a few rare occasions, no woman had ever evoked that emotion within him. But then, he'd never known a woman like Jeannie Alverson.

"I feel I must do everything possible to defuse this situation before it gets any worse." Jeannie stood behind Sam, staring at his broad shoulders, her hand itching to touch his back again.

"You've already talked to him once, and all it did was incite him to condemn you as a witch." Sam opened the back door. "Do you honestly think talking to him again will change his mind?"

"It might," Jeannie said. "Besides, I can't see where it can do any harm."

Cursing under his breath, Sam stepped out onto the back porch, leaving Jeannie standing in the open doorway. She had asked Reverend Religious-Fanatic Reeves for a little private tête-à-tête today, in the hope she could convince him she wasn't evil. A lot of damned good it would do! From the preliminary reports Sam had received on Reeves, the man didn't know the meaning of the word *compromise*. He was completely unwavering in his narrow-minded beliefs, which were his own warped interpretation of the Bible.

Jeannie followed Sam outside onto the patio. "I've already issued the invitation. He'll be here soon."

"He's already here," Sam said. "In spirit, if not in the flesh. Just listen, and you'll hear Reeves's own brand of evil at work."

Listening, she heard a soft breeze waltzing through the huge live oaks that spanned the width of the Howell property in the backyard. She heard the chirping of birds, the hum of traffic, the muted song of the Gulf waters. And she heard the sound of marching feet on the pavement out front, and the combined voices of the Righteous Light brethren in a familiar chant. "Witch, witch... Witch, witch..."

Pinpricks of dread chilled her. For the past three days, ever since the newspapers had printed the story about her "Sunday miracle" in the Monday morning newspaper, Reeves's followers had picketed her house. Twice the police had been called to disperse the crowd, but each time the reverend's disciples had returned in larger numbers.

From her bedroom window this morning, Jeannie had counted over twenty men and women, of various ages and races, carrying signs and spouting condemnation of her as they trooped up and down the sidewalk in front of her home. It had been at that precise moment that she decided to offer an olive branch to Maynard Reeves. He had accepted her invitation quite readily, almost as if he'd been expecting her to telephone him.

Sam opposed the meeting, and she understood his reservations, especially since the police lab's report plainly stated the blood on Jeannie's gift Bible and bookmark had been human. Reeves posed a real threat to her. She hoped that by meeting with him she could change his mind about her, remove the threat or, at the very least, lessen the man's hatred of her.

"I don't want you to be upset with me." Jeannie wished Sam would look at her, but he kept his back to her. "I know I should have discussed my decision with you before I called Reverend Reeves and invited him over here this morning."

"Yeah, you should have discussed it with me. I would have told you the idea was insane, just like so many of your other ideas have been."

Jeannie leaned on her cane. Although she had recovered from Sunday, she was still weaker than normal. "I don't think it's insane to want to reach a peaceful settlement with—"

"With a man who isn't going to compromise, a man who truly believes that if you aren't on his side, then you're against him, and if you're against him, you're against God." Sam turned quickly, his steely blue-gray eyes focusing directly on Jeannie's face. "My gut instincts tell me to keep you as far away from him as possible."

"If this meeting fails, I promise to stay away from Reeves, to never contact him again." She took a tentative step in Sam's direction, never breaking eye contact as she held out one hand, using the other to steady her cane. "Tell me you aren't really angry with me, and that we have a deal."

Sam glared at her. Dammit! A sweet, loving angel shouldn't have such a wide stubborn streak in her. He'd never had half as much trouble controlling wilder, more worldly, self-centered women. But the only thing other women could give or take away from him had been sex. If sex was all there was between Jeannie and him, he wouldn't feel so uneasy. But things weren't that simple.

He looked at her hand. Don't touch her, he told himself. Every time he touched her, he wanted her, and she knew it. And every time he touched her, it gave her an excuse to try to get inside his head.

Clenching and unclenching his hands repeatedly, Sam grunted. "After today, you stay out of harm's way. No more public appearances, no more invitations to the enemy. Do we have an agreement?"

"If I can't persuade Reverend Reeves to stop his persecution of me, then yes, no more public appearances." Jeannie sucked in air between her clenched teeth, then bit down on her bottom lip. "Except—"

"No exceptions!"

"Just one," she said. "I'm already obligated for tomorrow night. It's a private affair. Practically everyone there will be an old family acquaintance, many of them members of Julian's Fleur-de-lis Society."

"What are you talking about? What private affair? And what on earth is this Fleur-de-lis society?"

"The owner of the *Royale Belle* Casino has offered the riverboat for a charity night this Friday. All the proceeds from the invited guests' gambling losses will go directly to the Howell School."

While Sam listened to her explanation, Jeannie moved closer to him, taking one cautious step at a time. Her protector could be a bear at times, ferocious and growling. She'd learned to approach him slowly, gentling him gradually.

"There will be a dinner, followed by dancing and gambling." Jeannie stood beside Sam, only inches separating their bodies. "I'm the cochairman of this function. I have to be there." She raised her face, looking at him with her most pleading expression. "The Fleur-de-lis Society consists of descendants of the old French families who settled Biloxi. Julian's grandmothers were from two of the most prestigious families in this area."

"I see." A person's lineage had never impressed Sam. What the hell difference did it make who your great-great-grandfather had been? If you weren't in line for the throne of England, he couldn't see how your ancestry had any bearing on your life.

"After tomorrow night, I'll follow your rules and regulations, whether or not I agree with them." Jeannie lifted her hand, intending to caress Sam's stern face. He grabbed her hand in midair, manacling her wrist.

A current of awareness passed between them. Sam's stomach tightened; Jeannie shivered.

"Can't you control it?" Tugging on her slender wrist, he pulled her close, her breasts grazing his chest. "Can't you turn it off, keep it from happening?"

"It isn't just me, you know," she said. "It's you, too. It's both of us. That's what makes it so powerful. You're beginning to experience tiny little sparks of what I'm feeling."

He dropped her wrist, as if touching her flesh had burned him. He backed away from her. "I don't know what you're talking about."

"Yes, you do."

Ollie opened the back door, stuck out her head and called Jeannie's name. She turned to face the housekeeper. Sam moved in behind her, his big body forming a shadow of protection.

"That awful Maynard Reeves is at the front door. Says he's been invited." Ollie twisted her thin lips into a disapproving frown.

"Please show Reverend Reeves into the front parlor and offer him refreshments," Jeannie said.

"I'd like to offer him a cup of tea laced with arsenic," Ollie said.

Sam chuckled. Whipping her head around, Jeannie glared at

him. "Nothing can be accomplished unless we treat Reverend Reeves as a welcome guest," she said.

"I'll go invite the black-hearted devil into the parlor." Grumbling to herself, Ollie slammed the back door.

Sam gripped Jeannie's shoulder. "I'm going to stay with you every minute that man is in this house."

"But, Sam, you'll intimidate Reverend Reeves and put him on guard. If the two of us are alone, he might be more at ease and willing to accept—"

"I hope I do intimidate Reeves. I hope I intimidate the hell out of him. I want him to know that the only way he's ever going to be able to hurt you is by going through me."

Jeannie felt it again, that wild, primeval, possessive need inside Sam, that powerful protective instinct that claimed his soul whenever any thoughts of her came to his mind. And the strange thing was, she realized, Sam had absolutely no control over the way he felt, and that made him hate his feelings and fight against them all the more.

Knowing Sam would never agree to leave her alone with Maynard Reeves, she complied with his demand. "All right, Sam. I understand. You'll stay in the room with us. But, please, let me do all the talking."

"We'll see," Sam said.

WHEN SAM AND Jeannie walked into the hallway leading to the front parlor, they saw Ollie, hands on her hips, standing at the open front door, shaking her head. Then they heard Reeves's singsong, pulpitarian voice as he addressed the crowd. The man stood on the front veranda, facing his entranced followers, who stood at rapt attention on the sidewalk. Maynard Reeves had cultivated a pure, clean-cut look with his neat, well-tailored black suit and white shirt, his short sandy hair, and the silver cross he wore around his neck.

"I give you my solemn vow that I will be on guard during my exchange with the devil's daughter," Reeves shouted, his voice deep and clear. "And I will report back to you, my faithful brethren, on whether or not I was able to win back her soul from the evil one."

"Report back to the press, you mean, you scalawag preacher," Ollie mumbled, loud enough for Sam and Jeannie to hear her.

"You don't need to witness this spectacle." Sam tugged on Jeannie's arm. "Wait for him in the parlor. I'll personally escort the good reverend to you."

"Now, Sam, this is supposed to be a friendly meeting."

"Yeah, sure. You can't get much friendlier than soul-saving, can you?"

"Don't be sacrilegious."

"I'm not the one making a mockery of everything holy."

Jeannie nodded in agreement, admitting Sam was right. "I'll wait in the parlor."

Reeves continued his unholy message of hate. Sam laid his big hand on Reeves's shoulder; the man shuddered, then froze on the spot, halting his speech in midsentence.

"Ms. Alverson is waiting to see you," Sam said.

"I shall be with you momentarily, sir. I will not be summoned before I'm prepared. I need a moment of prayer before facing the powers of darkness."

Dropping his hand from Reeves's shoulder, Sam lowered his voice to a deadly whisper. "You're going to need more than a prayer if you keep Ms. Alverson waiting one more minute to continue this sideshow of yours."

Raising his arms in the air dramatically, Reeves closed his eyes. "Pray for me, brothers and sisters. Pray for me."

When Reeves turned around, Sam stepped aside to allow him entrance into the foyer. The moment the two men entered the house, Ollie closed and locked the front door behind them.

"She's waiting for us in the front parlor." Sam nodded the direction. "The doors to the left."

Reeves hesitated outside the double panel doors, but didn't

turn to face Sam. "Waiting for *us?*" he asked. "She led me to believe this would be a private meeting between the two of us."

"It will be." Sam slid open the panel doors. "I'm simply here to guard an angel while she tries to make peace with the devil."

Reeves gasped. His boyishly handsome face turned crimson beneath its dusting of freckles as he turned toward Sam. "How dare you!"

Sam looked at Jeannie's adversary; the man trembled. "Please, go right on in, Reverend. She's waiting for you."

Reeves obeyed instantly, entering the front parlor with the same caution he might have used in entering a den of lions. Before approaching Jeannie, who sat in a tapestry-upholstered rosewood chair, Reeves watched Sam Dundee take a protective stance across the room. Sam crossed his arms over his chest. Reeves glanced at Jeannie.

"Won't you please sit down, Reverend Reeves?" Jeannie glided her arm through the air, gesturing for her guest to sit across from her on the red velvet settee.

Reeves sat uneasily, perching on the edge of the Victorian sofa. "Little good will come of this meeting if I feel threatened." He dared a quick glance in Sam's direction.

Jeannie laughed. "You can't possibly be referring to Mr. Dundee."

Reeves jumped to his feet, obviously unnerved by her reaction. "I most certainly am. I came here in good faith, expecting a private audience with you."

"I have no secrets from Mr. Dundee. You see, he is my protector. His job is to make sure no harm comes to me. He isn't a threat to anyone, unless—"

"Yes, yes, I quite understand." Reeves sat down again, slowly, focusing his attention on Jeannie's smiling face. "When you called and asked to see me, I hoped that you'd changed your mind about joining my ministry. It isn't too late. All I have to do is go outside—" leaning toward Jeannie, Reeves lowered his voice "—and tell the Righteous Light brethren and the media that I fought the devil for your soul and won."

The urge to giggle would have overcome Jeannie if she hadn't been aware of the threat behind the reverend's offer. "But you haven't fought the devil for my soul, because my soul is my own, and my powers are not derived from any evil source."

"If you do not use your powers in his name, doing his work, then Satan controls you. There is much good you could do. You and I together could form a strong force to combat this sinful world."

Jeannie noticed the wild, glazed stare in Reeves's eyes, an almost otherworldly glimmer. Ripples of suspicion jangled her nerve endings.

In so many ways, Maynard Reeves reminded her of her stepfather, a man who had exploited her, never caring that his fanatical needs had condemned her to a living hell. She hated remembering those endless days and nights of pain from which she'd had no escape. Only in God's own good time and in his way had she been set free. She would never willingly be used to further an unscrupulous minister's career.

"I spent my childhood as the main attraction of my stepfather's ministry."

"And you would be the crown jewel in mine!" Reeves rose from the settee, lifting his arms as if to beseech heaven. "There is nothing that we couldn't do—together!"

Jeannie knew there was only one way to discover the truth, to prove or disprove her suspicions. But how would Sam react? His interference could prove disastrous. She had to make him understand that he was not to interrupt her probe, not even if she appeared to be in danger.

She called out to Sam silently. He didn't try to block her entrance into his mind, because he hadn't been expecting it. She glanced across the room at him; he gave her a quizzical look. Why wouldn't he open his mind and allow her to connect with him? If only he would admit that a telepathic link existed between them, it would be so easy.

I'm going to connect with Reverend Reeves, Jeannie told Sam telepathically, hoping he would open his mind to her.

Sam clenched his teeth. A muscle in his jaw twitched. He uncrossed his arms, lowered them to his sides, and knotted his hands into tight fists. He wouldn't listen to her. He had to shut her out once again.

Jeannie lifted her cane, braced the tip on the floor and rose from her chair. "Reverend Reeves, you understand all about possessing special powers, don't you?"

Spreading his arms in a circular motion as he brought them downward, Reeves stepped back, his legs bumping into the edge of the settee. "I know that there are powers from the devil and powers from God, and that those from the devil must be destroyed and those from God must be cultivated and used in his service."

Seemingly spellbound, Reeves watched her walk slowly toward him. He didn't so much as flinch when she reached out and touched him.

Jeannie held his hand with a strong but gentle clasp. Within seconds, she sensed a subdued energy pulsating weakly inside him. Gradually the sensations grew stronger, and the transference began in earnest. Fear. Pain. Anger. So much anger.

Sam moved inward from the far wall, stopping a few feet behind Reeves. She could not relay a telepathic message to Sam as long as she was connected to Reeves, and she dared not break the tenuous bond she had just formed.

Closing her eyes, Jeannie blocked out the world around her and concentrated on Maynard Reeves's emotions, on the haunted thoughts and painful memories swirling around in his mind. She sensed him trying to pull away, trying to break their link. But he was powerless against Jeannie's determination.

Sensing Maynard's fear, Jeannie connected to the memories

he was recalling. *Don't whip me again. Please, Mama, don't. I promise I'll never do it again. I'll be good.*

She felt the pain, the child's pain that had twisted and festered and rotted within Maynard Reeves.

She saw the blood dripping from welts on the little boy's buttocks. *No, Daddy. I'm sorry. I don't want the mean old devil inside me. I'll make him go away. I'll never use his evil powers again.*

Anger. He would rid the world of Satan's magic, the way his parents had beaten it out of him. But a residue of that power remained inside him. Nothing he did could make it go away. But no one knew. No one must ever know that, sometimes, he used the power. And sometimes he prayed for more.

Jeannie swayed on her feet as she slowly, patiently, drew the fear and pain and anger from Maynard Reeves's alter ego, a frightened and badly abused little boy. The pain was no longer physical, but a deep psychological hurt that tormented Reeves. Poor, poor little boy. Swaying unsteadily, Jeannie gripped her cane, then drew in deep, gasping breaths. Tears welled up in her eyes. Through the mist of her pain—sad, pitiful little Maynard's pain—she heard Sam moving closer. Not yet, she tried to tell him. Almost. Please wait. But she knew he hadn't heard her.

Sam grabbed Reeves by the back of his neck, jerking him away from Jeannie, tossing him down on the floor. Reeves cried out, covering his head, as if to protect himself from an expected blow.

Jeannie could no longer brace her weak legs with the aid of her cane. Her knees buckled, but before she slumped to the floor, Sam lifted her into his arms. She felt the strength that held her safely in its embrace, and knew nothing could harm her. The pain would pass, but it would take time to make its way through her mind, through her body, through her heart, before shattering into nothingness within her soul.

Reeves rose from the floor into a crouch, looking wild-eyed and frightened, like a cornered animal. "My God! My God!

Her power is strong, so strong. I could feel her draining my very soul out of me."

"You're out of your mind!" Sam didn't even look down at Reeves as he walked out of the parlor with Jeannie in his arms.

"Only a witch could possess such powers." Reeves stood, his legs trembling, his hands shaking. "Only Satan's child."

Sam ignored the man, his only thoughts of Jeannie's comfort and safety. "Ollie! Ollie!" He stopped at the foot of the stairs when Ollie Tyner came bustling down the hallway.

"What's wrong?" Seeing Jeannie in Sam's arms, Ollie gave Reeves a condemning stare. "What's he done to her?"

"Show Reverend Reeves to the door, Ollie," Sam said.

"Gladly." Flinging open the front door, Ollie planted her hand on her hip and waited for Reeves to depart.

"Thou shalt not suffer a witch to live!" Reeves shouted as he entered the foyer, his face suffused with color, his eyes glazed over with a rage born of realization.

"Get out of here!" Sam tilted his head just a fraction, just enough to glare at Reeves, giving the other man the full impact of his killer stare.

Standing in the open doorway leading to the porch, Reeves pointed an accusatory finger at Sam. "You protect the devil's daughter. When God destroys her, he will smite you down, also."

Ollie slammed the door on Reverend Reeves, hitting him squarely in the rear end. Swiping the palms of her hands together, she smiled. "Good riddance to bad rubbish."

"Activate the alarm system," Sam said. "We don't want any snakes trying to crawl back into the house. I'm taking Jeannie to her room."

"I'll bring her up some tea in a bit." Ollie shook her head sadly. "When she comes out of it, she'll be thirsty."

Sam nodded his agreement, then carried Jeannie upstairs and laid her on her bed. She clung to him, refusing to release her hold around his neck. Sitting down on the bed, with his back braced against the headboard, he lifted her onto his lap. She cuddled against him.

"Sam?" Her voice was weak, breathless.

"I'm here."

"Reeves…Reeves is…" She didn't have the strength to speak.

"Hush. It's all right. He's gone, and I'll never let him get close enough to touch you. Not ever again." Sam held her close, wishing that he could somehow absorb the aftershocks of pain hitting her now.

She lay quietly, her breathing gradually returning to normal as the color reappeared in her face. Sam stroked her back, soothing her, longing to give her his strength.

She opened her eyes and looked up at him. "I'm all right. Don't worry so."

"Don't talk. Just rest." He caressed her face with his fingertips, each touch filled with deep concern.

"Reeves was psychic as a child," she said.

"What?"

"His powers are very limited, but they do still exist."

"You tapped into those powers? Is that what happened?"

"Partly." Lifting her head off Sam's shoulder, she stared him directly in the eye. "Only his parents knew about his abilities, and they beat him severely anytime he used them. They—"

"Shh…shh… You're overexerting yourself." He placed his right index finger over her lips.

Jeannie covered his hand with hers and pulled it away from her face. "His parents thought little Maynard had received his psychic powers from the devil. They abused him unmercifully. There is so much pain and anger and fear inside him. I had just tapped into those emotions and had begun to drain them when you broke our connection."

"I'm sorry, but I can't waste my time worrying about what

happened to Reeves when he was a child, what psychological damage his parents caused that turned him into a lunatic."

Jeannie squeezed Sam's hand. "He sees me as a threat, now more so than before. I know his secret. I know that he believes, despite all that he's done and everything his parents did, that the devil still occasionally works through him."

"What are you not telling me?" Sam lifted her hand to his lips.

"He was willing to join forces with me, had I been agreeable. He knows that I know he was willing to sell his soul to the devil in order to share my power." Jeannie took a deep, cleansing breath, releasing all the residue of Reeves's emotions. "He cannot allow me to live. He sees me as an evil threat, a seducer with the devil's own power."

Sam buried his lips in Jeannie's open palm, then grabbed her into his arms, holding her with fierce protectiveness. "I'll never let him near you again. Whatever it takes, I'll keep you safe."

"Yes, Sam. I know you'll guard me with your life."

"Damn right about that!"

CHAPTER EIGHT

STEPPING ABOARD THE *Royal Belle* was like entering another world. Nineteenth-century charm and lavish elegance combined with the glitter and excitement of Las Vegas. The gambling casino, docked just off the Biloxi shore, was a security problem. Public access gave anyone the opportunity to come and go as they pleased. A quick and unobserved getaway would be simple—drive out of the parking lot and onto Beach Boulevard or escape by private boat. It would be easy to get lost in the horde of tourists who flooded the area from daylight to dark.

Three decks high, gaming on two levels and a restaurant-lounge on the third, the floating palace was ideal for a society charity function. Although two levels had been secured for the private affair, the bottom level of the riverboat remained open to the public, which meant it was possible for an uninvited guest to slip by security.

When Sam had been unable to dissuade Jeannie from attending this black-tie affair, he'd asked Rufus Painter to the Howell home for a private meeting. Painter agreed with Sam's opinion of Maynard Reeves as a fanatic, with the potential to become violent, but since the man stayed just within the law, Painter's hands were tied. Sam understood the officer's limitations. Before the police could do anything about Reeves, they needed some sort of proof that the man had broken the law.

Sam had stayed on the right side of the law all his life. He'd done a stint in the marines before college, and then joined the Drug Enforcement Administration. And since starting his own private security agency, he had, for the most part, adhered to government rules and regulations.

But to keep Jeannie Alverson safe, he was willing to do anything, and if that meant breaking a few rules, Sam wasn't about to lose any sleep over it. Yeah, he and Painter understood each other. They both had jobs to do; they were just bound by slightly different codes of conduct.

Yesterday, he'd had J.T. send down a couple of Dundee Private Security's newest recruits. He'd told J.T. the two-day stint would give the men some experience in the field and allow him to evaluate their performance. He knew J.T. didn't buy the excuse, but he was too good a friend to ask questions, even after Sam told him the agency would cover the cost.

Gabriel Hawk, a former CIA agent, and Morgan Kane, once a navy SEAL, hardly needed any field experience. Sam had evaluated their records thoroughly before bringing them into the business to replace two of his best men. Ashe McLaughlin wouldn't be returning. He had married his childhood best friend and decided to move back home and begin a new life. And Simon Roarke, who'd been severely wounded in the line of duty, needed several months to recover.

Upon their arrival from the airport yesterday morning, Sam had left Hawk at the Howell home to guard Jeannie while he and Kane checked out the *Royal Belle.*

EVEN WITH HIS own men assisting the private security provided by the *Royal Belle,* Sam felt uneasy. He had halfway expected to find a troop of Righteous Light brethren picketing the casino, but to his great relief, there hadn't been a sign of Reeves or his followers. Sam wasn't so sure that was a good sign. He'd much rather have these people out in the open than sneaking around in dark corners.

Constantly vigilant, Sam repeatedly scanned the room, which was filled with the Mississippi Gulf's elite, along with visitors from Mobile and New Orleans. Many of the people who belonged to Julian Howell's social circle, though cordial and nauseatingly polite to Jeannie, had watched her every move for the past hour during dinner. What the hell were they expecting? That she'd sprout wings and fly? Or cast a spell over the whole room? Unfortunately, there had been one dear old lady who, despite her breeding and sophistication, had been unable to refrain from requesting that Jeannie heal her spastic colon.

Julian rose from his chair, held out his hand to Marta Mc-Corkle and asked her to dance. The warmth of her smile softened the age lines around her eyes and mouth, making her appear years younger than sixty.

Sam noticed the way Jeannie watched the couples on the dance floor and couldn't help wondering if she had ever danced.

"Would you like to go downstairs and play the slot machines?" Sam asked.

"Not yet," she said. "I haven't finished my dessert." Lifting her spoon, she dipped into the chocolate mousse.

Sam concentrated on Jeannie's mouth. Full. Soft. A warm peach color. And so inviting. She ate the spoonful of mousse, then unconsciously licked her bottom lip. Sam swallowed, thinking of how her tongue had felt, mating with his, sampling his taste.

His gaze moved over her face, across her nose and her delicately tinted cheeks to her expressive brown eyes. When she smiled at him, her eyes smiled, too. Her pale eyes were almost identical in color to her beige-streaked ash brown hair.

Sam tried to return her smile, but somehow he had never perfected the art of smiling. Without opening his mouth, he curved his lips slightly. His niece Elizabeth had told him he needed to smile more, that he most certainly needed to laugh occasionally. And sometimes, with Elizabeth, he had.

"Everything's just perfect, isn't it?" Jeannie reached across the table, laying her hand flat, her palm open, gesturing for him to respond. "The weather is wonderful, not too hot, even for August. The casino is lovely, and everyone is having a good time."

Julian and Marta had kept a steady stream of conversation going during dinner, but Jeannie had been very quiet. He had noticed she wasn't prone to idle chitchat and that suited him fine. What didn't suit him was the way she kept getting inside his head. He had felt her probing a couple of times and had blocked her entrance. They were alone at the table now. If she had something to say to him, she could use the normal means of communication.

"Are you having a good time?" he asked, glancing at her hand, wanting to cover it with his. But if he touched her, she would connect with him. She would feel what he felt. And he'd be powerless to stop her.

"I'm pleased that we've had such a good turnout. If this function brings in a lot of money for the Howell School, Mr. VanDevere, the CEO of the company that owns the *Royal Belle,* has agreed to make it an annual affair."

Sam followed Jeannie's gaze to the dance floor, to Marta in Julian's arms. The older couple were gliding smoothly in a slow two-step.

Sam glanced down at Jeannie's hand again. She curled her fingers, relaxed them, curled them, relaxed them, signaling him to touch her. "How long have Julian and Marta been dating?"

"For several years. They've known each other since they were children. Julian and Miriam were close friends with Marta and her husband, who died a year after Miriam."

"Julian told me before we left the house that he wouldn't be coming home until morning." Sam watched her face for a reaction. "He said that you'd know where to reach him."

"He and Marta have been lovers for about a year now." Jeannie's smile widened. A sigh of humming laughter vibrated from her throat. "You aren't surprised, are you?"

"No. Besides, it's none of my business." He wished she'd

take her hand away; the temptation to accept her invitation overpowered his common sense.

He laid his hand in hers. She grasped it gently. He repeated the gesture. Sam stared directly into her compelling brown eyes and knew he'd have a hell of a time denying this woman anything. Just as a tingle of awareness passed between Jeannie and Sam, Hawk tapped him on the shoulder.

Sam released Jeannie's hand, scooted back his chair and stood. He stepped away from the table, making sure Jeannie couldn't overhear his conversation. "What's wrong?"

"Maynard Reeves just arrived with a lady named Danette Suddath." Hawk inclined his head to the left.

Sam scanned the area to their left, catching a glimpse of Reeves's sandy hair, gleaming in the muted lounge light. Swearing under his breath, he grabbed Hawk by the arm. "Why the hell did the guards let him in here?"

"The lady has an invitation, and he's her guest," Hawk said. "Kane is making a phone call to check on this Suddath woman, but she acts like she belongs here. She's spoken to several people, calling them by their first names."

"Reeves is a strong antigambling advocate." Sam repeatedly clenched and unclenched his hands. "I wonder how he'll justify socializing in this den of iniquity."

"I'll keep tabs on Reeves," Hawk assured Sam. "And as soon as Kane gets any information on the woman, I'll let you know."

"I don't want Reeves here, but there seems to be nothing we can do at the moment."

Turning around in her seat, Jeannie called out to Sam. "Is something wrong? Is there some problem I should know about?"

"Make sure he doesn't come anywhere near her," Sam told Hawk. "Stop him before I have to."

Hawk nodded, then made his way across the room, heading

directly to the lounge area. Sam held out his hand to Jeannie. Staring up at him, she gave him a quizzical look.

"No problems," he lied, and wondered how long it would take her to realize the truth. "Hawk was just checking in with me." Sam wiggled his fingers. "Come on, Jeannie, dance with me."

He saw the warm, glowing light in her eyes die. Dammit! Had she already seen through his lie? Was she aware of Reeves's presence?

"I—I don't dance," she said.

"What?"

"I don't dance, because of my legs." She bowed her head deliberately, to avoid looking at Sam. "You know I can't walk without my cane. I can't dance. I'd only make a spectacle of myself if I tried."

"Have you ever tried?"

"Once, when I was a teenager. Miriam tried to teach me, but we soon realized it was hopeless. I'm not able to move without bracing myself with my cane."

Sam lifted her walking stick and handed it to her. "How about a stroll around the deck instead?"

Raising her head, she nodded agreement, a flicker of a smile forming on her lips. She stood, supporting herself with her cane, and took Sam's hand. He slipped his arm around her waist and led her away from the lounge area and out onto the open deck of the riverboat.

It was not quite eight-thirty, and the sun had just set. The summer twilight spread gold across the sky, gilding the clouds, as the aureate Gulf waters rhythmically bathed the tawny shore. The evening breeze, pleasant and soothing, caressed Jeannie's hair; several loose tendrils blew across her cheeks.

They walked the length of the deck, reaching a secluded corner. The music from the live band echoed on the wind and water. Sam slowed their walk, then halted. Jeannie glanced up at him.

"Are you going to tell me why you rushed me outside so quickly?" she asked, sensing the tension in Sam's big body, knowing from merely touching him that he was concerned about something.

Tightening his hold around her waist, he turned her to face him. He lifted her left hand, placing it on his shoulder. "Hold on tight," he said, then took her cane out of her hand. Gasping loudly, she grabbed his other shoulder with her right hand. He hung her cane on the deck rail.

"What are you doing?"

"We're going to dance. I'll support you securely in my arms. Trust me. You can dance. You can dance with me."

"Sam, no, I—"

"No one can see us. We're all alone out here."

"I can't. I—"

"Kick off your shoes, then lift your left foot and put it on top of mine," he told her.

"What?"

"Don't ask questions. Just do as I say."

She obeyed his command, stepping out of her shoes and placing her left foot on top of his. "I don't see how my stepping on your feet is going to—"

"Haven't you ever seen little girls dancing with their fathers?"

"You can't mean…"

"Put your right foot on mine. We're going to dance."

"I'm not a little girl. I'm a grown woman. And I'm not light as a feather."

"I'm a big man, with big feet," he said. "And you're a small woman, with small feet. You'll feel as light as a feather to me."

Slowly, reluctantly, she lifted her right foot and placed it atop his. The moment the deed was completed, Sam moved, cautiously, without any sense of rhythm at first, allowing Jeannie a few moments to adjust to the new and unusual sensation of someone else actually walking for her. And that was all Sam did for a while, simply walked her backward and forward. With her arms draped around his neck, her body pressed intimately against his, she gradually relinquished all control to Sam. Her trust in him was that great.

"See how easy it is when you do what I tell you to do?"

She jerked her head up, glaring at him, but when he smiled, she smiled, too, unable to resist the magnetism of his smile. No wonder he didn't do it often, or so completely. His smile was devastating.

"You like being right, don't you?" Laying her head on his chest, she cuddled closer, and was pleased when she heard his indrawn breath.

"Yeah, I like being right." With one hand still bracing her back, he eased his other hand downward, from her waist to the curve of her buttocks.

The romantic strains of "I Love How You Love Me" floated on the night air, strings and brass blending into a sweet harmony. Sam moved his big body to the soft, slow melody, encompassing Jeannie in his embrace as he carried her across the deck, her small feet welded atop his much larger ones. Their bodies swayed in perfect unison, in tune with each other and the flow of the music.

She closed her eyes, absorbing the beauty of the moment, allowing herself to enjoy the pleasure of dancing and the joy of being in Sam Dundee's strong arms. She had never known anything like this incredible sensation. Dancing. Dancing in Sam's arms. Gliding across the floor as if she had wings on her feet.

Opening her eyes, she glanced over Sam's shoulder and saw the pale form of the moon, the darkening sky and the first glimmer of a twinkling star. She tilted her head.

Sam looked down at her. She smiled at him. Lowering his head, he rubbed his cheek against hers.

"Thank you," she said, then closed her eyes again, sighing,

wishing this moment could last forever. Sam had given her this gift. Dancing in the moonlight.

She could not imagine any woman not wanting to be in Sam Dundee's arms. He was so incredibly handsome, so big and powerful. So absolutely debonair in his black tux and unadorned white shirt. In the pale moonlight, his blond hair had turned to burnished flaxen silk, and his eyes had warmed to a smoldering slate blue.

As he waltzed her around the deck, Jeannie sensed the hazy glow she often felt just before connecting with another person's emotions. Then she felt the tiny electrical currents of awareness that came when she began picking up signals from within the other person. She could block these feelings if she tried hard enough, if she ended the physical contact. But this was Sam, unguarded and receptive. How could she not take the opportunity to share what he was feeling?

Jeannie. Sweet Jeannie. She was the very embodiment of femininity, of a woman's loving, nurturing nature. Her generous heart exposed her to the pain of others, and her healing touch absorbed that pain. How unfair life was, that a woman this gentle and kind had the ability to suffer the most excruciating pain for others, even healing them on a temporary basis, and yet was unable to ease her own pain, either physical or emotional.

Sam ran his hand over her buttocks, savoring the feel of the light peach silk covering her body. Pressing her against him, into his arousal, he kissed the top of her head. She sighed.

He wanted to take her mouth, to lift her in his arms and carry her away, to bury himself deep within her body. And he wanted her to know exactly how he felt. Slowing his movements, he danced her back against the wooden surface of the outer wall. She made no protest, verbally or telepathically. Indeed, she welcomed him, clinging to him, sending him a silent message of acceptance.

Lifting her off his feet, anchoring her between his hard body and the wall, supporting her with his arms, Sam circled her lips with the tip of his tongue. Her moist lips opened, issuing him an invitation. On the verge of losing his reason, he kissed her. She returned the kiss, enticing him with her body and her mind. He read her clearly, and knew she understood precisely what he wanted from her.

Her kisses were pure sweet fire, burning him in their intensity. Throwing caution to the wind, he devoured her, thrusting his tongue into her mouth, gripping her buttocks, straining against her. She clung to him, joining fully in the savagery of his kiss, returning full measure the heat of his passion.

He knew that she felt what he felt, wanted what he wanted. And in a sudden, blinding flash of realization, Sam sensed her physical yearning and her emotional desires. My God, it wasn't possible! He couldn't have actually tapped into her feelings.

The pleasure for both of them intensified, building higher and higher as they kissed and touched, their bodies undulating to the sensuous beat of primeval mating. He wanted to rip her clothes off her body and take her, here, now, with no thought of the consequences.

He had to stop, or there would be no turning back. He ended the kiss, his breathing ragged, his face and hands damp with sweat. Jeannie pressed her face against his shoulder.

"Oh, Sam…Sam…"

He eased her slowly to her feet, slipped his arm around her and held her close. He could feel the rapid beat of her heart. When she tried to comfort him by taking some of his throbbing need into her own body, he stopped her, knowing she ached with the same painful desire that racked him from head to toe.

"I can handle it," he said. "I may not be as strong as you are, angel, but I'll survive until—" he cupped the back of her head in his big hand "—until you take away this sweet ache when we make love."

"Tonight," she whispered, not knowing where his desire ended and hers began.

"Tonight," he agreed, kissing her again, but ending the kiss quickly. "Come on, Jeannie, dance with me again."

"Oh, yes, Sam, I'd like that. I'd like that very much."

With her arms draped around his neck and her feet atop his, Jeannie surrendered herself to the sensual pleasure of dancing with Sam. He glided her across the deck, the soft evening breeze caressing their bodies as the twilight shadows surrounded them.

Glancing over Jeannie's shoulder, Sam saw Hawk standing in the doorway. Hawk nodded, then returned inside the restaurant. Quickly Sam checked his watch. They'd been on deck nearly an hour; it was time for Hawk to report in. Was Reeves still aboard the *Royal Belle?* Sam wondered, still trying to figure out why the reverend had made an appearance tonight. There was something not quite right about Reeves showing up at this charity function.

Feeling the sudden jolt of unease that hit him in the stomach, Jeannie looked at him, willing him to explain. He walked her to the deck's rail, removed her cane and placed it in her hand. Bending on one knee, he lifted her foot and slipped on her shoe, then repeated the process with her other foot.

He started walking them around the deck, but she halted, and he had little choice but to stop. Trying to block his emotions so that she couldn't pick up on them, Sam refused to look at her.

"What's the problem?" she asked. "What do you not want me to know?"

"There's no problem. I've got everything under control. Enjoy the evening, and don't worry." There was no need for her to know that Maynard Reeves was on board the *Royal Belle*. Hawk and Kane would follow orders and keep the man away from Jeannie.

She knew Sam wasn't going to tell her what was bothering him. She appreciated his wanting to protect her from any un-pleasantness, but at the same time, she resented his treating her as if she were made of spun glass, some fragile, easily broken doll. With an unexpected flash of clarity, she heard the words *fragile angel,* and knew she'd read Sam's thoughts, without his knowledge.

He brushed the side of her face with the back of his hand, caressing her tenderly. "How long do you have to stay at this function in order to be socially correct?"

"I need to make an appearance in the gaming room." There was no point in pressing him about whatever was bothering him. Sooner or later, even if he chose not to share it with her, she would sense it. "We can play the slot machines or try the blackjack table. It doesn't matter, as long as I lose some money to set an example for the other guests."

"I suppose knowing their losses are going to a worthy cause will make losing a little easier."

Leading her inside to the restaurant level, Sam glanced toward the lounge. No sight of Maynard Reeves or Hawk, but Kane was headed in Sam's direction.

"I need to speak to Kane," Sam said. "Would you mind waiting back at the table for a few minutes?"

"All right." She patted him on the arm. "It's only a couple of yards away. I can walk over there without your help."

Acting as if he hadn't heard her, Sam escorted her to their table and seated her, then turned around and met his agent. Pulling Kane aside, making sure Jeannie couldn't overhear their conversation, Sam placed his hand on the other man's shoulder.

"Where's Reeves?"

"Hawk followed him and his lady friend downstairs into the gaming room," Kane said.

"Did you get any information on the woman?"

"She's an invited guest, a widow whose husband left her millions."

"Any idea what her connection is to Reeves?" Sam was aware of how charming Reeves might be to a lonely widow with plenty of money in the bank and the right social connections.

"She's a new convert to his Righteous Light Church." Kane hesitated, drew in a deep breath and looked Sam straight in the eye. "She has a daughter who's a student at the Howell School."

"Damn!"

"I've got a bad feeling about this, Sam. After your briefing on the situation, my instincts tell me Reeves has some sick reason for being here tonight."

"Yeah, my instincts tell me the same thing. But he hasn't tried to approach Jeannie. He hasn't even made a scene by preaching against the sins of gambling, when I know for a fact that he's given the casino owners hell for the past few years."

"There's something going on we don't know about."

"Go down and tell Hawk not to let Reeves out of his sight. I'll have to bring Jeannie downstairs. Even if I can't keep her from seeing him, I can make sure he doesn't come near her."

Nodding his agreement, Kane headed straight for the exit. Sam walked over to Jeannie, helped her to her feet and escorted her to the elevator.

They entered the elaborately decorated gaming room, which was crowded with the cream of Mississippi Gulf society. Sam spotted Hawk's black ponytail, then saw Maynard Reeves and his date standing a few feet to the agent's right, with colas in their hands, observing the gamblers.

Jeannie followed Sam's line of vision. Her muscles tensed, freezing her to the spot, the moment she saw Maynard Reeves. "That's what you didn't want me to know, isn't it?"

"He's not going to bother you. I promise." Sam squeezed her hand.

"How did he—? I don't believe it," she said. "He's with Danette Suddath. Her daughter Missy is a student at the Howell School. I've known Danette socially for years."

"She's a new convert to the Righteous Light Church," Sam told her.

"He's taking advantage of her." Jeannie gripped her cane

fiercely. "She's lonely and insecure, and trying to raise a Down's syndrome child alone. There's no telling what sort of lies that snake has told her."

"Danette Suddath isn't my concern," Sam said. "It's not that he's used her to get into this private party tonight that worries me, but why he's here."

"I can find out." She took a step away from Sam.

He held her back. "No!" He hissed the word between clenched teeth.

"Tell me that you don't feel the danger. It's all around us. There's something terribly wrong, and you know it as well as I do."

"Don't try to play mind games with Reeves," Sam said. "If anyone's powers come from the devil, I'd say his do."

"His psychic powers are limited, and very weak. I'm far stronger than he is." She noticed the skeptical frown on Sam's face. "Comparatively speaking, Reverend Reeves is a little squall and I'm a full-fledged hurricane."

"Well, Ms. Hurricane, you aren't going to—"

"I can do it from across the room, from where I'm standing now, but it would be easier if I were close enough to touch him. I can sense feelings and emotions without touching, but the sensations are usually very faint, too weak for me to completely connect with the person."

"No." He didn't give a damn about her ability to sense Reeves's emotions, and thus discern the reason he'd suckered some poor woman into bringing him here tonight. He wasn't going to let Jeannie anywhere near that lunatic.

She wouldn't argue with Sam now, Jeannie decided. She'd bide her time and figure out some way of getting closer to Maynard Reeves.

"Let's join Julian and Marta at the craps table." Jeannie waved at her foster father, who smiled and returned her wave.

Sam watched while Jeannie won a thousand dollars at craps,

then methodically lost two thousand. While he kept a close eye on her, he occasionally sought out Hawk, knowing Reeves would be within spitting distance. The good reverend and his date circled the gaming room slowly, Reeves smiling and laughing and flirting with the widow.

"I think we'll call it a night," Julian said, bending to kiss Jeannie on the cheek. "It's nearly eleven. Time for a man my age to be going to bed."

"See you tomorrow." Jeannie waved goodbye as the older couple left.

Ten minutes later, Sam escorted Jeannie to the ladies' room. Waiting outside impatiently, he noticed Hawk following Reeves and his date, who were coming in Sam's direction. His muscles tightened. His nerves came to full alert. When Reeves was within three feet of him, Sam stepped forward, but the other man ignored him, turning in the opposite direction, heading toward the doors leading out on deck. At that precise moment, Jeannie ventured out of the rest room. Sam stepped in front of her.

She walked around Sam and reached out, just grazing Reeve's sleeve before Sam grabbed her hand. Reeves jerked around, his gaze focusing on Jeannie as a wide smile spread across his face.

"Good evening, Jeannie," Reeves said. "What more appropriate place to find Satan's daughter than in one of his houses of sin?"

"Reeves, I'm warning you…" Sam said.

Reeves glanced behind him to where Hawk stood, then laughed aloud. "A host of fallen angels guarding the master's offspring. How appropriate."

"Danette, what are you doing with Maynard Reeves?" Jeannie asked.

Danette Suddath gasped, apparently startled by Jeannie's question. "Don't speak to me, you witch. Reverend Reeves has warned us all about your evil powers. If you ever return to the Howell School, I'll withdraw Missy immediately."

"Danette, how can you believe—" Jeannie reached out her hand "—this man's lies? You've known me for years."

Danette lifted her hand as if she intended to touch Jeannie, but Reeves slapped Danette's hand away, and when he did, Jeannie grasped his hand, threading her fingers through his. For a split second, he froze, fear etched on his face.

She sensed his anger and his hatred. Such cruel, ugly hatred. And a thirst for retribution.

Tonight they will die. All of these sinners will reap what they've sown. And the witch will burn with them. The flames will wipe them from the face of the earth and cleanse us of their evil.

Reeves jerked his hand away at the same moment Sam grabbed Jeannie. Hawk closed in, gripping the reverend by the shoulder. Reeves pulled out of Hawk's grasp. He whispered something to Danette Suddath, and the two of them rushed out the door.

"Let them go," Sam said.

"No!" Jeannie cried. "Stop Maynard Reeves!"

Sensing her need for him, Sam turned just as she swayed toward him and dropped her cane to the floor. He caught her in his arms. "Jeannie?"

Gripping the lapels of his tuxedo, she gazed up at Sam. He recognized the fear in her eyes. "What's wrong? You picked up something from his emotions when you touched him, didn't you?"

Jeannie gasped for air, the hatred and anger she had tapped into when she connected with Maynard Reeves still swirling around inside her. "Get everyone out… Get them off…now… Something's wrong. He—he's going to destroy this riverboat, and everyone on board."

CHAPTER NINE

SAM LIFTED JEANNIE into his arms, then turned to Hawk. "Contact Kane immediately. The two of you work with security to evacuate the casino."

"What the hell do I tell the security chief?" Hawk asked.

"Tell him—" Sam said.

"Fire. Flames. Destruction." Jeannie spoke the words as if reciting a chant.

"A bomb?" Hawk asked.

"Yeah." Sam nodded. "That would be my guess."

Hawk removed his small cellular phone from his jacket, speaking to Kane as he walked to the elevator with Sam and Jeannie. Redialing the phone, he spoke quickly, issuing orders. Returning the phone to his pocket, he held the elevator door.

"Kane's on his way to look for Reeves, and I've alerted the casino's security chief to the situation. I'll start evacuating this level as soon as I have a couple of men up here to help me keep everyone in line. Once this thing gets under way, more than one person is bound to panic."

"Sam?" Jeannie's voice was a little stronger, but she could barely open her eyes.

"I'm getting you out of here now," he said.

"Tell them… Hurry. Soon, I think. Soon."

Hawk looked at Sam, who nodded. Hawk stepped back, the elevator door closed, and Sam drew Jeannie closer to his body as she cuddled against him. When they reached the bottom level of the *Royal Belle,* Sam noticed the security guards in a huddle. Hawk and Kane weren't wasting any time. Good. If Jeannie's instincts were correct, and he had no doubt they were, disaster could strike at any moment. If Reeves intended destroying the gambling casino's patrons en masse, Jeannie included, the most likely means would be a bomb, or several bombs, strategically placed.

Sam carried Jeannie out on deck, down the wide gangplank that connected the *Royal Belle* to the dock, and onto shore.

"There's Marta and Julian," Sam said. "They're in the parking lot. Julian sees us."

"Take me to him, please. I'll—I'll have to explain what's happening."

Before they reached Marta's Mercedes, Julian was hurrying toward them, his eyes wide and questioning. "What's wrong?"

"Reeves…" Jeannie said. "I think he placed bombs on the riverboat."

"My God!" Julian touched Jeannie's cheek, his hand trembling, then looked at Sam. "You must get her away from here. And the casino must be evacuated."

"An evacuation is in the works as we speak." Sam lowered Jeannie to her feet, holding her close, bracing her against his body. "As soon as Kane apprehends Maynard Reeves, I'll send him with you and Marta to take Jeannie home."

"Sam?" Jeannie covered his hand with hers. He glanced at her and understood, without words, what she was asking.

"It could be dangerous if you stay here," he said.

"I can't leave. Not until everyone is safely onshore."

"If there is a bomb…" God, he hated the very thought of it. "Even if everyone gets out safely, once the bomb explodes, there's going to be a mad rush. You have no idea what the scene of a bombing looks like. And if people are hurt, you're going to want to help them. I can't let you do that. Can you understand? I won't let you suffer anyone else's pain."

"I have to wait. I can't leave." Not when you're staying, she wanted to say, but didn't.

Tilting his head back, Sam stared up at the starry night sky. Closing his eyes, he took several deep breaths. He couldn't allow her to stay and wait for the worst to happen. Enduring pain of that magnitude could kill her. Even if she was willing to take the chance, he wasn't.

Sam saw Morgan Kane searching the parking lot for him. Lifting his hand, Sam motioned to his agent. He didn't have Reeves with him. What had he done with the man?

Kane rushed over to Sam. "Reeves got away. He and his date were getting into her BMW by the time I found them. I tried to stop them, but the woman nearly ran me down. By the time I got to my car, they were lost in traffic on the boulevard."

"Damn! The police can't touch him without some evidence." Sam balled his right hand into a fist, wishing he could smash Reeves's pretty face. If he could have gotten hold of Reeves and questioned him before the police arrived, he might have been able to get the truth out of the bastard. "Look, Kane, make sure Jeannie gets home safe and sound. I'm going back in to help with the evacuation."

Jeannie lifted Sam's tight fist into her hand. "I'm not leaving. Not until everyone on board is safe and you can take me home yourself."

"Now is not the time to argue with me."

"Go do what you have to do, and take Mr. Kane with you. I'll be safe here with Julian and Marta."

"I don't think—"

"Give Julian your gun." Jeannie squeezed Sam's hand. "He knows how to use it. Don't you, Julian?"

"Give me the gun, and you two men go get those people off the riverboat," Julian said. "Maynard Reeves is nowhere around. I think I can protect Jeannie for the time being."

Music from the *Royal Belle* drifted in the air. The Gulf waters lapped at the sides of the big riverboat.

"Look!" Marta said. "People are crossing the gangplank by the dozens. The decks are filled with people."

Sam removed his Ruger from his holster and handed it to Julian. "If we're lucky, this will be a false alarm." He lifted Jeannie up onto the hood of Marta's Mercedes. "I wish to hell you'd go home, where I know you'd be safe."

She tugged on his sleeve, drawing him down toward her, then kissed his cheek. "Be careful."

Jeannie sat there watching Sam and Kane go back aboard the *Royal Belle*. Dear God, what if the bombs exploded while Sam was aboard? What if he died? No, no, no. She couldn't allow herself to think that way. She had to stay calm and prepare herself to help the injured.

"Julian, do you have your medical bag with you?" Jeannie asked.

"No," he said. "I was thinking the same thing. If there is an explosion, I'll be needed, won't I?"

As streams of people exited the casino, some running, some walking slowly, with dazed looks on their faces, a few women in tears, the loud wail of sirens could be heard in the distance. Within minutes, three police cars pulled up, each one blocking a gangplank entrance to the riverboat. Sam recognized Lieutenant Painter's bulky form and shock of silver hair.

The policemen, aided by the *Royal Belle*'s security force, kept order as best they could. Only a few people panicked, creating a disruptive scene that slowed the mass exodus from the riverboat.

"There's so much fear in the atmosphere," Jeannie said. "All those people are afraid they're going to die before they reach safety." She sensed impending doom. Closing her eyes, she said a silent prayer, asking for the strength to do all she could to help those who needed her. And she asked for Sam's safety.

People rushed into the parking area. Cars roared to life. Within minutes, a huge traffic jam existed, and a sleek black Jaguar collided with a Ford pickup truck.

Boom! Boom! The thundering roar of an explosion rent the night air. Jeannie screamed. Marta grabbed her hand as the three of them gazed at the *Royal Belle*. Fire shot straight up, lighting the darkness, streaking the sky with flames. The force of the explosion tossed the people on the gangplank forward. Most of them landed flat on their faces on the ground. A few were flung into the water. Terrified screams mingled with the sizzle of the fires and the echo of the bomb blasts.

Boom! Boom! Another explosion? Two bombs? Maybe more. This shouldn't be happening; it wouldn't be, if Maynard Reeves was not so determined to kill her.

Where was Sam? Please, dear God, let him be all right.

"Do you see Sam anywhere?" Jeannie asked.

"No," Julian said. "But you mustn't worry, my dear. Mr. Dundee can take care of himself."

Two ambulances arrived in quick succession. Lieutenant Painter issued orders in his gruff, commanding voice. Medics quickly attended to the injured, while two policemen tried to control the traffic.

Jeannie saw Morgan Kane in the middle of the panicked crowd, an unconscious woman in his arms. He handed her to a medic and returned to the forefront, immersing himself in the madness. Then she noticed a soaking-wet Hawk dragging himself out of the Gulf waters and onto shore.

"He's hurt," Jeannie said, straining forward, but unable to walk. "Please. I must do something. I can't just stand here and watch. Maynard Reeves did this because of me."

"This isn't your fault," Julian said. "You mustn't feel guilty."

"Please, Julian, I have to find Sam. I have to know he's all right. And I can help Mr. Hawk, and all these other people."

"You aren't going anywhere. Do you hear me? You aren't to try to search for Mr. Dundee. He'll make his way to you. And don't go trying to help these people. There will be too many injuries. You'll endanger your own life if you try to save them." Julian handed Marta Sam's Ruger. "I want you and Marta to wait inside the car. I'll go see what I can do to help."

"I should be helping, too." Jeannie looked at Julian with the wide-eyed innocence of a child, her voice pleading, her expression beseeching. "I will feel guilty if I don't try to help these people. Please, Julian. I'll only help those who are seriously injured, those in the most pain."

"Think what it would do to you," he said. "There are too many injured people for you to help them all."

"But if I don't try to help them, my mental torment will hurt me far worse."

"It would be too dangerous. You will stay in the car until Mr. Dundee comes for you."

Julian and Marta assisted Jeannie into the Mercedes, and then Julian rushed off, speaking to the ambulance attendants and medics.

Once Julian was out of sight, Jeannie turned to Marta. "I have to find Sam. Please, Marta. See if you can find him. If you speak to Mr. Hawk or Mr. Kane, maybe they can help you find Sam."

"I can't leave you here alone." Marta shook her head. "Don't ask me to go against Julian's wishes."

"I'll lock the door," Jeannie said. "You can leave Sam's gun with me. Please, Marta. I'm very worried about Sam. If something weren't terribly wrong, he would have come back by now."

"I don't know. Julian will be very upset with me."

SAM SWAM TO shore, dragging an elderly gentleman, one of over a dozen people he'd fished out of the water since the second explosion had hit. Hauling the unconscious man to shore, Sam called out for a passing medic, then saw Dr. Howell, down on one knee, giving a hysterical young woman an injection.

If Howell was helping the victims, who was guarding Jeannie? Lifting the wounded man in his arms, Sam carried him to where Dr. Howell and the medics had set up a makeshift emergency room in the parking lot while they waited for more ambulances to make return trips from the local hospitals.

Sam laid the man on the ground, then clasped Dr. Howell's shoulder. "Where's Jeannie?"

Julian gasped, then smiled when he saw Sam. "Thank God you're all right. Jeannie is beside herself with worry."

"Where is she?'

"She and Marta are in the car. Locked in. And Marta has your Ruger." Julian grabbed Sam's wrist. "She's bound and determined to help these people. I know Jeannie. If it's possible, she'll find a way."

"What would it do to her to try to help this many people?"

"It could kill her," Julian said.

Sam's chest tightened with fear. The sickening taste of panic rose in his throat. "I'll make sure she doesn't do anything stupid."

A weak smile faded from Julian's lips. He nodded. Sam made his way across the parking lot, stepping around people lying on the ground and speaking to the policemen he passed. He scanned the area, wondering where Kane and Hawk might be, hoping they were both all right.

Lieutenant Painter stopped Sam, questioning him about Maynard Reeves and how Jeannie had known there were bombs set to explode aboard the *Royal Belle*. Sam gave the lieutenant all the information he had, knowing it wouldn't be enough to arrest Reeves.

"I'll haul him in for questioning," Painter said. "But unless we can find some solid evidence to link him to this bombing, then he'll get off scot-free."

"Then you'd better find some sort of evidence, and soon," Sam said. "Otherwise—"

"Don't step over the line, Dundee. You're one of the good guys, remember?"

"Yeah, sure." Sam checked his watch. The damn thing was still running, even though the crystal was broken. Nearly two hours had passed since all hell had broken loose. Most of the parking lot had been cleared, and half a dozen ambulances had taken the injured to hospitals in Biloxi and surrounding towns. Several dozen people remained, waiting for returning ambulances.

Sam spotted Morgan Kane standing near the one remaining ambulance. As he drew near Kane's side, Sam looked inside the ambulance, and for one split second his heart stopped. Jeannie sat beside a badly burned dark-haired woman, holding her hand, absorbing her pain.

"What the hell's going on?" Sam gripped Kane's shoulder. "How did she get here?"

"Ms. Alverson sent Ms. McCorkle to look for you, and when she couldn't find you, she told me Ms. Alverson wanted to see me."

"You took Jeannie out of the car? You brought her here?" Sam's facial muscles tensed. He glared at Kane. "Do you have any idea what you've done?"

"She said she wanted to help these people, and she told me it would be all right with you as long as I was with her." Kane reached inside his jacket, pulled out Sam's Ruger and handed it to him. "She gave me this. It's yours, isn't it?"

Sam stuck the gun in his holster. "How many people has she helped?"

"How many?"

"Yeah, how many?"

"Ten, maybe twelve."

Sam cursed, the words strong and expressive.

"Hey, I don't know what the hell she's been doing," Kane said, "but every person she touched seemed to get better instantly."

"Didn't you happen to notice that she's been suffering more and more every time she *helped* another person?" Sam knew exactly what she'd been doing. She'd gone from person to person, alleviating their pain, absorbing enough of their suffering to reduce their chances of dying. Just thinking about what she'd put herself through tormented Sam.

"Where's Marta McCorkle?"

"She stayed with Ms. Alverson until a few minutes ago, then she left to look for Dr. Howell," Kane said. "Look, Sam, I'm sorry if by doing what Ms. Alverson asked I put her in some sort of danger. I haven't left her side for a second."

"Forget it," Sam said. "The damage's done. Besides, I know how persuasive Jeannie can be."

Releasing his hold on Kane, Sam stepped up into the ambulance. Jeannie was too deep into her healing trance to see him. Her colorless face was streaked with tears—the tears of others. He jerked her away from the burned woman. Jeannie groaned, then opened her eyes and stared at him.

"Sam, no. Please, just this one more. She's in so much pain." Jeannie tried to lift her hand to clutch Sam's sleeve. Her hand wouldn't cooperate. She let it fall to her side.

"You're in pain," he told her, pulling her out of the ambulance and lifting her into his arms. "You're so weak you can't even lift your hand. I'm taking you home. Now."

"But I can't—"

"We're not discussing it."

Standing just outside the open doors of the ambulance, Sam motioned to Kane. "After you and Hawk make your statements to the police and get a once-over in ER, fly back to Atlanta and take a few days off."

Jeannie squirmed in Sam's arms. "I don't want to leave. These people are suffering…because of me, because… Maynard Reeves wanted…to kill me."

Not only was Sam not going to allow Jeannie to do any more healing tonight, but once he took her home, he had no intention of allowing her out in public again. Somehow he'd persuade her to leave town. If Reeves was determined to see the "witch" burn, Jeannie wouldn't be safe anywhere Reeves could find her.

Ignoring Jeannie's pleas, Sam spoke to Kane again. "Phone J.T. and tell him to call in as many favors as need be, but I want something found on Reeves that can give the police reason to force him to stay away from Jeannie." Sam knew that, some-where out there, someone knew something about Reeves's past dealings. A thirty-two-year-old zealot with obvious mental problems was bound to have screwed up, at least once, in the past.

Jeannie took a deep breath. "Sam Dundee!" Her voice trem-bled. "If you don't let me help these people, I'll...I'll never forgive...you. Don't you see? It's my...fault."

He felt her exhaustion in every cell of his body, his nerve endings alert to her weakness. And he knew she was exerting her last ounce of strength to fight him.

"Lift your hand and touch my face," Sam told her. "Let's see if you have the strength to do more than you've already done."

She tried, but her hand would not cooperate. Tears welled up in her eyes. "Damn you, Sam. Damn...you." With that said, her energy expended, she closed her eyes and fell asleep.

Holding her close, Sam carried her away from the death and destruction that surrounded them.

SAM OPENED THE French doors that led out onto the upstairs balcony. Dawn light coated the eastern horizon, to the left of the Howell home. Overhead, a pink glow coated the charcoal sky. A warm, pleasant breeze blew in off the gulf. Sam looked across the road at the deserted beach and, just beyond, the pale gray water.

Turning his head, he glanced into the bedroom, checking once again on Jeannie. She had thrown off the sheet and light blanket, leaving her body, from the waist up, exposed to the early-morning air. She had slept fitfully the past few hours, occasionally moaning in her sleep. But she seemed peaceful for the moment, her face serene, her breathing evenly paced.

Beautiful beyond compare, Sam thought. With her waist-length hair spread out over her pillow and across her shoulder, she lay there in the floor-length cream silk gown Ollie had put on her early yesterday morning, when Sam brought her home from the *Royal Belle* disaster. She had been asleep more than twenty-four hours. When Julian rushed home yesterday, he had assured Sam that it was perfectly normal for Jeannie to require extended periods of rest after using her extraordinary skills, especially to the extent she'd used them after the casino bombing.

Sam had left Jeannie's side only long enough to shower and change clothes. Ollie had remained with her, bathing her and slipping her into a gown. Sam hadn't eaten all day yesterday, until Ollie brought him his dinner on a tray. She'd threatened his life if he didn't eat every bite of the hearty meal.

Julian had spent the past twenty hours at the hospital. Although officially retired, he was needed, because of the sheer number of patients brought in from the *Royal Belle*.

Last night, Sam had slept at Jeannie's side, holding her in his arms whenever she cried—and she'd cried often—never once waking. He had wondered how long it would take her to recover from the ordeal she'd experienced. What could it possibly be like to endure that much pain and anguish?

If he could have stopped her, he would have. When he should have been taking care of her, he'd been busy saving other people's lives—just as, in her own way, Jeannie had been.

Sam looked back at the vastness of the ocean, the endless water and sky. In a few hours, traffic would begin to move, the beach would slowly fill, the all-nighters would leave the casinos and the early-morning crowds would arrive. And the local and state authorities would continue to sift through the remains of the *Royal Belle* for evidence. They'd keep questioning employees and patrons alike, hoping someone could shed some light on whoever had planted the bombs.

Awaking with a start, Jeannie sat straight up in bed, her

mouth forming a silent cry. She glanced down at her body, then at her bed and around the room. Someone had removed her clothes, slipped on her gown and put her to bed. Sam? She smiled. Sam and Ollie.

A soft breeze surrounded her, chilling her bare arms. She hugged herself, took in a deep breath and blinked her eyes several times. The room lay in semidarkness, the only light coming from the windows, the faint, rosy illumination of daybreak.

She saw Sam standing on the balcony, his broad shoulders slightly drooped. He's tired, she thought, and worried. He wore dark slacks, slightly wrinkled. Had he slept beside her during the night? She had a vague memory of being held in his arms, a faded recollection of his wiping away her tears.

Usually the epitome of the well-dressed gentleman, Sam looked a bit disheveled in his wrinkled slacks, the tails of his pale blue shirt hanging around his hips, his hair windblown.

She searched the room, looking for a walking cane. Her favorite, a gift from Miriam, had probably burned inside the *Royal Belle.* Jeannie shuddered at the memory, the sound of the explosions echoing in her ears as well as the cries of wounded people. So many people in pain.

She wanted to go to Sam, to tell him that she was all right and that she forgave him for being so bossy and high-handed. She'd been so tired, so completely drained, that she hadn't been rational. Sam had done the right thing in forcing her to leave the disaster area.

Moving to the side of the bed, Jeannie slid her legs off the edge. She had no idea how she looked. She couldn't see a mirror from where she sat. Threading her fingers through her hair, she combed it to each side, allowing the mass to fall down her back. She lifted the twisted bodice of her gown to properly cover her breasts and smoothed out the wrinkles over her stomach and legs.

"Sam." Her voice sounded weak and very faint, even to her own ears.

He turned quickly. The moment he saw her, his lips curved into that seldom-used but devastating smile. "Jeannie." With a few giant steps, he was at her side, kneeling, slipping his arms around her.

She cradled his head in her lap and caressed his head, her fingers brushing over the stubble of his cheeks. He hadn't shaved, she realized. Since when? How long had she been asleep?

"This isn't the morning after the casino bombing, is it?" she asked.

Lifting his head, he looked up into her eyes, wanting nothing more than to protect her from the world, from all the ugliness, from a truth he could not change. "You've been asleep over twenty-four hours. Do you remember fainting in the back of the ambulance?"

"Yes, sort of. I remember telling you I'd never forgive you if you made me leave."

"I did what I thought was best for you. I brought you home." Sam rose to his feet, then sat down beside her on the bed. "Ollie undressed you and washed you and put you in your gown while I took a shower and changed clothes."

"You've stayed with me all this time, haven't you? You even slept with me last night."

"How do you know all that?"

"I sensed your presence." She leaned against him; he put his arm around her waist.

"How do you feel?" He kissed her forehead.

"Tired. But I'm all right."

"You did too much."

"It was a horrible disaster. So many injured people." She clutched Sam's hand. "Did anyone die?"

Sam took a deep breath. "Two of the casino's security men didn't make it off the riverboat. They were caught in the bottom-deck explosion. Only those two. There are about a dozen in critical condition, but, luckily, we had evacuated almost the entire casino when the bombs exploded."

"Have the police arrested Maynard Reeves?"

"They have no evidence against Reeves."

"But I know he's responsible." She bit her fingers into Sam's arm, tugging on his sleeve. "I sensed all those horrible emotions inside him. He couldn't block what he was feeling."

"I know, Jeannie. I know." Sam tried to soothe her, stroking her back with one hand while he cupped her chin in the other. "But they can't arrest Reeves just because you say you sensed his guilt."

She pulled away from Sam, covering her face with her hands as she bowed her head. She sat there for several minutes, then tossed back her head, squared her shoulders and turned to Sam. "I need some fresh air. Find me a cane, please. And walk out on the balcony with me."

"I can carry you outside." He stood, but before he could lift her, she threw up her hand to stop him.

"I want to walk." She nodded toward the huge, ornately carved wardrobe. "Look in the wardrobe. There should be two or three canes in there."

Sam obeyed her command without hesitation. He'd learned that sometimes it was easier not to fight Jeannie, especially when she was damned and determined to have her own way. He retrieved a black metal walking stick, with a gold tip and a fancy flower design engraved on the handle.

Handing her the cane, he watched while she positioned the tip on the floor and lifted herself to her feet. He walked behind her, not touching her, and followed her out onto the balcony. The downstairs veranda and the upstairs balcony surrounded the three-story antebellum-style house on all four sides.

"I never tire of looking at the ocean," she said. "This is a beautiful view, but nothing to compare with the view from the veranda of my house on Le Bijou Bleu."

Mention of the island where Sam had washed ashore six years ago brought back painful memories to him. Memories he had tried to erase from his mind.

"We should go to your island," Sam said. "There, I might be able to keep you safe."

She shivered from the chill of the early-morning breeze as it tickled her bare arms and shoulders. "Maynard Reeves wants to kill me, and he doesn't seem to care how many people he has to destroy to do it."

Sam wrapped his arms around her. "Julian told me that only a handful of people even know about Le Bijou Bleu, that when your parents bought the island they used it as a retreat and kept its location a secret."

"Julian's right. Other than Julian and I, and of course Manton, only our lawyer and Marta even know about the island. I've used the place as my personal retreat all these years. When Miriam was dying, we visited Le Bijou Bleu several times. The trip always seemed to revitalize her."

"You'd take her to the island and suffer her pain for her, wouldn't you?" Sam hugged Jeannie fiercely. "You'd take her away so that Julian wouldn't have to see the two of you in pain."

"I loved Miriam like a mother." Jeannie sighed. "She was far more a mother to me than my own ever was."

"Are you willing to go to Le Bijou Bleu and stay as long as it takes to free yourself from Reeves?" Sam asked.

"What if he won't give up? What if he waits us out? You have a life of your own, Sam. I can't expect you to move to Le Bijou Bleu and live with me indefinitely."

"We're digging into Reeves's past. Somewhere there has to be some information that will help us put a stop to him. Otherwise…"

She gripped Sam's forearms where they crisscrossed her waist. "Otherwise what?"

"Otherwise we'll have to find another way to get rid of the man."

"I can't help but believe that God will punish him. He has

committed so much evil in God's name. What greater sin could there be?"

"I'll make arrangements for us to leave Biloxi immediately. The sooner I can get you out of Reeves's grasp, the better."

"I can't leave yet," Jeannie said. "Not until…" She hesitated, turning her head and looking up at him. She wondered how he would react when she told him what she wanted.

"Not until what?"

"I want to stay a few more days, go to the hospitals and try to help the people who were injured in the bombing."

"No! Absolutely not!"

"Hear me out. Please."

Releasing Jeannie, Sam walked around her and over to the balcony's edge. With his back turned to her, he gripped the top of the banister. "You damn near killed yourself night before last, and you expect me to allow you to—"

"You do not *allow* me to do anything," Jeannie said. "Night before last, you were right. I had exhausted my energy. I wouldn't have been able to be of help to anyone. But I'm rested now. I need to help the people who are suffering because of me."

"You're being irrational, you know." He wished he could shake some sense into her compassionate little head. "You are not responsible for what happened to those people. Maynard Reeves is."

"And he bombed the riverboat because I was on board!"

"Dammit, Jeannie, what am I going to do with you?"

She walked over to the balcony's edge and laid her hand over his. "Night before last, you were going to bring me home and make love to me."

Every nerve in his body screamed. Neither of them spoke for endless moments. With her hand resting atop his, Sam and Jeannie watched the sun rise over Biloxi.

Jeannie had never wanted anything as much as she wanted Sam Dundee to be a part of her life forever, but she knew how impossible the dream was. Would any woman ever capture Sam Dundee's heart? Did a woman exist who was strong enough to be his equal?

Sam had never wanted anything as much as he wanted to protect Jeannie Alverson—from Reeves's insanity, from suffering the pain of others, and even from him. The desire he felt for this gentle, loving woman was so strong it could destroy her. He couldn't let that happen.

"It's all right, you know." She stroked his hand. "I want you, too."

"Jeannie?" His muscles tensed; his heartbeat accelerated.

"If there had been no explosions aboard the *Royal Belle,* you and I would have become lovers yesterday morning, when we got back here to the house," she said.

"You don't know that for sure."

"Yes, I do. And so do you. I haven't forgotten what happened out on deck when we danced. I remember exactly how we both felt, what we both wanted."

"Don't remind me."

He turned around and looked at her. Dear God, what was he going to do about Jeannie Alverson? She was driving him insane. He couldn't remember ever wanting a woman so badly or ever being so scared. Once her life was no longer in danger, he would return to Atlanta. He'd be safe there, far away from Jeannie.

She wanted too much from him. She wanted things that weren't in him to give. She thought he was a far better man than he actually was. She thought he was worth saving, worth suffering for, worth the pain of delving into his tormented soul. He'd never been a coward, never backed down from any challenge, but Jeannie was something else all together. What man was equal to the challenge of being Jeannie's mate, of understanding her enough to allow her to be the woman she was—an empath with a blessed talent? What man was strong enough to spend the rest of his life watching her suffer other people's pain.

"Sam?"

"Two things have been driving me crazy while you slept. I was worried sick that you'd suffered too much pain, that you might have permanently harmed yourself. And all the while I was worrying, I hated myself for wanting you so desperately, for thinking what might have been if—"

"Once we're on Le Bijou Bleu, we'll have all our days and nights to make love."

Sam swallowed hard. "When you're no longer in danger, I'm going back to Atlanta."

Jeannie sighed. "Yes, I know. I understand."

"Okay, then. I see no reason to delay our departure. We'll sail for your island today."

"I'll go with you to Le Bijou Bleu day after tomorrow, when I've had a chance to put things in order around here and do what I feel is right and necessary."

Dammit, he knew what she was planning to do. "I won't allow you to put yourself in any more danger."

"Everything is going to be all right," she said, only half believing her own words. "Somehow we'll find a way to make it right."

She slipped her arms around him, kissing him with a strength and passion that startled him. Within seconds, Sam had taken charge of the kiss, the power of his feelings ripping him apart inside. He needed to make love to Jeannie, and soon, or he was going to lose his mind. He'd never known desire so strong, passion so all-consuming, need so powerful. And somehow he knew Jeannie felt the same way, that even though sexual desire was a new experience for her, the desperation of her need matched his own.

But he would have to wait until she was fully recovered from the ordeal following the bombing of the *Royal Belle*. When they made love for the first time, Jeannie would need all her strength. When they made love, she would experience sexual fulfillment—both his and hers.

CHAPTER TEN

TAPPING THE CHINA rim with her fingernails, Jeannie stared into the teacup she held with both hands. She lifted the cup to her lips, took a sip of the warm, sweet liquid, then held the cup in front of her. Was she forgetting anything? She would go over her checklist again before she and Sam left in the morning. He had wanted to go to Le Bijou Bleu today, but she had insisted on waiting for tomorrow. That would give her enough time to get things in order around the house and make sure that, between Ollie and Marta, Julian would be taken care of properly. He insisted he could take care of himself, but Julian was one of those men who had always had a woman to handle life's daily annoyances.

And Jeannie really had wanted to visit the hospitals to see those injured in the explosion aboard the *Royal Belle*. But upon further discussion, she and Sam had compromised. She wouldn't go to the hospitals if he agreed to stay in Biloxi one more day so that she could put things in order before their departure. After all, what difference could one day make?

"There's no point in your worrying about things over which you have little or no control." Laying the medical journal he'd been reading in his lap, Julian looked at Jeannie. "What happened aboard the *Royal Belle* was an atrocity, but it could have been much worse. If you hadn't sensed that monster Reeves's emotions, everyone aboard the riverboat might have died. You did all you could to prevent the disaster and to ease the suffering of those who were injured."

"Sam has told me the same thing, but I can't forget that

if Reeves wasn't so determined to destroy me, he probably wouldn't have had bombs placed aboard the boat."

"You don't know that for sure. The man has been preaching against gambling ever since it was legalized and the casinos went into business along the Gulf."

"But he's never blown up one of the casinos before," Jeannie said. "He's never done anything violent, until now."

Sam Dundee entered the room, a sheaf of papers in his hand. "The man is totally irrational when it comes to you."

Jeannie's heart skipped a beat. Just the sound of his voice excited her, and one look into those steely gray eyes aroused her. She'd never known what it was like to want a man, to long for the feel of his hand in hers, the touch of his lips, the pleasure of his strong embrace.

"Reeves believes I'm a witch, possessed with powers from Satan." She set her teacup in its saucer on the mahogany table beside her chair. "I know he isn't going to leave me alone. He wants to destroy me." She shivered; the feel of Reeves's evil lingered inside her like a tiny sprinkling of ashes from a fire which had long since died.

"Reeves's obsession with destroying you is why it's imperative you leave Biloxi." Standing, Julian glanced down at the medical journal that had fallen from his lap. Grumbling under his breath, he reached down, picked up the magazine and laid it in the chair. "All the preparations have been made. I telephoned the Broadwater Marina. Your boat will be ready for your departure in the morning. And you've contacted Manton to let him know when to expect you and Mr. Dundee."

Jeannie nodded agreement. "I've packed a few things to take with me, but I keep so many things at the house there, I won't need much." She glanced across the room at Sam, who was standing by the windows, seemingly absorbed in reading the stapled sheets of paper in his hand. "And I've sent Ollie out to buy Sam a bathing suit and some shorts and stuff. The man brought nothing but business suits. Can you imagine? He came to Biloxi without a bathing suit."

Sam grunted, glanced up from his reading and gave Jeannie one of his half smiles. Already she'd learned that that was the usual extent of his smile, an upward curve of his lips that didn't show any teeth.

"I came to Biloxi to work," he said. "Not to play."

"What are you so interested in?" Jeannie looked at the papers in his hand.

"J.T. faxed me more information on Reeves." Sam walked over to where Jeannie sat and handed her the report. "There's only one new piece of information that might interest the police. Reeves is a known religious fanatic whose followers have been jailed time and again, but Reeves himself has a spotless record. He seems to always be on the fringes of anything his church does that's illegal. It's obvious someone else always does his dirty work and takes all the risks."

Julian placed his bony hand on Sam's shoulder. "What piece of information is suspicious?"

"It seems that when Reeves was sixteen, both of his parents died in a house fire. The fire inspector said it was out-and-out arson, but they never found the arsonists, never prosecuted anyone."

"Where was Reeves when his parents' house burned?" Julian asked.

"He had spent the night with a friend, a boy named Wayland Krenshaw. Krenshaw is a deacon in Reeves's Righteous Light Church, and the two are fast friends to this day."

Jeannie read through the report quickly, then handed it back to Sam. "The police suspected young Maynard Reeves, but they had no proof, and he had an alibi."

"Why would the police suspect Reeves?" Julian glanced from Jeannie to Sam.

"Two weeks before the fire, a next-door neighbor had heard Reeves threaten his father, telling him that if he ever beat him again, he'd kill him," Sam said. "And the elder Reeves, a hell-fire-and-brimstone preacher, told his son that the evil powers inside him would eventually destroy him. Then Reeves's father knocked him to the ground."

"My guess is that his father caught young Maynard using his psychic abilities," Jeannie said. "Obviously the man didn't realize that his son probably had little control over those abilities."

"And there are no other suspicious incidents in Reeves's past?" Julian pointed to the report in Sam's hand.

"There are countless suspicious incidents." Sam shook the sheaf of papers. "But that was the only time Reeves was directly linked to the happening. Our good reverend possibly has been behind numerous fires, bombings and even a couple of shootings, but there's no proof to link him to any of the incidents. And not once has one of his followers accused Reeves of any wrong-doing, even if it meant serving prison time themselves."

"Are you saying that this Righteous Light Church has members who are in prison because of—" Julian's dark eyes narrowed to mere slits. He slammed his hand down on the mahogany table beside Jeannie's chair, sending her empty teacup crashing to the floor.

Jeannie lifted herself, bracing herself with her cane. She grabbed Julian's arm. "You musn't get upset like this. It isn't good for your heart."

"Why can't the police do something to stop Reeves? It's obvious he's no man of God. If anyone is a child of the devil, he is!" Julian's swarthy olive complexion flushed with crimson. He knotted his hands into fists. "If I wasn't such an old man, I'd—"

"Calm yourself." Jeannie slipped her arm around her foster father's waist. "Sam is taking me away to Le Bijou Bleu in the morning. You, Ollie and Marta will be the only people who'll know where we are. Reeves doesn't know about my island, and the few people who know aren't about to tell him."

"I agree that the safest place for you is Le Bijou Bleu, but you can't hide out there for the rest of your life." Julian hugged Jeannie to his side. "If only the police could arrest the man. My God, he's threatened your life more than once."

"Technically, he hasn't," Jeannie said. "There is no law that prevents him from calling me names, and we have no proof that he sent me the Bible with the blood-spotted marker, or that he was responsible for the bombing of the *Royal Belle*."

Julian rubbed Jeannie's arm, then patted her tenderly on the shoulder. "If there's no other way to keep you safe, we'll leave Biloxi. We can go anywhere in the world. I'd do anything to protect you."

Jeannie hugged Julian. "I know you would, but I'm hoping that if I leave Biloxi for a few weeks, the media coverage on me will die down and perhaps Reeves will return to New Orleans and find some other poor soul to persecute."

When Sam grunted, Jeannie and Julian looked at him. Sam turned, picked up the report, folded it in half and stuffed it into his coat pocket. "In going to Le Bijou Bleu, we're taking Jeannie temporarily out of harm's way and buying us some time. If we can't legally nail Reeves's hide to the wall, then I'll have to find another way to handle him."

"What do you mean?" Jeannie asked, but really didn't want to know.

"There's no point in discussing alternatives until the present plan fails," Sam said.

"What present plan?" Julian asked.

"I've called in some favors." Sam tried not to look at Jeannie, who watched him closely. "I was a government agent for ten years. I know a lot of people. I have men on my payroll who are former CIA, former Green Berets and navy SEALS. My partner, J. T. Blackwood, left the Secret Service after he lost an eye and nearly died."

"What does who you know have to do with this plan to stop Maynard Reeves from…from killing me?" Jeannie willed Sam to face her, knowing he couldn't lie to her if he looked her in the eye.

Sensing her need for the complete truth, Sam made eye contact with Jeannie. "Since the bombing of the *Royal Belle,* the feds are involved. I've asked for and been promised one of their best men to head up the investigation. Dane Carmichael should be arriving today. He'll work directly with Lieutenant Painter. If there's any way to prove a connection between Reeves and the explosions aboard the *Royal Belle,* they'll find it. We just need to keep Jeannie out of harm's way until Reeves is behind bars. Painter and Carmichael are coming by to question us later this evening."

"Let's pray this plan works," Jeannie said. "I don't know if I could live with the alternative."

She tried to disguise her feelings, but they showed plainly on her face.

Knowing her so well, and caring for her so deeply, Julian could read her like a book. "We'll hope and pray Reeves will be found out and the police discover the proof they need to put him away." Gripping Jeannie by the shoulder, Julian stared at Sam. "But if it comes to—" Julian cleared his throat. "You'll do what must be done, what I'd do if I could. Her life is in your hands, my boy. I trust you to keep her safe."

"There's nothing I wouldn't do to protect her."

SAM COULDN'T SLEEP. If he hadn't been forced into a compromise with Jeannie, allowing her one extra day in Biloxi, he'd have taken her away today. Sam glanced at the bedside clock. Nearly midnight. They'd be out of the house before seven and on the gulf before eight.

Their talk with Lieutenant Painter and Dane Carmichael had lasted over an hour, with Jeannie reconstructing the events of three nights ago, aboard the *Royal Belle,* and explaining again and again why she knew Reeves had been behind the bombing.

Maybe, if they were lucky, Reeves had made a mistake, or perhaps someone in his organization would talk. Sam didn't know how long he'd have to keep Jeannie on Le Bijou Bleu, how long he'd have to act as her bodyguard, but he'd already asked J.T. to take control of Dundee Private Security. Sam hadn't had to tell J.T. that this case had become very personal. He'd just known. And J.T. was too astute to ask questions. Sam appreciated his friend and partner's keen perception. How the hell could he ever explain his feelings about Jeannie to someone else, when he didn't truly understand them himself?

Le Bijou Bleu. The Blue Jewel. Out there somewhere in the gulf. Sam drew back the curtains at the window and looked up at the star-filled sky. Tomorrow night they would be together on Jeannie's island retreat. Alone. Except for Manton. Sam had only the vaguest memory of the huge man. Dark skin. Bald head. How would Manton feel about Jeannie bringing Sam to the island? Would Manton instinctively know what was happening between Jeannie and Sam? Would he approve or disapprove?

Sam had no idea where Le Bijou Bleu was located. When he was tossed into the ocean six years ago, his body had washed ashore on Jeannie's uncharted island. Sam had checked and double-checked to make sure there was no way Reeves could discover the location of the island. Although Ollie and Marta knew about the island, as did the family lawyer, only Manton, Julian and Jeannie knew its exact location.

Years ago, the only means of communication had been a shortwave radio. With generators providing electricity to the house, Jeannie had provided Manton with a computer and fax-modem and had installed a telephone. One of the first things Jeannie had done after waking from her twenty-four-hour rest, was to fax Manton, something she did almost every day.

"He'll be worried if more than a couple of days pass without hearing from me," she'd said.

So like Jeannie, caring about others, worrying about the

people in her life, loving wholeheartedly, giving freely, taking on suffering that was not hers.

Sam didn't pretend to understand the depth of Jeannie's goodness, but the purity of her soul made him question his right to desire her. Of all the men in the world, why would she want him to be her first lover? She knew he could promise her nothing permanent, that he could offer her a physical relationship and nothing more. Why didn't she wait for some gentle, kind man whose soul would be in tune with hers? Why would she want a man who wasn't even sure he possessed a soul?

Sam heard the distant beeping sound and couldn't quite identify what it was was or where it was coming from. When he went out into the hall, he heard it more distinctly, a repetitive alert coming from somewhere downstairs.

Jeannie cried out his name. The beeping continued. Sam listened carefully. A smoke detector!

"Sam!" she cried again.

"I'll check it out," he said, knowing she could hear the alarm, too. "It could be nothing. I'll be right back."

He flew down the stairs, followed the warning signal into the smoky corridor leading to the kitchen and flung open the door. Growling at the sight before him, he swore loudly. Flames engulfed the kitchen, the curtains burning in seconds as he watched. Smoke filled the room.

Ollie touched Sam on the shoulder. He jerked around to face her. "Get out of the house. Fast. I'll send Julian and bring Jeannie down."

"Can't I help?" Ollie asked.

"Don't argue. No time. Get out!"

Sam slammed shut the door, raced back upstairs, calling Jeannie's name. Julian, wearing pajamas and a silk robe came out into the hall. "What's wrong? Is that the smoke detector?"

Ignoring Julian, Sam rushed into his bedroom, retrieved

his cellular phone from his jacket, went back into the hall and tossed the phone to Julian.

"Go downstairs and out the front door quickly. I've sent Ollie out. Dial 911. Get the fire department here before this old house burns to the ground."

"Jeannie?" Julian hesitated, but then he saw the look in Sam Dundee's eyes and, clutching the phone in his trembling hand, hurried downstairs.

Jeannie sat upright in bed, the lamp on the nightstand illuminating her frightened face. "The smoke alarm went off downstairs. Is there a fire?"

Sam lifted her into his arms. "The whole kitchen's on fire."

She had known somehow that the alarm hadn't gone off by accident, that it signaled a true danger. The moment she heard it, she'd called out to Sam, telepathically at first, but he hadn't responded.

She saw the panic in his eyes and realized how afraid he was for her. She held out her arms, waiting for him to rescue her. Nothing could ever truly harm her as long as she had Sam.

Although his mind functioned and he'd thought out every move in a reasonable fashion, one overriding emotion dictated Sam's actions—his concern for Jeannie. He had to get her to safety!

Jeannie clung to him as he rushed out of her room, dashing down the stairs, taking them two at a time. Billows of black smoke met them in the foyer. Fire licked at the walls. Jeannie closed her eyes against the destruction, coughing when the smoke filled her nostrils and crept into her throat. Ahead of them, the front door stood wide open. Sam didn't hesitate; he ran outside, down the steps and into the front yard, where Julian and Ollie stood huddled together.

"The fire department is on the way." Julian touched Jeannie's face and smiled. "Maybe they'll make it here in time to save the old place."

Jeannie knew how much Julian loved the house his grandfather had built, the home where he'd grown up, the house where he'd brought Miriam as a bride. To lose this magnificent old mansion would be like losing a part of himself.

"Could the fire have been an accident?" Jeannie asked Sam, her voice a whisper against his ear. "Or do you think Maynard Reeves—?" She swallowed, her emotions momentarily choking her.

"My gut instincts are shouting Reeves's name," Sam said. "We won't know for sure whether or not this was an accident until the fire inspector hands in his report."

Jeannie felt Sam's frustration, his fear for her and his savage anger at Reeves. She could hear his heartbeat, loud and strong and wild. Wild from the race away from what would have been certain death had he not carried her to safety. Wild with the desire to protect at all costs. Wild with the need to take revenge against anyone who would dare harm her.

"We're safe," she told him, and tried to draw the anger from him.

"Don't!" Tightening his hold on her, he lowered his head and nuzzled the side of her forehead. "I don't need calming or soothing. I don't want you to take away the hatred I feel. Save your strength. You'll need it later."

SAM WAS RIGHT. She did need her strength later. After the firemen doused the blaze and saved Julian's home from total destruction. After they stayed the night at Marta's, no one sleeping, all of them waiting to hear from the fire marshal. After they found out the house had been deliberately set afire. And after the police said they could do nothing more than question Maynard Reeves.

"He's sure to have an alibi," Lieutenant Painter had said.

Sam hadn't wanted to change their plans to leave at seven o'clock for Le Bijou Bleu, but she'd told him in no uncertain terms that she wasn't leaving the mainland until they knew more details about the fire and she saw Julian and Ollie settled.

She hadn't expected the fire marshal to detect the cause of the fire so quickly. The arsonist had done nothing to conceal his handiwork. And she certainly hadn't expected Marta to find Julian a temporary home that same morning.

Sam pulled Jeannie's Lexus up in the driveway behind Marta's Mercedes. The house, a small Victorian cottage between Long Beach and Gulfport, belonged to Marta's recently divorced son, who'd asked his mother to see about renting the place until he decided whether or not things would work out with his new job in Mobile.

Unlocking the front door, Marta stepped back and waited for everyone to enter. "All their furniture is still here. Joel hasn't touched a thing since Patsy Ruth left him."

The house wasn't half the size of Julian's home in Biloxi, but it was charming and homey and certainly large enough to accommodate Julian and Ollie for a few months until the restoration of their fire-damaged house was completed.

"I think the place is lovely," Jeannie said. "We're fortunate you hadn't already found a renter."

"The place is Julian's as long as he needs it." Marta turned to Jeannie. "We'll get everything set up today. A new computer and fax machine for Julian. Luckily, we hadn't had the power turned off or the telephone disconnected. Joel left for his new job in Mobile only last week."

"Yes, dear, you must contact me as soon as you arrive at Le Bijou Bleu and let me know all is well." Julian kissed Jeannie on the cheek, then offered his hand to Sam. "Take care of her. Her value cannot be assessed."

"I know that she's priceless." Sam shook Julian's hand, and the two men exchanged stares, one man pleading, the other promising.

"Get her beyond Maynard Reeves's grasp." Ollie placed her

hand on her hip. "If I ever see that scripture-quoting weasel again, I'll boil him in oil."

"You musn't delay any longer." Holding Jeannie's hand, Julian lifted it and placed it over his heart. "There's no telling what the man is capable of doing."

"But what about you, Julian?" Jeannie couldn't bear the thought of her foster father being in danger because of her. "What if Reeves tries to harm you?"

"I'm not his target, my dear, you are."

"But he's crazy, isn't he? That means he's unpredictable." Jeannie sighed. "Why don't you come to Le Bijou Bleu with us?"

"I'm not in any danger." Julian glanced at Sam, then shifted his attention back to Jeannie. "I'm needed here. I still consult at the hospital, you know, as well as being on the board. And since you can't continue your work at the Howell School, I'll keep an eye on Marta and the teachers for you." Looking over Jeannie's shoulder, he smiled at Marta, who nodded her head in amused agreement. "Besides, I'll have to be around to oversee the work on our home. I want everything rebuilt as close to the original as possible."

"We'll stay in daily contact," Jeannie said. "If you need me—"

"Take her away, now," Julian told Sam. "Before we're both in tears."

"I don't anticipate any problems for you," Sam said. "But if there is, let me know. I'll get Hawk or Kane back down here as quickly as possible."

Sam forcibly turned Jeannie, draped his arm around her shoulders and walked her outside to the car. When they reached the Lexus, she looked back, saw Julian in the doorway and waved goodbye.

Sam drove down highway 90, straight to the Broadwater Marina, where Jeannie's small cruiser awaited them. He had been anxious to get Jeannie out of Biloxi and away from Reeves before last night, but now, after the fire, he knew the only way to completely protect her was to keep her on Le Bijou Bleu until Reeves no longer posed a threat. And that meant until the authorities arrested him—or until Sam was forced to settle the matter himself.

CHAPTER ELEVEN

THEY ARRIVED AT Le Bijou Bleu late in the afternoon, just as the August sun began its descent into the western sky. A warm, humid wind surrounded them as they disembarked. Two smaller craft were anchored snugly a few feet away from the cruiser. All three rested in their slips. An enormous brown-skinned man, his bald head glistening in the sunshine, stood on the pier.

Sam swept Jeannie up into his arms, lifting her off the boat, then turning to face Manton. Remembering only bits and pieces of his hours on this island six years ago, Sam wasn't sure what to expect from the man who had helped Jeannie save his life. What he saw was a seven-foot giant, his huge, muscular arms crossed over his wide chest and his green eyes focused on Jeannie.

When Sam took a step forward, she tugged on his sleeve. "Put me down and give me my cane. I want you to meet Manton again, and then, after we've settled in and I've let Julian know we arrived safely, I want to show you my island."

Sam obeyed her request, wondering all the while if Manton would have tried to break him in half if he dared disagree with her.

Jeannie walked steadily toward Manton, who didn't move a muscle until she stood directly in front of him. A wide smile spread across his face, softening his hard features and putting a sparkle in his eyes. Opening her arms, Jeannie squealed with laughter when the gentle giant lifted her off her feet and into a bear hug.

Standing to the side, Sam watched the loving exchange and

saw an affection between Jeannie and Manton similar to that between her and Julian Howell. Though several years younger than the doctor, Manton was twice Jeannie's age and seemed to consider himself another substitute father.

When Manton set her back on her feet, Jeannie clutched her cane and turned her head. Smiling at Sam, she motioned him forward. "Sam, come meet the man who saved your life six years ago."

The two men sized each other up, taking a full inventory. Sam extended his hand; Manton saw Jeannie's happy smile and accepted Sam's handshake. Despite his size and obvious strength, Manton did not grip Sam's hand with any undue force. His handshake was firm, quick and nonaggressive.

Looking directly at Manton, Sam said, "I owe Jeannie and you my life. Thank you."

Manton nodded toward Jeannie, moving his hands rapidly, signing to her, then looked back at Sam.

"He's too modest to accept any thanks. He claims that all he did was help me get you to the hospital."

"That saved my life," Sam told him.

Manton grinned, signed again and waited for Jeannie to translate.

"He says that all the thanks he needs is for you to keep me safe."

"I'll do whatever it takes to protect her," Sam said.

Instinctively Sam knew that Manton understood his meaning without further words and knew, too, that this second substitute father was concerned about his and Jeannie's relationship.

He noticed that Jeannie and Manton seemed to be conversing, though Jeannie didn't speak and Manton didn't sign. They're talking telepathically, Sam thought, and wondered what they were saying.

Manton nodded, walked away and boarded the cruiser. Jeannie turned to Sam.

"He's getting our luggage." She held out her hand, motioning

Sam to her. "Manton usually carries me from the dock to the house. It's an uphill climb from here. See the steps over there?"

Sam took note of the curving set of rock steps that led up from the beach to the hill above. From where he stood, he couldn't see the house.

"What were you saying to him a few minutes ago?" Sam asked. "I know you were communicating with him."

"I told him to go ahead and get the luggage, that you would carry me up to the house."

An undeniable pleasure spread from the pit of Sam's stomach to his whole body. The sensation was ridiculous, he told himself, but he could not argue against the truth. Jeannie looked to him for care and protection. Not to Julian Howell, and not to Manton. Not any longer. The girl had become a woman, gently but firmly choosing Sam, instead of either surrogate father, to be her protector.

Sam lifted Jeannie into his arms, as he had done so many times recently, but this time the ritual was fraught with deep meaning. And they both knew it. Carrying her to the house was a symbolic giving of herself, a placing of herself into Sam's hands—not only to keep safe, but to possess, to pleasure, to love.

Sam had no idea the walk from the dock to the house would take so long. No wonder Manton had always carried Jeannie. Once at the top of the rock steps, Sam drew in his breath, an appreciative sigh escaping his lips. Green grass spread out as far as the eye could see. Live oaks climbed toward heaven, while some of the limbs curled downward and grew back into the earth. Spanish moss hung heavily on the trees, dripping almost to the ground here and there. Palm trees swayed in the summer wind. In the distance, blue sky and water met.

Sam couldn't remember anything about Le Bijou Bleu except the beach. He had no memory of the docks.

"Six years ago, I didn't wash up near the pier, did I?" he asked.

"No, I found your body on the other side of the island. Manton carried you to the boat."

"When they tossed me overboard, I didn't think I had a prayer." Sam caressed the top of her head with his chin, then turned his head sideways and rested his cheek against her hair.

"You have to put the past behind you," Jeannie said. "It can't be changed."

Halting his steps momentarily, Sam closed his eyes. With the hot sun and warm wind on his face, he allowed Jeannie entrance into his thoughts. The moment they connected, his eyes flew open and he gripped her fiercely. It would be so easy to let her take away the painful memories, at least for a while. He wanted to forget, but how could he allow her to experience the guilt for him?

"No," he said, mentally and emotionally withdrawing from her. "Don't. I can handle it."

"All right. If that's what you want. But sooner or later, you're going to have to deal with the pain you've buried deep inside you." She touched his cheek. He flinched. "If you share it with me, I can help you put the past to rest."

The sound of Manton climbing the rock steps reminded Sam that he and Jeannie were not completely alone. "Where's the house?" Sam asked.

"Look straight ahead. You can see the roof through that grove of trees."

With Manton at his side, Sam carried Jeannie across the wide, seemingly endless stretch of verdant ground leading to the house. The two-story raised French cottage had been built on the top of a rise, giving the occupants a view of the ocean from all sides.

A menagerie of animals greeted their arrival. A half-dozen cats of various sizes, colors and ages were curled around the banisters, their curious eyes staring at Sam. Four panting mixed-breed dogs, tails wagging playfully, rounded the side of the house.

Jeannie spoke to the animals, calling each by name. They purred and woofed in unison, welcoming their mistress.

Manton hurried ahead of them, rushing up the steps and onto the huge veranda to open the front doors. The rooms were large and airy, with floor-to-ceiling windows and double French doors leading to the veranda. The windows had been opened, and the warm breeze fluttered the lace curtains as it filled the rooms.

Jeannie reminded Sam to set her on her feet when they entered the front parlor, a spacious room with clean white walls, Victorian sofa and chairs upholstered in cream damask, and a baby grand piano in the corner.

He slid her slowly down the length of his body, allowing the intimate contact to linger. Wrapping her arms around his neck, she gazed up at him dreamily. He wanted to kiss her. She closed her eyes, waiting for his kiss.

Manton paused in the doorway long enough to make eye contact with Sam, then proceeded to carry the luggage down the hall to the bedrooms. Jeannie cleared her throat. Sam grinned.

"Is he going to be watching us the whole time we're here?" Sam asked.

Opening her eyes, Jeannie frowned. "Manton will be here all the time, but he won't be watching us. We'll feel his presence, because he is a part of this island. As much a part of it as the earth and the trees, the flowers, the birds, the animals."

"I think I'll have a difficult time considering him just part of the scenery." Sam kissed the tip of her nose, and chuckled when she wrinkled her nose and frowned at him. "Where does Manton sleep?"

A tentative smile began spreading across her face. "He has

rooms downstairs on the lower level." Her smile widened. "Our rooms are on the main level, just down the hall."

Lowering his head, his breath mingling with hers, he brushed a light kiss over her lips. "Are we going to need separate rooms?"

She drew in a quick breath, then released it on a deep sigh. "No." That one word said it all. The acceptance of the inevitable. The promise of ecstasy. The knowledge that no power on earth could keep them apart.

But as surely as Jeannie knew that Sam Dundee was destined to become her lover, she knew that he would never be free to love her as long as his past possessed his soul. Every time she touched him, she sensed his unease and uncertainty. He wanted her with a fierce and desperate hunger, but he was afraid of her, of her special talents—and he felt unworthy.

How could she ever make him understand that she was as afraid as he was? The power of Sam's primitive nature, his savage strength, his iron will, all just barely concealed beneath his sophisticated surface, made her doubt she could ever possess him, truly possess him, heart and soul.

Not only did the vast differences in their basic natures stand between them, but so did Sam's guilt-ridden conscience and Jeannie's endangered existence. No matter how they might long to be together, Jeannie knew she had no choice but to accept the likelihood that she and Sam had no future together.

Jeannie shuddered at the realization.

"What's wrong?" he asked when he felt her tremble.

"We're safe for now, aren't we? Here on my island, no one can harm us. We can be happy for a while."

His kiss combined the elements of passion and protectiveness and sent ripples of excitement through her, while at the same time, it soothed her concerns. Pulling away from Jeannie, Sam looked into her eyes. Warm, compassionate brown eyes that had haunted his dreams six long years.

"Yes, we're safe," Sam said. "You're safe here on your island,

and I'm going to make sure nothing goes wrong. The authorities back on the mainland will monitor Reeves. They'll know where he is at all times. Besides, he has no idea where we are."

"Then we can truly relax here on Le Bijou Bleu, and spend our days and nights—"

"Making love."

His next kiss sent shivers of desire rocketing through Jeannie's body, hardening her nipples, flushing her face, moistening her femininity.

Sam sensed her arousal and knew she had tapped into his, increasing her own passion. She gripped his shoulder with one hand. While standing on tiptoe, she dropped her cane onto the hardwood floor and caressed his neck with her fingertips. He lifted her off her feet, cupping her hips as she threaded her fingers through his hair and sighed deep in her throat as he deepened the kiss.

Manton knocked softly on the doorpost, announcing his presence. Slowly, reluctantly, Sam eased Jeannie back down on her feet, ending the kiss gradually. Holding on to his forearms, she stepped back, separating their bodies. Clasping Jeannie about the waist with one hand, Sam bent over and picked up her cane.

Manton glanced at Sam, giving him a brief but thorough inspection, then looked at Jeannie. Smiling, she nodded, then laughed aloud. Sam had no idea what they were saying to each other.

Jeannie wondered how long it would take Sam to realize that Manton approved of him, that he was actually encouraging Jeannie to explore her feelings for Sam.

I think a romantic dinner on the veranda would be appropriate, Jeannie told Manton telepathically.

Leave everything to me, Manton responded in the same nonverbal manner, his green eyes sparkling with delight. *He has returned to you, as I knew he would. Now, little one, you must claim him. Once you do, he will be yours forever.*

The danger hasn't ended for me, or for Sam, Jeannie said. *I don't know how much time we'll have here on the island together, but however long we have, I want to make that time special.*

I understand. Manton nodded.

Sam shook Jeannie's arm gently. "What's going on here?"

Turning her radiant smile on Sam, Jeannie hugged up to his side. "We were just planning dinner for tonight." She tugged on his hand. "Come on, let's change clothes before I give you a tour of the house and then the island."

"Change clothes?"

She looked him over from head to toe. "You don't plan on wearing a suit while we're here, do you? After all, Ollie went to a lot of trouble this morning, washing your new casual clothes before she repacked them."

"What should I wear?" He followed her out of the parlor, nodding cordially to Manton as he passed him in the doorway.

"Put on some shorts and a T-shirt. And sandals."

Jeannie led him down the hallway, stopping in front of an open door. "This is my room." She pointed to the next room down, directly beside hers. "And that's your room. To come to my room, all you have to do is walk out on the veranda. Every room in the house has access to the veranda."

He jerked her into his arms. Gasping, she gripped her cane, but did not resist him. "Why don't you come to my room with me?" he asked, with a playful leer.

"Go change clothes, and I'll meet you in your room." Pulling away from him, she gave him a shove in the right direction.

Turning around, not waiting to see if he obeyed her request, Jeannie slipped into her room and closed the door behind her. Sam waited for a couple of minutes, then walked to his room. Inside, he found a sunny space of beige-and-yellow warmth. The center point of the room was an old walnut tester bed without a canopy. Black-and-white ticking material had been fashioned into a coverlet and into pillows that mixed with beige-

and-yellow down pillows. Sam's clothes bag lay across the foot of the bed; his carryall rested on the seat of a large overstuffed chair.

Shorts, T-shirt and sandals. Jeannie wanted their time together to be a vacation, not an escape from danger. He intended to give her what she wanted. An interlude from the real world.

In the next room, Jeannie sat down on her bed, a huge white oak four-poster with a fancy black ironwork canopy. Hooking her cane over the bottom post, she lay down and breathed in the fresh salt air blowing in off the ocean. She looked around her room, loving every precious inch that she had decorated as a teenager. The heart-of-pine floors and planked ceilings gave this old house a country charm. While examining the room, she saw, lying on the floral chintz chaise longue, the clothes Manton had laid out for her. Her pale pink-and-lavender-striped sundress. Strapless, with a hem that fell to midcalf. A romantic dress. Beside the dress lay a wide-brimmed straw hat.

Hugging herself, Jeannie laughed.

MANTON SERVED THEIR dinner on the veranda. White linen tablecloth and napkins. Polished silver and glistening crystal. After placing their dessert of fruit with a light cream sauce before them, he lit the candles that flanked the small bouquet on the table, then excused himself. The sun hung like a ball of fire in the western horizon, its heat singeing the sky with radiant splashes of purple, magenta and golden orange.

The balmy ocean breeze surrounded Sam and Jeannie, gently flickering the candle flames. They lifted their wineglasses in a toast.

"To heaven here on earth," Sam said. "Thanks to you, my very own angel."

Her eyes glazed with tears. Happy tears. Accepting his toast, she sipped the wine.

"What do you think of Le Bijou Bleu?" She set her glass on the table.

"I see where it got its name. Blue sky and blue water everywhere. I suppose whoever christened this island considered it his own personal blue jewel."

"And now it's my blue jewel," she said. "*Our* blue jewel," she amended.

"I never thought I'd return to this island. The few memories I have of this place are bittersweet. I wanted to forget what happened before and after I was shot."

"I realized how difficult it was for you to come and see me six years ago, when you got out of the hospital." She looked down at the fresh tropical fruit resting in the crystal bowl. "You came only because you felt you owed your life to me."

"I did owe you my life," he said, watching her pick nervously at the linen tablecloth. "When I left Biloxi, I buried the past deep inside me." He tapped his chest with his fist.

"You didn't want to live." Jeannie lifted her eyes, meeting his gaze directly. "You felt you had no right to live."

"I don't want to talk about the past. Not now."

Casting her gaze downward, she hesitated. He was afraid of the complete truth. If he was ever going to heal, he would have to face a guilt too heavy for him to bear alone.

The sweet, melodic strands of a piano solo drifted in the air, like celestial background music. Sam cocked his head to one side, listening. He could have sworn the music wasn't taped, that someone was playing the baby grand in the front parlor. He glanced at Jeannie, his eyes questioning her.

"Manton plays beautifully, don't you think?"

"Manton? But how is it possible for him to play? He's deaf, isn't he?"

"Totally, irreversibly deaf. But he has the talent of a genius."

"I don't understand how—"

"He feels the music." Reaching across the table, Jeannie

clasped Sam's hand in hers. "He's played since childhood. A natural talent, one even he doesn't understand. The piece he's playing is his own creation. I believe his talent is truly a gift from God."

"He can't hear what he plays. He can't—"

"It defies explanation. Yes, I know. But so does my empathic ability." She looked into Sam's eyes and told him what she wanted. "There is magic on Le Bijou Bleu. It drew Manton here first, and then me. And now…" She did not allow herself to even think about what she knew in her heart, what Sam was not yet ready to accept.

He sensed her need to be in his arms, to move to Manton's mystical music—a twilight solo so utterly beautiful that Sam knew, without question, that the composition had been created for Jeannie.

Julian Howell's Jeannie. Manton's Jeannie. But, above all else, Sam Dundee's Jeannie. For she belonged to him now, and in ways she could never belong to another. This night would seal her fate. She would become his completely.

But not forever. Their affair here on Le Bijou Bleu would be days and nights out of time. He had no right to want or expect more. Jeannie was an ethereal creature, truly pure of heart, never meant to belong to a man whose hands were stained with blood. But he could not deny himself the chance to become her lover, to capture, if for only a brief while, the magic and wonder of possessing an angel.

Sam stood, rounded the table, pulled out Jeannie's chair and lifted her. Shivering with desire and anticipation, she kicked off her white sandals and allowed Sam to lift the soles of her small, delicate feet atop his big feet.

She wanted to dance the way they had the night on the riverboat. But here on the veranda of her home there would be no interruptions, nothing to intrude on the enchantment. They would be free to follow their hearts, to seek the fulfillment their bodies desired. Tonight was theirs.

Sam waltzed her around the veranda. Her skirt flowed in the breeze. They didn't speak aloud, but they communicated their feelings, exchanged their thoughts and shared their mutual desire.

Sam had opened his mind to her, no longer blocking her entrance into his privacy. Jeannie wondered if he had any idea that he had taken the first step in the healing process that could lead to his salvation. Only if he could trust her enough to share his guilt and pain could she help him face his demons and learn to forgive himself.

Did she have the strength and courage to be the woman Sam needed? Could she ever reach that golden core of goodness inside Sam and help him become the man he was meant to be?

The music swirled inside Jeannie's head as she gave herself over to the rhythm and surrendered completely to Sam, trusting him without hesitation. In his arms she took flight, experiencing once again the freedom she would never know without his support.

When Manton stopped playing and quiet descended, Sam led Jeannie back to the table. She retrieved her cane before they left the veranda for a moonlight stroll on the beach behind the cottage.

The new moon glimmered in the black sky, almost translucent in its pale beauty. A scattering of distant stars winked at them. The ocean waves spread their moon-kissed white foam across the beach, then, recalling the tide, washed away their tracks in the sand. Sam supported Jeannie with his arm around her waist as they stood on the beach, the water licking at their legs.

When Jeannie tired, her slow gait hampered by the sand, Sam lifted her in his arms and carried her to the top of the knoll that overlooked the beach where she'd found his nearly lifeless body six years ago. Placing her on the ground, he sat beside her and pulled her close. She laid her head on his shoulder.

Words were unnecessary. Each knew what the other thought and felt. Sam could not deny how he felt about Jeannie, how desperately he wanted her, how much a part of him she had become.

They sat on the knoll, their damp legs entwined, holding hands and listening to the ocean's gentle rumble as they looked at the night sky.

Then Sam turned to her, cupped her face with both hands and whispered her name aloud. She sighed. A lone teardrop fell from her eye onto his hand.

"It's all right, angel," he said. "This will be a totally new experience for both of us. I have no idea what will happen. The first time for most women is—"

She covered his lips with her index finger. "I'm not like most women. And you, Sam Dundee, are most definitely not like most men."

"I don't want to hurt you." He kissed her tenderly.

"The pain of wanting you without having you is far worse than any pain I'll feel. It will be a pain I'll soon forget in the pleasure that will follow." Curling her arms around his neck, she returned his kiss as their combined emotions began flowing inside her. "Sam?"

He rubbed his hand up and down the side of her thigh, bunching the cotton material of her full skirt, lifting it higher and higher with each upward motion. They fell back onto the ground. Lowering his head, Sam kissed the tops of her swollen breasts rounding above the strapless bodice of her sundress. He palmed her feminine mound through the silk of her panties. She arched up to meet his touch.

Sam leaned over her, his mouth and hands exploring the woman who lay beneath him. Jeannie. Sweet, beautiful, innocent Jeannie.

She moaned into his mouth when he kissed her again. Clinging to him, whimpering her need, stroking her body against his, she incited him to deepen the kiss. He ripped away the material covering her breasts, then slid his hand inside her panties and delved into her moist, welcoming heat.

Overwhelming desire claimed her. Desire so all-consuming she thought she would die from its intensity. Her desire. And Sam's desire.

Releasing her mouth, he breathed deeply. "Not here. Not on the hard ground, exposed like this. Not our first time."

"Then take me home, Sam. Take me home and make me yours."

With his heartbeat wild, his desire at fever pitch, he lifted her into his arms and carried her to the house. He opened the French doors leading from the veranda into her bedroom, walked into the moonlit sanctuary and laid her down on the pure white bed.

CHAPTER TWELVE

MOONLIGHT SUFFUSED THE room, coating the walls with pale luminance, casting a yellow-white glow over the floor and furniture, surrounding Jeannie like a body halo of purity. The summer breeze swept inside through the open windows and French doors, encompassing them in a warm cocoon. The ocean's undulatory melody drifted in on the night air.

Jeannie sat up in the middle of the bed and removed her sundress. Wearing only a pair of pink silk panties, her breasts thrusting forward as she braced the palms of her hands on each side of her hips, she smiled and called his name.

"Sam..."

She was a siren now, an enticing vixen with a woman's needs. And yet she was still an angel, so pure and innocent and compassionate.

Jeannie lay back on the bed, her heartbeat drumming in her ears, as she reached up, inviting Sam into her arms. She burned with a need she had never known before Sam Dundee entered her secure world. He had changed everything. After she saved his life, nothing had ever been the same again. And now that he had returned, possessed with a need to protect her, to care for her, their fate was sealed.

Since the night she had suffered agony for him, they had been partially united, their souls connected by a thin, invisible cord. With each passing day they were together, they became closer, their feelings for each other growing stronger. Tonight they would become one. There could be no going back, only forward, straight ahead into the bonding of their souls.

Sam could remember nothing in his life he'd ever wanted more than he wanted Jeannie. His Jeannie. His sweet, beautiful angel.

With arms uplifted, her face kissed with moonlight, she waited for him. He wanted to rip off his clothes and thrust into her with wild abandon. But Jeannie was no ordinary woman. What was happening between them was special, unique. Something to be experienced fully, savored lovingly. He could not rush their lovemaking. For her, this would be the first time. And it would be a first for him, too. Making love to a woman who could feel his every emotion, who could experience his desire and his pleasure. The very thought of what lay ahead scared him as much as it excited him.

Sam unbuttoned his short-sleeved cotton shirt, slid it off his shoulders and tossed it onto the floor at the foot of Jeannie's bed. The way she looked at him—her eyes caressing him, her lips tasting him, her hands tormenting him without once touching him—stirred his blood and hardened his body.

Thick, cascading strands of her silky brown hair covered one bare breast, leaving the other an uncovered temptation. Her breasts rose and fell as she breathed. Her lips parted on an indrawn sigh.

He sensed her longing, her need a viable force, strong enough to sweep them both over the edge of conscious action. He had to remain in control for just a while longer, until he was certain he wouldn't hurt her, wouldn't destroy her with the power of his desire.

Unzipping his navy blue shorts, Sam didn't take his eyes off Jeannie. He trembled, wanting her, needing her. Lured by her femininity, lost to her seductive charms, he surrendered to the desire he could no longer control.

Sliding his shorts down to his ankles, he kicked them aside. He stood before her, all power and masculine muscle, in a pair of navy blue briefs, his sex straining against the silk fabric. Perspiration moistened his hands and forehead; dots of sweat broke out across his upper lip. A white-hot need seared him to the bone.

Jeannie wanted to touch him, to run her hands over every inch of his body, caress every bulging muscle, kiss his tiny, pebble-hard nipples, thread her fingers through the thatch of thick brown hair on his chest. If only he would come to her, allow her to touch him.

Her magnificently beautiful, elegant savage.

Sam eased down on the bed, placing his knees on either side of her feet. Crawling slowly up her body, bracing himself with his hands so that the contact was whisper light, he covered her body with his. She touched him hesitantly at first, sweeping her hands across his shoulders. He shuddered; she trembled.

And then exactly what she had been waiting for happened. The connection. The blending. Gradually, with just faint glimmers of awareness, Jeannie felt Sam's hunger and knew that it more than equaled hers. He was a virile man, experienced in the ways of the world, and yet he was uncertain. He was afraid his desire would be too much for her to handle, that it would be too powerful for her fragile innocence.

He needed her reassurance. She had to do more than issue an invitation; she would have to be the persuader, seducing him beyond the point of no return.

Arching her body, lifting herself closer to Sam, she kissed his chest, then drew a damp circle around first one and then his other nipple. He sucked in a deep, excruciating breath.

She felt the first crack in his iron control. She kissed his shoulder. He eased his body lower, his chest brushing her breasts. She gasped when her breasts tightened, almost painfully, and sent a signal straight to her core.

Slipping her arms around his waist, she buried her face in his shoulder. Her tongue drew spiraling circles from his shoulder, up his neck and to his ear. She squirmed beneath him, well aware of what her movements were doing to him. He was holding back, trying to be patient. And it was killing him!

Didn't he know, she wondered, that she felt every painful throb of his sex, every pulsating ache? Had he no idea that the longer he postponed their lovemaking, the more painfully aroused she would become?

She kissed his cheek. The pulse in his neck twitched. She covered his mouth, licking like a kitten lapping cream until he opened to her insistent little tongue, taking her inside as he followed her lead. Intensifying the kiss, Sam devoured her as he gripped her hips, lifting her up and against his arousal. She cried out, the sound trapped in his mouth, as shudders of intense pleasure skyrocketed through her.

Continuing the kiss, he divested her of her pink panties and eased his hand between her legs, parting her thighs. With an equal amount of urgency, she tugged on his briefs, pulling them down and over his firm, rounded buttocks, pausing to stroke him lovingly. Using her foot, she slid his briefs to his ankles and off onto the floor.

With each touch, each kiss, each urgent moan, the link between them grew stronger, until Sam, too, faintly sensed Jeannie's feelings. Knowing she wanted him as much as he wanted her only added fuel to the blazing flame of his passion.

He touched her nipple, already beaded and throbbing. She swallowed a moan. He placed his mouth on her, suckling her breast. She wrapped herself around him, her soft little cries a plea for release.

"Please, don't wait any longer," she whispered as he suckled her other breast. "Oh, Sam, put an end to our pain."

Too soon! Too soon! his mind told him. *Now!* his body urged. *She feels what you feel,* his heart told him.

"I need to protect you," he said.

"I need no protection from you, Sam."

And then he sensed her probing, seeking entrance inside his mind. He allowed her to come in, and when their minds joined, each realized the searing-hot fire and uncontrollable force of their combined madness. Knowing he would hurt her, if only briefly, Sam tried to be gentle, lifting her hips, entering her by slow degrees.

He was so big; she was so small.

He was a savage brute; she was a gentle angel.

No! she cried out silently. *I'm as savage as you are and you are as gentle as I am. Take me, Sam. Please take me now!*

Sam responded by thrusting to the hilt, giving her all of himself. She groaned, accepting the quick, hot pain. He stopped, his breathing ragged, sweat dripping from his body onto hers.

Heaven help him, but he'd felt her pain. How was that possible? It wasn't.

The pain subsided. She knew he'd felt it, too, but had dismissed it as impossible.

Jeannie moved, lifting up, wrapping her legs around Sam's hips, urging him to resume. Pleasure rippled through him as the pressure built. Pulling partly out of her, he hesitated only a second before plunging deeply again and starting the primeval mating dance.

His iron control cracked in a dozen places, weakening his defenses, making him more vulnerable, open to her possession. The agony intensified, the pressure inside them close to exploding. Jeannie clung to him, whispering his name in gasping little chants. Sam moaned dark, desperate, erotic words to her.

Release hit them simultaneously, or so Jeannie thought, but she soon realized that the fulfillment she felt was Sam's. Wild, hot, savage. He emptied his seed into her, shudders of pleasure jerking his big body. The sensations rocketed through her, and she cried out, trembling with the aftershocks.

Agony turned to ecstasy. But before she fell from the heights of rapture, she gripped his hips, lifting herself up against him, stroking her body against his frantically. Strong, forceful spasms clutched her sex, then threw her headlong into the heaven of carnal fulfillment. She clung to him as wave after wave of joyous release washed over her.

Sam held her, aware of her completion, and fully aware

that in some way, though faint and subdued, he shared her release.

Easing off her and onto his side, he drew her into his arms and kissed her forehead. They lay there in the aftermath of a loving so profound neither of them could find the words to express how they felt. When their ragged breathing settled to normal, Sam got out of bed, lifted Jeannie in his arms and smothered her with passionate kisses. She clung to him, knowing that she was now Sam Dundee's woman in every sense of the word. She had never felt closer to anyone in her life.

Sam carried her across the bedroom, kicked open the bathroom door and stepped into the shower. When he turned the faucets, a spray of cold water hit their naked bodies. Jeannie squealed. Sam held her with one hand while adjusting the water temperature. The shower poured over them with refreshing warmth. He picked up a bar of white soap, smelled its sweet perfume, then grinned.

"If I use this stuff, I'll smell like you," he said.

"You already do."

He laughed. She loved the sound of his laughter. So hearty. So genuine. She had to make sure he laughed more.

"And you smell like me." Lowering his head, he licked her breasts, from one nipple to the other. "And you taste like me."

He lathered her body slowly, taking special care to be gentle as he cleaned away the residue of her innocence. He braced her against the ceramic wall, washing her thoroughly.

Lowering himself to his knees, he held her hip with one hand while he spread her legs farther apart. She gripped his shoulders. Her body clenched, released, then repeated the process. While the warm water cascaded down Jeannie's body and onto Sam's back, he sought her feminine core and began a sensual assault that left her breathless and pleading. His mouth covered her, his tongue driving her crazy with its strong, sensuous attack.

She swelled and tightened, then turned to liquid fire. She cried out; he groaned, the sound rumbling from deep in his chest. She splintered into a million pieces of indescribable pleasure; his sex hardened painfully when fragments of her fulfillment sizzled through his body. Tiny sparks of white-hot ecstasy claimed him as surely as they had Jeannie.

During the moments of downward-spiraling release, Jeannie squeezed Sam's shoulders, urging him to stand. He stood slowly, sliding himself up and against her. She circled him with her hand. He gritted his teeth, trying not to cry out, and covered her hand with his, instructing her movements. Once. Twice. Three times. He thrust his tongue inside her mouth at the precise moment he erupted into completion. He threw back his head as a deep, guttural cry escaped from his lips, torn from his body with the force of his release. Experiencing to an infinite degree the explosion of Sam's sensations and emotions, Jeannie wrapped her arms around his waist. They clung to each other, weak and exhausted, as the water washed over them. Finally, Sam reached out and shut off the water.

Covering Jeannie in a huge white towel, he dried her with the patience of a parent tending to a child. She reciprocated, drying him, delighting in his playful growl when she stroked him intimately.

Naked, clean and sated, they gazed longingly into each other's eyes. At that precise moment, words were redundant. He kissed her gently; she returned the kiss. Lifting her in his arms, he carried her back to her bed, stripped away the soiled coverlet and jerked the floral blanket up into the air. He flung the blanket over his shoulder, half of it covering Jeannie. She peeked out from beneath the blanket as he carried her outside, onto the veranda. He kissed her on the nose. She giggled.

Sam covered a huge wicker rocker with the floral blanket, then sat down, Jeannie in his lap. She cuddled in his arms, their naked bodies warm against each other. They sat in the wicker rocker on the veranda, man and woman, lovers for the first time, and the bonding that had begun on the beach six years ago grew stronger. They both felt what was happening. She acknowledged it in her heart; he fought the truth, unable to relinquish complete control.

For endless moments, time having become meaningless, they absorbed the beauty of the night, the moon and stars, the soft, balmy breeze, the ocean's song.

Hours later, Jeannie awoke in his arms and lifted her head, seeking his mouth, initiating a kiss that quickly turned passionate. Turning her body, she rose over him, straddling him, bracing her knees on each side of him. "Make love to me again, Sam." She nuzzled his ear with her nose.

"It's too soon. You're sore, and I don't want to hurt you again." He stroked her hip.

"I'm not that sore," she told him. "I ache with the wanting, and I know you do, too."

Gripping her buttocks, he lifted her as he stood and carried her across the porch, resting her on the top of the wide banister. She kept her arms locked around his neck as he positioned himself, bending his knees, pulling her forward. The joining was swift and complete. Jeannie gasped; Sam moaned. Clutching her hips in his big hands, he guided her back and forth, lifting her completely off the banister. She wrapped her legs around him, clinging to him as the hard, hot plunges stroked her to an unbearable pleasure. She spiraled out of control, crying out her completion. Sam shook from the sensations he experienced, then fell headlong into oblivion with one final, forceful lunge. While he trembled, she quivered, and he held her in his arms, her legs and arms wrapped around him, their mouths locked in a passionate kiss. And the intimate bonding of their hearts and souls continued, binding them together, strengthening their ability to share every feeling.

From inside the house, they heard the soft, sweet strains of piano music. Jeannie's song. Manton knew. And he was paying tribute to their love.

JEANNIE KICKED THE sand with her bare toes. Sam rubbed suntan lotion on her delicate skin, coating her back and arms thoroughly, then starting on her legs. Beautiful, silky legs. But physically weak, unable to fully support her slender weight. He kissed her inner thigh. She ruffled his thick blond hair.

Sam looked up at her and smiled. "I promise you, my childhood was boring and meaningless. I don't know why you want to hear about it."

"Because I picture you as this serious little boy who went around with a frown on his face." Jeannie giggled when he tickled her foot. "Come on, tell me. This is called getting to know each other. You go first."

Sam completed his suntan detail, recapped the bottle and tossed it on the blanket beside the picnic hamper. "My father was a career soldier, so I didn't see much of him, even before he died. After our mother's death, James and I lived with an aunt and uncle, and I stayed on with them when James joined the marines. Aunt Harriet and Uncle Pete are both gone now."

"Were you a happy child?" Jeannie rummaged around inside the picnic basket, retrieved a bottle of wine and two clear plastic glasses. She handed the wine to Sam.

He opened the bottle, filled their glasses, then reached around Jeannie to place the wine back in the hamper. "I guess I enjoyed my childhood as much as any kid does, but I never had a lot of friends. I was a bit of a loner." Jeannie handed Sam a glass of wine. "I idolized my father. So did James. I thought my dad was a real hero. I wanted to be just like him."

"I never knew my real father." Jeannie placed cheese, apples and wheat crackers on a plastic plate. "My mother got pregnant when she was sixteen. She was only twenty-two when she married Randy Foley." Jeannie shook her head from side to side, making her long ponytail bounce from shoulder blade to shoulder blade. "Julian and Manton have both been like fathers to me."

"Yeah, well, when our old man died, James became my

substitute father. I followed him into the marines as soon as I turned eighteen. And when he got married, James's wife told me that their home would always be mine. Sandra was a special lady."

Jeannie clasped Sam's hand. "It's all right to still feel sad about their dying so young."

"Elizabeth was only twelve. She really needed her parents, but she was lucky. She had a great-aunt who understood what it meant to be psychic. Legally, I was Elizabeth's guardian, but her great-aunt Margaret was the one who raised her."

"You love Elizabeth dearly, don't you?"

Sam brought Jeannie's hand to his lips, kissed the open palm and laid it over his heart. "She's the only person I had in my life to love." He gazed down into the wine, sighed, then took a sip. "But she's a grown woman now, married and a mother. Every time I look at her little boy—"

"You want a child of your own, don't you, Sam?" She sensed the need in him, tapping into his emotions simply by touching him. Big, macho, hard-edged soldier, government agent and bodyguard, Sam Dundee had a central core of goodness, a wellspring of pure golden love just waiting to be lavished on a child.

He jerked away from her, spilling his wine. Standing, he faced the sun, then shaded his eyes with his big hand. She watched him, his broad shoulders moving slightly when he breathed.

"I'm sorry," she said. "I couldn't help picking up on what you were feeling. I didn't mean to intrude on something that's obviously painful for you."

She knew! Dear God, she knew. She had gotten that deep inside him.

Sam willed himself not to think about what had happened six years ago, about what had happened to the child who might have been his. "Your childhood was pretty rotten, wasn't it?"

he asked her, deliberately changing the subject. "Until you went to live with Julian and Miriam Howell."

"You can't imagine." Jeannie sipped the wine slowly. "From when I was six and Mama married Randy Foley, until I was thirteen and they died in the car crash that crippled me, I lived in pain every day of my life. Except…"

Sam sat down again on the quilt beside Jeannie, cupped her chin in his hand and tilted her face upward. She stared into his eyes. "Except when you came to Le Bijou Bleu for vacations."

"This island was my heaven. And Manton was my guardian angel. He was the first person I communicated with telepathically. I never told Mama and Randy. It would have been one more thing they would have tried to exploit. And I didn't try to develop the talent. It never happened again until Miriam became sick and…" Tears gathered in Jeannie's eyes; she bit her bottom lip. "I loved her so dearly."

"Cancer can be a horrible way to die," Sam said.

"She suffered unbearably near the end." Jeannie swallowed her tears as the memories of Miriam's final days flooded her memory.

"And you shared that suffering. You made it bearable." He pulled her into his arms, stroking her back, resting his head atop hers, his cheek brushing her hair. "It must have been terrible for you."

"Yes and no. It would have been worse for me if I hadn't been able to absorb some of her pain, to take away the suffering for just a few hours, to give her a little relief. There came a time when the drugs didn't help."

"She was very fortunate to have you." Sam kissed the side of Jeannie's face.

She slipped her arms around his waist, touching his naked skin beneath his loose cotton shirt. "I was fortunate to have her for a mother for so many years. She was an extraordinary woman. Beautiful. Brilliant. Compassionate. I would have done anything for her."

"And you did." He soothed her with his hands, caressing her tenderly.

"Can't you understand?" She looked at him, asking him to put himself in her place. "If you saw someone you loved in excruciating pain, wouldn't you want to make the pain go away? Wouldn't you, if you could, suffer that pain for them?"

Sam kissed her. Hot. Fierce. Demanding. Yes, he understood what it meant to care so deeply for someone, to be willing to die for that person if necessary. When he released her mouth, she gasped for air.

"Sam?" She'd felt it, that tiny kernel of emotion called love. It was there, buried so deep within Sam that he wasn't even consciously aware it existed. All these years, there had been no one to keep love alive in Sam, no one except Elizabeth.

But Sam had never been deeply in love, had never bonded with a woman. Not until— But their bonding was incomplete, despite a week of making love and sharing private thoughts and feelings. He wouldn't allow himself to love her. The risk was too great. And as much as he wanted a child—even if he denied that great desire—he had not made love to Jeannie again, after that first night, without using protection.

And just who was he protecting, she wondered, her or himself?

Sam peeled off his shirt, dropped it on the quilt and nodded toward the ocean. "How about a swim before we eat lunch?"

Jeannie held up her arms to him. He lifted her, carried her across the beach, and together they dived into the water. Within minutes, his dark mood lightened and the sadness left her eyes. They frolicked in the Gulf like two playful children. Later they sat in the shade of a huge old live oak with branches that drooped to the ground and had taken root. They ate the cheese and fruit, drank the wine and made slow, sweet love.

With each passing day, with each shared intimacy, Sam and

Jeannie's joining became stronger. If Sam could ever bring himself to love her, truly love her, they would become one. Every beat of his heart, hers. Every breath she took, his. Her thoughts, her emotions, her feelings, would belong to him, and his to her. How deep the bonding would go, even Jeannie did not know.

CHAPTER THIRTEEN

JEANNIE CUDDLED IN Sam's arms. The late-afternoon sun was behind them, the ocean breeze soft and warm on their bare skin. With an occasional backward sweep of his foot, Sam kept the wooden porch swing in slow but continuous motion as he held Jeannie close. Caressing her shoulder with one hand, he rested his cheek against the side of her head. Her fresh, clean smell surrounded him. Turning her head just a fraction, she glanced up at him and smiled. Bringing his mouth down on hers, he kissed her with the wonderful sweetness of familiarity. In the twenty days they'd spent on Le Bijou Bleu, Sam had allowed himself to drown in the pleasure of loving Jeannie, of being at her side night and day, of discovering the incredible sensations of having his lover experience his every emotion, just as he was beginning to experience hers.

They hadn't spoken about what was happening to him, the fact that he was becoming more and more attuned to Jeannie's thoughts and feelings with each passing day. Although Sam didn't scoff at the idea of psychic powers, having been exposed to Elizabeth's psychic talents for so many years, he'd never experienced any himself. Until now, with Jeannie. Although whatever was happening to him was on a limited basis, he had to admit that he could communicate with Jeannie telepathically, to a certain extent. And each time they made love, the sensation of feeling what she felt grew stronger and stronger. He couldn't imagine what it was like for her, experiencing his fulfillment and her own.

Manton's piano music drifted through the open French doors.

Every afternoon, without fail, the gentle giant of a man played his sentimental compositions.

"Listen," Jeannie said. "That's something new. He's never played it before."

The tune seeped into Sam's mind, and for some odd reason, its sweet, vibrant melody resurrected long-buried memories. That night six years ago, a three-piece band had played on the riverboat nightclub owned by Louis Herriot, a man the DEA wanted badly enough to place Sam and new agent Brock Holmes in a dangerous undercover operation. And everything had gone exactly as planned, until Connie Bell inadvertently walked into the middle of things as the sting was coming down.

"Sam?" Jeannie touched his face.

He jumped, then stared at her, suddenly aware of where his thoughts were leading him. "I'm all right."

"No, you're not." She caressed his cheek.

Closing his eyes, loving the feel of her, he covered her hand. "There's no point in talking about what happened. It's over and done with, and I'll have to live with the consequences the rest of my life. All the talking in the world won't change anything."

"Talking might help you deal with the grief and the guilt." She sensed his resistance, his fear, his guilt. Several times she had been right on the verge of telling him she was aware of the terrible pain eating away at his soul, but he'd sealed himself off from her, and she had respected his privacy.

"Don't you know you can share anything with me and I'll understand? If you'll only let me, I can ease your suffering."

Releasing his hold on her, he moved away, then stood, keeping his back to her. He thrust his hands into the front pockets of the cutoff jeans he wore. "Like you did the day you saved my life?"

She shivered with the force of his anger as it spiraled inside her. Reaching for her cane that rested against the wall, she slid to the edge of the swing. "Yes, like I did the day I found you on the beach. You felt guilty for two people's deaths. You didn't think you deserved to live."

"Yeah." Sam walked down the veranda, stopping several feet away from her. "I thought I was dying, and when I came to and saw you, I thought you were an angel." He emitted a grunting laugh. "Ironic, isn't it? As it turned out, that's exactly what you were."

"You can't spend the rest of your life blaming yourself, hating yourself, letting that guilt destroy your ability to live and love." Positioning her cane, Jeannie stood and took several steps toward Sam. She laid her hand on his back. He flinched.

"Don't do this," he said. "I don't want you to suffer for me. I don't want you to know what it feels like."

"Please trust me, Sam." She slipped her arms around his waist, holding tight when he started to withdraw from her. "You must know how much you mean to me. You're the one person in this world I most want to help."

His unrelenting guilt hit her with shattering force. She clung to Sam, resting her head on his back. Dear God, the pain inside him was unbearable. Dark, bitter rage simmered in his soul. Damned forever. Oh, her poor Sam. A lesser man would never know such guilt.

"Stop it!" He realized what had happened, what he had allowed to happen. Dammit, he wasn't going to let her absorb any more of the tormenting grief from which he could never escape. His grief and guilt were his punishment, not hers. She was innocent, so very innocent.

"Talk to me about what happened. Let it go. Give it to me and let me share your burden. Allow me to help you." While she held him with the fierceness of that abiding protective devotion, she gave those very feelings over to him, allowing him to experience the great depth of her emotions.

"I don't want your help!" Jerking out of her embrace, he stalked off the veranda and across the wide expanse of lush green lawn.

Jeannie stood on the veranda and watched him walk away. Tears filled her eyes, ran down her cheeks, trickled off her nose and over her lips. She couldn't force him to come to her, expose his heart's deepest emotions and bare his soul. But neither could she let him suffer alone, as he had done for the past six years. If he would not allow her to take away his guilt and grief for a few hours, she could still be at his side, supporting him while he grieved anew.

She took one step down from the veranda, then heard Manton call to her. Turning around, she saw him standing behind her.

Did you like the new composition I played for you and Sam today? he asked telepathically.

It was lovely, but—

It made Sam very sad, didn't it?

Yes. It made him think of something he would like to forget.

I wrote the song for your child, Jeannie. For your and Sam Dundee's child.

Jeannie stared directly into Manton's piercing green eyes. Several days ago, she had made the first connection with the new life growing inside her. If she had not been so overwhelmed with all the new feelings she'd experienced the first time she and Sam made love, she would have known immediately that she had conceived his child.

"I knew I couldn't keep the child a secret from you," she said, her lips moving silently.

You should not keep her a secret from her father, either.

Jeannie laid her hand tenderly over her flat stomach. Sam's child. The most precious gift God could have given her. She had been given so much. Dare she ask for Sam's salvation from guilt and grief? Dare she ask that he be freed from the past so that he could open his heart and love her? Perhaps she had been blessed with more than enough. Perhaps what she and Sam had already been given was all heaven would allow.

I can't tell Sam now. It's too soon. He has to deal with his old grief first.

Then go to him, Manton said. *He will never be able to come to terms with what is destroying him without your help.*

Jeannie embraced Manton, her heart filled with love for him. He was the dearest of men, his soul so pure that it was on its final journey to completion.

She walked down the steps and into the yard. She knew where Sam had gone. Back to the beach where he had washed ashore six years ago.

She found him looking out at the ocean, his body statue-hard, the wind whipping his hair into his eyes, his face etched with tense lines of agony.

When she approached him, she didn't touch him, but he sensed her presence. Turning around, he looked at her with dead eyes, eyes of pure gray steel. She took a tentative step forward; he didn't move. Another step. And another.

He watched her, his gaze fixed to hers. She stood directly in front of him, one hand holding her walking stick, the other clutching the side of her peach gauze skirt. A muscle in his neck throbbed. His lips parted. He sucked in a deep breath.

Tearstains marred her face. The hand with which she held the cane trembled, the movement barely discernible. She looked at him with eyes of love and understanding and compassion. His big shoulders slumped ever so slightly. His eyes softened from steel to blue-gray.

He was losing this battle, and he knew it. He might be twice Jeannie's size, his body far more powerful, but inside that fragile body, within that enormous heart of hers, lived a strength for which Sam was no match.

A fine glaze of moisture covered his eyes. He blinked away the evidence of emotion, but he could not turn away from Jeannie. He pulled her into his arms. She went willingly, gladly, dropping her cane onto the sandy beach. She wrapped him in the warmth of her embrace, petting his back with gentle up-

and-down strokes. After six long years of running away from a truth that tormented him, Sam knew the time had come to exorcise the demon.

But, dear God, how could he endure watching her hurt for him? How could he, once again, be the recipient of her tender mercy?

"I knew better." He spoke softly, the words a mere whisper on the wind. "If I hadn't been so damned stupid!"

"You made a mistake, Sam. Everyone makes mistakes." She hugged him, absorbing his feelings.

"But not everyone's mistakes cost two people their lives." Clinging to her, he allowed her inside his mind and heart and body. He held back nothing.

Releasing her hold around his waist, she reached up and took his face in her hands. Every muscle in his body tensed. Jeannie held his face, forcing him to look directly into her eyes. "Say it. You blame yourself for Brock Holmes's death. He was a rookie agent, and you felt responsible for him. You blame yourself for the death of Connie Bell, the woman you were having an affair with, the woman who was a nightclub singer in Louie Herriot's employ. You knew better than to become personally involved with someone while you were on an assignment. If you hadn't been sleeping with her, she wouldn't have shown up at the wrong place and the wrong time and gotten shot.

"But it isn't Brock's death, or even Connie's, that you can never forgive yourself for causing. Tell me, Sam. Say it aloud. You've never done that, have you? You keep the truth hidden so deep inside you that it's festered into a rotting sore."

He glared at her, his big body shaking, his eyes dry, his face crumpling before her very eyes. "Dammit, she was pregnant!"

"I know." Jeannie slid her hands down Sam's neck and out to his shoulders, gripping them firmly. "Say it. Just this once, and you'll never have to say it again."

The pain inside him carried him to his knees, Jeannie with

him. She could feel the guilt, the anguish, the gut-wrenching pain, as it began to leave him and make its way into her.

"Don't you see, the child could have been mine? I didn't have any idea she was pregnant. After I woke up in the Biloxi hospital, I found out about her being pregnant from another agent who'd been sent in to wrap up the case. Connie was two months pregnant. That baby—" he clutched Jeannie's hands, holding them between their bodies "—was probably mine."

"Say it!" Jeannie cried the tears Sam could not shed. The pain eased from him; she took it upon herself.

"It's my fault that child was never born. I'm responsible for the death of my own child!"

A heavy weight of guilt lifted from Sam. Pain and grief cleared from his heart and soul. He breathed deeply, drawing fresh air into his lungs, cleaning out the dark, dank recesses of his heart, allowing his soul a brief hint of reprieve.

At sunset, Jeannie sat in Sam's lap on the beach, cocooned in the security of his strong arms. Sam held her, never wanting to let her go.

"The grief and the guilt will always be there," she said. "You know that, don't you? But now that you've faced them, you can learn to deal with them."

"I can't change the past."

"No, but you must learn to live with it."

"I wasn't in love with Connie, and she wasn't in love with me. She'd just broken off with another guy, and I knew he was still around."

"The child could have been his or yours, and you'll never know." Jeannie took Sam's hand and laid it on her stomach, covering his hand with hers. "But the guilt is the same, because there's a good chance the child was yours."

"If I hadn't let my... I knew better. I screwed up and it cost two...three people's lives."

"The only way to atone for that mistake is to make the most

of *your* life. Give all that's good and strong within you to others. Forgive yourself, and find the love buried deep inside you."

"I don't know if there's any love in me," he said.

"You love Elizabeth and her child." Jeannie leaned back, letting her head rest on his shoulder. "I know there's more love inside you, if you'll only release it. But no one else can do that for you, Sam. Not even me."

No, not even Jeannie, sweet, angelic Jeannie, could save him. Hell, he wasn't sure he wanted to be saved. He had become accustomed to his guilt and remorse. To the pain. And the price of salvation was too high. If a man didn't care too much, he didn't put his emotions on the line. If caring for others to the extent Jeannie cared, and being willing to open himself up to his deepest emotions, was the only recourse, Sam knew he was damned. Jeannie Alverson was expecting too much from him. He could never be the man she wanted or needed.

Turning in his arms quickly, Jeannie kissed him. A tender, loving kiss. "It's all right. I'm not asking for more than you can give." She caressed his cheek, knowing in her heart that her words were a lie. She wanted Sam Dundee. All of him. His body. His heart. His mind. His very soul. And she wanted him forever. But he hadn't promised her forever. All they had was today.

THE RINGING TELEPHONE awoke them before dawn. Within minutes, Manton knocked softly on Jeannie's bedroom door.

"Something's wrong." Jeannie sat upright, the pastel floral sheet sliding off her naked breasts to rest at her waist. "We've received a fax from the mainland."

Sam slipped into his shorts and stepped out into the hallway. Manton handed him the faxed communication. Scanning the message quickly, Sam groaned. His stomach muscles tightened. Hell! He wished he didn't have to tell Jeannie. There would be no way to keep her on the island once she knew what had happened.

"I'll tell her." Sam looked directly at Manton so that the big man could read his lips.

Manton nodded, then signed to Sam. In the three weeks they'd been on the island, Sam had tried to learn a few basic words in sign. The best he could make out, Manton was saying he'd prepare some coffee and would bring it to them.

Jeannie pulled her pastel yellow gown over her head, lifting her body to ease the silky material down her hips. Swinging her legs off the side of the bed, she looked up at Sam when he returned with the fax message in his hand.

"It's Julian. What's happened? Did Maynard Reeves—? Oh, no, it's Julian's heart."

Sitting on the edge of the bed beside her, Sam took her hands in his. "Julian's had a heart attack. He's in intensive care. The fax is from Marta. She's with him."

"I've got to get to Biloxi." She squeezed Sam's hands. "Julian needs me. No one else can help him the way I can."

"Maynard Reeves still poses as much of a threat to you as he ever did. If you return to Biloxi, you'll be in danger."

"I know that." She bowed her head, praying silently.

"The doctors will take care of Julian. If they can't save his life, then there's nothing you can do."

She snapped her head up, glaring at Sam. "I'm going back to Biloxi. If Julian dies, I want to be there with him. And if he lives, I can help."

Sam wondered why he had even tried to reason with Jeannie. Why couldn't he just accept the fact that her compassionate heart would always win any battle against logic? For there was no logic to Jeannie's powers, no reasonable explanation. Somehow she had been blessed, or perhaps she'd been cursed, with the ability to truly bestow loving kindness on others. He, of all people, knew what it meant to be the recipient of her tender mercy.

Sam nodded. Jeannie's glare softened to a gentle stare.

"I'll take care of Julian," she said. "And you will take care of me."

He kissed her on the forehead. "I'll take good care of you." Standing, he helped her to her feet and into her silk robe, then handed her a cane. "Manton's fixing coffee."

"I'm sorry our days in paradise have to come to an end," Jeannie said, looking at him lovingly.

"Anywhere I am with you is paradise. Don't you know that?"

Manton knocked on the door, then came in carrying a tray, which he placed on Jeannie's desk, an antique of white-painted wood, with a sailing ship surrounded by a circle of roses stenciled on the back. He poured Jeannie a cup, placing cream and sugar in the coffee, then handed it to her. He poured another cup and handed the black liquid to Sam.

Immediately he signed to Sam, looking to Jeannie to translate whatever wasn't immediately understood.

"He wants you to keep me safe," Jeannie said. "He senses danger for both of us. He doesn't want us to leave the island, but he understands that we must."

Jeannie patted Manton's enormous hand, then lifted it to her lips and kissed it. "We'll come back to Le Bijou Bleu as soon as Julian is well." She glanced over at Sam. "Won't we?"

Sam nodded agreement, but he wasn't sure he'd ever return to this island. Once they were back in Biloxi, he would have to deal with Maynard Reeves. After three weeks of searching for any type of evidence that would warrant Reeves's arrest, the local and federal authorities still had nothing concrete. Reeves was still a free man, waiting for Jeannie Alverson to come out of hiding.

MARTA MCCORKLE KISSED Julian's pale cheek, then thanked the young nurse who stood by his bedside. She walked out of the ICU unit and right past the man who stood with his back to her. Maynard Reeves had been told of Julian's heart attack by a

Righteous Light disciple, a hospital janitor who'd been working when the medics rushed Julian into the emergency room.

Maynard had been waiting patiently for Marta McCorkle to leave the ICU. All he needed was a few moments alone with Julian Howell. For twenty days, he had tried by every method possible to discover Jeannie Alverson's whereabouts. Dundee had taken her away, was hiding her, keeping her safe. Maynard knew his only hope of finding Jeannie was to get the information from the one person who would know where she was. Julian Howell. But he hadn't been able to get anywhere near Dr. Howell, and making a psychic link with someone he couldn't touch was beyond his capabilities.

No one, except Jeannie and his old friend Wayland Krenshaw, knew he was psychic. Wayland was his right-hand man, a trusted deacon in the church they had founded together. But Jeannie was his enemy. She had refused to join his great cause, to use her talent, as he used his, in the service of the Lord.

He deeply regretted that his psychic abilities were so limited. He knew God had meant for his powers to be greater, but his stupid parents had stifled the natural growth of his powers. If only Jeannie Alverson had joined him, there would have been no limit to the heights he could have reached. Together, they could have been the most powerful force for good in the world.

But Jeannie had shown her true colors. She dared not use her powers in the Lord's service, when her real master was the devil. The woman was a witch, not a saint, as he had hoped. She and her guardian, Dundee, would annihilate him if they could. Satan had given her enormous power, power far greater than those Maynard himself had been blessed with. He had no choice but to destroy her, before she destroyed him.

"May I help you, Father?" the nurse asked.

"Yes, my child. I've come to see Julian Howell." Reeves stood tall and straight in his priest's disguise, one he knew might gain him an audience with Dr. Howell.

"Are you his priest?"

"My parish is near New Orleans," Reeves lied. "I'm a family friend who has been called in for special prayers."

"Dr. Howell's daughter hasn't arrived yet," the nurse said. "And Ms. McCorkle has gone to make a few phone calls. I really need the family's permission before I allow you to visit Dr. Howell."

"My dear child, I am here at the family's request." He lifted the white Bible he held in his hand. "They know I will be a comfort to Julian."

"Well, I don't suppose there would be anything wrong with letting you come in for a few minutes."

Maynard flashed her his most charming smile, the smile he had used often to persuade ladies to donate large sums of money to the Righteous Light Church. "I need only a few minutes."

Maynard found Julian Howell resting comfortably, his every bodily function monitored. The young nurse stayed with him, still a bit uneasy about allowing someone other than immediate family to visit an ICU patient.

Placing his hand over Julian's, Maynard closed his eyes and began mumbling something he hoped would sound like a prayer. He lowered his voice, allowing it to drift off into silence. Closing his eyes, he concentrated on Julian. Hazy, sleepy, surreal thoughts and images clouded Julian's mind. Maynard probed deeper.

Jeannie is safe, Maynard said telepathically. *Far away from Biloxi and any danger. Think about where she is and how safe she is.*

Visions of blue sky and water formed in Maynard's mind, then an island, lush and green, a big raised French cottage resting high on a hill.

Dundee had taken her to an island. But where?

When Maynard tried to delve deeper into Julian's

subconscious mind, he realized Jeannie's foster father was fighting him, trying to keep him out before he acquired the much-needed information.

Julian thrashed about in the bed. The nurse rushed to his side. "I'm afraid you'll have to leave. Something's wrong. Dr. Howell is becoming quite agitated."

Maynard forced his way past the barrier in Julian's mind. Le Bijou Bleu. The distance from Biloxi and the location of the island flashed through Julian's thoughts, and then his mind closed.

"Father, please leave," the nurse repeated her request.

Opening his eyes, Maynard smiled. "Yes, of course. I'll return later, when he's awake and calm."

When Maynard opened the door to exit the ICU unit, Lieutenant Painter met him. How had that idiot found him? He'd been certain he'd ditched the policeman following him.

"Changed religious affiliations, Reverend Reeves?" Painter asked. "Or should I call you Father Reeves now?"

"Reverend Reeves will do. What are you doing here, Lieutenant?"

"I was about to ask you the same question."

"Visiting the sick, of course."

"I'm sure I could hold you in jail overnight, Reverend. Impersonating a priest might not stick in court, but I could drum up some other charges to go with it so we could haul your butt in for questioning."

"The clothing I choose to wear in my role as a minster of the gospel is my business, and the fact that a young nurse mistook me for a priest is not my fault." Maynard wasn't afraid of the police. He had outsmarted them time and again. No, he didn't have anything to fear from the likes of Rufus Painter.

"What the hell is he doing here?" A deep voice roared from the doorway leading into the waiting room.

Maynard jerked around, his eyes widening with surprise.

Sam Dundee. And, at his side, Jeannie Alverson. Maynard smiled. So, he would not have to go in search of the witch after all. She had returned. No doubt to cast a spell to cure her foster father.

Jeannie clung to her protector's arm. She was so sure he could guard her from the inevitable. Well, she was wrong. Sam Dundee was indeed a formidable opponent, but all Maynard needed was a little time to figure out how to bring the big man down.

"I thought y'all were watching him," Jeannie said. "How did he get in here to see Julian?"

"He's leaving right now," Painter said. "I'm driving him to the station, where he can call his lawyer before answering a few questions for us."

"This is all a waste of time," Maynard told them. "You cannot condemn an innocent man. And you have no evidence that I've committed any crime."

"Lieutenant, would you mind going with Jeannie to see Dr. Howell?" Sam asked. "Reeves is right. Taking him in would be a waste of time. Yours and his."

"How wise of you to understand," Maynard said.

"Please, Lieutenant, go with Jeannie. She's anxious to see her father."

"Sam?" Jeannie said, questioning his intentions.

"Go on. See about Julian."

Lieutenant Painter escorted a reluctant Jeannie into the private ICU cubicle, leaving Maynard alone in the waiting area with Sam.

"Watch her day and night, Dundee." Maynard laughed, the sound robust and confident. "You know not the hour or the day I will strike."

Sam grabbed Maynard by the neck, dragging his face up to his. My God, what did the man intend to do? Kill him on the spot? Maynard lifted his trembling hands, desperately trying to dislodge himself from Dundee's choking hold. Maynard gasped, then struggled for air when Sam tightened the pressure on his windpipe.

"Know this, Reeves—if any harm comes to Jeannie, you will die. And a soul as black as yours will surely rot in hell forever."

CHAPTER FOURTEEN

JEANNIE SAT AT Julian's bedside, his hand clasped in hers. She had stayed with him since her return to Biloxi, thirty-six hours earlier. Sam had done everything short of knocking her out and throwing her over his shoulder to get her to leave for a short rest, but she had refused. The doctors had told them Julian was out of any immediate danger, but with a heart-attack victim, nothing could be certain.

Jeannie had been given special permission to stay with Julian in ICU, but Sam had been banished to the waiting area, except for regularly scheduled visits. The past thirty-six hours had been an exercise in torture for him. Keeping guard at a distance was not Sam's style of protection.

The ICU door opened and Jeannie walked out, a wide smile on her face. "They're moving Julian to a private room. He's improving quickly. The doctors are astonished."

Sam dropped the newspaper he'd been scanning, stood and walked over to Jeannie. "They don't realize Julian's had a little extra help in his recovery." He slipped his arm around her; she leaned her body against his.

"Julian loves roses. While they're moving him, I want to order some flowers for him. Two or three dozen roses. And you can run by the house...no, not by the house, by the cottage, and pick up some pajamas and a robe for Julian, and—"

Sam kissed her into silence, then released her quickly. "I'm not going anywhere. Call Ollie and have her bring over Julian's things."

"Julian gave Ollie a much-needed vacation to visit her sister in Tupelo, while the repairs are being done on our house. Don't you remember my telling you?"

"Then have Marta pick up Julian's stuff." With his arm around her shoulders, he turned her toward the outer waiting room door. "And you can order flowers after you've eaten something. You haven't left Julian's side, except to use the bathroom and drink a few cups of coffee. You haven't eaten anything except a doughnut one of the nurses brought you." He brushed away an errant strand of hair that had come loose from her ponytail. "And as soon as you check on Julian, after he's in a private room, I'm taking you to the cottage for some rest."

"I'll eat soon. I promise. And I'll rest as soon as I'm sure Julian will be all right without me." She knew Sam was right. She needed food and rest. She was thankful Sam had been forced to remain in the waiting area. If he'd seen her faint twice, he would have taken her away from Julian, despite her protests. And if he knew about her condition—that she was carrying his child—he wouldn't allow her to give Julian the peace of mind and pain-free rest he so desperately needed.

"Dammit, Jeannie, you can't go on this way. Not eating. Not sleeping. Julian wouldn't want you to endanger your health to help him."

"The choice is mine. Not Julian's. And not yours." But there was more to consider than her own health; she had to think about her child. "Please, Sam. I'll order the flowers, then call Marta. And I'll eat something in Julian's room. You choose my menu, and I'll eat every bite. But I must stay with Julian until I'm certain he doesn't need me anymore."

How could she make Sam understand how much she owed Julian? He had been the surgeon who saved her life after the car wreck, when she was thirteen. Later, he and Miriam had taken her into their home, helped her through years of therapy and made her the daughter they'd never had. The Howells had given Jeannie the beautiful, peaceful existence that had been hers before the truth about her past had been revealed. There was nothing she wouldn't do for Julian or for Manton, just as there had been nothing she wouldn't do for Miriam.

"You're going home tonight." His statement left no room for argument. Regardless of her protests, Sam was determined to save her from her own stubbornness.

Jeannie reached up, caressed his cheek and looked into his eyes. "When I love someone, I love them completely, with no reservations, no limitations. Like you, Sam, I haven't given my love often. I love Julian and Manton the way you love Elizabeth and her little Jimmy."

"I know how you feel," Sam said. "But understand this— I'm taking you home tonight, if I have to drag you out of this hospital kicking and screaming."

She smiled, stretched on tiptoe to drag his face down to hers, then kissed him. "See if the cafeteria is serving spaghetti. With lots of Parmesan cheese."

Sam swatted her behind. She giggled. God, how he loved the sound of her happy giggles.

JEANNIE DEVOURED THE plate of spaghetti Sam had had delivered from a restaurant, along with chocolate cheesecake and ice tea.

"I don't think I can eat another bite." She shoved the plate aside. "I'll save the cheesecake for later."

"You'll take it home with you," Julian told her, then looked at Sam. "You should have made her leave long before now. She's exhausted. See those dark circles under her eyes? She's done too much for me already."

"You know Jeannie. She wouldn't leave willingly," Sam said. "But she's going home tonight, willing or not."

Julian chuckled. "I'm so sorry this happened. My heart attack brought her right back to Biloxi, and put her within Maynard Reeves's grasp."

"Sam will protect me from the good reverend." Jeannie

finished off the tall glass of ice tea, wiped her mouth with a paper napkin and shoved back her chair. "And as soon as the doctors say it's all right, we'll all go to Le Bijou Bleu."

Julian pointed to the television, which he'd set to the weather channel. "If that tropical depression off the coast of Africa moves in our direction, we might be in for a hurricane, or at the least a bad storm. You might be stuck here in Biloxi."

Jeannie turned her attention to the weatherman's forecast. "Or it could die out before it gets here, or move north or farther south and miss us completely."

"Nevertheless, you'll want to warn Manton to keep an eye on the weather," Julian said. "Is the storm shelter on the island in good repair?"

"Stop worrying. Everything on Le Bijou Bleu is in tip-top shape." Jeannie had been in the storm shelter only once, when she was ten and a tropical storm hit the Gulf Coast. She'd heard Julian talk about what devastation Hurricane Camille had caused back in 1969 and thanked God that Manton had survived in the storm shelter, located in the basement of the cottage.

"I don't like your being back here in Biloxi," Julian said. "It's too dangerous for you as long as Maynard Reeves walks around a free man."

"You musn't worry about me. You let Sam do that. I want you to concentrate on getting well."

"I know about Reeves's visit." Julian glanced from Jeannie to Sam. "Don't go looking for someone to blame. I overheard a conversation about the reverend passing himself off as a priest."

"I didn't want you to know," Jeannie said. "At least not until after you were fully recovered."

"I don't remember seeing him," Julian said. "I have no idea what his reason for coming to the hospital might have been."

"You were his only connection to me." Jeannie walked over

and sat down in a chair beside Julian's bed. "Perhaps he thought he could threaten you into revealing where Sam had taken me."

"I can't believe the police haven't come up with something that can put that man away." Lifting himself into a sitting position, Julian clutched the bed's rails. His cheeks flushed. Beads of sweat broke out on his face. "There has to be something they can do!"

"Julian, please don't upset yourself." Jeannie grabbed his hand, instantly feeling the surge of anger shooting through him, the rise in his blood pressure, his accelerated heartbeat.

"I'll be…all…right. Don't…don't…" Julian gripped her hand when the first sharp pain struck him.

Clasping his hand tightly, Jeannie cried out as the pain entered her. She trembled from the force of his suffering.

Sam flew across the room, halting behind Jeannie's chair as he placed his big hands over her shoulders, cupping her upper arms. What the hell had happened? "Jeannie?" She didn't respond. "Dammit, don't do this. You're too weak."

Shivering, she closed her eyes and absorbed all Julian's pain, stopping the onset of another heart attack. His anger and fear trickled into her mind, leaving him at peace. Jeannie cried out; tears streamed down her face. Sam ripped Julian's hand out of Jeannie's, jerked her chair around and fell to his knees in front of her.

The anguish on her face told him all he needed to know. She was hurting, hurting badly, and all he could do was watch her suffer. If only he could give her some of his strength. If only he could absorb her pain, the way she had absorbed Julian's. He took her hands in his. She felt ice-cold. Rubbing her hands, he concentrated on mentally connecting with her. Just as he sensed the link beginning to form, a nurse rushed into Julian's room, quickly followed by an entourage prepared to administer lifesaving techniques. The moment the nurse shouted orders for Sam to move, the fragile link to Jeannie's mind shattered.

Sam pulled Jeannie up into his arms and kicked the chair aside. She lay there like a rag doll; Sam realized that she had fainted. The group of technicians hovered around Julian's bed.

"I don't understand," the nurse said. "His heart monitor showed signs of another attack."

"Machines make mistakes." Sam glanced at the nurse with cold gray eyes.

"Damnedest thing I've ever seen," a male nurse said. "Dr. Howell is fine. He's sleeping peaceful. All his vital signs are normal."

"Arrange for a private-duty nurse for Dr. Howell," Sam said. "I'm taking Ms. Alverson home. You have the number of Dr. Howell's rental house, don't you? If his condition changes, contact me."

SAM UNDRESSED JEANNIE and laid her, naked and exhausted, in the bed. She had regained consciousness briefly on the drive to the cottage, but once Sam assured her that Julian was fine, she'd drifted off to sleep, unable to fight the total depletion of her strength.

Both beds in the two-bedroom cottage were doubles, neither really long enough or large enough to accommodate Sam's height and size. He'd chosen the room on the back of the house, the quieter, more secluded one, the one that would be sheltered from the morning sun. He didn't want anything disturbing Jeannie's rest.

He'd found some expensive brandy in the kitchen, obviously belonging to Julian. Sam poured himself a shot, downed it in one swallow, then put the liquor away. He didn't want anything dulling his senses, putting him at any disadvantage if he had to confront Reeves. After making a ham sandwich, he devoured it quickly and returned to the bedroom. Jeannie had thrown off the covers and lay in the middle of the bed, her small, sleek, naked body tossing back and forth.

She moaned as she squirmed about in the bed. "Sam... Sam..."

Leaning over the bed, he brushed the hair out of her face, then kissed her forehead. "I'm here, angel. I'm here."

Sighing, she turned toward him, cuddling into a ball. Sam placed his Ruger on the bedside table, then removed his clothes. His body throbbed with desire. Straightening the covers, he folded them at the foot of the bed, lay down beside Jeannie and drew her into his arms.

He didn't fall asleep until nearly dawn, awakening only when the phone rang at ten-fifteen. Jeannie moaned and cuddled closer to his back, but didn't awaken. When he reached for the telephone, his hand grasped his Ruger. He shoved it aside and picked up the receiver.

"Dundee here."

"Mr. Dundee, this is Marta McCorkle. I'm at the hospital with Julian. He's fine, but he's concerned about Jeannie."

Sam glanced at the sleeping beauty curled against him. "She's all right, but still sleeping."

"Would it be all right if I stop by to see her after I leave the hospital?" Marta asked. "I know she'll be eager for an update on Julian, and a report on the Howell School children."

"If she's awake, you can see her," Sam said. "I won't wake her. She needs her rest."

"Of course. I'll stop by sometime after noon. When she wakes, give her Julian's love. And mine."

"I'll do that." Sam hung up the phone.

Sam's stomach growled. He was hungry as a bear. He'd eaten twice in the past forty-eight hours. Easing away from Jeannie so that he wouldn't disturb her, he got out of bed, pulled the cover up to her shoulders, and picked up his wrinkled slacks. Dressing hurriedly, he went into the kitchen. Within minutes he'd set the coffee machine, put bacon on to fry and cracked six eggs into a skillet.

Jeannie found him cooking breakfast in his bare feet,

wearing rumpled trousers and an unbuttoned shirt that hung open, showing the center of his broad, hairy chest.

"Are you fixing enough for two?" she asked from where she stood in the doorway.

He continued scrambling the eggs. "How long have you been standing there?" he asked, knowing precisely the moment she'd walked out of the bedroom three minutes ago.

Jeannie tightened the belt on her silk robe. "I can't imagine a more charming sight than a man busy at his domestic duties."

Sam guffawed as a wide grin spread across his face. He glanced up from his cooking, and his heart stopped for one breath-robbing moment. Jeannie stood in the doorway, her long hair falling down her back and over her left shoulder. Leaning on her cane, she put one foot in front of the other, exposing her right thigh between the open folds of her robe. Her round, full breasts pressed against the silk material, her nipples plainly outlined.

His body tightened. His heartbeat drummed in his ears. He wanted to forget breakfast, forget everything, and take Jeannie back to bed and make slow, sweet love to her all day.

"Come on in and take a seat," he said, trying to control his baser instincts. "I think I can spare a few bites for you."

She walked toward him, her gaze moving from his face over every inch of his body, returning to the bulge in his pants. "Breakfast could wait, couldn't it?" She stopped a foot away from him and smiled. "I woke up hungry." She laid her hand on his chest, then smoothed her way downward. "But not for food."

Drawing in a deep breath, Sam grabbed her hand a second before she reached her destination. "I'd like nothing better than to feed that hunger." He slid his arm around her, pulling her up against him as he lifted her hand to his lips. "But for now, you'll have to settle for scrambled eggs and bacon. Marta's on her way over here. If we hurry, we might be able to finish breakfast and catch a quick shower before she gets here."

"We could skip breakfast and go straight to the shower." Spreading apart his unbuttoned shirt, Jeannie smeared a row of tongue-moist kisses across his chest.

He cupped her buttocks, lifting her up and into his arousal. "Angel, you're being a very bad girl this morning."

"I like being bad with you, Sam."

"After you eat a good breakfast, take a shower and visit with Marta, I'll let you be as bad as you want to be." Releasing her, he grunted, then breathed deeply and gave her a gentle shove backward, keeping his hands on her arms to make sure she didn't lose her balance.

"Promise?" she asked. "I'm fine, you know. If you're worried that I'm not recovered from—"

"Stop talking, Jeannie," he said. "I'm having a hard enough time keeping myself from laying you down on the kitchen table and taking you right here and now, without your trying to persuade me to make love to you."

"I like knowing how much you want me. I like it even better when you tell me."

"Yeah, well…" Sam seated her at the table, then turned back to the stove, dished up the scrambled eggs and added three strips of bacon to Jeannie's plate. "Eat up." He placed the food on the table. "I'll get you some coffee."

They ate in silence, occasionally glancing at each other. Jeannie smiled; Sam frowned. She took her shower first, while he cleaned up the kitchen. He showered while she called Julian.

Marta arrived at one o'clock on the dot, hugging Jeannie profusely, assuring her that Julian looked the picture of health. While Marta visited, Sam took the opportunity to survey the cottage and the surrounding yard.

"Everyone at the school misses you terribly," Marta said. "The children ask about you continuously. They really didn't understand exactly how you were helping them, but they're well aware that things have changed since you've been gone."

"As soon as this problem with Maynard Reeves is solved, I'll return to work. I miss the children. I miss all of you."

"Will he be staying?" Marta nodded toward the yard, where they could see Sam surveying his surroundings.

"You mean, will he stay after I'm no longer in danger, when I don't need a bodyguard?"

"Yes. Will he?"

"I don't know."

"You're in love with him, aren't you?"

Jeannie lowered her head, avoiding Marta's direct stare. "Am I that obvious?"

"Only to those who know you well and love you dearly." Marta rose, walked across the living room and sat down on the sofa beside Jeannie. "Somehow I never pictured you with a man like Sam Dundee. He's too...too—"

"Too much a man."

"Well, yes." Cool, calm, controlled Marta blushed. "He's quite sophisticated, and very elegant, but... Oh, my dear, he's so big and brutal-looking, despite being so handsome. And what he does for a living! A bodyguard. You must know that there's every likelihood he's killed someone at some point in his life."

"Yes, you're probably right." Jeannie covered Marta's hand with her own. "But what you don't understand is that Sam needs me and I have so much to give him. And his strengths are my weaknesses and my strengths are his weaknesses."

"You must be careful not to let him break your heart." Squeezing Jeannie's hand, Marta forced a weak smile.

"Julian's worried, isn't he?" Jeannie sensed the truth as Marta clung to her hand. "I think Julian saw me married to a doctor or a lawyer. Someone local, the son of one of his friends or associates. Perhaps a member of the Fleur-de-lis Society."

"Julian loves you as dearly as if you were his own flesh and blood." Releasing Jeannie's hand, Marta stood and looked down at the floor. "Julian believes you and Mr. Dundee are lovers."

"I'll talk to Julian," Jeannie said. "Sam is taking me to visit him after dinner this evening. I'll make Julian understand how much I love Sam."

"He wants only your happiness."

"Sam makes me happy."

"Has he mentioned marriage?" Marta looked at Jeannie.

"No."

"I see."

"Come back and sit down." Jeannie patted the sofa cushion beside her. "I want to hear about every Howell School child. Give me details on progress and setbacks. How is Cassie Mills? And little Justin Walker? And Missy Suddath? Her mother hasn't taken her out of school, has she?"

"That crazy woman!" Marta sat down beside Jeannie. "She comes inside the school every day when she brings Missy, and looks around to make sure you aren't there. We've told her that you are no longer working at the school."

"I want you to continue allowing her some leeway," Jeannie said. "I know Danette has joined the Righteous Light Church and thinks I'm a witch, but I don't want Missy to suffer for her mother's ignorance."

"I've told the staff how you feel and given them instructions to make allowances for Danette Suddath's odd behavior, but I'm telling you, the woman is unbalanced."

"I wish I could help Danette, but she would never allow me near her. The most we can do is take care of Missy."

The front door opened, and Sam Dundee stepped into the living room. Jeannie and Marta looked up at him, Jeannie smiling as Marta patted her on the knee.

"There's a beautiful little secluded garden at the back of the house," Sam said. "How would you like to have supper out there?"

"My son's ex-wife loved the garden," Marta said. "I think it was the main reason they bought this house."

"Well, it's something to see." Sam sat down in the Chippendale armchair to the right of the sofa. "I can see where a woman might find it a selling point when buying a house."

"I think supper in the garden is a lovely idea." Jeannie hoped Marta saw the significance in Sam's suggestion of a romantic supper in a secluded garden. She wanted Julian and Marta to understand why she loved Sam, why she was happy to be carrying his child.

"Well, I need to stop by school and check on things." Marta hugged Jeannie, then stood. "I've neglected my job the last few days."

Standing, Sam walked Marta to the door. She turned to him when he stepped outside with her.

"I'll see y'all at the hospital later this evening," Marta said, and walked down the stone sidewalk. She stopped abruptly, turned around and looked Sam in the eye. "She's in love with you, you know. Please, don't hurt her." Marta rushed to her car, got inside and backed into the street.

Sam watched her drive away, his back to the porch. He heard Jeannie as she approached him, her cane tapping on the wooden porch and steps.

"You musn't let what she said bother you." Jeannie laid her hand on Sam's back.

"How can I not worry?"

"No matter what happens, you'll never hurt me."

He turned, looked at her and closed his eyes, the pain inside him shattering in its intensity. How could she trust him so completely, love him so unselfishly, when he'd made no lasting commitment to her? How could he tell her he loved her, when he wasn't sure he was capable of truly loving a woman the way Jeannie deserved to be loved?

"Show me the garden in the backyard." Bracing herself with her cane, she held out her other hand, inviting his touch.

If he touched her, she'd know exactly how he felt. She'd sense his confusion and uncertainty. And she would feel the desperate need burning inside him.

He took her hand in his and led her around the house to the backyard. All the while they walked—slowly, to accommodate her hampered gait—he allowed her to understand how he felt.

She realized he was unaware of how far he'd come in trusting his innermost thoughts and emotions to her. He'd gone from fighting the tiniest link to full acceptance of their joining. As always, she sensed his protectiveness and his possessiveness. A raging hunger. An overwhelming sexual desire. A deep, unrestrained need. And a sweet, tender caring. Gratitude. Unworthiness. Uncertainty. And fear. She picked up on every delicate nuance of his emotions. But she could not connect to the depths of his heart, to that place where the truth of his feelings lay buried so completely that it was a secret, even to Sam.

The garden wrapped around the back of the cottage like an emerald shawl of dense foliage and lush shade. Opening the wrought-iron gate, they entered beneath a clematis-covered arch and walked down a stone pathway leading to a fully enclosed piece of paradise. A concrete table and benches had been placed in the corner of a climbing-rosebush arbor.

"This *is* beautiful," Jeannie said.

"You're beautiful." Sam slipped his arm around her waist, urging her to turn.

She went into his arms, knowing what he wanted, admitting to herself that she wanted the same. He wrapped her in his embrace; she snuggled close, loving the feel of his powerful arms holding her.

"Jeannie?"

Make love to me, Sam. Here. Now. In the privacy of our little garden.

He heard her as clearly as if she'd spoken the words aloud.

And the moment he took her lips in an all-consuming kiss of possession, he felt the wild, uncontrollable need within him come alive within Jeannie, too.

Slow and easy, he told himself. Don't frighten her. Don't hurt her.

"It's all right," she said, reaching out to slide first one side of his jacket and then the other off his shoulders.

He let the expensive silk jacket fall to the ground, to rest atop a tiny sculptured shrub. He grabbed her by the waist to support her. She dropped her cane on the stone path. Restraining himself, just barely controlling his need to take her like the savage he was, Sam allowed her to undress him. She whipped off his tie and flung it into the air. Unbuttoning his shirt seemed to take forever. She threw it down beside his jacket, then unbuckled his belt.

Sam sucked in a deep breath. His arousal throbbed painfully. Every muscle in his body strained; every nerve screamed.

"Oh, Sam…" Swaying from the force of the sensations she received from his body, she grabbed his forearms.

"You're in charge, angel. We'll do this your way, but I don't think you'll last much longer."

Gulping air, she smiled at him. Perspiration coated her flushed face. She unzipped his slacks and pulled them down his hips. When they hit the ground, Sam kicked them aside. She tugged on his briefs. Taking one hand from her waist, he assisted her in removing the last strip of his clothing.

He stood there, his big body hard, his sex pulsating with life. He felt her longing, knew she was unraveling by slow degrees, just as he was. The passion grew stronger and stronger, becoming raw and uncivilized as it developed.

"Please, Sam," she said aloud.

He pulled her green cotton sweater over her head, loosening her hair. Sliding the pins from her hair, he let it fall free. With shaky fingers, he unlatched the hook on her bra, removed the silken garment and cupped her naked breasts in his hands.

She shivered from head to toe. If he didn't take her soon, she was going to explode. Her sex throbbed painfully. She needed release, needed Sam inside her, giving her all of himself.

"Soon, sweet angel." He kissed each nipple in turn, feeling the spiraling tension in her breasts as it gripped her femininity. She was on fire; he was on fire. Together they would burn themselves out, dissolving into ashes of completion.

Unzipping her slacks, he watched her face. He wanted to kiss her. She was alive in every fiber of her body, on fire with a heat that seared him as completely as it did her. Holding her by the hips, he knelt and slid her green-and-white-striped slacks and beige silk panties down her legs.

He kissed her stomach, burying his face in her warm, soft flesh. He felt her closing off, shutting him out of her thoughts. Why had she done that? he wondered.

She had to keep her secret. Sam's child was nestled there inside her, in her womb, safe and secure. But now was not the time to share her happy news with him. There would be time enough when Maynard Reeves was no longer a part of their lives.

She pushed the thoughts of their child deep into her heart, closing them off from her conscious thoughts. Threading her fingers through Sam's hair, she moaned as he delved his fingers deeply into her body.

She gripped his shoulders, urging him to stand. He kissed her intimately. She shuddered. Sam rose, lifted her off her feet and carried her into the rose arbor. A lush bed of grass and moss beckoned him. Placing her on the ground, he lay down beside her and pulled her on top of him. She stared down into searing blue-gray eyes and had no doubt what joy awaited the two of them. Holding her hips, petting her buttocks with his fingertips, Sam eased her down onto him, entering her with a forceful thrust.

Jeannie cried out with the pleasure of their joining, lowering her head to reach his lips. She plunged her tongue into his mouth; he reciprocated with equal fervor. They devoured each other as he stroked her back and buttocks. Placing her hands on either side of his head, she pushed herself upward until her breasts hung over his mouth, a luscious temptation.

She set the pace, moving with restless need, her own desire so strong she didn't know whether she could handle his, as well as hers. When he took her nipple into his mouth, sucking greedily, the first warning of release clenched her sex. While his mouth toyed with one breast, he lifted his hand to cup the other, then pinched the nipple between his thumb and forefinger. Fulfillment claimed her, rocking her to the core. Sam caught her cries in his mouth as her release rippled through him.

He changed the pace of their lovemaking, increasing the tempo, deepening his thrusts. He was on the verge, and so was she. Together they splintered into shards of unequaled ecstasy, Jeannie sharing his pleasure as he shared hers. Panting heavily, their bodies dripping with perspiration, Sam rolled over onto his side, holding her in his arms, kissing her again and again.

"I love you, Sam. I love you with all my heart."

"Ah, Jeannie…Jeannie…my sweet angel."

CHAPTER FIFTEEN

SAM MOANED WITH pleasure. Jeannie smiled at him as she slowly pulled the fork out of his mouth. He chewed the scrumptious bite of blueberry pancake dripping in syrup that she had fed him. They gazed into each other's eyes, silently conveying words of erotic intent as they remembered their night of passionate loving.

Looking at him sitting there in nothing but his slacks, his broad chest bare, Jeannie sighed as her body recalled Sam Dundee's savage possession.

He grinned, enjoying the sight of her, her flawless skin, soft peach lips and warm brown eyes. Tendrils of sun-streaked brown hair curled about her forehead and ears. His body hardened when he thought about her being naked beneath her robe.

Turning his fork sideways, Sam sliced off a piece of his pancake, speared it and lifted it toward Jeannie's mouth. With her gaze focused on Sam, she parted her lips. He slid the morsel into her mouth, watching while she chewed. Laying his fork on his plate, Sam reached across the table and, using the tip of his finger, wiped a trickle of syrup from the corner of Jeannie's mouth. Inclining her head, she captured Sam's finger between her lips and licked off the syrup.

Groaning deep in his throat, he jerked his finger out of her mouth. He knocked over his chair as he stood quickly, then rounded the table and lifted a laughing Jeannie out of her chair. Shoving her breakfast plate, cup and silverware across the table with the back of his hand, he set her on the edge of the table, opened her silk robe and parted her thighs. In one swift motion, he unzipped his slacks and discarded them.

She gripped his shoulders. He took her mouth at the exact same moment he lifted her hips and plunged into her. The joining was instant, jolting both of them with its power. As their bodies united, their hearts and minds entwined, each experiencing the pure ecstasy of their combined loving.

When they reached fever pitch, Sam groaned hot, shameless words to her, and she responded by abandoning herself to the sheer, pulse-pounding glory of their simultaneous twofold release.

She clung to him in the aftermath, kissing his shoulder as he lifted her and carried her to the bathroom. He drew her a bubble bath and slid her into the tub, then tossed her a washcloth.

"I'll clean up in the kitchen while you take your bath." He kissed her on the tip of her nose.

The telephone rang. Jeannie tensed. Sam winked at her, the action meant to reassure her that all was well. He closed the door behind him, leaving her alone.

She eased back, resting her head against the tiled wall. They'd been back in Biloxi five days. Julian was definitely on the road to recovery and would probably be coming home in a couple of days. Despite the possibility of a storm brewing in the Atlantic, heading toward the Caribbean, she hadn't given up her hope that Sam and she could take Julian back to Le Bijou Bleu to fully recuperate.

But she couldn't hide away on the island forever, and Sam had a life in Atlanta. Sooner or later, he would have to leave.

Although no doctor had confirmed her pregnancy and she hadn't bothered with a home test kit, Jeannie knew she was carrying Sam's child. She had been able to link with the baby and experience the first stages of her daughter's existence. She was almost four weeks pregnant now, and she still hadn't told Sam. How could she add to his burden of worry? He would want this child, and he would be even more protective and possessive if he knew. Until the situation with Maynard Reeves was settled, she would wait, keeping her precious secret in the deepest, most private part of her heart.

Sam opened the door, walked in and handed her the portable phone. "It's Marta. She sounds a little odd, but she says everything's all right. She needs to talk to you about one of the students."

Jeannie took the phone in her hand, then waved goodbye to Sam as he went back into the bedroom. "Hello, Marta."

"Jeannie, please don't let Mr. Dundee know what I'm saying to you."

"All right." Jeannie sensed Marta's fear. "Why don't you tell me what's wrong?"

"When Danette Suddath brought Missy to school this morning, two other women came with her." Marta swallowed. "We allowed her free access, just as you'd instructed."

"Are you alone in your office?" Jeannie asked, realizing that something was terribly wrong.

"Yes. They've allowed me to come in here alone. But Jeannie... Oh, dear God, they have guns! They're holding the children hostage."

Jeannie heard Marta sobbing. "What do you mean, they're holding the children hostage?"

"During our before-school free time in the cafeteria, Danette Suddath and these two other women pulled their guns, each one grabbed a child, and they're holding the whole school hostage."

"What do they want?" Jeannie asked, but she knew. She glanced at the partially open door, wondering if Sam had gone back into the kitchen.

"They want you, Jeannie," Marta said. "They're all members of the Righteous Light Church. Danette told me that—that they won't hurt any of the children, if you'll come down to the school."

"Call the police, Marta. Tell them what's happened. Sam and I will be there as soon as possible."

"No! I can't call the police, and Sam Dundee must not come here. They said if I called the police or if Mr. Dundee comes with you, they'll start sacrificing the children. That's the exact word Danette used. *Sacrificing.*"

"They want me to come alone?" Jeannie's mind splintered into a dozen different thoughts, the prime one being the question of how she would ever escape from Sam.

"I don't know what to do, Jeannie. If you come down here, they'll turn you over to Maynard Reeves." Marta's voice quavered more with each word she spoke. "I think they're expecting him to come here and get you."

"I understand. I'll find a way to get there. Alone. We can't allow any harm to come to those precious children in our charge."

"There must be some other way," Marta said. "If only—"

"Everything will be all right," Jeannie said. "I'll do what I have to do."

Jeannie punched the Off button and laid the telephone down on the bath mat beside the tub. Closing her eyes, she said a quiet prayer, allowing her mind to relax and her nerves to calm. She would have to lie to Sam, and she would have to trick him. She hated doing it, but she had no choice. The lives of forty-five children were at stake. Innocent, helpless children with physical and mental limitations that made them even more special to Jeannie. She knew so well the pain these children endured, especially their emotional suffering.

"Sam! Sam, I'm ready to get out of the tub now."

Within a minute, Sam was at her side, lifting her out of the tub and drying her with a large, fluffy towel. She wrapped her arm around his neck.

"Why don't you go ahead and enjoy my bubble bath? It's still warm," she said.

"I haven't finished up in the kitchen." He carried her into the bedroom and placed her on the edge of the bed.

"After I get dressed, I'll take care of that." She pulled him down toward her, rubbing her cheek against his. "Go on. You need a bath. You smell like…well, you smell."

Sam laughed. "I smell like you and me. I smell like sex."

"Yes, you do. You smell like sex."

"Need any help getting dressed?" he asked.

"You're better at helping me undress." She shoved him away from her. "Now go get your bath. I can dress myself and finish cleaning up the kitchen without your help."

"Your wish is my command." He stripped out of his slacks, which he'd put on again when he returned to the kitchen.

Jeannie watched while he walked to the bathroom. He stopped in the doorway, turned and smiled at her. When he closed the door, she lifted her cane from its resting place against the nightstand and hurried to the closet. She dressed as quickly as she could, dug the keys to her Lexus from her purse and walked out of the bedroom.

Easing the front door closed, she breathed a sigh of relief when it made only a faint clicking sound. She slid behind the wheel, started the engine and backed out of the driveway, holding her breath all the while.

"Please, forgive me, Sam. I have no other choice." She whispered the words aloud, knowing that Sam had already sensed that something wasn't quite right.

When she pulled out into the street, she glanced in her rearview mirror. Sam Dundee ran into the yard, a towel draped around his hips. He screamed her name.

Tears blurred Jeannie's vision as she pressed the accelerator. The Lexus flew down the street and out of Sam's sight.

CHILDREN'S WHIMPERS AND muted cries drifted down the hallway. Jeannie gripped her cane as she walked along the empty corridor. She hesitated at the closed cafeteria doors, uncertain what she would find once she entered, but knowing she was willing to make whatever sacrifice was necessary to save the children.

She flung open the double doors and stepped inside, halting immediately. The children had been divided into three groups. The groups huddled on the floor in three corners of the cafeteria, each group guarded by a woman with a gun. Danette Suddath held her own daughter in front of her as a shield as she brandished a semiautomatic weapon.

"Hi, Jeannie." Missy Suddath smiled, her round face wrinkling in pleasure lines when she saw Jeannie. "My mama's playing a game with us. It's like cops and robbers. Did you come to play with us?"

"Yes, Missy, I came to play with you." Jeannie clenched her teeth, willing herself to stay calm and unemotional for the sake of the children.

"Come on in, Jeannie Alverson!" Danette shouted. "Your days of evil are about to end."

"Suffer not a witch to live!" A plump middle-aged woman with long, straight salt-and-pepper hair tightened her hold on little seven-year-old Amelia Carson, who'd been born marginally retarded. Clasping a small-caliber gun in her hand, she laid it across Amelia's chest.

"I've followed your instructions," Jeannie said. "I've come alone, without the police or Sam Dundee. You have what you want. Please release the children."

"Such concern for these little ones." The baritone voice came from a tall, slender woman who held the third group of children in the far right corner. She lifted six-year-old Justin Walker, blind since birth, up on her hip. Justin screamed. The woman placed her hand, which held a gun, over the little boy's mouth.

Jeannie sucked in a deep breath. "Please, put him down. You're frightening him."

"Hush now, child," the tall woman, who was wearing a

frumpy floral-print dress, said. "If Jeannie loves you, really loves you, none of you will need to be sacrificed."

Jeannie couldn't bear the thought of a child being harmed because of her. How could these women threaten the children, when they claimed to be believers in a religion of love and compassion?

"I'll leave with you," Jeannie said. "I'll go with you to Maynard Reeves without protest."

All the teachers had been lined up against the wall on the far side of the cafeteria. Jeannie looked at them, one at a time, hoping to convey hope and love. Marta McCorkle was conspicuously absent.

"Where's Marta?" Jeannie asked.

"Ms. McCorkle is in her office," Danette Suddath said. "She's there to answer the phone and make sure the outside world thinks everything is normal here at the Howell School."

Jeannie sighed with relief. For one split second, she had feared for Marta's life. "My car is outside. The keys are in the ignition. We can walk out of here, and you can take me to Reverend Reeves. Right now."

"We won't need your car," Danette said, forcing her daughter to walk around her classmates sitting on the floor. "Our plans are already made."

"All right." Jeannie walked into the room, slowly moving toward Danette. "I'm prepared to go with you, on your terms."

Missy Suddath took a step toward Jeannie. "Are you a bad guy?" the child asked. "They're calling you ugly names. I don't like you playing bad, Jeannie."

"I'm not really bad. Remember, this is just a game." Jeannie reached out her hand to Missy.

"No! Don't touch her!" Danette jerked her daughter close to her side, the gun she held resting over the child's body. "I won't have you contaminate her with your evil."

"Danette, surely you know I'd never do anything to harm

Missy," Jeannie said. "She's been attending the Howell School for four years, and she's made excellent progress. All of us here love her."

"Enough talk." The tall, deep-voiced woman marched around her charges. Justin shivered in the big woman's arms, tears streaming down his face as he sobbed.

"Justin, don't be afraid," Jeannie said. "I'm here in the room with you."

"I don't like this game," Justin said, choking back his tears. "I don't wanna play anymore."

The woman holding Amelia walked toward Jeannie. "The game will end soon," she said. "As long as Jeannie does exactly as she's told."

"What do you want me to do?" Jeannie asked.

"You'll come with us. My friends and I will walk out of the school to the parking area, where our cars are waiting." The woman in the floral-print dress secured her hold on Justin and lifted her gun to the child's head.

Jeannie was thankful Justin couldn't see, that he really didn't understand what was happening. "Yes, I'll come with you. Just put Justin down, and don't harm any of the children."

The tall woman grinned. Jeannie gasped, suddenly realizing that the person holding Justin was a man disguised as a woman. Maynard Reeves!

His grin widened when he looked directly into Jeannie's eyes. She knew he was aware that she'd recognized him.

"Danette will take her daughter with her," Reeves said. "I'll take Justin. Nora will take the little girl with the blond pigtails. And we'll need five or six more children as escorts. All of us will walk out of here together."

"There's no need to take the children. You don'

"You'll let the children go as soon as we get outside?"

"All except Missy and Justin," Reeves said. "They'll go with us. Once I make sure we haven't been followed, I'll release Justin, somewhere you can be certain he'll be safe."

"Don't do this. Please. No one has called the police, and Sam Dundee has no idea where I am."

"I tend to believe you. However, I'm not a person who takes chances." Reeves waved his gun in the air, then pointed it to the door leading to the hallway. "Shall we go?"

Jeannie watched, feeling totally helpless, as Danette and the plump middle-aged woman gathered up six children, instructing them to form a single line beside Reeves. Confused and crying, the children ran to Jeannie, completely ignoring Danette's directions. Kneeling, Jeannie touched each child, placing them in a circle around her. They reached out, laying their hands on her. She absorbed their fear and frustration, and within minutes all six children had quieted.

"Look at the witch's power!" Reeves bellowed, storming across the few feet that separated him from Jeannie. "She controls the minds of the innocent!"

He set Justin on his feet, then pulled the six children away from Jeannie. She reached for her cane, grabbing it up off the floor just as Reeves dragged her to her feet.

Turning to his two faithful helpers, Reeves motioned them toward him. "She controls these children." He pointed at the four boys and two girls Jeannie had soothed with her touch. "They are useless to us. Take only the child you have with you, and go to your car. Wait for me outside." He looked at Justin, who had found his way to Jeannie and was holding on to her leg. "Take his hand, and bring him with you. And don't try any of your witchcraft on him. If you do, I'll have to destroy him when I destroy you."

"Please, don't—"

"Take his hand! Now!" Reeves screamed.

Jeannie lifted Justin's hand, grasping it firmly, then looked to Reeves for instructions.

Reeves placed his arm around her shoulders. "We'll walk into the hallway and through the school to the back door."

Jeannie nodded her agreement. Danette and her cohort left the room, taking Missy and Amelia Carson with them. Reeves stuck his gun in Jeannie's ribs, motioning her forward. With each step she took, Jeannie prayed. The moment she exited the cafeteria and entered the corridor, she felt Sam Dundee's presence. Dear God, how had he found her? And what was he going to do? Had he called Marta? Had she been unable to hide the truth from him?

Danette and the other woman left the building, Missy and Amelia with them. Halting abruptly halfway down the long central hallway, Reeves squeezed Jeannie's shoulder.

"Wait," he said.

Her breathing quickened. She clasped Justin's hand tightly. Whatever happened, she'd need to move at a moment's notice. If ever she had wished she could run, it was now.

"You and Justin will walk out in front of me," Reeves told her. "Just remember that I'll be right behind you, with a gun aimed at the boy."

Jeannie nodded, swallowed hard, squeezed Justin's hand and walked them toward the back door.

Grab Justin. Drop to the floor and roll into the open class-room on your left. Now! She heard Sam's orders as clearly as if he'd spoken. Not hesitating, she obeyed, grabbing Justin around the waist and throwing them both onto the floor.

"What are you doing?" Reeves fired his gun, but a big hand knocked the weapon upward, and the bullet lodged in the ceiling.

"Don't move a muscle," Sam Dundee said.

With her arms wrapped around Justin, protecting him with her body, Jeannie rolled them directly across the hall. Curling her body into a fetal position as she rolled, she tumbled them through the open classroom door. She caught a glimpse of the female-disguised Reeves, Sam Dundee towering behind him, his Ruger pointed directly at the reverend's head.

With his free hand, Sam jerked Reeves's wig off his head. "Looks like you've been caught in the act."

"Let me go, Dundee, or two innocent children will have to be sacrificed."

"What the hell are you talking about?" Sam flung the wig to the floor, then thrust his big arm around Reeves's neck, bringing the man's back up against his chest.

"Ask your precious little witch," Reeves said. "She'll tell you. Two of my disciples have potential sacrifices with them, and if I give the order to destroy these children for the greater good of the Righteous Light Church, they'll shoot them."

"Sam?" Jeannie called out to him silently. "Danette Suddath has her daughter, Missy, but I'm not sure she wouldn't harm her. And the other woman has Amelia—"

"All right, Reeves, let's you and me go outside," Sam said. "If what you say is true, I'll exchange you for the children."

Reeves's maniacal laughter reverberated in the hushed stillness of the corridor. "You give me Jeannie, and I'll give you the children."

Sam didn't hesitate before giving his reply. "No deal."

"Jeannie, Dundee is willing to sacrifice the children to save you!" Reeves shouted. "Is that what you want?"

"Sam?" she said aloud.

"Stay where you are. Trust me to handle this," Sam said.

Reeves taunted her. "Jeannie, I won't hesitate to sacrifice the children."

She didn't reply. Sam gave Maynard Reeves a tight jerk, choking him momentarily, then loosed his hold and shoved him toward the back door.

than Jeannie's. You got that? You do whatever you have to do, but if you issue an order to kill those children, I won't have any qualms about blowing your head off."

"Jeannie? Answer me, you witch, you seed of the devil!"

Reeves struggled. Sam pressed his muscular arm into Reeve's windpipe, cutting off his oxygen. He ceased struggling and stood perfectly still.

Sam waited in the hallway for a moment, allowing Reeves to listen to the silence. "What's it going to be?" Sam asked. "Do you and two innocent children die, or do I exchange your life for theirs?"

"Let me go, and I'll send the children in when I reach my car."

"No deal." Sam rubbed the Ruger's barrel up and down the side of Reeves's sweaty face.

"State your terms."

"We'll walk outside. You'll tell your disciples to release the children. As soon as they're within touching distance of me, I'll release you."

"How do I know you'll keep your word?" Reeves asked.

"You don't. You'll just have to trust me, won't you?"

Sam walked Reeves out into the parking lot behind the school. Danette Suddath and an older woman sat inside a dark blue sedan, two children sandwiched between them in the front seat.

"Tell them to let the children out of the car," Sam said.

"Danette. Nora. Release the children."

Once Danette and Nora saw that their beloved reverend's life was in Sam's hands, they opened the car door and ushered the children out, telling them to go to the man with the gun. Missy clasped Amelia's hand, and the two girls walked toward Sam. The moment the girls came within his grasp, Sam shoved Reeves forward as hard as he could, then grabbed both girls up in his arms. Missy and Amelia clung to him.

Reeves ran toward his Lincoln Continental, parked beside

Danette's sedan. He started the engine, shifted the gears and roared out of the parking lot. Danette followed him quickly.

Police sirens screamed in the distance. Sam turned around and walked back toward the Howell School. Jeannie stood in the doorway, her eyes swimming with tears. Sam set the two little girls on their feet and pulled Jeannie into his arms. Within minutes the corridor had filled with children and teachers, all of them crying.

Marta rushed out of her office, dropped to her knees and embraced the children closest to her. "Thank God you didn't believe me, Mr. Dundee. I hope you understand why I couldn't risk telling you the truth when you called."

"You saved us all, Sam." Jeannie wrapped her arms around his neck. "I was so afraid, but I knew you wouldn't let anything happen to Missy or Amelia."

"Don't you ever do something like this again." He covered her mouth with his, claiming her, the kiss one of rejoicing and affirmation.

CHAPTER SIXTEEN

SAM HAD BEEN unsuccessful in persuading Jeannie to allow Marta and the teachers to care for the children. Her compassionate heart would not allow her a moment's concern for herself; her every thought was of the frightened, confused boys and girls who crowded around her, seeking comfort. And she gave them comfort, and so much more, in a way only Jeannie could. One by one, she hugged the children, absorbing their anxieties, freeing them from the trauma they had experienced.

With each child's unburdening, Jeannie grew weaker and weaker. Sam sat down beside her, wrapping his arms around her, wanting desperately to give her some of his strength. The moment Marta lifted the last child out of Jeannie's arms, Jeannie turned to Sam, her eyelids drooping and her lips parting on a sigh. She tried to lift her hand to caress his worry-lined face, but she didn't possess enough strength. When she dropped her hand to her side, Sam lifted it, brought it to his lips and kissed her open palm.

"Take care of me, now, Sam." She closed her eyes and fell immediately into a deep sleep.

With Jeannie in his arms, Sam stood and carried her out of the Howell School. Lieutenant Painter met them in the parking lot, halting Sam before he reached the Lexus.

"Is Ms. Alverson all right?"

"She will be after she gets some rest," Sam said.

"I'll need to speak with her as soon as she's able to answer a few questions."

"Give me a call this evening and I'll let you know."

"Tell her that we apprehended Danette Suddath and Nora Dill. And we've put out an all-points bulletin on Maynard Reeves. He finally made a big mistake. We can throw the book at the reverend. He must have lost his mind, taking a school full of disabled children hostage."

"Reeves is obsessed with destroying Jeannie. He's convinced himself and his followers that she really is a witch."

"Tell Ms. Alverson that we'll get Reeves. We've set up road-blocks and are doing an all-out search." Lieutenant Painter glanced down at Jeannie, lying in Sam's arms. "She's for real, isn't she? I mean she actually can take away other people's pain."

"Yeah," Sam said. "She's for real."

He walked away, carrying Jeannie to her car. He opened the door, reclined the seat and laid her down, then closed the door. He got inside, started the engine and drove out into the street. The noonday sun heated the road, creating a shimmering glare. Reaching inside his coat pocket, Sam pulled out his sunglasses and put them on.

She's for real, isn't she? He heard Lieutenant Painter's question echoing in his mind on the drive to Julian's rented cottage. Oh, yeah, Jeannie Alverson was most definitely for real. A real angel of mercy. A real empath who considered it her sacred duty to relieve the suffering of others. A real healer of the human heart.

When they reached the cottage, Sam carried her straight inside to bed. After undressing her, he sat down on the bed and scooted up to rest his back on the headboard, then closed his eyes.

Reeves was out there somewhere, a hunted animal. He would be even more dangerous than before. Now he had nothing to lose. Sam knew what he had to do if the law didn't apprehend Reeves soon.

Reeves had finally crossed the line from mental instability to insanity. Sam had seen it in his eyes. He'd seen that look before, in the eyes of other men, men who had completely lost their hold on reality.

Jeannie moaned in her sleep and turned over, her hands searching. Sam slumped down in the bed, took her in his arms and held her close. Cuddling against him, she returned to a restful sleep. Sam trembled as he held her, the reality of how close he'd come to losing her finally hitting him. He clung to her, stroking her back, dotting tiny kisses over her forehead and cheeks. An ache formed in the pit of his stomach and spread upward, lodging in his throat. Emotions so vast, so forceful that they threatened his sanity consumed him.

Guarding Jeannie was his first priority. Nothing was more important than keeping her safe. *Take care of me, now, Sam. Take care of me, now, Sam.* Her words replayed over and over in his mind. She had taken care of each one of the forty-five students at the Howell School, depleting her energy, putting her own physical and mental health in jeopardy. And then she had turned to him, trusting him completely, never doubting that she was safe in his hands.

He would take care of her, protect her at all costs, but the one thing from which he could not protect her was her own compassionate heart.

Laying her hand on his chest, she wrapped herself around his big body. Sam drew in a deep breath. How had this happened? How the hell had he allowed himself to become captured by a sweet innocent, by an angel whose tender mercy ruled her life? How could such purity be so sensual, such spirituality be so human, such etherealness be so totally erotic?

Six years ago, when he washed ashore on Le Bijou Bleu, Jeannie had done far more than save his life—she had taken possession of his soul. He had never been able to forget her. The sound of her voice. The feel of her comforting hands. The look in her gentle brown eyes.

He had tried to stop thinking about her, willed himself not to remember the powerful connection that existed between them, but deep inside he'd always known that he could not escape the inevitable. Even his niece Elizabeth, when he stayed with her to recuperate from the nearly fatal gunshot wounds, had sensed he was running away from more than his guilt and remorse over Brock's and Connie's deaths. And Elizabeth, who possessed strong psychic powers, had predicted that Sam would return to Biloxi, and to the woman who had saved his life.

He had not allowed Elizabeth to tell him any more of what she'd seen in his future. He hadn't wanted to know, and he still didn't want to know. He felt unworthy, undeserving of being loved by Jeannie. Didn't she know the kind of man he was, the type of life he'd lived? Of course she knew. She even knew he'd been responsible for the death of his unborn child. And yet she loved him.

JEANNIE SLEPT THE day away, waking with a ravenous appetite for both food and Sam. He made slow, tender love to her, and she blossomed under his loving care, seeming to gain strength from their physical joining. Later he prepared hearty salads, serving them with wine and bread. They ate in the garden again, isolated from the world, nestled in their own tiny piece of paradise. After dinner, she asked him about the morning's events, and he told her everything he knew.

"Don't ever run away by yourself again, the way you did this morning," he said. "I died a thousand deaths when I saw you drive off and knew I couldn't stop you."

"How did you figure out where I'd gone? And how did you know Reeves was at the school?"

"I knew something Marta had said must have triggered your actions." Tilting his head to one side, Sam rested his cheek against the top of her head. "When I phoned the school and spoke to Marta, I could tell something was wrong. She was acting strange. I put two and two together and figured Reeves was involved."

"I know it was foolish of me to go alone to the school."

She covered his hands, which lay across her stomach, with her own. Would Sam ever have forgiven her, or himself, if Reeves had killed her and, in doing so, destroyed their unborn child? "I couldn't let Maynard Reeves hurt the students. I did what I had to do. Please understand."

"I understand." He hugged her, encompassing her in his embrace, wishing he could absorb her into himself and keep her safe. "You don't have the capacity to put your needs before those of others. You give and give and give, no matter what the cost is to you."

"You would do the same." Tilting her face, she reached up and kissed him, wanting him to look inside himself and see the truth.

"Not me," he said. "I'm not as strong as you are, angel. I don't have your guts. Besides, the powers that be knew I was the last person on earth who should have the ability to heal the suffering of others. I don't even know how to love."

"That's where you're wrong. You have a great capacity to love. But before you can use that wellspring of goodness inside you, you must come to terms with all the negative feelings keeping that love trapped."

"Oh, Jeannie you don't know me."

"I know you better than you know yourself," she said. "I'm a part of your soul, as you are mine."

He had no response to her statement. Intense emotion gripped him, holding him captive. Jeannie saw the best in him, sensing a goodness he could not see. Dear God, was he worthy of the trust she placed in him? Could he be the man she thought he was, the man she expected him to be? Or would he let her down?

When Lieutenant Painter arrived at eight-thirty that night, he found Sam and Jeannie watching the weather channel on television. The depression that had begun near the Cape Verde Islands, off the coast of Africa, had moved into the Caribbean and was building up speed and intensity. A tropical storm with high winds and heavy rain was expected to hit the islands southeast of the Gulf by early morning.

"Come on in." Sam opened the door and led the lieutenant into the living room. "Jeannie's concerned about the tropical storm headed our way. She has a close friend living on one of the islands in the gulf."

"Yeah, I hear they think this thing has a good chance of turning into a full-fledged hurricane before she hits the coast." Painter nodded at Jeannie when she glanced up from the television and smiled at him.

"Give me just a moment, Lieutenant," Jeannie said. "I'd like to hear the rest of this report from the National Hurricane Center. I've already contacted my friend to make sure he's aware of the storm headed his way, but I want to stay updated on what's happening."

"Sure. I can wait," Painter said.

When the report ended several minutes later, Jeannie switched off the set and turned to the police officer. "Thank you for being so patient. Sam has told me that you arrested Danette Suddath and the other woman."

"Nora Dill. Yes, we arrested them. But members of the Righteous Light Church posted bond for them, and they're out on bail until their trials."

"Missy hasn't been given to her mother, has she?"

"No." Sam walked over and stood behind Jeannie's chair, placing his hand on her shoulder.

"Social services will place Missy in a foster home until after her mother's trial," Lieutenant Painter said. "And she'll remain in one if—or should I say when—Danette Suddath is found guilty and sent to prison."

"Y'all haven't found Maynard Reeves, have you?" Jeannie reached up, placing her hand atop Sam's on her shoulder.

"I swear, Ms. Alverson, it's as if the man vanished off the face of the earth." Shrugging, Lieutenant Painter shook his head. "The best we can figure it, he must have left Biloxi by boat. Since his church is headquartered in New Orleans, the authorities there have been alerted. The feds have pretty well taken over this case, but we're working with them."

"Too bad someone in his organization isn't willing to turn him in," Sam said. "It amazes me how gullible some people are."

"None of his followers will betray him." Jeannie patted Sam's hand. "People want to believe in something, in a higher power, and that's why they can sometimes be brainwashed by a charismatic leader like Reverend Reeves. He feeds on their fears and prejudices, teaching them hatred and intolerance."

"I want you to know, Ms. Alverson, that we've posted a man at the hospital to guard Dr. Howell, and one at the school to make sure the children are safe. And even though you're well taken care of—" Rufus Painter glanced at Sam "—we're sending a patrol around the block here every hour."

Jeannie clasped Lieutenant Painter's hand. "Thank you for all you've done."

Painter grinned; it was a lopsided, boyish grin. "Yes, ma'am. You're entirely welcome. Just wish we could have done more."

"I believe we have some business to take care of, don't we, Lieutenant?" Jeannie asked.

Flushing, Painter cleared his throat. "Yes, ma'am, we do. I've got someone outside ready to take your statement concerning the events at the Howell School this morning."

"Are you sure you're up to this?" Sam moved around to the side of her chair, placing his hand on her arm.

"Yes," she said. "I have to do all that I can to help remove Maynard Reeves from society, to put him away where he can't harm anyone."

After the police left, Jeannie tuned in the weather channel for an update on the tropical storm, then contacted Manton again before she and Sam went to bed.

As they lay together, the room dark and quiet except for the moonlight filtering through the curtains and the hum of traffic a few blocks away on the highway, Sam held Jeannie in his arms.

"Stop worrying," Sam said. "You told me Manton has weathered storms, and even a few hurricanes, on Le Bijou Bleu."

"I know. But I can't help worrying." Jeannie kissed Sam's naked shoulder. "He's assured me the storm shelter is stocked with the basic necessities to last several days."

"Manton will be all right. The man has a sixth sense about things. If the storm hits the island, he'll wait it out in the storm shelter."

"Sam?" She lifted her head off his shoulder and looked down into his blue-gray eyes.

"What is it, angel?" He rubbed his hand up and down her arm, from shoulder to wrist.

"I have an uneasy feeling I can't explain. I'm afraid, Sam. I'm so very, very afraid."

He enclosed her in the strength and safety of his arms, lowering her head to the pillow and kissing her eyelids closed. "Julian suffered a heart attack, the students and staff of the Howell School were held captive, a tropical storm is probably going to hit Le Bijou Bleu while Manton's there alone, and Maynard Reeves is out there somewhere plotting your destruction. I'd say something would be wrong with you if you weren't feeling uneasy and if you weren't scared half out of your mind."

"No, it's more than the obvious things."

With her eyes still closed, she snuggled against Sam, absorbing the warmth and force of his big, powerful body. She had noticed that for weeks now she had been able not only to connect with Sam's thoughts and feelings, but also, in a limited sense, to draw strength from him. She knew he was totally unaware when it happened, that he had no idea the link between them grew stronger, more intricate and complicated, with each contact. Mental. Physical. Emotional. Spiritual.

"Everything is going to be all right," Sam said. "Julian will be home in a few days. The children and teachers at the school are safe now. Manton and Le Bijou Bleu will weather the storm. The authorities will capture Maynard Reeves. And I'll take good care of you."

When his lips touched hers, she responded wholeheartedly. When his body covered hers, she arched upward, encouraging his possession. And when he thrust into her moist heat, she welcomed him, clasping him tightly. They mated in a fast, furious frenzy, sharing their pleasure, then fell into a deep, sated sleep.

Jeannie woke early. The morning sky was red, warning of bad weather. She got out of bed, slipped into her robe and set her cane on the floor.

"Come back to bed, angel. It's still early." Sam patted her pillow.

"I want to check the weather and contact Manton before the storm hits and blocks our communication."

"All right," Sam said. "You check the weather and get in touch with Manton, and I'll put on some coffee. Or would you rather have tea?"

"Coffee will be fine."

Sam slipped into a pair of trousers and headed for the bathroom.

A few minutes later, on his way to the kitchen, he paused in the doorway to the living room. The weather forecaster was predicting that hurricane-force winds would sweep the Gulf Coast by nightfall.

"Get in touch with Manton," Sam said. "Make sure he's all right, and that he's prepared to take shelter."

"I wish I could shake this uneasy feeling."

"You'll feel better after you've been in touch with Manton."

"I hope so."

Sam filled the coffee machine with bottled water, then

spooned the gourmet blend into the filter. His stomach growled, reminding him his dinner salad had been a light repast for a man of his size. Omelets, he thought, ham-and-cheese omelets.

He was turning an enormous omelet over in the skillet when Jeannie came into the kitchen. Smiling, he looked up from his chore. Pale-faced, wide-eyed, she walked over to him and gripped his arm. She swallowed, then bit down on her lower lip.

"What's wrong?" He turned off the stove and grabbed Jeannie's shoulders.

"I can't get a response from Manton. I've been trying for the last ten minutes."

"Maybe the storm has already hit Le Bijou Bleu."

"No, it's not possible. The storm couldn't possibly hit the island before late this afternoon." Tears gathered in her eyes. She squeezed his arm. "Something's wrong. Bad wrong. Manton would not have left the house this morning. He would have brought the dogs and cats inside last night."

"We'll keep trying to contact him."

"If I don't get a response soon, I'm going to the island."

"No, you're not." Sam jerked her into his arms; her cane hit the floor with a resounding thump. "There's a damn hurricane headed this way!"

"Something has happened to Manton. Don't you understand? I have to go to him."

"If anyone goes, I'll go," Sam said. "I'll have Lieutenant Painter send an officer over here to guard you until J.T. or Hawk can fly in from Atlanta. I'll go to Le Bijou Bleu and make sure Manton is all right."

"No. If he's hurt, he'll need me."

"Dammit, Jeannie, you are not going to Le Bijou Bleu, and that's all there is to it!"

Three hours later, Jeannie docked the cruiser, and Sam lifted her onto the pier. Dark storm clouds swirled overhead. An angry wind gusted around them, blowing windrows of sand along the beach. Faint, almost indiscernible raindrops fell from the sky.

Sam carried her up the steps to the top of the hill. The wind whistled through the trees, whipping the branches.

"Stop!" Jeannie raised her voice to fight the howl of the wind. "Manton won't answer me!"

"What?" Sam shouted, knowing damn well they couldn't stay out here in the violent wind much longer.

"I've called to him repeatedly since we docked, and he isn't responding."

Sam lowered his head, putting his mouth near her ear. "Hasn't there ever been a time when you couldn't connect telepathically with him?"

"Never. Not since the first time our minds linked, when I was nine years old." She clutched Sam's shoulder. "He's hurt. I know he's hurt. He'd have to be unconscious not to hear me, not to be able to answer."

"Calm down, angel. We'll find Manton and take care of him. Whatever's wrong, you'll fix it until we can get him back to Biloxi."

Sam rushed toward the house as heavy drops of rain began falling. They were both drenched by the time he stepped up on the veranda. The front door stood wide open. Sam carried Jeannie inside. An eerie quiet filled the rooms, though the fury of the rain and wind blasted the outside of the house, making the walls tremble.

Not one dog welcomed them; not one cat slinked about their legs. Where the hell was Manton? Sam wondered. What could have happened to him? Had he taken ill? Had there been an accident?

Sam set Jeannie down on the sofa in the living room. "I'll go get ... ... ch downstairs and I'll search upstairs. ...

Jeanni ...

return. He brought her cane and helped her to her feet, then cupped her face in his hands.

"Stay in touch with me, angel." He looked deep into her gentle brown eyes.

I love you, Sam Dundee.

Swallowing hard, he closed his eyes. *My sweet Jeannie.* He kissed her on the mouth, quickly, then turned around and walked up the front staircase. Jeannie began her search in the dining room, then moved into the kitchen.

Manton. Please answer me.

She checked the downstairs twice, thoroughly searching every nook and cranny. She spoke to Sam telepathically, letting him know that she hadn't found Manton. He told her that he'd found nothing upstairs. No sign of Manton or his animals.

Was it possible Manton had gone down into the basement? she wondered. Had he already moved into the storm shelter when something had happened to him? Or could he have gone outside, be somewhere out there now, injured and alone?

The old stables at the back of the house! The animals bedded there, and Manton carried food and fresh water out to them every day. Perhaps he'd accidentally fallen and hit his head last night or early this morning.

I'm going out to the old stables behind the house, Jeannie told Sam telepathically. *Meet me out there.*

Wait for me, he said.

Manton's in the stables, Sam. I know it. I can feel it.

He repeated his telepathic message. *Wait for me.*

Jeannie's need to find Manton urged her through the house and out onto the back veranda. A row of trees in the backyard arched over in the wind, many of their tops touching the ground. Bending in the wind, a young sapling groaned, then toppled over, its roots lifting and falling, finally tearing loose.

Jeannie fought the wind as she made her way off the veranda. The stable doors hung open, creaking as they slammed open and shut. With the wind stinging her eyes, Jeannie squinted and gripped her cane tightly. The black sky emptied heavy rain onto the earth, and the wind roared a warning. Instinctively Jeannie knew the tropical storm had graduated to a hurricane, and it was only a matter of time until its full force hit Le Bijou Bleu.

She made her way to the stables, slipping inside as one big door swung open. Darkness surrounded her. She felt Manton's presence. He was somewhere nearby, but he was still unconscious.

Suddenly cold, menacing evil surrounded her. For one brief second, she forgot to breathe. Her heart stood still. And in that moment she knew. *Sam!* her mind screamed. *Help me, Sam!*

"I've been waiting for you," the voice said.

Jeannie spun around. There in the doorway behind her, the faint light from outside casting shadows across his handsome freckled face, stood Maynard Reeves.

CHAPTER SEVENTEEN

"So NICE OF you to come out in this bad weather to meet me." Reeves took a step forward, his toothy, charismatic smile spreading across his face.

Jeannie stepped backward, away from the threatening presence. "I'm not alone. Manton's here, and so is Sam."

"I've already taken care of that stupid giant you call Manton."

"What have you done to him?"

"He's sleeping peacefully, him and his dogs. I used a tranquilizer gun to bring your Manton down. I shot him twice, so he'll sleep a long, long time."

Reeves moved toward her. A flash of lightning struck nearby. Jeannie gasped. Reeves laughed. Shards of light flashed through the open doors and the wide cracks in the rotting wooden walls of the old stables. A shiny 9 mm handgun glistened in Reeves's hand.

"Sam will come out here to find me." Jeannie felt something warm and soft curl around her leg. One of Manton's cats.

"Let him come on out. I want him to find us. The witch's guardian doesn't deserve to live. I'll destroy him first, before I punish you for your evil."

Reeves moved closer and closer. Jeannie backed farther and farther into the darkness, her escape hampered by her inability to maneuver without her cane.

Sam! Sam! Hurry. Please hurry. And be careful. Maynard Reeves has me trapped in the stables.

As she backed away from the approaching madman, Jeannie

lost her balance. The raging wind battered the old wooden stables. Lightning zigzagged from heaven to earth. Hard, heavy rain pelted the island. Jeannie fell, landing on her backside, her cane hitting the dirt floor, just out of arm's reach.

Reeves hovered, glaring down at her, his smile wide, showing all his teeth. His eyes glowed in the darkness. Jeannie scooted backward. Her heart hammered, rumbling in her ears like a hundred bass drums. The damp earth stuck to her palms as she used her hands to propel herself backward.

Reeves stomped one big foot down beside her hip. She clenched her teeth. He lowered the other foot, straddling her as he bent over, reached out and seized her. She sucked in air. He jerked her up off the floor. She hit him, her hands flailing against his chest. Reeves grabbed her by her hair, pulling her face against his, so close their noses touched. The more she struggled, the tighter he clasped her hair and the deeper his fingers bit into the gun he held pressed against her back.

Reeves licked her face, from chin to forehead. Jeannie closed her eyes, struggling to make contact with her attacker's inner thoughts and feelings. Anger! Hatred! Passion to possess her power! If only she could hook onto his emotions more firmly, she could begin drawing them from him.

"No!" Reeves screamed, shoving her away from him with such force that she fell backward onto the floor, her fragile body hitting the damp earth with a jarring thud. "You will not use your wicked talents to possess me, witch! I will destroy you, and then God will bless me with your powers."

From her position on the floor, all Jeannie could see was the trembling outline of Reeves's body. Even from several feet away, she could feel his rage. His murderous intent swirled around her, more powerful and far uglier than the raging storm assaulting the island.

The metallic taste of fear coated her tongue. A sour, salty bile rose in her throat.

Stay where you are, Jeannie. Don't move. Don't make a

sound. Act as if nothing has changed. Sam cautioned Jeannie telepathically as he entered the stables, his footsteps indiscernible, masked by the storm's fury.

Be careful, Sam. Reeves has a gun.

Reeves held the 9 mm in his shaky hand, aiming it directly at Jeannie. He laughed, the sound hysterical and shrill. "Shooting you would be so easy, but not appropriate for you, Jeannie Alverson, spawn of Satan. No, a witch must burn. You will be a sacrifice to the Lord."

Sam Dundee swooped down on Reeves like a hawk clawing its helpless prey. Grabbing Reeves by the shoulders, Sam lifted him and tossed him into the air. Reeves shrieked as he landed against the wall, his gun sailing out of his hand and disappearing in the darkness.

Stay where you are, Jeannie, Sam told her.

A slash of lightning illuminated the stables momentarily. In a split second, Jeannie saw Sam, his face contorted with rage, his Ruger aimed in Reeves's general direction. He fired a shot. Reeves bellowed. When a second and then a third brilliant explosion of lightning hit the island, she saw it glimmer off Reeves's gun, which lay halfway between Sam and him. Reeves grappled for the gun with one hand while he clutched at his bloody shoulder with the other.

Another shot rang out, then another. She had no idea who was doing the shooting or whether either bullet had hit its target. Pushing herself up into a sitting position, she watched while two shadowy figures lunged headlong at each other. She could distinguish which man was which solely from Sam Dundee's massive size. He was a couple of inches taller and much heavier than Maynard Reeves.

The sound of fists hitting flesh reverberated inside the stables. Thuds. Thumps. Knocks. Ragged breathing. Sam Dundee, his back to the outer wall, landed a resounding blow to Reeve's midsection, knocking the breath out of him and laying him out flat on his back.

Sam stood over Reeves, his chest heaving. Jeannie waited for Reeves to stand. He didn't. Another shot rang out. Sam's body jerked from the impact as the bullet ripped through his side. Jeannie screamed.

Reeves lifted his shoulders off the floor, gripping the 9 mm in his trembling hands. "God is on my side! He will help me destroy both the witch and her guardian."

In one quick, practiced move, Sam lifted his leg, pivoted around and slammed his foot into Reeves's hands, plummeting his gun into dark oblivion. Before Reeves had a chance to react, Sam brought his foot around again and knocked his opponent flat on the floor.

The roar of the hurricane-force winds shook the stables. The wall directly behind Sam collapsed. Jeannie screamed again. The old timbers fell on top of Sam, knocking him to his knees, then flat on his face, covering his body completely.

The wind roared like a mighty jet plane. Rain poured into the stables, washing over the remains of the toppled outer wall.

"Sam!"

No response.

Sam!

She tried again to contact Sam, but he didn't answer. He had to be unconscious. And with the weight of those heavy old boards crushing his body, he was probably seriously injured. She had to go to him. Help him. Save him.

Lifting herself onto her knees, she felt around the damp dirt floor for her walking stick. Suddenly she saw her cane, lying several feet to her left. Then realization dawned on her. There was light inside the stables, pouring in from outside.

The deafening rumble subsided. The wind stopped. The air became perfectly calm. Jeannie knew enough about tropical storms to know that the island was encased in the eye of the storm, that eerie, calm core in the center of the massive, spiraling clouds and driving rain.

Jeannie crawled on her knees across the stables, clutched

her cane and lifted herself up off the floor. She scurried to the pile of heavy boards lying in a heap, completely covering Sam Dundee.

Sam, you're going to be all right. I'll take care of you. I promise.

She had to remove enough of the debris to touch some part of his body, to clasp his hand, to caress his head. Only then could she begin her loving ministrations; only then could she work her magic and save Sam's life. Balancing herself with her cane, she eased down on her knees and laid her cane aside. Finding the intact boards far too heavy to lift, she clawed at the rubble. She saw Sam's hand. She reached for him.

"You're not going to save him!" Maynard Reeves jerked Jeannie off the ground.

She gasped. It couldn't be. Sam had shot Reeves and knocked him unconscious.

Fighting Reeves proved fruitless, but Jeannie fought him all the same. Although he'd been no match for Sam, he was much larger and far stronger than she was. He dragged her out of the stables, through the huge opening made by the wall's collapse. Jeannie hit him repeatedly; he didn't seem to feel her blows.

All the while he tugged her around the house and toward the beach, Jeannie struggled. She could not—would not—allow this monster, who called himself a man of God, to triumph. If he succeeded in getting her off the island, they were both doomed to drown in the storm, and there would be no one to save Sam and Manton. Even if help arrived in a day or two, it might well be too late for these two men she so dearly loved.

Sam. Sam. Oh, my darling, please hear me.

Silence.

Reeves halted at the top of the hill overlooking the far side of the island, where he'd docked his small boat. "I'm taking you straight to the Righteous Light Church, where my disciples are preparing for your sacrifice."

"No!" Jeannie screamed. "Don't you realize we'll be killed if we leave the island?"

"The storm has passed," Reeves said. "God has calmed the seas for my safe passage."

"The storm hasn't passed. We're right in the middle of the eye of the storm. Don't you know what that means?"

"You can't trick me with your lies, witch."

Reeves pulled her into his arms. Jeannie struggled. Threading his fingers through her hair, he cupped her scalp. "When you draw your last breath, the Almighty will bestow your powers on me. He will cleanse them of evil and infuse them with his glory."

Manton. Manton, can you hear me? If only she could rouse Manton. He was in the stables, not far from Sam. If she could make him hear her, she could tell him that Sam needed him. *Manton!*

Jeannie? Manton asked, their link wavering and fragile because of his grogginess. *Jeannie, where are you? Are you all right?*

The stable wall fell in on Sam. He's hurt. Maynard Reeves is trying to take me off the island. I need your help. Jeannie closed her eyes and said a silent prayer of thanks that Manton was alive and conscious enough for the two of them to communicate. *We're in the eye of the storm, and Reeves doesn't realize that we can't sail to the mainland. Sam will die without my help.*

You must overpower Reeves, Manton told her.

But how? she asked. *I'm not strong enough.*

Yes, you are strong enough. Far stronger than you know. Reach inside yourself. Draw strength from the depth of your love for Sam, Manton said. *Concentrate. Focus all your energy on saving Sam, on saving his life.*

Can you help Sam? Jeannie asked. *Are you able to move?*

Not yet. But soon. The feeling is returning to my body. Be strong, little one.

Reeves licked Jeannie's face. She cringed.

"If you won't listen to me, won't believe what I'm telling you about the storm—" Jeannie looked heavenward, wondering just how long they had before the eye passed and the storm's fury consumed the island once again "—then at least consider the possibility that we'd be safer in my cruiser than in your small boat."

Reeves licked her face again. "I can taste the evil in you, but I can also taste the power. The power that will soon be mine."

"We'll never make it to the mainland alive in your little boat."

"Perhaps you're right about taking your cruiser." Gripping her painfully about the waist, Reeves tugged her in the opposite direction, toward the other side of the island.

Manton?

Yes, Jeannie?

I have to find the strength to stop Reeves and save Sam.

Your love for Sam is your strength. No power on earth is greater.

Jeannie focused on the incredible power surging through her body. She had to overpower Reeves; it was the only way she would be free to go to Sam and save his life. Nothing mattered except saving Sam.

She felt the tightening of her muscles, the hardening of her biceps. She could hardly believe what was happening to her. A few times with Sam, she had realized she was absorbing a small fraction of his strength, but nothing this forceful. Manton had been right. There was no power on earth greater than love.

Jeannie grabbed Maynard Reeves by his shoulders, tightening her hands, lifting him off his feet and away from her. He yelped aloud, fear and amazement bright in his eyes.

"Put me down, you demon-possessed witch!"

Jeannie flung Reeves from her. His body landed on a muddy

patch of ground several feet from her. Jeannie slumped to her knees, her crippled legs as weak as ever.

Rising into a sitting position, Reeves glared at her. "I am not afraid to fight the devil, for the Lord—" Reeves lifted his arms toward the sky "—will give me the victory." Reeves stood, his once charismatic, boyish smile twisted into an evil leer.

Raindrops hit Jeannie on the face. The wind whistled through the trees. The eye had passed quickly; the storm would be upon them again in a matter of minutes.

Reeves took a step toward Jeannie. She looked to his left, where a row of palm trees swayed in the wind, bending their heads as if awaiting execution. Lightning crackled in the sky, followed by the rumble of thunder. In the distance, Jeannie heard the storm's deadly roar.

Reeves took another step, and then another. Jeannie scooted backward. *Concentrate on saving Sam, on the depth of your love for him,* she told herself.

When Reeves was upon her, Jeannie prayed for help. A bolt of lightning hit the enormous old live oak directly behind Reeves, splitting it apart as if it had been hacked in two by a giant ax. Jeannie watched in horror and fascination as one half of the tree uprooted and toppled, crushing Maynard Reeves in its downward path. He screamed once, then fell silent. Blood oozed from his mouth. His sightless eyes stared off into space.

Jeannie's battle with Reeves had ended. A higher power had indeed decided the outcome.

Jeannie crawled toward the unmoving man lying beneath the weight of the severed tree. She placed her fingers on the pulse point in his neck. She sighed. Maynard Reeves was dead.

Sam! She had to get to Sam. In her frustration, she struggled to connect her mind to Manton's. God had granted her one miracle. Would he grant her another?

Help me. Please help me get to Sam before it's too late.

She crawled away from Reeves, knowing there was only one way to reach Sam. She would have to crawl, on her knees, back to the stables. The rain poured down, drenching her. The wind toppled her, facedown, into the saturated grass. She lifted herself and continued crawling across the vast front lawn, away from the ocean and toward the house.

She'd made her way to within twenty feet of the front veranda when she saw an enormous dark form running toward her. Manton! She stopped, the pain in her knees radiating up her thighs and into her body.

She lifted up her arms. Manton hauled her up, pressing her wet body against his.

I'm still groggy from the tranquilizer, Manton told her. *I'm weak, and my brain is fuzzy.*

I'm so thankful you're all right, she said. *Now, please, take me to Sam. I can't lose him.*

Manton carried her to the stables, depositing her beside the rubble burying Sam Dundee's big body. Manton cleared the boards off Sam. Jeannie laid both her hands on Sam's back. Tears gathered in her eyes.

Manton picked up a piece of splintered board, laid it over his knee and broke it in half, then handed it to Jeannie.

Use this as a cane. We need to get to the storm shelter. I'll carry Sam.

The wind and rain attacked them mercilessly on their trek from the stables to the house. Completely drenched, their skin bleeding from blowing-sand cuts, they went down the dark flight of stairs leading to the storm shelter in the basement, Manton carrying Sam.

The storm must have damaged the generator, Manton said. *We have no power of any kind. Try to find the kerosene lamps and light them. A box of matches will be beside one of the lamps.*

Once inside the shelter, Manton and Jeannie felt their way around in the pitch-blackness. The fronts of Manton's calves bumped into the cot. He laid Sam down gently. Jeannie found the matches, struck one to find the kerosene lamp on the table.

She removed the globe, lit the wick and turned to seek out the other lamp. Manton took the matches from her, nodding toward Sam.

Jeannie hobbled over to Sam and sat down on the floor. She lifted his hand, encompassing it in hers. Concentrating totally on making the connection, she focused her every thought on entering Sam's body, on linking herself to his injuries.

Manton lit the other lamp. The two sources of light, situated on opposite ends of the room, cast a soft glow that illuminated the entire twelve-by-twelve storm shelter. Walking over to where Jeannie sat on the floor, Manton placed his hands on her shoulders.

Sam is very weak, she said. Rising up on her haunches, she reached out and wiped away the blood trickling down Sam's bruised and cut forehead. She wiped the blood across her skirt. *He's bleeding, and his ribs are broken.*

I know you want to save him. Manton squeezed her shoulders gently. *But you must not endanger your life and your child's. Sam would not want you to sacrifice yourself and the child to save his life.*

I cannot—I will not—let him die!

Releasing her shoulders, Manton stepped away from her and sat down in a chair at the table.

Jeannie knelt over Sam, embracing him. The faint pulses of his pain seeped into her body. She moaned as the pain increased, moving gradually out of Sam and into her.

Sam's eyelids fluttered. Still embracing him, Jeannie lifted her head and looked at his pale, blood-smeared face. He opened his eyes.

"Hello," she said.

"Jeannie…don't…" His eyes closed, and he drifted back into a semiconscious state.

She kissed his lips with the utmost tenderness. "Hush, now, my love. You're going to be all right."

His injuries were extensive, and the bleeding was severe and life-threatening. She had to stop the bleeding! He would die if she didn't help him.

The pain doubled her over. She cried out, the sound a harsh plea for endurance. As spasm after spasm of torturous cramps racked her body, Jeannie balled her hands into fists and slid off Sam, down the side of the cot and onto the floor. Her eyes closed. She moaned again and again, biting her lower lip to contain the sound.

Manton jumped up, rushing to her aid, lifting her into his arms. She shivered, once, twice, then opened her eyes. *I haven't finished. Carry me back to Sam. I have to help him.*

Be careful, Manton cautioned, then complied with her request and set her back down on the floor at Sam's side.

She laid her head on Sam's arm where it rested on the edge of the cot. She lifted his limp hand, brought it to her lips and kissed each finger. Squeezing his hand, she focused again. Sam's injuries became hers, ripping her apart, then dissolving as the pain suffused her body. Tears of agony streamed down her face. Anguished moans rose from her throat.

Exhausted and close to losing consciousness, Jeannie clung to Sam's hand. He opened his eyes and looked at her.

"My God, Jeannie, what are you doing?" Lifting his head off the pillow, he glanced at their clasped hands. He jerked his hand away.

She tried to smile, to speak, to tell him that there was nothing she would not do to save his life. Didn't he know that he was her life, that without him she did not want to live?

He heard her words as clearly as if she'd spoken them aloud. "You're killing yourself. I want you to stop." Sam looked around for Manton and found him standing a few feet away, his eyes filled with tears as he watched Jeannie's suffering. "Why the hell don't you stop this? Keep her away from me!"

Sam tried to sit up, but weakness overcame him and he fell back on the cot. Jeannie reached for him. He slapped her hand away. "Get away, dammit! If I die, I die, but you're not going to die with me."

"You're already stronger. Your injuries have stopped bleeding." With great effort, she rose up on her knees, her body hovering over his. "When the pain returns and the bleeding starts again, I'll have to help you. To keep you alive. We can't get off Le Bijou Bleu until the storm passes."

"If you take my pain into your body, it will kill you," Sam said. "Don't you think I know that? My God, Jeannie, I don't want you to die for me."

Covering her mouth with her hand, she cried silently, her body trembling with her hushed sobs.

"Promise me," Sam said. "Promise me that you—" his eyelids fluttered, and his voice faltered "—you won't do it again."

"I love you," she said.

"Promise me..." He sank back into a semiconscious state.

Jeannie rested, closing her eyes, laying her hand next to his, careful not to touch him. With his injuries temporarily, partially healed, he would sleep, drifting in and out of consciousness. And Jeannie would sleep, restoring her depleted strength, until Sam's pain from his internal wounds returned and the bleeding began again.

Jeannie covered her stomach with the palm of her other hand. Would saving Sam's life cost them their baby? Could she save both father and child?

In the last conscious moments before sleep overcame her, Jeannie pleaded for the strength to endure, and for the blessing of life for Sam, herself and their unborn child.

CHAPTER EIGHTEEN

SLEEPY, EXHAUSTED AND nearly depleted of her energy, Jeannie held Sam's hand and listened to his uneven breathing. She would have to join with him again. She had no other choice; without her help, Sam would die.

When she called to Manton, he came to her and placed his hands on her shoulders. She drew strength from him. Manton's strength was the only thing maintaining her consciousness and enabling her to continue keeping Sam alive. If only Manton possessed the power to share her pain and suffering...but he did not. She, and she alone, had to bear the burden.

When I have finished, Jeannie told Manton, *cover me with a blanket and let me rest, but don't move me away from Sam.*

I'll take care of you, Manton said. *And while you rest, I will go upstairs and try once again to contact the mainland. It's daylight now, and the storm passed hours ago. Perhaps someone can get to the island soon and take you and Sam to the hospital.*

Within minutes, Jeannie had made the connection again and began her miracle of healing.

As she withdrew his pain and stopped the bleeding once again, Sam opened his eyes. Jeannie lay in a huddled mass against the cot, writhing in pain. Weak, dizzy and disoriented, Sam struggled over to her.

"Jeannie...Jeannie..."

Drenched in sweat, groaning in agony, Jeannie barely heard Sam calling her name. She tried to respond verbally, but could not, and when she tried to convey her thoughts to him telepathically, she found she lacked the strength.

Sam saw Manton standing over them, and realized the gentle giant was dying inside as he watched Jeannie suffering and knew he could do nothing to alleviate her pain.

Sam reached over and enclosed Jeannie's trembling, pain-racked body in his arms. On some level of consciousness, Jeannie felt Sam's embrace, sensed his concern. He ached with the need to help her, to share her pain, not realizing that the emotional torment he endured was transferred to Jeannie, weakening her all the more. And she could not relate to him what was happening, that his very nearness was creating more pain inside her, draining her of what little strength she had left.

Manton grabbed Sam by the shoulders, pulling him away from Jeannie. Sam hit out at the other man, dazed by the suddenness of his attack. Manton pushed Sam back down on the cot and signed to him. Sam glared up at Manton, wondering what the hell he was trying to tell him.

He watched closely while Manton jabbed his index fingers toward each other repeatedly.

"Hurt?" Sam asked.

Manton nodded, then signed again, thrusting his right index finger under his prone left palm. Sam didn't understand. Manton repeated the procedure.

"Kill," Sam said, realization dawning on him. "Holding her hurts her? Is killing her?"

Manton nodded repeatedly.

"Then do something to help her."

With his hands prone, Manton struck his left index finger with his right index finger. Tears filled his green eyes and streamed down his bronze cheeks.

"You can't." Sam balled his hands into fists.

Sam huddled on the far side of the cot, forcing himself not to touch Jeannie again. While he lay there helpless, watching her endure his pain, he felt as if his life were being drained out of him. He had begged her not to help him, but she hadn't listened. Dammit, why hadn't she listened to him? Why hadn't she done what he'd asked?

He would rather die a thousand times over than see her suffering this way and know he was powerless to help her. Was this his true damnation? Had the guilt and remorse he'd endured for six years been only a preliminary to this final atonement? Was having to watch the woman he loved die by slow degrees his punishment for Brock's and Connie's deaths? For the death of his unborn child?

It wasn't right that Jeannie had to pay for his sins, to suffer because of his crimes. She was innocent, so completely pure and good. *This isn't fair,* his heart cried. An angel of mercy given no mercy herself.

Sam's angry, savage cry pierced the very gates of heaven.

Minutes dragged by, seeming like hours. Eventually Jeannie fell into a deep sleep. Manton drew the blanket up around her and slipped a pillow under her head. Drained and weak, Sam closed his eyes.

When he awoke, he and Jeannie were alone in the storm shelter. A sudden, sharp pang hit him in the chest. His pain was returning.

Sam heard footsteps on the stairs. J. T. Blackwood swept into the room, Manton following him.

"I've got a float plane waiting to take you back to Biloxi," J.T. said. "The storm missed Biloxi and lost a lot of steam before it hit the Louisiana coast."

"Get Jeannie to the hospital." Sam tried to stand, but swayed on his feet and fell backward onto the cot.

"We'll get you both to the hospital." J.T. glanced down at Jeannie, lying on the floor. "What the hell happened to you two? Did you get caught out in the storm? I don't read sign, so I have no idea what this big fellow's been trying to tell me."

"You carry Jeannie out to the plane," Sam said. "Manton can help me."

Sam watched while J.T. lifted a lifeless Jeannie into his arms. When J.T. walked past Sam, Sam reached out. J.T. stopped. Sam let his hand hover over her face, and died a little inside because he didn't dare touch her.

"A wall fell on me," Sam said. "It should have killed me. I'd be dead now if Jeannie hadn't saved my life."

Manton's cats and dogs, who had followed them out of the stables the evening before, now followed them up from the storm shelter into the house. J.T. stepped around the shards of glass from several blown-out windowpanes and stomped through the water puddles marring the wooden floors.

Outside, the sun shone faintly from behind a mass of clouds. The paint on the north side of the house had been sanded down to the bare wood, and several window shutters lay scattered on the ground. A small section of the roof had blown off, and debris was strewn in every direction. Uprooted trees marred the landscape. Huge sandpiles dotted the beach.

Maynard Reeves's body lay beneath the severed trunk of an old oak tree. Manton stopped abruptly when Sam tugged on his arm.

"Not a very pretty sight," J.T. said. "Looks like lightning struck the tree, splitting it in two. Then half of it fell on the reverend."

"He was out of his mind," Sam said. "He thought if he killed Jeannie, he would somehow gain her empathic abilities. He thought God would give them to him as a gift for destroying a witch."

"Well, it looks like a higher power made a judgment call." J.T. glanced down at Jeannie, lying unconscious in his arms. "I'd say somebody up there was watching out for one of his own."

Every muscle in Sam's body strained toward Jeannie; his need to touch her was overwhelming. "Let's get off this island and take Jeannie to a hospital." A sharp, stabbing ache sliced through Sam's midsection. He doubled over in pain.

"Hang on," J.T. said "The plane's right down here."

He led them down the steps to the beach. Lifting Jeannie up high in his arms, he handed her to the float plane's pilot, then turned to help Manton with Sam. Once Sam was seated and Jeannie rested in Manton's arms, J.T. jumped on board and gave the pilot orders to get them to Biloxi as quickly as possible.

Jeannie did not awaken from her deep sleep on the flight to Biloxi. Sam watched her for any sign of recovery, but she lay in Manton's arms, unmoving, looking like a limp rag doll. If only he could hold her in *his* arms, kiss those pale lips, stroke her tearstained cheeks. As pain radiated through his own body, Sam felt himself slipping away. He tried to stay conscious, not wanting to sever that last link—visual contact—with Jeannie.

AFTER SURGERY, SAM awoke calling for Jeannie. J.T. assured him that everything possible was being done for her, but Sam wanted to see her, needed to know for sure that she was going to be all right. J.T. and an orderly forcibly held Sam down on the bed while a nurse injected him with a sedative.

He awoke again sometime during the night. Glancing around the hospital room, he saw J.T. sitting in a chair, his tan Stetson covering the upper part of his face as he slept.

Jeannie. Where was Jeannie? Was she all right? He had to find her.

Sam took note of the tubes stuck in his body, then dismissed them, sitting up in bed and sliding his feet over the side. Dizziness swirled around inside his head. He took several deep breaths trying to overcome his disorientation. On wobbly legs, he struggled to stand.

J. T. Blackwood clamped his big hand down on Sam's shoulder. "Where the hell do you think you're going?"

"Jeannie." The one word said everything.

"The shape you're in, you can't do her any good," J.T. said. "Stay in bed. The doctors are doing everything they can for her."

"I've got to see her." Sam jerked away from J.T., took three steps and passed out cold.

Sam floated in and out of a drug-induced sleep, realizing that each time he fought them, begging to see Jeannie, they sedated him again. His gut instincts told him something was horribly wrong, but he couldn't fight the sedatives they gave him to keep him calm and allow him to heal.

Three days after his arrival, Sam awoke at midday, his mouth as dry as cotton balls, his eyes gritty and his mind still a bit foggy. Glancing around the room, he saw J.T. first, standing at the foot of his bed. Manton and Julian Howell stood in the open doorway.

"What's going on? Why aren't you with Jeannie?" Sam sat straight up. His head throbbed. He shut his eyes, trying to block out the sudden pain.

Julian Howell approached the side of Sam's bed. "The doctors felt it was necessary to keep you sedated in order to give you a few days to heal." Julian laid his hand on Sam's shoulder. "Every time you woke, you tried to get out of bed and find Jeannie."

"Yeah, I get the picture," Sam slid his legs off the bed, jerked the tubes out of his arms and stood. "I take it that y'all have finally decided to let me see her."

"You couldn't have done anything for her," Julian said. "She's been unconscious since—" Julian swallowed his tears.

"You mean she hasn't woken up yet?" Sam glanced at J.T. "What is it? What are y'all not telling me?"

J.T. exchanged a concerned look with Julian. Sam glanced at Manton. The gentle giant signed to him. He placed his hands on his shoulders, then moved them outward, the action mimicking the smoothing of feathers on the wings.

Angel. One of the first words Jeannie had taught Sam in sign language. His pet name for her.

Sam didn't understand the next word, although Manton repeated it several times, placing his hands palm to palm, then turning both hands over.

"What's he saying about Jeannie?" Sam asked.

"He said, 'Our angel is dying.'" Julian wiped tears from his eyes.

"No, she can't be dying." Sam gripped Julian's thin arm. "I won't let her die!"

J.T. grabbed Sam's shoulder, turning Sam to face him. "The doctors don't know what the hell is wrong. Like Dr. Howell said, she's been unconscious for days. Her vital signs are growing steadily weaker. They've run every test imaginable on her. They can't treat her, because they don't know what's wrong with her."

"I know." Sam tried to pull away from J.T., but his friend held him fast. "Dammit, I know what's wrong with her. I killed her. In saving me, in healing me again and again just to keep me alive, she used up all her energy. She has nothing to build on. She's depleted her life force."

He realized that J.T. might think he'd gone mad, but he knew Julian and Manton would understand. He looked at Julian. "Tell him I'm right."

"It's possible that's what happened." Julian turned from them, burying his face in his hands as his body shook with sobs.

"She's been drifting in and out of consciousness for the last hour," J.T. said. "She keeps calling your name. Over and over."

"Take me to her, J.T. Please."

Sam Dundee never begged, never pleaded. But he was begging now.

Manton shook his head, stepping in front of Sam, signing

furiously. Sam reached out, grasping Manton's enormous hands, halting him.

"I know what you're trying to tell me." Sam patted Manton's hands. "But if she's dying, I can't hurt her, can I? And she's calling for me. I need to be with her."

Manton nodded, agreeing with Sam.

Julian Howell, tears coating his face, his voice shaky, turned around and said, "Take him to her, Mr. Blackwood. She wants him with her. She loves him so."

"He needs to be told before he goes to her," J.T. said.

"Yes, of course he does," Julian agreed.

Fear like nothing Sam had ever known invaded his mind and body, trapping the screaming rage inside him. "What haven't you told me?"

J.T. closed his eyes momentarily, blew out his breath, then opened his eyes and looked directly at Sam. "She's pregnant. Four or five weeks pregnant."

Sam's blood chilled. His nerves burned. His muscles knotted painfully. Jeannie was carrying his child. And they were both dying. Because of him. She had sacrificed herself and their child to save his life.

"No!" The word roared from his body like the cry of a dying animal, his pain more than he could bear.

Sam turned, balled his hands into fists and pounded the wall so hard his hands burst through the Sheetrock. Pulling out his hands, he squared his shoulders and faced J.T.

"Let's go," Sam said.

J.T. walked Sam down the hall to Jeannie's room, Manton and Julian following. She rested on the pristine white sheets, her face devoid of color, her eyes closed. Dressed in a hospital gown, she lay perfectly still.

"I want to go in alone," Sam said. "I can make it without any help."

Sam entered her room, leaving the door behind him open. J.T., Manton and Julian hovered in the doorway. Sam walked slowly over to Jeannie and sat down in the chair beside her bed, then lifted her hand and pressed it against his lips.

"I'm here, angel. I'm right here with you," he told her. "Come on, Jeannie, wake up."

Her eyelids fluttered.

"That's it, come on, wake up." Standing, he clasped her hand to his heart.

She opened her eyes and looked at him. A faint smile curved her lips. "Sam."

Holding her hand, he leaned down and kissed her lips, the touch feather-light. "You've got to fight, angel. You can't let go. You have to live. What would I do without you?"

"You…you're…all right?"

"I'm fine." He rubbed the back of her fragile hand across his cheek. "You saved my life again." Tears lodged in Sam's throat.

"I love…you," Jeannie whispered.

"Please, Jeannie, don't die." Sitting down on the edge of the bed, he lifted her into his arms, kissing her tenderly on her forehead and cheeks. "I don't want to live without you."

"The baby…she's all right." Jeannie brought Sam's trembling hand down across her stomach. "We need you, Sam. Your little girl and I. You can save us."

"How? Dear God, Jeannie, tell me how!"

"You know how…you know…" Her voice drifted away as she closed her eyes and sank once again into an unnatural sleep.

"I don't know!" Sam shouted. "Tell me! I don't know!"

He clasped her to him, holding her against his chest, stroking her back, whispering her name. Tears welled up in Sam's eyes. A drop fell on his cheek. He swallowed hard. Another tear fell, then another, and another. Tears flooded his eyes, ran into his mouth, dripped off his chin.

Sam allowed his mind to delve into Jeannie's, seeking a response when he telepathically called her name.

I'm here, Sam. Help me. Save me. Save our baby. Take care of us.

"How?" he asked aloud, then repeated the question silently. *How?*

You know how.

He held her close, strengthening their physical connection as he kept their mental link intact.

I love you, Jeannie, my angel. I love you. Please don't leave me.

He felt her love invade his mind, conquer his heart and lay claim to his soul. *Don't let us go, Sam. Give us your strength. Take away our weakness.*

"I'll do anything to save you." Clutching her in his arms, holding her weak, lifeless body against the strength of his, Sam trembled with sorrow, crying from the depths of his soul as he had never cried before in his life. Not even when he was a child and his mother died.

"Please. Please. She's suffered so much for so many people. She gives and gives and asks nothing in return. She's saved my life twice, and shown me the meaning of real love. I can't live without her. If she dies, I die."

J.T. touched Sam on the back. "Come on, Sam. Don't do this. You aren't helping her."

Sam eased Jeannie down on the bed, stood up and turned to J.T. "I would give anything, even my soul, if I could do for her what she's done for so many others. If I could just reach inside and take away her suffering, make her whole again, give her all my strength."

"You're asking for a miracle," J.T. said.

"Yes, I know." Sam shoved J.T. away. "I'm not leaving her. She believes I can save her and our baby." Sam clamped his teeth together, choking on his pain, tears pouring down his face.

Sam fell to his knees beside Jeannie's bed in a mirror image of her vigil at his side in the storm shelter on Le Bijou Bleu. He held her hand.

"I love you. Do you hear me, Jeannie? I love you."

Manton and Julian entered the room and stood next to J.T., all three men standing by helplessly. Several nurses stood in the doorway, tears in their eyes.

"Just this once, angel, let someone hurt for you. Let me remove all that suffering inside you. I'm strong enough for both of us, and for our baby. Give me your pain, Jeannie. Do it for us. Do it for…our little girl."

Sam felt the first faint glimmer of pain, a deep, emotional need, and a physical weakness so great that he cried aloud when Jeannie's suffering began slowly draining from her body.

"That's it, angel. Let it all go. Don't be afraid. Our love is more powerful than anything. We can do this. Together."

Her pain swirled around inside him, sharp and jagged, ripping him apart. He moaned in agony. Suddenly he felt her withdrawal.

"Don't, angel. You've suffered far more for me. Love me enough to give me your pain. Please."

She returned to him, allowing him to take more of her suffering into his body and mind and heart. And when the deed was completed, Sam fell to the floor, unconscious, as his soul joined with Jeannie's forever.

Slowly, Jeannie opened her eyes. "Don't touch him. Leave him where he is," she ordered the others.

She eased off the bed, dragging the sheet and blanket with her. She crawled over to Sam, lifting the sheet over them as she put her arms around him.

"Everyone, please leave," she whispered. "He's all right. He just needs rest."

When the nurses tried to enter Jeannie's room, J.T. demanded they leave. "I don't think Jeannie and Sam need any medical assistance right now."

"Mr. Blackwood is right," Julian said. "Jeannie and Sam

will be all right. The miracle of love has proven to be more powerful than medical science." Julian gripped Manton's arm, and guided him out the door. The room emptied quickly. J.T. closed the door when he stepped into the hallway.

Jeannie kissed the side of Sam's face, then drew his head into her lap. Placing her hand over her stomach, she smiled, knowing their baby was safe.

Sam's eyelids quivered, and then he opened his eyes slowly. "I'll always take care of you." Lifting his hand, he laid it over hers on her stomach. "Both of you."

"Your love saved us," Jeannie told him.

"*Your* love saved all three of us," he said, then closed his eyes and drifted off into a restorative sleep. When his limp hand slipped off hers, she grasped it and laid it on her stomach.

"Everything is all right, sweetheart," Jeannie told their unborn child. "Mommy and Daddy are here, and we love you as much as we love each other."

EPILOGUE

THEY MARRIED A month later in the small Congregational church on Beach Boulevard. Sam was devastatingly handsome in a gray striped morning suit, and Jeannie angelically lovely in Miriam Howell's ivory satin wedding gown. They honeymooned on Le Bijou Bleu, putting the horrors of Maynard Reeves's madness behind them.

Seven months later, little Miss Samantha Dundee came howling into the world, after having made her mother and father suffer together through ten hours of labor. But once they held their daughter in their arms, they agreed that they just might give her a brother or sister in a few years.

After enduring the torment of the damned, Sam and Jeannie found heaven on earth. They loved deeply and completely, sharing every joy, every sorrow, every pleasure and every pain. He would forever be her elegant savage, and she his angel of mercy.

Sam didn't take their happiness for granted. As he had once guarded Jeannie from a world gone mad, he now guarded Jeannie and Samantha, making it his mission in life to surround them with the shield of his loving protection.

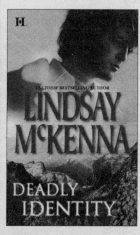

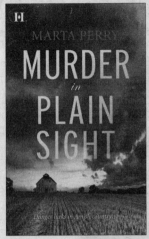

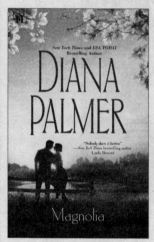